Fated Warriors

Book Six of the Dragon Spawn Chronicles
By Dawn Ross
© 2024

"There's no fate but what we make for ourselves."
– John Connor (Terminator 2: Judgment Day)

Fated Warriors

Book Six of the Dragon Spawn Chronicles

by Dawn Ross

Cover
Cover art by Jon Stubbington. The starry background is a public domain image from NASA. Images combined by germancreative on fiverr.com.

Special Thanks
I'd like to extend a thank you to all the beta readers and editors who helped me make this novel shine. Special thanks to Brett Linley and Grace Bridges, who have been with me through every single book and have been instrumental in helping me make these stories so great.

Reviews for StarFire Dragons

"A thoughtful novel that owes a debt to
Star Trek but works on its own terms."
—Kirkus Reviews

"A subtle space opera that explores the ethical
conundrums of intergalactic relations with main
characters who are worth rooting for."
—Becca Saffier, *Reedsy Discovery*

"Fans of epic sci-fi that look for realistic characters and complex
yet believable settings will find *Starfire Dragons*
a powerful introductory story that promises more, yet
nicely concludes its immediate dilemmas."
—D. Donovan, Senior Reviewer, *Midwest Book Review*

Fated Warriors

Book Six of the Dragon Spawn Chronicles

by Dawn Ross

1
Separated

The rising star turned the sky a shade of pink that generally would've inspired awe. All Commander J.D. Hapker noticed was how the clouds appeared to be dipped in blood. With the universe flipped on its head, they might as well be.

He released a long sigh, then sipped his tea. He'd been sitting here by the window for a while, dreading the upcoming day.

As the dawn brightened, his reflection on the glass faded. *Good.* He was tired of seeing his crooked frown and haggard features. It was probably his imagination, but his eyes seemed more wrinkled and his sandy blond hair more greyish. He was only thirty-six, yet the past year had taken its toll. Not even the hotel's simple homey décor eased the somber weight bearing down on him.

A tingle sizzled up his arm. He flexed his new fingers, amazed but also disconcerted at the medical technology that had grown him a new limb. Although the procedure used his own cells, it felt more like a prosthetic than his own flesh and blood. It didn't help that the scar on his index finger was gone or that his skin looked younger.

He still couldn't believe he'd lost his arm. In a fight against long-since outlawed MEGA super-soldiers, no less.

MEGA. The acronym made him scoff. *Mechanically enhanced, genetically altered.* People who considered augmentation a step up in human evolution had coined it. Yet many of the MEGAs he'd met seemed to have lost their humanity. Gottfried especially.

The MEGA Injunction barred MEGAs from positions of power and political influence, yet Gottfried and a squad of super-soldiers had risen high within the Prontaean Cooperative ranks. After their murderous plot fell apart, an investigation revealed even more MEGA operatives working among them.

Hapker ignored the flashing news icon on his tablet. The stories were all the same. MEGA Insurgence, they called it, and it sent everyone into hysteria. Frightened people accused neighbors of having unnatural abilities, hateful rhetoric against anyone with augmentations spewed from the mouths of citizens and government officials alike, and riots broke out across the galaxy.

Neither losing his arm nor the political instability bothered him as much as losing Jori.

The tranquility presented by the wooded scenery outside did nothing to soothe him. The transport ships rising in the distance only served to remind him he'd have to leave soon and abandon his search. He ran his hand down his face and rested his bare chin on his palm. Maybe he shouldn't return to the *Odyssey*.

The thought saddened him. He was just coming to enjoy his position as the second-in-command of a spacefaring starship. The purpose of this Prontaean Colonial Cooperative vessel satisfied his desire to explore the universe. It also complemented his Pholatian Protector ideals of public service. Rescuing broken-down ships, offering medical aid to travelers, and promoting peace between different worlds were but a fragment of all this ship's workload.

But none of those things would bring the same sense of purpose if Jori wasn't there.

A pang twisted in his gut as he remembered the first time he'd met the boy. An enemy Tredon ship had crashed, and from its flaming guts appeared a young warrior with a deadly starfire phaser aimed at Hapker's face. The intensity of Jori's dark eyes had been as steady as the hand holding the weapon.

Despite that initial hostile encounter, he and Jori became friends. No. More than friends. Hapker would've adopted him had the Cooperative Council not intervened. It didn't matter that Jori was just a child, that he'd defied his warmongering father to save the lives of several Cooperative PG-Force officers, or that he was the one who uncovered Gottfried's MEGA plot. The Cooperative Council took advantage of Hapker's medical trauma to send Jori to some out-of-the-way planet.

Even if it meant giving up his career with the Cooperative, Hapker had to get him back. He'd promised to provide him with a better life away from his abusive father, but all he'd managed to do was leave him at the mercy of hate and prejudice. Why couldn't anyone see that just because Jori's people were the Cooperative's enemy didn't mean that *he* was the enemy? Warrior or no, Jori had a good heart... And he deserved better.

Hapker swallowed. The video message on his tablet had ended long ago, but it begged to be replayed. He didn't want to torture himself by watching it again, but he kept hoping Jori had left a clue telling him where the Cooperative planned to send him.

His finger hesitated over the play icon. Just when his heart told him he'd had enough grief, an impulse betrayed him and he tapped it.

"J.D." Jori filled his lungs, the sound coming through the feed like a wind at the head of a storm. His normally piercing eyes were somber, and his youthful features seemed to have aged. "I hear you're on your way to a full recovery. A new arm. Wow. The Cooperative has some amazing technology."

Hapker rubbed his arm, trying not to think of it as an alien appendage.

"I'm glad you're alright," Jori continued. "I am too. The council exonerated me. I'm free—as free as I can be. They're sending me to a children's home. I'm not allowed to say what planet it's on, and I won't be able to contact you or anyone else in the Cooperative. They said it's for my safety, but well… You know." His throat bobbed. "I'm alright with that, though. Not that I don't want to live with you. You've been a great friend—the best, really. But I wouldn't want you to give up your career for me. The Cooperative needs someone like you."

Hapker's face scrunched in anguish. His sinuses burned as tears threatened to form.

Jori cleared his throat. "I'm sad about having to say—" He choked back a sob. Hapker did too. "I'm sad about having to say goodbye." Jori sighed. "But this is best for both of us. You know I don't lie. I believe the council when they say I'll be safe. At least no one will know who I am. They won't even be aware that I'm from Toradon. That will help me start over. Maybe I can be a scientist or an engineer or something." He shrugged. "I'm not sure yet, but I'll figure it out. Thank you for being there for me. And take care of yourself."

The video ended. Hapker clenched his fists to hold back the flood of sorrow.

Jori was wrong. This wasn't what was best. The Cooperative might've given him a new identity, but they were likely keeping a close eye on him. They might even have a hand in the type of parents who adopt him. Hapker imagined a strict military man who thought enforcing obedience was the most effective way to handle a child who'd grown up a soldier. But that wasn't what Jori needed. He needed someone who understood him. Someone who accepted him just as he was.

An intrusive knock on the door snapped him out of his despair. It was time to go. His transport ship would arrive soon. It was the only one heading to the Mirlian space station this month, and the *Odyssey* couldn't wait there for him for too long.

Even a little late, and the transport would leave without him. As depressing as this hotel was, at least he'd have more time to figure out where the Cooperative had sent Jori.

No doubt the ones at the door were retrieving him for that very reason. The Cooperative couldn't afford to lose him. Not with MEGAs being found at every rank and in every government facility.

He wondered if they'd forcibly make him go. Probably not, but it wouldn't do any good to resist. He had no way to track Jori down. But if Jori got the chance, the first place he'd reach out to would be the *Odyssey*.

Hapker rose with a heavy groan. As much as he wanted to run off on a search and rescue, going back to his ship was the best bet. He grabbed his bag and headed out with a dark cloud hovering over him.

This doesn't mean I'm giving up, Jori. We'll find each other again. I promise.

2
Matters of the Heart

The sun burned like a thousand torches, blinding and relentless. Day in and day out, it scorched the earth and dried up the lakes. Parched dirt blew around in mini dust storms while the stifling air created shimmering mirages in the distance. Groves of trees and shrubs dotted parts of the landscape of Hisui Island, but their brown leaves hung off their skeletal remains like dead skin.

Terkeshi wiped sticky sweat from his brow. He would have cursed the island's perpetual hot weather had he dared to open his mouth and release what little moisture he had left. Besides, he'd be damned if he complained before anyone else. Baba Airi was a withered old woman, but she worked just as hard as the others. Anxi grunted now and then as she shoveled heaps of rocky soil out of the trench, but determination etched her wide freckled face. Even the usually chatty Yuan labored in committed silence.

I guess only spoiled princes whine about work. Well, he wasn't a prince anymore. He was a farmer now, just like the others. Almost. He was still a warrior, despite having a minor handicap.

He wiped off the sweat that'd pooled over the patch covering his empty eye socket. A nearly imperceptible prickle rippled through his scarred hand. With a silent, despondent sigh, he shook it away and heaved another shovelful of baked dirt from the trench. A trickle of water appeared at the bottom, barely enough to hydrate a chicken. It'd been their hope that the bit of rain up in the hills would drain here, but this was looking like a wasted effort.

Damn you, Father, for making these people suffer.

Since this island was where the nobility often banished those with too much political clout to execute, his father had always questioned Lord Qing's governance. All the recent betrayals from Fujishin to Jori likely contributed to an increased distrust. *More like an escalating madness.*

Terk wasn't privy to how distrust had led to the threat of war. All he knew was his father's latest embargo didn't hurt Lord Qing as much as it did these villagers. With the island preparing for an invasion, water deliveries from the solar still had become sporadic, creating the need for the four of them to dig a trench. Sure, they had an entire ocean to distill water from, but Baba Airi's homemade still couldn't keep up with all the farm's needs.

A few months ago, Terk wouldn't have given a damn about this place. A prince shouldn't have to work on some old lady's pig farm. But her persistent cheerfulness and enduring, hard-working spirit made him realize what a self-centered ass he was. Before long, he was helping her. He hated the endless drudgery, but he hated himself more when he let her do it all. She deserved better, so he kept his complaints to himself, heaved another shovelful of dirt out of the trench, and tried to be better.

Baba Airi grunted as she dug. Wisps of her white hair had come out of her ponytail and fallen in sweaty tangles over her ice-blue eyes. Yet her brows furrowed in doggedness as she hefted a decent amount of dirt.

"Baba," Terk said. "Didn't you say you needed to cook the beans for canning today?"

"Don't you be trying to get rid of me, young man," she replied in mock sternness. "I may be an old crone, but I am perfectly capable of digging a hole."

He quirked a smile at her. He'd called her an old crone once, intending to hurt her feelings because that was the sort of chima he was. She'd laughed and told him he was right. Then she adopted it as a nickname. It didn't stop her from working, though. Even after he'd taken over many of the hardest jobs, she always found other things that demanded her attention.

"It's you three who should be doing something else," she said. "Something far more important than helping an old lady."

Terk shot an anxious glance at the sky. In a way, she was right. No one was certain whether the emperor would attack, but they still needed to be prepared for it.

He'd taken the two assignments Washi had given him earlier this year with the utmost diligence. Although the defense training of a handful of villagers proved challenging, the escape drills had better results. Anxi was his best student for both. She had the tenacity of a lone pongamia tree in a typhoon and the fighting spirit of a blackbeast. The former would pay off if she needed to rescue the villagers. And if fighting became necessary, she'd tear the enemy apart before they realized she was a woman.

"This is important, too," Terk replied. "We can't help anyone if we all die of thirst."

"Sheesh, Terk," Yuan said with a half-cocked smile. "Can you be any more morbid?"

Terk responded with a shrug. In the past, he would've snapped at him for being so naïve. But it wasn't Yuan's fault that the only pains in his life were the ones earned by hard work.

A dog yapped from the other side of the barn. Terk's imagination saw Dragon Warriors and his nerves tripped into alarm. He almost abandoned his work to run over, but his senses detected something else. Gaichu, his pup, was just playing.

Baba Airi wasn't the only one who'd pulled him out of his surly attitude after being banished to this shitty village. Somehow, Gaichu had needled his way into Terk's heart. The annoying pup would follow him everywhere and often nuzzled him with his wet nose. At some point, Terk caved to those damned innocent eyes filled with curiosity and devotion. He wasn't worthy but tried to be anyway.

With his tension released, he went back to work. He thrust his shovel into thick mud. A pang struck the center of his chest, making him drop the shovel and gasp. Baba Airi doubled over at the same time, clutching her own chest. He realized then that the pain wasn't his own. His sensing ability had picked up on her agony.

"Baba!" Anxi's emotions carried more concern than the tough old woman's. "Are you alright?"

Terk's alarm kicked in, banishing all other sensations. He grasped Baba before she collapsed and eased her to the ground. Her mouth opened as though she wanted to speak, but words didn't come.

Yuan rushed over, his forehead wrinkled with worry. Then came Gaichu. Somehow, the mottled black and white pup knew something was wrong and abandoned his silly antics to investigate.

Anxi knelt by the woman's other side. "What's wrong, Baba?"

Terk probed with his ability, sensing her pain and determining the source. "I think it's her heart."

"No!" Anxi cried.

Yuan bent over her with stricken brows. "What do we do?"

Terk shook his head, having encountered nothing like this before. "Get help."

"The constable?" Yuan poised to go.

"No," Terk replied, stopping him in his tracks. "He's in the city." *Preparing for war.*

"What about Leichen?" Anxi asked.

A crushing despair hardened in Terk's gut. "She's too far away." *Who else?* An idea snapped in his brain. Only one person had the means to help in time. Even as an exiled noblewoman, she had more privileges than these farmers, including access to medical supplies. But would it look suspicious if he mentioned her?

To hell with that. Baba Airi needed aid.

"Try Lady Amarante." His own heart panged at saying her name. He'd been permitted to speak to his mother as a villager a couple of weeks ago, but not as her son. This time would be no different, but it'd still be good to see her again.

Yuan took off. Terk envied him. If only he had an excuse to visit with her more often—a reason besides this one.

He and Anxi carried Baba Airi to the shade and laid her down on a brown patch of grass. Gaichu followed with a whine, his fuzzy face wrinkled into a troubled expression. Terk shared his concern but dared not let it show.

"Baba, can you hear me?" Anxi asked.

The woman nodded. "Chest… Hurts."

"Just hang on," Terk said, clasping her hand and noting its unusual cool dampness. "We're getting help."

"I'll be fine," she replied with a stubborn conviction, her worry nowhere near as strong as Terk's or Anxi's. She squeezed her eyes shut. Her wizened, sun-darkened skin wrinkled further, punctuating her anguish.

Terk gripped her hand harder. His insides pinched, but more out of fear than from taking in her pain. "Take it easy."

"Got too much work," she croaked.

She moved to rise, but Terk held her down. "Don't be stubborn," he chided gently. "We'll finish this. You just rest."

That she didn't protest intensified his concern. The moments ticked by in agonizing slowness. He watched her with the intensity of a hawk, noting every wince and hitched breath with a lump in his throat.

Eventually, her pain ebbed. When her breathing evened out, he handed her his canteen. "Here. Drink."

She wagged her head. "No. It's yours."

"Just drink it." In better circumstances, Terk would've quirked a smile at her selflessness.

At first, he'd resented getting stuck living with an old woman. He'd come to this island expecting to be reunited with his mother and his old personal guards only to get sent to this farm instead. He thought it was because Washi and Michio had been angry with him for getting Jori and Sensei Jeruko killed. But the real reason was because his father would come after him if he found out he was alive. And as much as Terk grumbled about his demotion from a prince to a pig farmer, he'd rather put up with dirt and pig shit than live under his father's thumb again.

Besides, this place might be hotter than a blue star and the biting insects more irritating than an ill-fitting enviro-suit, but he'd come to appreciate the people around him. He'd never had real friends before.

Although he was close in age with Yuan and Anxi, they had little in common. Yuan could be annoyingly chatty, but he was friendly, helpful, and honest. Anxi was a girl, but her fiery spirit had earned his respect when they'd fought together against pirate-slavers.

He considered Baba Airi a friend too, though their friendship was different. The thought of her dying tore more fear through his chest than the dread that his father might find him.

"I'm fine," she said as she tried to push his arm away and rise. "I'm fine."

Determined or not, she might as well be a kitten pawing at a tiger. "Good." He gently pressed against her shoulder. "But I'm not letting you up until Lady Amarante gets here."

She grumbled but obeyed, and Terk relaxed at seeing the color return to her cheeks.

Yuan returned, red-faced and panting, and his messy black hair more askew than before. "She's coming."

Terk's heart leapt. He redirected his sensing ability and detected the warmth of her lifeforce a short distance away. "She's got medical supplies?"

Yuan nodded, still breathless. Even now, he didn't say much. Earlier, it might've been due to fatigue. Now, a worry exuded from him in a wave that was almost as powerful as this heat. He knelt beside Anxi, his skinny frame and boyish features a contrast to her thicker build and serious demeanor.

Anyone looking at the three of them wouldn't have guessed Terk, with his taller and more athletic physique, was the youngest at fifteen. Yet they still looked to him for direction—like he magically knew how to heal as well as fight.

"What if… What if…" Yuan hesitated, probably reluctant to speak his thoughts out loud with Baba Airi there.

"It won't come to that," Terk replied firmly. "She's too stubborn to let anything stop her."

Baba Airi chuckled, knowing they were discussing her wellbeing. "Darn right."

Terk swelled with optimism. His relief intensified as his mother neared. Although worry laced through her emotions, her overall lifeforce radiated a liveliness he'd never felt from her before. Back home, her spirit had always been burdened by his father's domination. Whenever Terk had visited her in the harem, despondency had been her primary emotion—even when she tried to hide it with smiles and tenderness.

It made his heart swell to know she was happy here. He caught her eye, but this wasn't the time for a mother-son exchange. He dipped his head, then stepped aside to give her space.

She knelt with grace beside Baba Airi, the hem of her light-colored dress settling in the dirt. "Sit her up," she said to Anxi.

Anxi eased the old woman into a sitting position.

"I'm fine," Baba Airi replied in a disgruntled tone that Terk sensed as embarrassment. "These young ones overreacted, is all. You shouldn't have had to come all this way, my Lady."

His mother smiled in sympathy. "It's quite alright, my dear." She held out her cupped hand. "You should take these." She pulled a canteen from around her shoulder. "Drink as much as you want."

A pang twinged Terk's gut. He hadn't expected to miss his mother so much after Father had exiled her. Back home, he'd been so determined to grow up and be a warrior that he'd eschewed her affections. Now, he wished differently. She was stronger than he'd imagined. And more intelligent than he'd ever given her credit for.

And she cared about people—the same ones he'd come to care about. From providing old man Puyi with supplies to repair his storm-damaged house to making sure Beiye got the medicine she needed to treat her arthritis.

Baba Airi shook her head. "Take it," Terk ordered, knowing she'd deny help even to the brink of death unless he was firm.

"I have more than enough," his mother insisted softly. With her dignified demeanor coupled by her graceful features, Terk wouldn't be surprised if the rumors that Lord Qing wanted to make her his concubine were true. He loathed the idea of her becoming someone else's property again, but there wasn't much he could do about it.

"Will she be alright?" Anxi asked, wringing her hands as Baba Airi swallowed the pills. "Will the medicine help?"

His mother shook her head. "I'm not sure. She may need surgery. I'll see what I can do to get a doctor here."

"I'm alright now, everyone." Baba Airi planted her palm on her knee and tried to push herself up.

"Oh no you don't," Terk's mother said. "You must rest." She turned to Terk. "Will you carry her inside?"

Terk dipped his head and obeyed. Baba Airi protested, but only a little. He lifted her easily, noting her scrawny frame. How someone so small could be so tough amazed him. This thought led to a reminder of his younger brother Jori, and a pang swelled in his chest. "I've got you," he said as a promise to let no one he cared about down again.

She rested her head on his shoulder. "Such a good boy."

Terk's cheeks burned. She wouldn't be saying that if she knew who he was—how many people he'd murdered.

A horrendous boom followed by a rumble in the sky halted Terk in his tracks. He glanced up, following a contrail to a pointy-nosed fighter, and cursed, "Chusho."

Baba Airi clutched him. Anxi cursed too. His mother's and Yuan's eyes widened. They all understood what this meant. The Dragon Emperor had finally brought his warmongering madness to this island.

Damn you, Father.

3

A New Warden

An ugly transport vessel eased into the docking bay of the *Black Thresher*. The live feed on the monitor revealed its bulbous nose and fat body. The rear propulsion units resembled giant pimples. There was nothing sinister about this ridiculously shaped ship yet Jori still wanted to slam the entrance hatch shut and crush it.

The thought of having to deal with another damned MEGA made him want to both spit and cry. Would this new arrival be a psychotic monster like Vance? Or a jealous conniver like Major Blakesley? Or an overconfident liar like Gottfried?

Rather than activate the remote controller, he balled his fists. MEGA-Man wouldn't try the same tactic twice, so this newcomer was bound to be worse. As long as no one thought to control him by hurting the people he cared about, he'd face whatever came.

A whisper of coolness from the nearby vent sent a chill down the back of his neck. He scooted his chair forward and made a mental note to either move his desk or adjust the direction of the airflow. A few more changes to Vance's old office, and it might finally be comfortable.

He'd already had this once ostentatious room stripped bare. Gone were the ornate knick-knacks and gaudy furniture. The tapestries had been taken down and the plush rug removed. And all of it discarded into the recycler. The walls were still a headache-inducing yellow and the fancy tiled flooring remained, but at least it no longer reflected the inflated ego of its previous—and now deceased—occupant.

Jori had replaced the oversized desk with its elaborate trimmings and ornamental handles with a more modest one. He'd fabricated it to be the same size as the other, but the electronics were more efficiently arranged with some systems hidden in the side cabinets and the main console able to fold into the tabletop.

Although rearranging this place offered a welcome distraction, he swallowed against the lump of loneliness growing inside him. Everyone in his life was gone: His mother exiled, his brother and his mentor left behind then killed because of his father's madness, and Commander Hapker swept away to a medical facility while the Cooperative Council banished Jori to a faraway planet.

Not that he ever made it there. He and Zaina, his new advocate, had been tricked into boarding this MEGA ship. It'd been an awful experience, but at least he'd found a friend in her. His heart still ached at sending her away, but it had to be done. MEGA-Man wouldn't allow Jori to leave but agreed to let Zaina go if he promised to stay here and travel to Cybernation to meet MEGA-Man in person. He had no idea what to expect. Since he had nothing left to hold on to, he embraced his fate.

He shoved his melancholy aside and scrolled through a document displayed on his monitor. Working provided a minor distraction. As part of the agreement with MEGA-Man, he'd been promoted to the captain of this ship. An eleven-year-old in charge of a spaceship wasn't all that impressive since he was still a prisoner and didn't have the authority to change the ship's course. He didn't even have much control over the crew given that most were mindless cyborgs. All his empty title gave him was a few administrative tasks.

He spent most of his time either repairing bots in the workshop or studying all Vance's files. The latter was tedious, but interesting in its own way. The more he learned about his situation, this ship, the planet Cybernation, and MEGA-Man, the better.

Jori sat back with a sigh. All the information he'd gleaned thus far was rudimentary at best. The only details Vance had on him were his test results or things he already knew. Same with the ship. Vance hadn't hidden the fact that the *Black Thresher* acted as both a warship and a science vessel. Or that its exterior design bore some resemblance to Cooperative ships like the *Odyssey* while its arc drive and other systems ran on different technology.

He'd gleaned more information about Cybernation, but it proved basic as well. A private enterprise had funded the terraforming process. The first colony had arrived about five hundred years ago. Today it was as densely populated as most societies at its age. A pretentious MEGA who called himself MEGA-Man ruled it. And unlike the vast majority of civilizations throughout the galaxy, it didn't adhere to any of the precepts recommended by the MEGA Injunction.

He glanced at the monitor showing the docking bay and swallowed. The transport ship had docked. The only thing left to do was restore atmospheric conditions and pressurize the compartment.

Kiyoshi awoke as though sensing his anxiety. The white-and-tan-blotched rat rose from the plush bed set on the corner of the desk and stretched. With a waddle that made his ugly bald tail sway behind him, he climbed up Jori's arm to his shoulder and nuzzled his cheek. Jori scratched his side, taking comfort as a bit of his loneliness abated.

Kiyoshi had adopted him in a way. Before the conflict with Vance, Jori had let many of the lab animals loose. With his sensing ability, he'd used them to deduce the location of MEGAs with no lifeforce. Afterward, he'd programmed the pest bots to recapture them, but Kiyoshi was too clever. Jori somehow befriended him and they'd been near-constant companions ever since.

Kiyoshi's snuggles turned into curiosity. He shoved his nose down Jori's collar, his whiskers tickling his neck. Jori pulled the necklace out from under his shirt so they could both look at it. The pendant glimmered with copper flecks and the gold chain radiated a warmth that reminded him of his mother. It'd been hers once, but she'd left it behind when Father exiled her. It was the only thing he had as a reminder of her besides memories.

Tears welled in his eyes. He'd likely never hear from her again. If she was safe, maybe even happier now that she no longer had to deal with his father, he'd never know. All he could do was hope she fared better than him.

The door comm chimed. Kiyoshi scrambled down and out of view. Jori wiped his cheeks and tucked his necklace back under his shirt. He didn't detect a lifeforce beyond his door, but only one MEGA ever bothered him nowadays.

"Enter," he said through a tightening throat.

The door swished open, revealing a young man once known as Rodrigo, or Rigo for short. He still had cropped reddish-brown hair and a square jaw. His real eye looked the same—narrow like Jori's though more elongated and heavier lidded. But Rigo had transformed himself by undergoing gene therapy—using Jori's DNA, no less—and getting cybernetic implants.

His once lean physique had filled out and he stood tall rather than hunched like a meek mouse. His happy, eager-to-please demeanor was gone, leaving only a base-model robot in its place. Even his lifeforce had been stripped away. Everything he said or did now was a pre-programmed response.

"Docking complete," Rigo announced in a monotone voice.

Jori sighed and pushed back from his desk, his worries churning like a hurricane. He'd gotten MEGA-Man's first agent arrested and killed the last one. What sort of agent did MEGA-Man send this time?

Jori wiped the sweat from his brow. *Stop being a coward.* He filled his lungs, jutted his chin, and left to meet his next warden.

4
Rescue

The sky rumbled with violence. Rattler jets streaked through the air like a swarm of angry killer bees. Cracks louder than thunder resounded from the direction of the city. Terkeshi's eardrums pounded, along with his speeding heart.

With a small jerk of his head, he gestured for Yuan and Anxi to go ahead. They acknowledged with a tilt of their own, tossed away their tools, and took off to assist their assigned neighbors. Terk glanced about, panic seizing him as he wondered what to do with Baba Airi. He had others to help too, but running with her in his arms couldn't be good for her, and neither was making her run.

"I'll take her," his mother said.

"You can't carry her."

"Can I use that?" She pointed to the wheelbarrow leaning up against the barn.

Terk hesitated. He didn't want to leave her to do this alone.

Without waiting for his reply, she marched over to it and turned it on its wheel. "Put her in."

Still unsure, Terk obeyed anyway.

His mother flicked her hand. "Now go. Do what you trained for. I know where to go."

Her tone brooked no nonsense so he ran to the cottage, grabbed his bow and quiver of arrows, then fled to his neighbor's house.

Gaichu raced alongside him. Leggier now, the pup kept up without tripping over his oversized paws. Determination wrinkled his forehead while his emotions emitted urgency. It didn't matter that he didn't understand what was going on. The pup understood enough to want to help. Terk threw him a pitied look. Gaichu had no clue that he'd have to stay behind.

As he ran, hot, dry air filled his lungs and fueled a frenzied energy. Brittle blades of grass and desiccated branches slapped or sliced his skin as he sprinted down the narrow dirt path, his muscles burning in desperation.

Emergency sirens keened with a nerve-jarring whine while missiles whistled and Rattler jets thundered through the air toward the city. The sounds of war that generally stirred his soul filled him with trepidation instead. Although the emperor's attack focused on the urban area, these villagers were far from safe. In addition to the Dragon Warriors on the warship, his father had undoubtedly ordered his allies to send him additional infantry. Those chimas tended to be more thuggish than the elite soldiers.

He glanced at the Anaconda carrier dominating the sky where hundreds of troop transport ships spewed from its sides like sparks from a flame. Once the destruction of the city was complete, warriors still high on battle lust would spread out in search of more prey.

They wouldn't find any here.

The training Terk had been conducting would save them. In martial defense, Yuan had the grace of a drunken goat. But his aptitude for logistics had been a tremendous help in organizing the drills. Thanks to him, Terk and his other trainees were rescuing the most vulnerable villagers at this very moment.

He smacked a dead branch out of the way and broke from the woods. In the clearing sat a rundown cottage beside a struggling garden. A woman wearing a tattered linen shirt and pants waited out front with an infant balanced on her hip. A twelve-year-old girl stood at her side while a toddler played in the dirt at their feet.

Relief spread over Lili's gaunt face even while she frantically waved him over. Terk ran up and grabbed her tote bag, suppressing a scowl at its heaviness. With no time to remove the nonessentials, he hefted it over his shoulder and scooped up the toddler. The boy yelped. A Rattler zoomed by, starting him into silence. Dozens more missiles and jets ripped through the sky, sending him into a wail.

"It's alright, Yingying," Lili said to him, panic stricken through her voice.

Terk took off. She strived to keep up. Although they'd practiced this scenario many times before, she was having a harder time running with the wailing infant than he was with the toddler and all this stuff.

The little girl kept up better than her mother. Her brow curled with unwavering determination. Anxiousness pervaded her emotions but not with the same intensity as Lili's. Perhaps because she didn't have a full understanding of her fate if soldiers found her.

He spotted his own mother on the path ahead. Her sensing ability undoubtedly told her he was there, but she didn't slow—not that she was going fast. Pushing Baba Airi in a wheelbarrow through the dry, rocky dirt couldn't be easy.

The cries of the younger children had ebbed by the time Terk caught up. Baba Airi's eyes lit up at seeing him and the others. He suspected the prospect of Lady Amarante ferrying her around had mortified her, but the urgency of the situation seemed to have subdued her embarrassment. Now her gaze darted from the sky back to the path as she clutched the sides of the wheelbarrow.

In the drills, Baba Airi had run on her own and his mother had taken a different escape. The wheelbarrow hampered them, but he wasn't about to complain. He swallowed down his trepidation, helped wherever he could, and kept everyone moving.

A trickle of unfamiliar lifeforces pricked his senses. *Soldiers.* They could've been island guards like Washi and Michio, but they exuded the odiousness of thugs and the intensity of predators, marking them as the enemy.

"Stop," he ordered the others before they entered the clearing. He glanced at his mother.

She dipped her head, acknowledging she sensed them too. Since only Washi, Michio, and possibly Major Jingyu were aware of her abilities, she signaled what she detected by showing four fingers and pointing to the right.

"What is it?" Lili asked.

"I think someone's heading this way," Terk replied, speaking the truth without giving away how he knew. "Over here." He waved for them to follow him and led them into the brush. "Behind this rock."

The boulder reached his chest and was just as wide. Dry grass and a gnarl of leafless bushes surrounded it. His mother's gown snagged on a branch, creating a loud snap that made him flinch.

At least the children were quiet now. He suspected his mother might've used her imperium ability to convince them to be calm but dared not verify. Lili's terror-stricken emotions would double if she knew Lady Amarante could not only read minds, but also put suggestions into them. Not that she'd ever do that except in the direst of circumstances—like this one.

"Stay down," he told them. "I'll be over there." He pointed to the opposite side of the trail.

"Don't leave us," Lili whined.

He dropped her bag and handed her the toddler. "Don't worry. If they get close, I'll distract them."

"Be careful." His mother touched his arm, emitting both concern and pride.

Terk squared his shoulders, her faith in him bolstering his confidence.

He hid them well, then backed out, hurrying to pull up the broken reeds they'd trampled on.

The soldiers neared. He pulled an arrow from his quiver and ducked. "Gaichu." He tilted his head, signaling for the dog to come to his side. The pup obeyed, even lying low as though understanding the need for stealth.

Terk's senses told him they'd split up. Two veered away but the others headed this way, exuding a predatory darkness. Terk made a shushing signal at Gaichu. The pup rested his head between his paws, although his ears remained perked and his eyes roved with expectancy.

Terk nocked his arrow and peeked between the blades of grass. Two men, one larger and bald and the other wearing a battered helmet, prowled through the trees. Both bore hardened expressions that made his heart hammer. Their older-model phaser rifles and tattered, mismatched uniforms defined them as lowlife infantry, not Dragon Warriors.

Good. He'd have a better chance of taking out non-professionals. He scoffed inwardly. A *better chance* still wasn't much considering all he had was a shitty bow against their rifles.

They swiveled their heads as they stalked down the path, carrying their rifles low but ready. "Here's a trail," the helmeted one said.

"Check it."

"What do you think?" The man pointed to the ground. "Footsteps or animal tracks?"

Terk froze. Sweat pooled over his brows and dampened his shirt. The acrid smell of his body tweaked his nostrils.

"Who the hell knows," the bald one replied.

Terk slowly exhaled, thankful that the dry dirt didn't hold distinctive impressions.

"I don't know how they expect us to find anyone in this damned wilderness."

"Yeah. Those fuckers in the city got it good."

The men neared Terk's hiding spot. He held his breath while his heart pounded like a mad drummer. His shoulders tensed, ready to shoot if they spotted him.

The rim of the man's helmet appeared above the grass line. If he'd been a Dragon Warrior, his headgear would have sensors. Fortunately, these were just the grunts.

Terk kept his bow taut and crouched lower as they stalked by him. Gaichu must've sensed the need to keep still because even his ears stopped twitching.

The men passed him but advanced closer to where the women hid. The larger man scanned that area for too long. Terk clenched his teeth and prayed the children stayed quiet.

"What do you think? Does that look like another trail?" the helmeted one asked.

The bald soldier narrowed his eyes. "Yeah, I think so."

"Should we follow it?"

The other man made a show of looking beyond. Terk sensed his indecision and wondered whether his mother was using her imperium ability to influence him.

"Naw," the soldier eventually replied. "Let's just stick to the main trail. There's shade up ahead."

"Yeah, if we have to patrol the ass end of his island, might as well stay cooler doing it."

The men moved on. Terk allowed himself to take in a new breath but remained motionless with his muscles still coiled. It wasn't until the lifeforces of those soldiers became a whisper in his mind that he finally relaxed.

"Terk?" came a hushed query.

"Here." He eased his cramped legs into a standing position. "Is everyone alright?"

His mother's head appeared above the boulder, then Lili's. Their shoulders sagged at seeing him.

"It's safe," he said. "Let's go."

Gaichu hopped to his feet with puppyish buoyancy but retained the worried wrinkles in his forehead. Terk helped his mother get Baba Airi and her wheelbarrow out from the brush, then retrieved the toddler from Lili. Careful to keep his senses sharp, he led them down a smaller path, away from the soldiers. The blistering heat lessened somewhat when they reached the other end of the clearing and into a copse of evergreen trees.

"I should get out and walk," Baba Airi said, expressing a concern he was sure she'd meant for them and not herself.

He detected no pain from her, but he didn't want to risk her heart giving out again. "Walk, possibly. But run?" He shook his head. "Stay there."

She didn't protest. They forged ahead. Yuan's idea to clear the trails helped them keep up a decent pace. After coming across those soldiers, he second-guessed whether that had been a wise decision. If the enemy caught sight of them, the women wouldn't be able to outrun them.

The trees thinned, revealing the precipice that led down to the beach. The faint sound of phaser fire trickling along the breeze kept him from feeling relief. He extended his sensing ability. Multiple lifeforces filled his mind. He couldn't discern details but detected several fearful people surrounded by aggression.

"Chusho."

"What?" Lili asked, her sweaty forehead wrinkled and pale.

"I think our people are in trouble down there," he replied. "Go hide." He handed her the toddler and pointed to a thick, brushy area.

She carried her two youngest children and led her daughter over. Before his mother wheeled Baba Airi over too, he stopped her with a hand to her forearm. Since she had the ability to read minds, he asked her for details about the situation with a thought.

Unfortunately, he couldn't read hers in return. They had a secret way of communicating, one that he, Jori, and his mother had created to keep their conversations private, but she didn't use it now—not with Baba Airi there to wonder how they both knew the same unfamiliar words.

Rather than speak, she pointed toward their hidden escape vessel and signed that there were six attackers and eighteen villagers.

Damn. Six was more than enough against farmers.

He gave Baba Airi the bag and sent her and his mother with Lili. With his bow and an arrow in hand, he snuck to the edge of the cliff. Gaichu mimicked him, his crouch becoming a crawl. Together, they peered over the rim.

A thickly wooded and rocky area lay below. Then beyond that, a bare sandy beach where their small spaceship awaited. Covered in tarps the same color as the sand, it was invisible from the sky. But anyone with eyes could see it from here.

The side hatch lay open. Of the five bodies splayed out before it, one was a child.

Those chimas!

He located the six attackers, one patrolling the perimeter on the beach and the rest spread out and taking cover in the trees. Flashes of light erupted from the ship's opening indicating at least one villager was actively on defense. The four closest enemies returned fire.

Chusho!

He hated leaving his mother and others by themselves, but if he didn't stop those soldiers, they'd pick off the villagers one by one. He pressed himself up off the ground and slunk over the side of the rocky ledge.

Damn you, Father. Why do you have to be such a chima?

5

The Beach

A hot breeze blew in from the sea. The salty air carried a sultry scent of fish spiked with the tangy odor of phaser fire. Terkeshi slunk low, then hunkered down behind a clump of bushes. Hopefully, the rustling leaves created a disjointed pattern that'd disguise him even if someone looked his way. If not, he'd be in deep shit.

He glanced at the cliff he'd just descended. Gaichu hid up there, his mottled coat mixing in well with the dry grass and dark shadows. Terk couldn't see him but felt his eyes staring down with reluctant concern.

Stay there, you dummy.

He'd gotten used to the pup following him everywhere, but now wasn't the time. Leaving him there hurt like hell, though. When Terk and the others managed to get on that ship, Gaichu would be stuck here. With no clue how to hunt, he'd wander around and wonder why he'd been abandoned—until he starved to death.

Terk swallowed against the hardness in his throat and shoved the image aside. There were more important things to worry about than a stupid dog—like Baba Airi and his mother, and Lili and her children.

He'd left them up there too, but only for a little while—until he eliminated the six men blocking their way. *Starting with this chima.*

A warrior patrolled the narrow beach that led to the villagers' only means of escape. He paused and yawned, then peered eagerly toward the fight. Terk eyed him with disdain. *"Never let your guard down,"* Sensei Jeruko used to say.

Terk gritted his teeth, scrutinizing the situation. The M-TAK rifle clutched in the warrior's hands bore much usage. His black armor looked sturdier than the earlier soldiers, but he also wore no helmet. Old and tattered boots clad his feet. All this was the strict opposite of the Dragon Warriors with their top-of-the-line weaponry, sharp uniforms, and polished boots. This man did a half-assed job of looking like a soldier—and acting like one. He spent more time kicking up the stones in his path than watching the woods.

Terk nocked his arrow and considered his options. The man's head was the most vulnerable. Jori could've struck true from here, but Terk wasn't so confident. Although he'd been practicing his aim, having only one eye still hindered him.

When the soldier turned away for another pass, he darted closer. Adrenaline shot through him, shifting him into battle-focus. With light steps that would've made his old mentor proud, he advanced. His shoulders strained with tension as he pulled back the arrow. Breathing deep and even, he aimed for the softest part of the man's head—his eyes.

The soldier turned. Terk loosed the arrow. It thwacked into the man's face, dropping him like a sack of pig feed. The pain of death seared into Terk's senses and darkened his vision.

Chusho! His sensing ability had its advantages, but taking in other people's suffering wasn't one of them. If another enemy spotted him, he wouldn't be able to react. He scurried over, almost blindly, and plopped into the sand beside the body. With deep breaths, he gathered his wits enough to see that his arrow had struck true. The pain of death vanished but a lingering sensation remained. The smell of the man's excrement banished it.

Terk swallowed a glob of saliva. With reluctance, he set his bow aside and unslung the quiver. They'd once belonged to Baba Airi's deceased husband. He hated leaving them behind, but taking them with him made little sense. He covered them with dried brush instead—in case they ever came back here.

He confiscated the soldier's rifle, slipping its threadbare sling over his shoulder while keeping it at the ready. A quick inspection of the energy magazine showed it at full power. That still wasn't much. As old as it was, he doubted it held more than a dozen shots. The gun had no variant settings either, meaning no stun, kill, or rapid-shot features. It'd emit one blast at a time and would only kill if it hit just right.

Terk groaned inwardly at the prospect of fighting at such a severe disadvantage. He puffed and gathered his resolve. Using the advantage of his ability, he detected two soldiers nearby. He tiptoed through the brush, careful not to step on twigs or dried leaves. His breathing slowed. Blood rushed to his ears.

There you are, you chimas. The two soldiers knelt behind a fallen tree and looked out to the beach where the ship sat. They weren't wearing headgear either, making them vulnerable—assuming he hit them on his first try.

He crouched and took aim. *No good.* He needed to get closer. He rose. One step. Two. He swallowed. Sweat dripped from his brow, stinging his eye. His lungs screamed for air, but he dared not make even a whisper.

Nearer now, he stooped beside a low-lying boulder and aimed once more. He risked a few readying breaths, lined up the rifle's sights, and fired—twice in quick succession. The warriors slumped over dead before they had a chance to cry out.

"Hey!" someone shouted. "We got another one over here!"

Terk dove behind a bigger rock as phaser fire whipped around him. The smell of ozone intensified as trees and stones bore the brunt of the assault.

The warrior ducked as more blasts spewed from the ship. Terk detected Anxi's tenacious lifeforce. Rage erupted from her like a volcano as she provided a distraction.

Terk contorted himself into a better firing position. He peeked between two boulders where a thick clump of dry grass offered camouflage. The soldier crouched low but not low enough. Terk targeted his head and fired. The man's pain of death echoed through his skull. *Four down, two to go.*

The last two warriors hid behind a rocky outcropping. Their attention on Anxi kept them from noticing Terk as he snuck up on them. From tree to boulder to another tree, he slunk through the woods. If he came up from the rear, they'd have to choose between shielding themselves from Anxi or from him.

A blast struck a branch beside him and snapped it. He slammed his back against the trunk. Burnt linen tweaked his nostrils. Heat seared his upper arm, but it didn't hurt. He tucked in his arms as more phaser fire erupted around him.

His senses weren't acute enough to tell him much. He had a vague idea that one warrior still fired at Anxi while the other had his sights on Terk. But where was he? Had he remained with the other soldier or stalked closer?

The risk of taking another look was too great. But Terk had discovered a new skill back when he and Anxi fought pirate-slavers. His sentio ability had amplified to where he saw the world through his foes' eyes. Literally. It'd served him before, it'd serve him now. He closed his eye and willed his mind to settle.

"Come out, you," the warrior drawled. "Come out and I won't hurt you."

The lie broke Terk's focus. *Concentrate, damn it!*

The intensity of the warrior's drive to kill clashed with Terk's desire to end this chima and save his friends. Sensei Jeruko had always warned him about killing out of hate. In this moment, he understood why. The lifeforce of this warrior had twisted into something more like an animal than a man. Then again, no animal he'd ever encountered carried malevolence.

Like a splash of icy water, Terk's perception snapped into a different perspective as he looked out from the man's eyes. There was the tree Terk hid behind. And there was the hem of Terk's shirt sticking out from one side.

"Come out, little man," the warrior cooed. With his finger poised over the trigger, he waited for his prey to poke his head out.

Terk ignored the warrior's burning emotions and took in all his other sensations. One knee sank into the wet ground. Sweat trickled down his temples. His elbow rested on a stone, keeping his rifle level. A narrow tree was all he had for cover. He was about one hundred sixty degrees from Terk's backside and fifteen meters away.

Terk gritted his teeth. While that wasn't far, he'd have to dart from his position and hit his target before his opponent returned the favor. *Damn it!*

Jori could've done it—easily. A pang twisted in Terk's gut. In the past, he'd been jealous of his younger brother's martial abilities. But now, he'd do anything to have him back. And not because he'd be helpful in situation. Jori had a way of seeing the best in people. He would've loved Baba Airi. Too bad he was dead.

Focus, you idiot! Terk shoved the pain aside. He'd lost his brother to his hateful father, and he wasn't about to lose his mother to that chima as well.

Think! His newfound skill hadn't given him enough edge, but maybe there was more to it. After his fight with the pirate-slavers, he'd told his mother about his new skill. It didn't work the same way as her ability to manipulate people, but perhaps it did something similar.

He snapped back into the man's head and focused on his legs. *You're getting uncomfortable. You need to shift your feet. They're growing achy and cramped.*

Nothing happened. As far as he could tell, the man didn't notice a thing. Terk switched back to himself. His choices were to take a risk or wait the warrior out.

"Argh!" Neither option gave him much of a chance, but he had to do something before reinforcements arrived.

He dived into the soldier's perspective once more. In the past, his own body had locked in place. But perhaps that had been from the shock of the new experience. What if he could be in two places at once?

Staying inside the man, he willed his elbow out from behind the tree. A weird shifting and crawling sensation came over him, but it worked. The soldier saw his arm. Eagerness sprouted through him, but it quickly turned to irritation when Terk didn't expose a more vulnerable body part.

Alright. Now what? Terk pulled his elbow back in and maneuvered his rifle. The peculiar experience of being both himself and the warrior hindered his movements, but by watching through the soldier's eyes, he saw the barrel of his weapon poke from behind the tree.

The soldier smiled when he noticed it, likely thinking how ridiculous and unlikely it was for shooting blindly to work. But Terk used the man's vision to line up his rifle. Holding his breath, he verified his aim and fired.

A twinge sliced through Terk's senses, catapulting his consciousness back to himself. The soldier cried out. A thump followed. Terk huffed in relief. He hoisted his weapon, ducked low, and peeked out. The man remained kneeling but had dropped his rifle. He clutched the side of his head, trying to hold back the blood spilling between his fingers.

The warrior exuded pain, but it wasn't the pain of death. Terk aimed and fired—and missed. Twice more. The man slumped over but his lifeforce still flared. Terk bounded to another tree trunk, then a boulder, firing in rapid succession along the way.

The pain of death shot to the fore, making Terk stumble. He fell behind a thick bush. Fighting through the sensation, he scooted his back against it, his chest heaving.

The soldier's lifeforce disappeared. The spots dancing across Terk's vision dissipated.

After catching his breath, he checked his weapon. Less than half the power remained. It should be enough for one more man. He refocused his ability. The last warrior had all his attention on Anxi.

Something else tickled his senses. He spanned his awareness outward.

Chusho! More warriors headed this way—maybe a half-dozen. His shoulders fell. Despite the extra help from Anxi, the odds were too great. She had to protect the villagers already on the ship. And— damn it—all he had was a shitty rifle and an even shittier aim.

He clenched his teeth, summoning his resolve. Fuck these chimas and fuck his father. He'd be damned before he gave up. Too many people were counting on him.

Determination thundered through him. He huffed, then crept from his hiding place, keeping his rifle level. If he got this one soldier out of the way, he had a better chance of defeating the newcomers. But first, he needed to replenish his supply.

He came upon the body of the warrior and grabbed his ankle. With a grunt, he pulled him behind a rock that barely reached his thigh. The dead man wore a utility belt. Protruding from each of the little pockets for easy access was an array of useful items: a first-aid bundle, a dagger, a grenade, and a full energy magazine. This man wasn't a Dragon Warrior either, but he ranked higher than the other thugs.

Rather than remove all the stuff, Terk pinched the belt's buckle and snapped it open. He rolled the dead man over to take it off it and found a holster carrying an old-fashioned firearm and a pouch containing one clip of about a dozen bullets. *Perfect.*

"Haru!" the last warrior bellowed. "Get your ass back over here!"

Terk's heart sped as he secured the belt around his waist. It hung awkwardly on his hips, but he couldn't tighten it. It would have to do. He familiarized himself with the location of all the items in the pouches, then hoisted his new rifle. This one had a stun setting, but these chimas deserved nothing less than a full kill shot.

He crept to the edge of the rocky area. The last warrior lay within his sights but too much underbrush prevented a clear shot. He tiptoed between trees and boulders, keeping as close to the larger ones as possible.

"Haru!" the last soldier called out again. "Where the hell are you? I'm getting hammered here."

Terk's breaths fell shallow. He eased around a tall outcropping. The ground wasn't level here, but it kept him covered.

"Mother," he said in his head, hoping she'd be able to read his mind from her location. *"Make sure Anxi knows it's me."* Anxi wouldn't hear her, but his mother's ability might help her understand the other person out there was on her side. Terk realized his mother might've been doing this all along. Not that Anxi needed prompting to protect the people on the ship, but the timing of her distractions had coincided with his actions.

Even now, her irregular potshots kept the warrior's attention. Either that, she was getting low on ammo.

"Damn it, Haru!" A crunching sound indicated the man moved around, possibly preparing to investigate.

"Mother, I need you." He prayed she heard him. Then he prayed she had the skill to do what he needed. He wasn't sure how strong her imperium ability was or to what extent she could force someone to do her bidding, but he had to try. *"Can you distract him?"*

Nothing happened. He swallowed, scraping the dryness of his throat. Was she having trouble? Or maybe she didn't hear him. *Mother, can you—*

The man grunted. Terk poked his head out. The warrior doubled over, his firing arm held over his gut. Assuming his mother had given him a shot of agony, Terk positioned himself for better aim. The warrior's eyes caught his and widened as a phaser blast struck him in the face. Terk pulled back, squeezing his one eye shut until the pain of death subsided.

Blasts crackled around him. The other soldiers were too far to get a good view, but close enough for him to detect five distinct lifeforces.

He pulled the single grenade from his belt and waited. He didn't know when, but Anxi had stopped firing. Except for the periodic crunch of footsteps, the beach lay silent. His senses told him the warriors were spreading out. He couldn't let them get too far from one another. Nor could he allow them to flank him. He gripped the grenade in his sweaty palm.

If he lobbed it, he'd expose himself. And his mother couldn't distract all five at once.

Anxi, please tell me you have more ammo.

As if in response, more phaser fire spewed from the ship. One warrior fell, his pain penetrating Terk's senses. Terk took advantage of the diversion and dove into a roll. He landed behind a shorter boulder and tossed his grenade. An explosion rocked the ground beneath him, hurtling shards of timber, rubble, and shrapnel.

He ducked, covering his head. Sharp pricks pelted his back and hands. But three warriors expired, one was unconscious, and the last one cried out in pain.

"Cease fire!" he bellowed to Anxi. "Cease fire! It's me! Terk!"

She stopped. Terk bolted to his feet, spotted the writhing soldier, and fired. The man died. Adrenaline kept Terk going despite the pain of death as he raced to the unconscious one. As soon as his vision cleared, he shot point blank and killed him too.

The debris settled. Except for the ringing in his ears, a deafening silence fell over the beach. This battle was over, but there was more to come.

6
MEGA-Doctor

The stark white walls and tables put Jori on edge. He hated this ship. Why did everything have to be so sterile? He'd never minded simplicity, but this was extreme. A cafeteria shouldn't feel like a damned operation room.

At Doctor Percy Sokolov's suggestion, they'd come here. "*I prefer a more comfortable environment to get to know one another*," he'd said. The request seemed sincere, so Jori agreed.

The doctor, whose black hair graced his head like a helmet, put on a genuinely kind smile. Unlike Gottfried or Vance, he had a strong lifeforce—and it didn't radiate a hint of deceit or malice.

Jori wasn't about to let that fool him. Gottfried had pretended niceness too.

Keeping his eye on the exit and his guard up, he stayed on his feet until the short and squat man sat before taking a chair himself.

Doctor Sokolov winked and smiled again, the breadth of his mouth proportional to his wide head. "I sincerely apologize for what Vance did to you," he said, his words ringing with sincerity.

Jori maintained a blank façade while waiting for the inevitable shift in tone.

"His treatment of you and your friends was done entirely without permission," the doctor continued with an earnestness that put Jori off balance. "It was not at all condoned by my boss."

Yeah, right. "So why is MEGA-Man so intent on keeping me?" Jori asked, wanting to skip the friendly overture.

Doctor Sokolov folded his hands and leaned in as though to tell a secret. "You have so many wonderful qualities, making you one of MEGA-Man's most important allies."

Jori frowned. With Gottfried and Vance, he'd gotten a sense that his value lay in his abilities as well as his bloodline, but this level of importance made his insides writhe. Just how desperate was MEGA-

Man to use him? Determined enough to force him? Or kill him if he didn't comply?

"He knows you are reluctant," the doctor continued, "and he understands. His last two agents have terribly wronged you. His regret is great, as is mine. We want to make it up to you."

"Then let me go," Jori retorted.

"Of course. Once you meet MEGA-Man in person, you will be free to leave."

Jori harrumphed, doubting it would be so simple. "I don't trust MEGA-Man enough to believe he'll keep that promise."

"Hmm." The doctor glanced up and tapped his cheek. "Yes. I can see why." He filled his lungs. "What if we arrange for you to return to Commander Hapker?"

Jori's breath hitched. "How?"

"I'm not sure yet. But despite the adverse consequences brought about by Gottfried, we still have influence within the Cooperative."

Jori had suspected as much but schooled his emotions. His thoughts spun with all the things that'd happened because of Gottfried and Vance as well as the upheaval on the space station caused by the MEGA-Haters.

Being with Hapker again tugged at the strings around his heart, but he wasn't sure whether he could sacrifice the rest of the galaxy for him. Zaina came to mind too. Had she made it home? Was she safe?

He planted a solid glare into the doctor's eyes. "But you and the Cooperative are at war. How can I be sure he won't get killed in the chaos MEGA-Man is causing?"

The doctor tapped his cheek again. "That's a good question, but I'm sure MEGA-Man will see that he stays away from the fighting."

Jori scoffed. "I can't trust MEGA-Man so long as he's killing innocent people."

Doctor Sokolov winked, implying a shared secret. "The Cooperative isn't innocent."

This resonated when Jori thought about certain individuals like Calloway or Sergeant Banks. But he reflected on the friends he'd made on the *Defender* despite being considered a criminal. Lieutenant Gresher, Sergeant Ortega, and others were part of the Prontaean PG-Force, making them fair targets in war. But the sneakiness of Gottfried's attacks still amounted to murder.

"What about those on the Avalon space station?"

"We didn't kill anyone who wasn't innocent."

Jori cocked his brows. "I watched your soldiers open fire into the docking bay."

"They only targeted the ones who had attacked you."

Jori narrowed his eyes. "But Vance fired this ship's weapons at the entire station. You can't tell me innocent people didn't die because of it. Vance planned on attacking other places too. I'm not stupid. I know MEGA-Man sanctioned it."

"Hmm. Yes." The doctor pinched his lip, then puffed. "But you should understand better than anyone, there are sometimes casualties of war that cannot be prevented."

Jori firmed his jaw. "A war you started."

"Only because of how society treats our people. That makes society our enemy."

"The governing bodies are your enemy. Not the people in it. Not everyone in the Cooperative believes MEGAs are bad." He wasn't sure how true that was. Commander Hapker wasn't the type of person to mistreat anyone, not even if they were the son of a homicidal maniac. But he wasn't sure how many others shared his values. "And what about the children? Do you consider them your enemies too?"

The doctor met Jori's scowl with a sympathetic look. "This bothers you, hmm? May I ask why, considering how horribly the Cooperative has treated you?"

"Not everyone there has mistreated me."

"But those who have been good to you are few, yes?"

Jori scowled, unable to deny it. He wanted to hate MEGA-Man's new agent, but the doctor wasn't making it easy.

"There's another reason it bothers me," he said, trying another tactic. "You know I'm a sentio-animi, right? I don't just sense emotions, I also feel it when someone dies. It's painful. Worse than anything you can imagine."

The doctor pulled away. "Oh. Oh my. I wasn't aware of that. That certainly adds a different perspective." He leaned back in, his forehead wrinkled downward. "So you sympathize with others because you endure their suffering?"

"That's not the only reason," Jori snapped. "My father's murdered many people, all in the name of *his cause*. And it's always felt wrong."

"If this sort of thing bothers you, perhaps we can provide you with—."

"An emotion chip like Doctor Claessen's? Forget it." Sometimes he hated having to feel everything, but he was also glad. "If I didn't experience other people's pain, I might've ended up like my father."

"Who you despise," the doctor said. "Yes. This is all making sense now. I see why you are so wary of us. If only Gottfried and Vance had spoken more with you about this, perhaps MEGA-Man could've understood."

The doctor's empathy grated on Jori's nerves. He'd expected MEGA-Man to send someone who'd overwhelm him with justification, but this tactic to win him over with genuine understanding muddled his resolve. "I tried to tell Gottfried."

"Yes, well, he was a bit of a fanatic."

Jori harrumphed.

"I'm afraid there's not much you and I can do here and now to remedy that, but I truly want to make things better going forward. I'm here to listen to you, to learn your perspective."

"And what good will that do? You're not the one in charge. MEGA-Man is."

"Quite true but consider me an emissary. Help me understand your point of view, I will share it with MEGA-Man, and perhaps we can find some common ground."

Although the doctor radiated sincerity, Jori expected nothing to change. He wasn't about to give up, though. If this agent was willing to listen, he might as well put it to the test. "Tell him I don't like what was done to Rodrigo. I get that he wants to recruit more people but the man who existed before the augmentations is dead."

"It was his choice."

"He didn't have all the information! You took advantage of his ignorance." *And his idiocy.*

"I see. Hmm. I wasn't aware of that. We rarely screen people for the procedure, though."

"Major Blakesley tried to stop it, but Vance overruled him."

The doctor shook his head. "Vance was good at many things, but relations wasn't one of them." He sighed. "I will certainly bring this issue up with MEGA-Man."

Jori growled. Although the doctor concurred, he was merely the middleman. "Why are you even here? MEGA-Man sent you to replace Vance, but why? Did he think that by sending someone nicer that I'd agree to be used?"

Doctor Sokolov tilted his head apologetically. "We just want to help you."

Jori almost scoffed again. "I don't *need* your help. I wouldn't even be here if it wasn't for Gottfried."

The doctor splayed his hands. "I'm so sorry, young man. Things really weren't supposed to happen this way."

Jori lurched forward with a scowl. "And how *was* it supposed to happen?"

Doctor Sokolov's features wrinkled with sympathy. "The fight for MEGA rights was supposed to be peaceful. MEGA-Man was playing the long game. He'd discreetly placed his people into positions of authority so they could change policy from the inside. But then Gottfried got found out, and plans changed."

"Are you saying this war is my fault?" Jori barked. Anger spewed out but guilt churned within.

The doctor put up his hands. "Not at all. It was Gottfried's fault. He wasn't supposed to get caught."

"You mean he was supposed to get away with killing all those people and stealing the schematics to the perantium emitter." Jori curled his lip. "That doesn't sound like a peaceful transition to me."

For the first time since the conversation began, Doctor Sokolov emitted frustration. It didn't show on his face, but he paused as though trying to rein in his emotions and collect his thoughts.

After a minute or so, he sucked in a lungful of air and bobbed his head. "I see we have a lot of work to do to make things right."

"To convince me you're not a bunch of warmongering chimas like my father, you mean," Jori mumbled.

The doctor pretended not to hear. "I don't want to hurt anyone, least of all you. I just want the same rights as everyone else—to be accepted by society and to be free to make my own choices."

Jori bit the inside of his cheek. Doctor Sokolov's words made sense. In a way, they shared similar circumstances. Society didn't accept either of them and neither had the freedom to make their own decisions.

"So why become a MEGA in the first place?"

The doctor harrumphed. "It wasn't my choice. My mother had a hard time getting pregnant, so when she finally did and found out it was a girl, she had me genetically altered. All she did was to convert the XX chromosomes to an XY pair but it was enough to get her in trouble and have me labeled."

Jori's eyes widened. Was the MEGA Injunction that strict? Could such a simple modification really get someone condemned? It didn't seem fair.

"That's right," Doctor Sokolov said with a wink. "They marked me for life and limited my future. I still received a public education but no college would admit me. I landed a decent job on an independent freighter. My non-MEGA crew mates gave me flack sometimes but nothing terrible." Despondency trickled through the doctor's emotions. "Then my captain died and the second officer booted me. He'd always disliked me. I'm not sure if it was just a personality clash or because I'm a MEGA. Either way, he spread the word that I was no good. I couldn't find a job anywhere after that. I was near starvation when one of MEGA-Man's operatives found me. He helped me find my purpose."

"Which is?"

"To give people like me a fair chance."

"By killing."

"When necessary, yes."

"Have you ever killed anyone?"

"Not directly, but I've taken part in a few missions." Doctor Sokolov leaned back and folded his hands over his belly. "What about you? Have you ever killed anyone?"

Jori scowled, refusing to answer. His self-righteous debate crumbled to dust.

7
Odyssey

The tendrils of a headache spiked in Captain Silas Arden's temple. It'd been one stressful incident after another. This most recent had his wife in tears. It broke his heart to see her this way, especially since there was little he could do to help.

Symphonia stood beside him, out of view of the video call opened on his desk, and dabbed her red-rimmed eyes with a tissue. He generally admired how her bright-flowered dress brought out the glow in her warm brown skin and exemplified her sunny demeanor, but today it clashed with her distress.

Not four days ago, she'd been crying for a different reason. After a month-long visit, her sister and nephew had said a teary goodbye, then transferred to a cruise liner for their new jobs as part of the entertainment staff. A few hours earlier, Director Sengupta had brought him news that MEGAs had attacked the liner. Those who survived were taken as prisoners.

"I'm sorry, Captain," Councilor Alvia said in the live video feed. Her forehead wrinkled all the way to the top of her bald head. The purple bags under her eyes hinted at her exhaustion. "That boy you rescued has thrown everything into disarray."

"Jori?" Arden asked, a twinge of consternation intensifying the ache in his skull. "He was the one who revealed the infiltration. Is there something you're not telling me?"

The councilor shook her head and waved her hand. "I didn't mean to say he'd caused it. Merely that his discovery has set off a chain reaction that we're hard pressed to contain."

Arden frowned. Jori was a hero. Yet because he was the son of another dangerous enemy, no one would acknowledge it. Arden had mixed feelings himself, but he shouldn't. Yes, the boy had commandeered his ship once. However, that was Admiral Zimmer's fault for insisting on detaining him and his brother even though they'd done nothing wrong. After that, the child had nearly died while rescuing several Cooperative officers. He'd saved more people after finding out Gottfried, an admiral's aide, was a MEGA.

He wondered where Jori was now, but only briefly. Councilor Alvia was right about one thing—everything was in disarray. But she still hadn't answered his question. "I'm not sure I understand, Councilor. Are you saying nothing can be done to help them?"

Councilor Alvia's forehead creased again. "I'm afraid we don't have the resources."

Symphonia sucked in air. He froze his end of the video and pinched the bridge of his nose as the headache sharpened.

"Is there anything we can do?" Symphonia asked him.

Arden tossed her an apologetic glance, then resumed the feed. "I understand the PG-Force is busy defending against MEGAs, but surely this is a priority too."

"Priorities are popping up on every planet, space station, and ship under our domain." She raised her hands in helplessness. "The Avalon space station was destroyed. Archelians discovered their president and many of its government officials are MEGAs. The communication hubs in the Zendian sector have been disabled. A ship of unknown and superior design attempted to attack the Tanirian Protectorate." She sighed. "I'm truly sorry, Captain. We're on the lookout for MEGA ships, but we don't know how to detect them through their disguises."

"They're likely taking our people somewhere. My guess would be Cybernation," he replied using the planet's slang term over its formal name. "It's the MEGA's homeworld, and it's probably where MEGA-Man resides. I realize it'd be risky to send a rescue party, but many of those prisoners are civilians… Some are children."

"We've sent a few ships out for reconnaissance but haven't heard from them yet."

For a moment he wondered if the ships had simply failed to check in, but her tone and eyes said it all. He suppressed a groan. "Do we know what the MEGAs are doing with all the people they've taken?"

Councilor Alvia's features fell, making her wrinkled skin sag. "We can only guess. Since there've been no hostage declarations, I suspect…" She glanced away with brows tilted in despair.

Symphonia leaned in, still out of view of the feed. She didn't say anything but Arden knew what she was thinking. "They're turning them into MEGAs," he said.

Symphonia covered her mouth. Tears welled in her eyes. Arden harbored the same horror but kept it at bay. All his life he'd been told any form of augmentation was bad. Worse, Lieutenant Gresher had reported that the soldiers who tried to take over the *Defender* seemed soulless.

"I'm afraid so," the councilor replied.

Arden's chest constricted. "We'll lose this war if they convert all our people."

"Trust me, rescuing our people is *high* on our list of priorities." Her brows furrowed with the intensity of a promise.

Arden believed her sincerity. And although he understood, his instinct to run off and try to rescue his family himself released a drowning helplessness. His large expedition vessel had weaponry and powerful shields. It even had a small PG-Force presence. But the *Odyssey* wasn't a military ship. The weaponry and shields were for defense. And the PG-Force offers functioned as security. Only a handful of them had offensive training.

"Thank you," Arden replied, though he had nothing to thank her for. He disconnected the feed and slumped back in his chair with a heaving sigh.

Symphonia grasped his shoulder and squeezed. He met her eyes and patted her hand. "I'm sorry," he said, knowing the words sounded hollow.

A tear ran down her cheek. "Perhaps Commander Hapker will have some insight."

Arden nodded. She might be right. It was a dim hope, but it was all he had.

8

The Dusty Rose

The ship was called the *Dusty Rose*. It might've been aptly named at one time, but no longer. Now it was a heap of junk. Hidden here weeks ago in anticipation of an assault, it lay like a dead slug in the sand. A sandy-colored tarp camouflaged the top, but nothing disguised its battered belly. Grime festooned the once silvery hull. The place where its name and emblem had once been now looked like a festering pimple. The hatch's hydraulic pistons and hinges showed signs of rust. And the flooring inside was as uneven as old man Huang's teeth.

Terkeshi's lips curled. Assuming this damned ship hadn't perished while rotting here like a beached whale, it was supposed to take thirty or so villagers up into space. But he couldn't imagine this piece of shit flying.

He heaved a sigh. This was the only way to get away from the rampage of the Dragon Emperor's soldiers, so he had to try it.

"Anxi!" he called out. "The area's secure. You're safe!"

Anxi poked her head out. So did Huang. A few wisps of his hair stood in disarray on his tan, balding scalp. His lean body swayed unsteadily as he ambled down the gangplank. "Dead? All of them?"

Terk stepped from the treeline. "Only the ones here. I don't know what's happening on the rest of the island."

Huang arched his neck, peering up and down the beach and behind Terk. "Where are the others?"

"It's just me," Terk replied, knowing the man was asking after the other defenders. "Baba Airi and a few other villagers are still on the cliff but they'll be down shortly."

"Just you?" Huang glanced at the dead soldier, then eyed the rifle in Terk's hands. "Where'd you get that?"

"I took it from an attacker."

Yuan came out. "Terk has had some training. He's the one who's been helping us learn to defend ourselves."

Huang's gaze narrowed as he studied him. Terk skipped the explanation and turned to Yuan. "Status?"

"Everyone is here except the families across the bridge. They'd already been overrun."

"Chusho," Terk cursed. "Where's Chenwei and Tingtai?" They were the ones who were supposed to retrieve them.

"Huang said Tingtai was killed."

Terk's shoulders fell. He was about to ask after Chenwei when the willowy twenty-year-old appeared with his head hanging. "There were too many. I barely got away myself."

"Your father?"

"I-I was out in the field when the attack came. I ran for the house, but soldiers were already there."

Terk scowled. His sensing ability told him that Chenwei had spoken the truth, but he'd always had a cowardly aura. Even Yuan, who wasn't much of a fighter, was braver than this wimp.

"Anxi," he called and she exited. "Baba Airi, Lili, and Lady Amarante are still up on the cliff. Go help them. Baba will need to be carried." Anxi darted off. Terk turned to Yuan. "Search the dead soldiers. Pull all the weapons you can. And hurry. We must get off this island."

Yuan's breath hitched. "Rui was killed. I saw him get shot down. We don't have a pilot."

"I'll take care of that," Terk replied.

Yuan and Huang's brows tilted into a question, but he didn't give them a chance to ask. "Get going," he said to Yuan. "Huang, get everyone in the ship secured. Quickly, before reinforcements arrive."

They hopped to it. Terk helped confiscate weaponry. Most of the energy magazines were low on power, but it was better than nothing. He found more knives and another grenade, plus a couple of flash bombs. No more pistols, though. One man had feet about Terk's size, so he took his shoes. He removed an armored vest from another warrior.

A cracking branch sent him ducking and reading his weapon. He extended his senses. Two people headed this way. Their benevolent lifeforces marked them as Guozhi and his wife, Beiye—the ones Tingtai was supposed to help.

Terk lowered his rifle and ran over, calling their names so they'd know it was him. Guozhi, a thin old man with bushy brows, saw him first and frantically waved him over. Beiye kept her curly, grey-haired head pointed down and stepped gingerly around the larger rocks. She slipped. Guozhi gripped her upper arm and steadied her.

Terk helped from the other side. Between the two of them, they brought her to the clearing.

"Thank you," Guozhi said. "I wasn't sure she'd make it this far, but I wouldn't leave without her." His light brown eyes warmed as he smiled at her. She returned it with a loving expression.

Terk made a small smile himself. The way they doted on one another was touching, even if it sparked a little envy.

After leading them to safety, he and Yuan swept sand and kelp away from the intake portions of the ship.

"What about them?" Yuan asked about the five bodies spread out over the sand.

Terk used his sensing ability and determined they were indeed dead. Two of them had nearly made it to the open hatch before they were killed. There was the child, too. Bibi was only seven years old. Now she was dead, her lifeless eyes seeming to gaze at the wooden doll that'd rolled beyond her grasp. *Chimas*.

Terk swallowed. "We don't have time to bury them."

Yuan opened his mouth in protest, but a Rattler jet zoomed by and he snapped it shut. "Can you really fly this thing?" he asked instead.

"Yes," Terk replied, not wanting to explain how he'd trained in simulators on the very warship waging war on them now, and how he was a better pilot than most of those flying the Rattlers above.

To his surprise, Yuan didn't pester him with more questions. He undoubtedly would at some point. Others would too, but he'd worry about that later.

His mother arrived. Relief brightened her features, then her expression turned pained. He gave her a consoling look, knowing she didn't feel good about helping him kill those warriors. She likely felt bad about him having to take lives as well.

Gaichu bounded after her, his pink tongue hanging out with joy.

"Gaichu!" Terk yelled. "I told you to stay."

"You mean to leave him behind?" his mother asked.

Terk ignored the pain in his chest. "I can't bring him with us."

"Why not?"

"We don't have a way to secure him."

"This is your dog, right?"

A couple months ago he would have denied it. But if he said it now, his mother would know he was lying. "Yes."

She smiled. "Then we'll find a solution."

Terk's insides did a flip. He couldn't have decided for himself. Not after telling all the other villagers they had to abandon their livelihoods, which included their own pets and livestock. But she was a noblewoman. Nobody would contradict her.

"Thank you," he said in his head, smiling back.

Inside the ship, the cargo area had been fitted with two dozen seats, each with a harness system salvaged from other ships or handmade by the villagers. Not everyone would get one. The children wouldn't fit in them anyway. But they'd created padded areas with makeshift straps along the hull.

There weren't enough bunks either. Six cramped quarters took up the rear half of the habitable fore sections of the ship. Each only had four beds, leaving some people to share or sleep on the floor. This ship didn't have much of a common area either. Two bathrooms flanked a tiny kitchenette with little counter space and no dining tables.

He had no idea of their destination, but this would be a long trip regardless.

Nearly everyone was secured. Desperate faces met his. Some eyed his new rifle and utility belt. Others looked beyond him, likely hoping for the island guards to come in after him. But the only ones to arrive were Lili and her children, followed by Anxi with Baba Airi.

"I haven't seen Rui," Anxi said as she set the old woman in a chair.

"Yuan says he's dead."

Anxi gasped. "Then how will we get away from here?"

"I know how to fly."

Her shoulders sagged and her anxiety waned. He liked how she didn't push for more answers. That wasn't the same for the others. Several questions came at him at once.

Terk put up his hand. "I don't have time to explain so you'll just have to take my word for it."

Faces fell in a combination of dismay and disbelief. Terk ignored their whispers. After everyone was buckled in, including Gaichu with the children, Terk went to the cockpit. He did a cursory inspection, noting all the essential controls. They were outdated, but everything seemed in good order.

"You sure you can fly this thing?" Huang asked as he took the copilot's seat.

"Positive," Terk replied. He plopped into the pilot's seat. "Do you know where we're going?"

"I do. Do you know how to navigate so we can get there?"

Terk wanted to reply that he was probably a much better pilot than Rui but settled for lifting his eyebrow instead.

He prepped the engine and reviewed the gauges. Despite how rundown this ship was, everything checked out. The engines started out soft, then built to a roar. *So far, so good.*

"Should we remove the cover from the ship?" Huang asked.

"No. Once we lift off, all that will fall off."

He pressed the liftoff button. The ship jerked up. It was normal, especially since part of the landing gear had gotten covered by sand, but yelps resounded from the hold. If they thought that was bad, it was about to get worse. He pulled the lever to make the ship rise, doing it slowly to ensure he didn't hit any of the nearby trees. The *Rose* jostled. More cried out. Huang gripped the arms of his chair.

"This is normal!" Terk yelled back, trying to contain his annoyance.

After clearing the trees, he engaged the throttle. The ship took off, rising at a slant. Terk prepped the booster. The thrill of flying consumed all his senses. It was as though a gust of cool wind had pushed him over the ridge of a mountaintop and sent him gliding like a bird. His face flushed. His skin tingled. He no longer heard anyone in the back cry out. It was just him and the ship—a crappy one, but still a ship. Damn, he loved to fly.

Pressure built in his ears. Realizing these people wouldn't understand what was happening, he yelled out assurances and instructions on how to pop them.

The SRS beeped. Terk tapped the screen. A red dot flashed in the upper right corner.

"What's that?" Huang asked.

"A Rattler." *Damn it*. The flutter in his chest constricted. This ship barely had any defenses. He prayed the *Dusty Rose* would make it to where he could ignite the boosters—assuming it didn't fall apart on its own beforehand.

No simulation had prepared him for this.

9
Dogfight

The *Dusty Rose* rattled violently as it approached escape velocity. A high-pitched whine keened from the aft section. The control panel shuddered, rendering the gauges impossible to read. The passengers cried out, believing the ship was about to fall apart. They were probably right… But that wasn't their biggest worry.

Energy blasts bombarded the *Rose*. The shields dropped from ninety to less than seventy percent in a matter of seconds. Terkeshi faced a tactical dilemma. Executing evasive maneuvers might disrupt his attempt to escape this planet. But if he stayed his course, and if their defenses held, they'd be in space where the Rattlers couldn't follow.

Sixty percent. *Chusho!* There was no way those shields would last long enough. He manipulated the thrusters into a serpentine path that maintained their ascent. With any luck the enemy would have a more difficult time targeting them since energy cannons couldn't change course.

It worked. A few blasts struck, but most missed. Shield depletion slowed. At fifty-five percent now, he had a better chance of flying this piece-of-shit ship beyond the exosphere.

The green icon representing the enemy fighter still closed in. Curiously, it stopped firing. Maybe it'd depleted its capacitors during the dogfight against the island's air force. *I sure as hell hope so.*

His optimism burst into a million pieces as vector lines depicting incoming missiles appeared on the screen. The *Rose*'s shields, now at forty-seven percent, offered no protection against kinetic weapons. And this damned ship's point-defense system was rudimentary at best—if it was even operational.

Only one way to find out. He'd prepped them earlier but held off on using them until the missiles came within optimal range.

Huang's brows folded over his eyes as he tried to decipher the various readings on the display. "What's this red light for?"

Terk groaned inwardly. "Don't talk while I'm flying."

"Does this mean they're getting closer?" Huang persisted, either not hearing him or ignoring him.

That's the QR gauge, idiot. But he kept the comment to himself and concentrated on their escape vector.

The *Rose* accelerated through the thinning atmosphere. Terk clenched his thighs and tightened his gut to counter the g-force effects. His mouth watered at the taste of freedom glittering ahead. A rear-facing camera displayed the receding planet on an auxiliary screen. From the now imperceptible Hisui Island to the oceanic expanse to the continental landmasses, the farmer's life fell behind him. Leaving triggered the same twisting feelings of loss as when he'd lost Jori and fled from his father.

"Are those missiles?" Huang asked as he leaned toward the screen with nervousness radiating from him like the spikes of the sea creatures Baba Airi liked to cook. "Can we evade them?"

"No. They're guided by AI."

"But they're getting closer."

Terk growled. "I know! Now be quiet so I can concentrate."

The *Rose* strained against the planet's gravitational well. G-forces pinned Terk to his seat. The engines squealed, burning off the last vestiges of their fuel like a dying star.

"Aren't we going to do something about them?" Huang's tone elevated as high as his distress.

Shut up, damn it.

The relentless missiles closed the gap. Terk willed the spaceship to hurry as the backup fuel drained faster than Senshi Rumio's liquor bottle.

The warheads crossed the proximity threshold. An annoying beeping filled the cabin.

"What's that?" Huang asked.

Terk gritted his teeth as he assessed the weapons status display. Four of the eight readiness indicators glowed green. *Chusho.* Each weapon port housed one set of five anti-ballistics, totaling twenty questionable countermeasures. If only he'd been able to convince Washi and Michio to let him inspect the ship before they hid it there.

Four shots were still better than zero. He didn't believe in luck, but he poured his faith into it now as he fired the first set of anti-ballistics.

The ship rocked. Five mini disruptors deployed from the *Rose*. Two kilometers. One-and-a-half. One. *Come on. Come on.*

Three struck the lead missile, disrupting its guidance system and neutralizing it. Terk wiped the sweat from his brow.

Two more incoming warheads followed. Terk targeted them and fired. The indicator light turned red, signifying the launch mechanism had malfunctioned. He gritted his teeth and shot at the next one.

One and a half kilometers. One. *Almost there.*

One of the two missiles disappeared from the screen. Terk held his breath. The second blinked out. "Yes!"

His elation was short-lived. His heart pattered as four more enemy warheads closed in. Huang's emotions spiked. The passengers groaned as the Gs pressed in on them. Someone puked and the odor wafted into the cockpit.

Terk fired the last set of disruptors. Nothing happened. The light remained green so he tried again. Nothing.

He smacked his hand on the edge of the console but kept his curses behind his lips for the sake of the stressed passengers. He gripped the flight controls instead and prayed.

One missile fell away, likely malfunctioning because of the thinning atmosphere, but the other three were mere meters from impact.

"Hold on!" he yelled back.

The spaceship continued its ascent. Gravitational influence from the planet waned. The jostling of the ship lessened. A tapestry of stars and galaxies sharpened into focus like a blast of cool water on a hot day.

The missiles, designed for atmospheric operation, dropped away. The Rattler veered off before it too failed to operate.

Terk cut off the *Rose*'s engines and expelled a huff. His body wanted to drift in the microgravity, but the straps held him in. He would've celebrated their escape, but he'd merely exchanged one enemy for an even greater one.

Another alarm sounded. An additional signal appeared at the curvature of the planet. An inherent fear reached up from Terk's gut and clutched his throat. All the will he'd summoned to save himself and these people crumbled and died as the information about the oncoming ship came in.

He was a child once more, helpless against the violent rage of a dragon. There was no escape as the *Dragon*, his father's ship, advanced like a wrathful monster.

10
Emptiness

The scenes swirled and shifted. Jori pitched from one savage fight to another, each worse than the last. Fists, knives, and phaser fire came at him from all sides. He flailed in desperate helplessness, but the barrage of attacks kept coming. From Corporal Calloway on the *Odyssey* to his father on the *Dragon*, super-soldiers on the *Defender* and Vance on the *Black Thresher*, they all wore masks of either sadistic coldness or infinite rage as they tried to kill him.

The nightmare spun around and around, like a typhoon of biting wind and sharp-edged debris. *It's not real. It's not real!* He turned to run only to face Vance once more. He clenched his fists and roared, "I killed you already!"

Vance's mouth spread into a chilling smile. "I'll never die."

Jori dropped to his knees in hopeless exhaustion. Vance zoomed closer with ethereal swiftness. Jori flinched but refused to back away. He jutted his chin instead. "Do your worst, you chima."

Vance bellowed. Jori tried to close his eyes but the nightmare didn't let him. He braced himself against the inevitable. The man's giant fist came down in a slow-motion arc. Jori's heart thudded. Vance's sinister smile turned to boiling rage. Jori flared his nostrils and bared his teeth in defiance.

Vance's knuckles struck in a blinding flash of white. Jori gasped. Physical sensations bombarded him, but none of them pain. Reality coalesced around him.

His chest heaved in ragged breaths. The relentless pounding of his heart threatened to burst. He blinked until his eyes adjusted. Familiar shadows formed in the darkness, offered comfort. Each intake of air subdued the turbulent storm inside him. His trembling body subsided into a minor fluttering. The rivers of sweat running down his face cooled and evaporated. His racing heart diminished into heavy beats.

As his terror retreated, another powerful emotion filtered in. Instead of being battered by a savage tempest, an emptiness as deep and as dark as space swelled inside him. If he'd been back home on the *Dragon*, his mother would've comforted him. On the *Odyssey* or *Defender*, Commander Hapker would've been there. Here he had no one—except a rat who'd likely fled through the vents at the first physical manifestations of the nightmare.

The darkness that'd provided a reprieve moments before closed in like a smothering specter. The deep pit of loneliness inside him grew tenfold. He crossed his arms over his gut and squeezed his eyes shut. Crying wouldn't do any good, so he pushed against the hollowness until it retreated to the back of his mind.

"Lights," he croaked.

The room brightened slowly. When the lights reached their full strength, he tossed his crumpled blankets aside. With an inward sigh, he swung his feet over the edge of the bed.

Rodrigo stood by his door, as silent as the dead.

Jori nearly jumped out of his skin. "Chusho! What the hell are you doing in here?"

"I detected an elevated heartrate and heightened stress levels."

"What?" Jori bellowed. "So after you saw it was a nightmare, you just lurked by my door?"

"Yes."

"Why didn't you wake me?"

"You were in no danger."

Jori palmed his forehead. "Then why did you remain in here?"

Rigo paused. "Unknown."

The response sparked a bit of hope. "Did you stay because you were worried about me?"

"Negative."

Jori's shoulders fell. There had to be something left of this man in there somewhere. Maybe if he kept trying, he'd find it. "Do you remember why you opted for your upgrades?"

"To become more."

"Yes, but why?"

"To improve myself."

Jori clenched his teeth. "You told me you wanted to be like me. You even enhanced your genes using *my* genes. Do you remember that?"

"Yes."

"And why did you want to be like me?"

"To improve myself."

"No!" Jori huffed. "But why me? Was it because you admired me? Cared about me? Why?"

"Because you are more."

"So not because you admired me?"

"Admire. To respect or look up to with a pleasant or affectionate manner."

"Yes. Did you feel admiration?"

"Emotions are not quantifiable."

Jori bit his lip in frustration, drawing blood. Did the chip implants in Rigo's brain destroy the amygdala or just sever the connection? If the latter, new synapses might form. "Do you still enjoy playing tenisi?" he asked, hoping to encourage a reconnection to his past.

"Enjoyment is not quantifiable."

Jori huffed again. "Will you play tenisi with me?"

"Yes."

Neither reluctance nor eagerness carried through his tone, but it was a start.

Jori dressed, his loneliness abating with a sense of purpose. Exercise tended to settle his spirit, and he looked forward to seeing if this experience could trigger the old Rodrigo. Rigo hadn't been a friend exactly, but he wasn't a bad person either. He didn't deserve to live the rest of his life as a mindless robot.

*****

The ball hurtled across the court. Jori dove for it and missed, then stumbled to the floor. His anger spiked, but not because he was losing. This was not how the old Rodrigo had played.

Before the procedure, it'd been Jori hitting the balls over the net and Rodrigo failing to hit them. Computer chips and gene enhancements had turned him from a hopeless klutz into a professional athlete with actions and reactions too contrasting to give Jori much hope in getting the old Rigo back. The man was an empty vessel, operating solely on his programming.

A deep-seated ache smothered the thrill of facing a worthy opponent. It wasn't his fault the man had chosen this path. Rodrigo was a complete idiot who thought being like Jori would make him worth something. No amount of pleading or arguing the facts had changed his mind. Not even Major Blakesley had convinced him. Yet Rigo's words about wanting to be like Jori kept echoing in his skull.

He wasn't a MEGA, yet MEGAs considered him one of them. It made little sense. He'd been doing some things better than his fourteen-year-old brother but only because Terk was more laid back while Jori practiced every day for hours. Surely his DNA wasn't the only factor. Terk had a similar genetic code. Jori's mental drive contributed to his skills, which wasn't something a series of nucleotides could duplicate. These MEGAs must be desperate to use him as their base for creating super-soldiers.

Jori leapt and stretched as another ball zoomed over to his side of the court. The ball smacked in the center of his racquet but it bounced upward into a high arc. *Chusho*. Technically, he wasn't supposed to hit the ball more than once in a turn, but he swung and thwacked it on its way down and sent it over the net.

Rigo caught the ball in his hand. "Game," he said with no glee.

Jori sighed. It was hopeless. Rodrigo was gone.

11
The Dragon

The elated satisfaction from escaping the planet plummeted into despair. Although shields held at just under fifty percent, they wouldn't last long against the *Dragon* warship. The gauge for the rocket engines showed them in the red. The dry heat radiating into the cabin was much like the climate on Hisui Island except tainted with a fuel smell. Sections of the flight operations console had stopped working.

Terkeshi held his breath and activated the backup power. The dead gauges flickered back to life. He puffed and rerouted power to the engine coolant systems. At first, it didn't seem to do any good. But the gauge fell into the orange zone less than a minute later.

Having done everything possible to ensure the ship kept running, Terk refocused on the *Dragon*. Heat borne of fury swelled in his chest. *Damn you, Father! Don't you have anything better to do than assault a bunch of farmers? Coward.* Just when he'd found peace in his life, that chima had to show up and ruin it.

Fear that his father had come because of him undermined his defiance. Washi had told him his father believed the cyborgs had killed him. But what if Major Jingyu had betrayed the truth?

No. It made little sense. If Jingyu was the sort of man to help someone with one hand and stab them in the back with the other, his mother would've detected it and said something to Washi and Michio.

Terk clutched the logic that his father believed him dead. But maybe he was here for his mother. From what Terkeshi had heard from Washi, the emperor had once accused her of causing the so-called rebellious actions of the populace. But how could he know she was here on this specific ship?

No. This had to be just his father's warmongering desire to quash all his enemies, no matter how small.

"What now?" Huang asked.

Terk didn't answer. He switched to the impulse engines and prayed the components shared with the rocket engines held up. Outrunning the warship would be impossible but if he got this ship far enough away, he could activate the arc drive. Surely the war on the planet kept the *Dragon* too preoccupied to worry about this piece of crap.

His concentration slipped as a familiar lifeforce approached the cockpit.

His mother poked her head in, the microgravity causing her to float at a weird angle. "Are we free?"

"Not quite," Terk replied without facing her. "We've broken through the atmosphere but the *Dragon* is heading our way." Her emotions billowed with panic, but she cut them off.

"I think we can get away, though," he added, trying to convey confidence. *Assuming this crappy ship holds up… And the arc drive works.*

"The passengers are doing alright," she said. "A little scared. Some got sick. But they'll all be fine."

He used his sensing ability to check on his friends. Baba Airi felt a bit shaken up, but worriment was her primary emotion. Yuan harbored distress but did well at hiding it. Anxi didn't emit any fear. Curiosity wafted from her. Whether it was because she'd never traveled on a ship before or that he knew how to fly it, he wasn't sure. A curiousness borne of confused anxiety exuded from Gaichu too.

"Good. Keep them calm," he told his mother, unintentionally giving her orders.

"I will handle it back there. You take care of yourself up here," she replied. "Is there anything I can get you to make this easier?"

"No. Just let me concentrate."

Her gown swished as she twisted around and floated away.

"You should be more respectful," Huang whispered. "She's a lady of the nobility."

Terk almost smirked. *If only* you *knew.*

But Huang was right. It didn't matter that emotions were running high. She was a noblewoman—and his mother. Not a soldier to be barked at.

He verified the shield's strength once more. The *Dragon*'s energy cannons would deplete them faster than the ones from the

Rattler. At least the warship's trajectory wasn't on intercept. Perhaps the *Rose* would go unnoticed after all.

He shook his head, not willing to take it on faith. The same rule applied about the inability of an energy blast to change course, so the more Terk maneuvered the *Rose*, the less likely it'd get struck. Then again, the closer the *Dragon* got, the harder it would be for it to miss.

Terk increased the thrust of the impulse engines by adjusting the throttle. The acceleration pressed him into his seat, though not as strongly as before. By maintaining optimum output, it'd take them seven long-ass minutes to reach the point where he could activate the arc drive. He dared not push the engines much harder. It wouldn't buy them more than thirty seconds anyway.

"Why are we still here?" Huang asked. "I was told this ship traveled at the speed of light."

Terk huffed at the oversimplification. "That's not exactly how it works." Manipulating spacetime made it easier to travel long distances without breaking the laws of physics, but certain laws still applied. "I can't activate the arc drive until we're far enough away from the planet."

"Why not?"

Terk clenched his teeth. *Doesn't he get how hard it is to fly and answer all his damned questions too?* "Because its gravity has too much influence on this ship, and it'll tear us apart."

He'd risk it with a better ship, but not the *Crappy Rose*.

The evasion sequence he'd programmed in increased their travel time to the arc zone to eight minutes, but it was necessary. "Mo— Lady Amarante!" he called. It'd be hard to explain how he knew how to fight and fly, but he couldn't do it by revealing his relation to her.

She swept to the cockpit entry. "Yes?"

"This ship is about to make a lot of erratic moves. Be sure everyone stays in their seats. You included."

Huang choked at the way he gave orders again, but his mother replied deferentially, "Yes, Sir."

Terk blinked. She was undoubtedly keeping up pretenses, but *sir*? That was a stretch, even if he *was* in charge at the moment. It confused and warmed him at the same time. Despite his faults, despite getting her youngest son killed, and despite everything else he'd done, she still believed in him. It was enough to make his sinuses burn.

He gathered a hold of himself. "Alright, give me our destination," he ordered Huang.

The man rattled off the coordinates.

Terk entered the information and examined the location on the star map. "Are you sure?"

"Memorized it until I was saying it in my sleep."

Terk believed him, but it was in the middle of nowhere. "What's there?"

"I don't know."

Chusho. It made sense to go to a place not labeled on the charts, but what if Huang was wrong? They couldn't afford for this shitty ship to break down so far from any source of help.

An alarm sounded. Huang jumped in his seat and Terk released a string of curses.

"What now?" Huang asked.

"They've targeted us."

Huang gripped his armrests. "What do we do?"

Nothing. "It's about to get rough!" he called back.

He manipulated the thrusters, adding more erratic movements to the ship's meandering trajectory. The *Rose* tugged to the left, then jerked to the right. He pulled up, then down, side to side, diagonal, every which way possible to keep the *Dragon*'s AI from predicting his moves. His gut churned with it all. A pressure built in his head. Bile welled up in his throat, but he swallowed it, the burning sensation exacerbating his already searing anxiety.

"I don't see anything on the screen," Huang said. "Why aren't they firing?"

"They *are*," Terk replied, irritation laced through his tone. "You don't see their energy blasts because they're traveling at the speed of light."

Huang emitted confusion. Before he could ask yet another question, Terk barked.

"Now quit talking so I can concentrate!"

He glanced at the shield status and the ES-sensors. Both indicated they'd been hit twice now. An additional alarm sounded and the gauge for the arc engines flashed yellow. The ship rocked and shield strength fell to thirty-two percent. *Fuck!* If the *Dragon* didn't kill them, the *Rose* would.

Despite his queasy stomach, he increased the intensity of the maneuvers. People moaned, screamed, and cursed. Irritation spiked through Terk's nerves. Afraid or not, these villagers needed to shut the hell up or they'd all die.

The shields fell to sixteen percent. Two more hits and they wouldn't have enough protection. A third blast would fry them. Against his better judgment, he pushed the engines to the red. The g-forces tunneled his vision and drove him to the brink of unconsciousness. Blood trickled down his nose. The ship juddered, making it difficult to apply the breathing techniques that'd help him stay alert.

The passengers probably fared worse. It was possible Baba Airi would die. His heart ached at the thought, but he had no choice but to risk it.

Another blast impacted the shields. They were now at eight percent. Blackness closed in on Terk's vision, but he managed to read the display. Two-and-a-half minutes to arc. He poised his hand over the arc activation—or tried to. The jerking of the ship hindered him.

The *Rose* shuddered with tremendous force. He didn't need to look at the shield-strength indicator to know the enemy had hit them again. Or that they still had more than a minute to go before they reached arc.

We're not going to make it. The blackness pressed around like a lid trying to close. If he didn't activate the arc drive before he lost consciousness, the *Dragon* would destroy them.

Fuck it. He slammed his hand down on the activation button. The ship lurched. The force pulled his insides outward and his outsides inward. He screamed in agony, then blacked out.

12
Drifting

Terkeshi snapped into consciousness. His gut roiled violently. An acidic liquid shot from his mouth, spewing like a pressurized gasket. An excruciating pain bloomed in his skull. Had he hit his head? No. He was still secured in the pilot crash couch, headrest and all. *Crash couch.* The memories of fleeing the planet swept in. He'd jumped into arc before it was time and the g-forces had strained his entire body.

Dizziness slammed into him, making his stomach tumble in another protest. Vomit spilled down his chin. He grasped for stability and found the cockpit console. A slimy yet textured wetness coated his fingers. *Gross.*

Several groans issued from the cabin along with the sound of more retching. Terk closed his eye, in part from vertigo and as a prayer. If anything happened to Baba Airi, his mother, or his friends, he'd never forgive himself.

The urge to check on them cut short when a light flashed on the console. He peered through the mess he'd caused and located the source—a misalignment in the inertial dampeners. The slight shift in gravity perception would cause nothing more than minor discomfort or unsteadiness—unless they found themselves the victims of another attack.

Terk's anxiety diminished as he reviewed the other readings. They'd made it into arc and were traveling smoothly. All the indicator lights read normal, including the engine temperature gauge. No ships were within range either. Hell, nothing was in range. If not for the navigation system, he would've thought they were drifting through nothingness instead of flying toward what he hoped was safety.

His chest deflated. "We did it."

"Guozhi!" a woman cried out, her anguish striking Terk's senses like a slap. "Guozhi, wake up!"

Terk's throat caught. *What happened to Guozhi?* He frantically searched for the man's lifeforce, finding nothing. It had to be a mistake, so he tried again, concentrating harder. Still nothing.

Knowing what that meant, his chest caved in. Guozhi, the genial old man who loved his wife, was dead. Terk had killed him.

Beiye's grief tore at his soul. *I'm so sorry!* If only they hadn't been so desperate to get away. *But I didn't have a choice.* If he hadn't activated the arc drive, his father would have killed every single person, including his—

His heart jumped to his throat. "*Mother!*" he screamed in his head. Her lifeforce flared. She was alive. Both discomfort and concern issued from her but no pain, telling him she was likely tending to the shaken passengers.

Terk didn't have time to be relieved. He used his sensing skill to find his friends next. His personal connection to them made it easy. Seeing beyond his own hurt hindered his ability to determine specifics, but he fought through it.

Anxi didn't seem fazed, but she would keep a firm grip on her emotions even through immense stress. Regardless, her lifeforce would resonate an alarm if she were in danger of dying. Terk allowed some of his tension to depart.

Fear came from Yuan, but it wasn't death-gripping. *He's probably alright.* Terk relaxed a bit more.

Baba Airi seemed fine as well, but she could be downplaying her condition like she had with the heart attack. *Stubborn old woman.* If not for her strong lifeforce, he would've continued to worry.

Huang moaned. Nasty green vomit clung to his chin and the front of his shirt.

Terk shook his shoulder. "Are you alright?"

Huang coughed. It sounded juicy, like he was going to throw up again. Terk nudged his cheek aside so he wouldn't add more gunk to the console. Huang gurgled. A gushing followed as the man spilled the contents of his stomach into the side of his chair. Since his lifeforce didn't register a medical emergency, Terk left him there to check on the others.

Another bout of dizziness swept over him as he floated upward. He braced himself at the cockpit entry. *I hope this shit passes soon.* This interlude didn't mean they were out of danger.

At first glance, the cabin seemed unremarkable. The villagers were all strapped in. Their harnesses still secured them in the crash couches. And nothing from the supply closets had gotten loose and caused damage. But his senses bombarded him with overwhelming distress. The children wailed. Adults cried too. Those who remained silent were too disoriented to speak.

His mother was the only one not strapped in. She bent over the lifeless form of Guozhi, hopeful as her fingers pressed to the side of his neck. Her ensuing sadness told Terk all he needed to know. He clenched his fists and looked away.

Baba Airi caught his eye. She didn't seem to have had the same sickly reaction as everyone else. Her clothing was dry. And instead of being shaken, a weary smile creased her face. He knelt before her. "How are you doing, Baba?"

"My stomach hurts a little, but I'll be alright in a few minutes."

Terk shook his head. "You could be dying, and you'd still say that."

She patted his hand. "Don't pay me any mind. Plenty of others here are in more need."

Terk shot his mother a questioning look.

She came over and examined Baba Airi by checking her pulse, looking into her eyes, and pinching her fingertips. "She seems fine," she said as she tucked a bit of loose, white hair over Baba Airi's ear. "That medicine I gave her probably helped with this too."

Terk scanned his friends, confirming what he'd sensed from them earlier. Then there was Gaichu… The moment Terk's eye fell on him, his tail thwacked on the floor in furious enthusiasm, eliciting a similar—yet not as openly ridiculous—sensation within himself. Gaichu had thrown up too, but it was in a neat little pile between his paws. It even looked as though he'd eaten some of it. *Disgusting mutt*, he thought with a smile.

Terk spread his gaze over the rest of the passengers, skipping the grieving Beiye but still feeling a twang in his gut. Everyone else was in various states of misery but otherwise seemed fine.

That provided only a little consolation. He'd escaped his chima-of-a-father twice now, both times at a great cost. He hadn't yet recovered from losing Jori when Sensei Jeruko's life had faded into oblivion. This planet had offered succor, but it also exemplified his failure. Hisui Island was a sunny place, but he'd faced a storm. He remembered the terrifying sensation of drowning as he told first his mother then Washi and Michio that Jori and Sensei Jeruko were dead… And it was all his fault.

Although Jori was the one who decided to save Commander Hapker no matter the cost, but Terk should've done a better job of protecting him. He should've killed his asshole father and saved everyone from this murderous rampage.

Then there was Washi and Michio's father. Sensei Jeruko wasn't even supposed to be there when he blew up that ship housing the perantium emitter. But Terk ought to have known his mentor would come to the rescue.

And now Guozhi was dead.

He clenched his fists and reminded himself that none of these things would've happened if his father hadn't been such a hateful chima. Terk had suffered enough at his father's hand. It was time to stop feeling guilty for matters he had no control over and put the blame where it belonged.

After a deep breath in and out, he called out, "Attention everyone!" The adults quieted, their faces contorted into a mixture of fear and hope. "We're safe now. No one is chasing us. I'll activate the gravity controls soon. After that, you can leave your seats. There are beds in the back. Claim one and get some rest. I'll go over the safety protocols later."

"Who in the hell put you in charge?" Lixin called out.

"He saved our lives," Anxi said.

"And killed Guozhi!" Lixin replied.

Despite his remorse for the man's death, Terk bristled. He imagined punching the sneer from Lixin's face. How he hated that stupid, ugly-ass bully. Then his eyes fell on Beiye and his mouth went dry. "I'm sorry, Beiye. I truly am."

She dipped her head but didn't reply as tears spilled anew.

Lixin scoffed at Terk. "It doesn't change the fact that's he's dead and you are acting like you're some lofty hero who thinks he should be our boss."

"Are you angling to be in charge?" Anxi turned from Lixin to the others. "I'd like to remind everyone of how the first thing Lixin did when he got here was run in and hide."

Figures. Terk suppressed a smirk.

"Fuck you," Lixin replied, red-faced. "At least I didn't get anyone killed."

Sympathy radiated from his mother as she placed a hand on Terk's forearm and addressed the passengers. "This ship is old. Piloting it under these circumstances would've been difficult for anyone, and this young man here did better than any of us expected." She turned to the grieving widow. "I'm so sorry, Beiye. Guozhi was a good man. And the only one to blame for his death is the Dragon Emperor."

Lixin crossed his arms and sulked. "That still doesn't mean a fifteen-year-old gets to tell us what to do just because he can fly a ship."

Terk swallowed down his hurt over Guozhi and his hatred for Lixin. "I don't care who's in charge. If anyone else feels up to the task, by all means."

Heads swiveled. A range of uncertainty and timidity wafted from the villagers. Some people turned to Terk with hope while others looked at him with doubt.

"What about Lady Amarante?" Lili asked. "She's a noblewoman."

"I'm not listening to some woman," Lixin snapped.

Terk's nostrils flared as he contemplated kicking that chima's ass. Although the farmer caste held women in a higher regard than the warrior caste, the overall view of their society was that women didn't belong in a position of authority unless it was over other women. *Which is stupid.*

"What about Huang?" someone asked.

Huang, unsteady in the microgravity, clutched the cockpit door jamb. "Don't look at me. I have no idea what comes next."

"You're kidding," Lixin said sourly. "So the only one here who knows what they're doing is this interloper? We don't even know this chima."

Dread spread through Terk's gut as questions formed on people's faces. In the beginning, they thought he was a refugee. Then they'd learned about his fighting skills. What did they think now that he could also fly a spaceship?

He struggled for a way to put them at ease without divulging too many details. "It's true that I have experiences beyond the island," he said carefully. "But I want to survive just as much as you do."

The cabin silenced. Doubts remained but they mostly sobered. Only Lixin still looked at him accusingly.

"Where are we going?" Lili asked as she tried to clean vomitus from the baby's swaddling.

"Huang gave me coordinates to a…" Terk replied. "I'm not sure what it is—a ship, a space station, a planet—but I'm told we have allies there."

"Rebels?" someone else asked.

"Maybe." It would explain part of his father's behavior, but what that chima considered rebellious another would consider survival. "But I doubt they call themselves that."

Whispers filled the cabin. Some were worried, others were relieved, none were angry. His father had done too much for them to care that they'd be committing treason. What did treason mean to a bunch of farmers struggling to survive anyway?

You don't deserve the loyalty of these people, Father.

"I don't know what awaits us," his mother said, "But Lord Qing wouldn't have provided us with a means to escape if he didn't have a plan. Wherever we're going, I'm sure we'll be safe." She turned to Terk and bowed. "You helped save us too. And I trust you'll continue to take good care of us—as our leader."

Terk hid his burning face by turning away. His chest swelled at the same time. Doubt about whether he could handle all the challenges ahead squirmed through his insides, but her faith bolstered his determination to try.

13
Dragon Prince

A miniature man wearing black-scaled Crathean armor threw a punch. Jori ducked and punched upward into the holo-man's kidney. The image doubled over. Jori elbowed the back of its bald head. The haptic feedback allowed him to feel the impact, though it was tempered for safety.

The holo-man disappeared. Jori stepped aside and lowered his fists. A digitized scoreboard appeared, *Level Ten* displayed in green text.

I did it. His mood lifted, but only a little. This was just *one* win. He needed to beat this level consistently before being considered a master. Even then, real-world application didn't work as well with a child's strength.

He deactivated the machine, ignoring Doctor Sokolov who'd been watching from the sideline. His effort was in vain as the man followed him to the hydration station along the wall. Heat that had nothing to do with the workout billowed in Jori's chest. Apparently, the doctor having more of a lifeforce than other MEGAs didn't make him any less weird.

The doctor sidled up beside him and winked. "That was most impressive. Few of our own MEGAs are able to perform such a feat."

Jori wiped the water from his mouth and faced the man with a scowl. Although MEGA-Man had agreed not to use Jori's genetic profile to make more people like Rodrigo, Doctor Sokolov's compliment hinted that he still coveted it. Doctor Stephen Stenson had sworn he'd altered the record of Jori's genomic sequence before sending it to MEGA-Man and had purged the original data from the ship's databanks. So far as Jori knew, no one had attempted to recover this information. Yet, he suspected MEGA-Man might still have it and was making clones of him right now. There wasn't much he could do about it, but he put on a stern expression anyway. "I won't help him make soldiers."

"And you don't have to. You have a lot of other useful talents that will benefit mankind."

"Or harm them. I won't be used in *any* way."

The doctor nodded. "I understand your stance, but I find the sentiment illogical. Society has no trouble passing on our genes to our children yet balks at the idea of sharing their genes through scientific means."

The doctor's nonchalant attitude set Jori's teeth on edge. Or maybe it was because his words had a ring of truth to it. "It's not natural."

"No, but it's more precise and controllable. Genetic engineering has the potential to eliminate all sorts of hereditary disorders while enhancing beneficial traits such as intelligence and physical wellbeing."

Jori clenched his fists. "That's not how MEGA-Man is using it! He's creating super-soldiers so he can impose his will on others." He'd vowed that next time he spoke with the doctor, he'd pretend to be more compliant and get more information from him, but this tactic of spouting reason while skirting the facts set him off.

Doctor Sokolov opened his mouth as though to argue but hesitated. "I see your point. But we need soldiers. The men and women who opted to join our army did so because they were tired of feeling so helpless. We're in a fight for our right to live as we please, but the Cooperative isn't making it easy for us."

Jori growled. It made too much damned sense, yet the man still wasn't getting it. "No one should get to decide how to use my genetic profile except *me*."

The doctor dipped his head. "Perhaps this is why he's agreed to not use it just yet."

Just yet? "If he keeps his promise, am I still *important*?" He practically spit out the last word.

"Yes," the doctor replied, unfazed. "I believe it has more to do with your heritage."

"You mean that I'm the heir to the Dragon Empire," Jori said, rebelling against the implications.

"Yes. The *last surviving* Dragon Prince." Doctor Sokolov put on a wistful smile and winked.

Jori reined in the urge to punch him. Beneath that was the ache over Terk's death. He took in a deep breath and calmed his mind. Emotion wasn't always a weakness, but it was this time. Since gathering intel from files proved elusive, he had to school his anger and engender the doctor's trust. Sharing opinions wasn't enough. He needed to find weaknesses so he could get the hell away from these manipulative people.

"MEGA-Man wants me because he believes he can use me to take control of our military," he said, attempting to avoid sounding argumentative. But *I won't let him.*

"The Dragon Warriors would certainly provide a boost to MEGA-Man's influence."

"You mean his rule." Jori wanted to kick himself. *Be agreeable, you idiot. You can't get information if you keep arguing.*

"MEGA-Man's quest for power is more of a quest for change." Doctor Sokolov's eyes tilted imploringly. "Many quests for equal rights require a fight. Think about the history of ancient Earth. The wars against slavery. Protests revolving around religious freedom and women's rights. Battles of indigenous people against colonizers. The Lunar War, Miner's War, I could go on and on and that's just Earth. Every planet we've colonized has had to re-fight all these battles, including those in Toradon territory."

Jori wasn't well versed in history, but surely there'd been some equality wins that didn't involve violence. It was worth looking into.

"There's another reason you should take your father's place," Doctor Sokolov said before Jori could think of a way to turn this conversation to his favor. "Come with me."

The man turned about, his emotions giving nothing away. Jori begrudgingly followed him to a workroom filled with identical workstations, each equipped with wide monitors and standardized consoles. He'd nicknamed it the *Newsroom* since it was the only place on the ship that accessed the public broadcasts transmitted via the galactic communication hub network.

One person occupied the room today. A brown-haired man with four arms, one pair real and the other cybernetic, operated two stations simultaneously. The doctor breezed by without a glance. He activated a station in the rear and queried Toradon news. Several feeds popped up at once, including one from a rogue broadcaster known for uncovering classified information. Jori had viewed one of those reports many times already. It speculated that both the emperor's sons were dead. Though wrong about Jori, the footage of Terk caught in an explosion was undeniable.

He stifled his tears as Doctor Sokolov bypassed it and selected another feed. The video flickered to life. People with dark hair and the Toradon features of the lower castes raced away from a formation of Rattler jets zipping across the sky. Buildings made from crude material burst into balls of flames and rubble. Debris scattered and smoke plumed on the ground, forcing people to duck for cover.

"Reports from Meixing say the Dragon Emperor has launched an attack," a male with a deep and somber voice said. "Footage of what we believe is the *Dragon* warship, shown here, is in synchronous orbit over the ocean."

Jori's chest constricted as the screen flicked to a view of his father's ship. Even from this distance, the monstrous vessel looked sinister.

"It's rumored that a rebel force has hidden out on one of the many islands in Meixing's Shuijing ocean, and the emperor is determined to wipe it out—even at the cost of his loyal citizens."

Jori couldn't breathe. His throat locked up. His mother was on an island in the Shuijing ocean. But this footage could be any Toradon village. And the *Dragon* visiting Meixing wasn't unusual.

Who was he kidding? At the faintest whisper of treachery, his father wouldn't hesitate to destroy the place where she lived.

Doctor Sokolov planted a hand on Jori's shoulder. "The news doesn't say, but we have information from one of our sources that he's sent troops down to this island and is killing villagers."

"Which island?" Jori managed to ask through his tight throat.

"We're not sure yet."

A heat rose through Jori's core and exploded out of his mouth. "Why are you showing me this?"

"This..." The doctor tapped the screen. "This is why you should take your father's place. It isn't the first time he's massacred innocent people."

Jori swallowed. Doctor Sokolov was right. His father would call for violence over *any* perceived slight. He remembered when Lord Taguchi had made a tasteless joke about his father's inability to sire more children. Not long after, Taguchi was accused of selling weapons to a rebel group. Jori didn't partake in that battle, but his father had forced him to witness Taguchi's execution. The man had pleaded for the lives of his family, then for his own life, swearing that he never sold anything to the emperor's enemies. Jori sensed the truth of his words and told his father as much, but to no avail. Taguchi, his wife, his three sons and four daughters had been executed. One child was Terk's age.

Jori tightened his fists. If he had the power, he'd put an end to his father's madness.

14
Negotiations

Galactic Dominions. Why were MEGAs the only people Jori ever played this game with? First Gottfried. Then Vance. And now Doctor Sokolov. Despite the thrill of solving a strategic puzzle, he hated this game. Although earlier games imparted important lessons, its association with MEGAs left a bitter taste in his mouth. But he played anyway, hoping the distraction would keep him from dwelling on the fate of his mother.

It had worked so far. For once, he was winning. He initially suspected Doctor Sokolov was letting him, but the man's careful consideration before each move suggested otherwise. Perhaps his lack of cybernetic enhancements put him at a disadvantage. Or maybe the lessons Jori learned from Gottfried and Vance were finally paying off. Now if he could only apply the knowledge and figure out how to help his mother without becoming MEGA-Man's puppet.

It's too late to do something, so stop thinking about it!

The game came back into focus. Jori represented the fictional rulers of Babilios who waged war against the inhabitants of Enlilum, a large moon within the same star system. He loved how no two of these games were ever alike. Territories, cultures, military assets, and more varied. The cause of war did as well. This one was fought over the resources Enlilum had and Babilios insisted it had a right to, since Enlilum was its territory.

Jori tried to ignore the politics of it. It was about winning, not about who was right. However, it was his turn and his best move required him to destroy a manufacturing plant. Although this was a valid military tactic, it reminded him of Vance's plan to attack an entire city just because an influential organization that supported the Cooperative resided there. Even if this was merely a game, in real life there'd be workers in that factory who had little to do with government policies.

He sat back and studied the three-dimensional holo-board, trying to figure out how to fight a war without murdering innocent people.

"Is everything okay?" the doctor asked. "You seem troubled."

Jori frowned. Although the game's circumstances differed from the situation between Prontaean Cooperative and the MEGAs, a few similarities stood out. What right did Babilios or the Cooperative have to decree what others should do? And why did the Enlilums or the MEGAs need to take the fight beyond their borders?

"This game is stupid. If this were a real problem, shouldn't the two sides compromise instead of resorting to war?"

The doctor winked. "Sometimes one side doesn't listen and war becomes inevitable."

Jori narrowed his eyes. The game spit out random circumstances, but he suspected the doctor might've manipulated it to make a point. "It still seems stupid," Jori muttered.

"Agreed. But the necessity of war has existed since the dawn of man. Take our cause for example."

I knew it. The parallel of this game to current events couldn't be a coincidence. But he suppressed his irritation and listened for an opportunity to garner more information.

"MEGAs have been trying to get the authorities to listen to them for decades," the doctor continued. "Placing our people within their ranks to advocate for change didn't work either."

"That's because Gottfried committed murder," Jori snapped. "If he hadn't done that and hadn't planned on killing more, I might've kept his secret."

"Yes. We've had this discussion before and I concede your point. The opportunity was too good to pass up, I'm afraid. But the long game of getting society to see us differently also costs innocent lives. Even before this war, MEGAs died every day at the hands of MEGA haters."

The doctor's words rang true, but Gottfried's actions still felt wrong. Jori just wasn't sure how to articulate why. "Let's keep playing," he grumbled.

"You know," the doctor said, "negotiation sounds easy. But what do you do when someone like your father, for example, refuses to negotiate?"

Jori's mood plummeted. Father would never compromise.

"The only way to end the Tredon war is to eliminate its leader and replace him with a better one."

A chill fell over Jori's body. The doctor was right, but that meant giving himself over to MEGA-Man. *Pretend to be agreeable, damn it.* "What do I have to do?"

Doctor Sokolov shrugged. "Just tell me you want to do it, and MEGA-Man will see that it's done."

"No implants?"

"Of course not."

Jori narrowed his eyes. The doctor spoke the truth, but only as he knew it. MEGA-Man might have other plans.

"You don't believe me," Doctor Sokolov said.

Jori clamped his mouth shut. *Be agreeable.*

"Think about Doctor Celine Stenson," the doctor explained anyway. "She was forced and the results were detrimental."

Jori's insides twisted. According to Doctor Stephen Stenson, she'd been a much different and happier person before the procedure.

Doctor Sokolov leaned in with eyes full of sincerity. "MEGA-Man doesn't want that to happen to you."

Jori scoffed inwardly. That might be true in the beginning, but he had no doubt things would change once he gave MEGA-Man what he wanted. There must be another way to help his mother.

The game resumed. Jori did well until the doctor took out his presidential leader. Babilios' army still outnumbered Enlilum's, yet Jori's soldiers fought worse while Doctor Sokolov's rallied.

Jori tapped his lips, trying to understand why. He'd read of battles lost by superior armies after a psychological defeat but didn't grasp how it worked. Did people really put so much confidence in their leader that losing them diminished their will to fight?

He almost laughed out loud. Senshi warriors wouldn't care if something happened to his father.

An idea sparked. The people of Toradon might not give a second thought about the demise of their ruthless ruler, but Doctor Sokolov and others like him worshipped theirs—not just with confidence but with a profound devotion. So could ending MEGA-Man end the war?

This line of thinking clashed with his desire to stop his father, but he still wasn't foolish enough to subject himself to MEGA-Man to do it.

His mood heightened. Of all the strategies used in this game thus far, the least assuming was the one that'd win. His mind churned with real-world applications. He was just one person, but he was closer to this than most. He only needed to bide his time and gather information.

"Why aren't you connected to the Great Commune like Rodrigo?" he asked, portraying curiosity while doing recon.

The doctor shrugged. "The direct connection requires intensive surgery, and I've opted not to undergo the procedure."

Jori sensed evasiveness from the man. "Because you're afraid of surgery or because you know implanting hardware affects your brain, possibly deprives you of your soul?"

Doctor Sokolov grunted. "I'm not concerned about my soul, but you are correct about me being worried that it'll affect my personality."

"I never believed in the soul until I met a MEGA with no lifeforce," Jori replied. "How does the Great Commune work, anyway? Its communications are instantaneous, just like with the communication hubs, right?"

"Very much so."

"But how? Doesn't Rodrigo have to be close to a hub?"

Doctor Sokolov tilted his head, emitting reservation. He probably figured out Jori was fishing for information. "Yes," he answered, perhaps realizing trust required him to be more forthcoming.

"But we weren't near a hub when he communicated with MEGA-Man before."

"Oh." The doctor paused with his mouth open. "Well, that's because we have our own."

Jori's eyes widened. "Your own?"

"Yes, well." Doctor Sokolov quirked his lips. "I'm not sure I should be telling you these things."

Jori crossed his arms. "Why not? I thought you wanted me as an ally?"

The doctor bobbed his head though his reluctance remained. "I suppose you'll find out soon enough." He sighed. "The technology of our hubs is much more advanced than the Cooperative's. They have a greater range and are more reliable."

Jori schooled his eagerness. This was precisely the type of information he needed. He doubted Doctor Sokolov had sentio abilities, but he'd already been too obvious. "So you can speak to MEGA-Man as well, just not in your head like Rodrigo?"

"Correct."

"Can MEGA-Man also give Rodrigo orders, like right now?"

"Certainly."

Jori hid his unease. He'd programmed Rigo to protect him but if MEGA-Man had access, he could override it. He thought back to the mindless soldiers on the *Defender*. They likely had internal contact with MEGA-Man as well.

"How many people have a direct connection to the Great Commune?"

The doctor pursed his lips, reminding Jori to be more subtle. But this supply of answers was more than he'd hoped for. Besides, if MEGA-Man was so desperate to use him, why not take advantage of it? *Because his suspicions might turn against you.*

"I'm not sure," Doctor Sokolov finally said. "Perhaps several thousand. Why do you ask?"

"I'm curious," Jori replied, speaking a partial truth. "It's not a tech that anyone else in the galaxy uses."

"That's because the MEGA Injunction prohibits people from implanting any type of tech, which is ridiculous. Implants have the potential to simplify so many tasks. People could talk to one another without those pesky ear-comms. They'd easily be able to download new information if they had immediate access to something like the Cooperative's Main Data Stream."

"Does MEGA-Man have his own MDS?"

The doctor shifted in his seat.

Jori gritted his teeth, unable to keep up the agreeable façade. If he wanted answers, he had to take a risk. "Why the hesitation? If your cause is so righteous, why hide things from me?"

Doctor Sokolov still emitted reservation but smiled. "You're right. Yes, he has his own version of the MDS, one that all of us have access to. It's part of the Great Commune."

Jori swallowed. MEGA-Man and this Great Commune sounded like a central processor or a hive mind. And if that was the case, his idea of eliminating MEGA-Man would have an effect beyond reducing the morale of his followers.

But what about his mother and the other people? His father must be stopped.

What if I do both? MEGA-Man wanted to use him, so why not let it work to his benefit? Let MEGA-Man take care of his father, then eliminate MEGA-Man himself. The prospect of ending MEGA-Man didn't bother him. The way Gottfried had described him, he was probably as soulless as Rodrigo. But killing his own father, even indirectly, didn't sit well with him. Did he really hate the man that much? But what about all those innocent people his father kept murdering? He needed to think about this more before deciding.

"It's your turn," Doctor Sokolov prodded.

Jori propped his cheek on his fist and tried to focus. If he couldn't defeat the doctor, he held little hope for outsmarting MEGA-Man.

15
Research

Jori's shoulders sagged under the crushing weight of his worries. His problems loomed impossibly large, making him feel like a leaf tossed about in a relentless storm. What hope did he have against a raging emperor or a super-MEGA who commanded legions of devoted followers? Short of surrendering himself to his enemies, not a damned thing. Every option required the same thing—to let the storm throw him into the jaws of the enemy.

His office was quiet but not silent. Although he was lonely, he wasn't alone. He leaned back in his chair and watched Kiyoshi play on the floor beside him. The rat's curiosity over the old delivery bot converted into a toy should've put a smile on his face. He envied the rat, wishing his own research triggered the same exuberance.

With a sigh, he returned his focus to his monitor. He'd confirmed the Great Commune and MEGA-Man's version of a main data stream were all interconnected. The doctor had helped him access it, only it wasn't as useful as he hoped. Since those who could plug directly into it were the primary users, it dispensed information in a flood. If he were a MEGA, his internal processor would take it all in and filter it. Instead, he had to do it manually.

It was too much and most of it was beyond his intellect. He'd learned more about how this ship's arc drive and other systems worked, but he didn't have the skill to figure out how to use that information to his advantage. Other things he'd queried, such as what MEGA-Man was like, what his plans were, how many MEGAs had infiltrated the Cooperative, and so on, weren't available. Or if they were, he didn't know how to find them.

"Rigo," he said.

"Yes, Captain," the man replied from the door with a flat inflection.

"Are you always connected to the Great Commune?"

"I have access to the Great Commune eighty-four percent of the time on average."

"Are you connected to it right now?"

"Yes."

Jori shouldn't have been surprised, but a worm of discomfort wriggled through him. "Are you able to contact MEGA-Man through it?"

"Yes."

Jori's spine tingled. "Can you reach out to him whenever you want?"

"I am only permitted to communicate directly with him when certain criteria are met."

"But he can communicate with you at any time, right?" *Please let the answer be no.*

"Yes, but only if I'm in contact with the Great Commune."

Chusho. He suspected as much but the implications made his blood turn cold. Rodrigo's cybernetic eye wasn't just an enhancement—it likely also served as a constant surveillance device. It explained why Jori's decision to keep him as a personal guard had gone unchallenged. Undoubtedly, MEGA-Man monitored his activities through his connection to the main data stream.

He hid his uneasiness and altered his tactics in case MEGA-Man was watching right now. Rather than look for specific information, he browsed through the cascading menus, tapping into anything that looked interesting, relevant or not.

Hundreds of options popped up, eliciting a groan. He might as well be a shark pursuing a school of frenzied fish. The menu ranged from innocuous topics such as nutritional formulas and the grooming habits of Sambadian lemurs, to more comprehensive ones like terraforming, medical advances, tech manuals, the location of valuable resources, the customs and immigration laws of various nations, and the defense systems of several planets. That last one caught his breath.

A communications menu appeared, seemingly out of order considering the otherwise logical arrangement. Clicking it revealed a list of files labeled with numbers and symbols. He scrolled through, wondering what they meant. One folder stood out. It read *Sokolov.*

MEGA-Man wants me to see this. He hated being manipulated, but curiosity got the better of him as he navigated to another directory of folders. He clicked one at random, surprised that it opened without a password prompt. It was a transcript of a communication between the doctor and MEGA-Man.

His pulse quickened at the prospect of finally discovering their secrets. Those chimas wouldn't be able to trick him. He'd figure out their plans and thwart them.

His enthusiasm waned as he read through a monotonous stream of benign information. The file from another day revealed the same thing. Doctor Sokolov did most of the communicating by relaying his daily activities, and nothing he'd said hinted at malice or deceit.

Jori frowned. If he'd come across this on his own, he might've believed it. This seemed contrived.

The next conversation made Jori straighten in his seat.

> <Sokolov> We overestimated Gottfried's and Vance's abilities in this matter. And we grossly underestimated the princes.

Jori's throat caught. *Princes, as in plural?* What did Terk have to do with MEGA Man?

> <MEGA-Man> Agreed.

Jori frowned at MEGA-Man's lack of an explanation. Instead, the conversation moved on with the doctor sharing all that'd happened since he'd arrived, including all his conversations with Jori. Overall, he presented the information objectively. MEGA-Man provided no instructions and offered no opinions, making Jori wonder whether parts had been altered or deleted.

He closed the folder and huffed. *So much for finding answers.*

Another folder appeared. Once again, Jori felt like he was being led. But opening it revealed a live conversation.

> <Sokolov> Jori and I have had more conversations. He's curious, which is good, but I fear he still doesn't trust us. I'm not having any luck

convincing him we're fighting for a just cause.
What do I do?

<MEGA-Man> Detour to these coordinates.

Jori tensed. He couldn't determine the precise location without looking it up, but it was within Cooperative territory. His imagination went wild. Vance had taken him to an asteroid to purchase a powerful weapon. Then to a planet to lay waste to an entire city. Did MEGA-Man have another similar plan?

<Sokolov> There's nothing at that location.

Jori almost relaxed but MEGA-Man's response gave him pause.

<MEGA-Man> There is. I will provide more details
     later.

<Sokolov> Very good. But how do you want me to
     proceed? I allowed Jori to remain in charge here.
     Am I to take it over now? I'm not sure that will
     go over well.

Jori clenched his fists. The doctor's concern seemed hollow since Jori had no authority over anything important anyway.

<MEGA-Man> No. Ask him. Assure him it'll be safe
     and that he'll have more answers to his questions.

Jori blinked. Was it true? Would he be safe? Would he get answers? Too bad his sentio ability didn't work electronically.
He crossed his arms. He should refuse the doctor's *request* and see what happened—find out how far he could deviate from MEGA-Man's plans before consequences set in. But this piqued his curiosity. The lure of more information tantalized him too much to say no. When the doctor asked, he'd agree—albeit reluctantly.

16
Tatawar

Terkeshi huffed, his breath forming a mist of fog in the frigid air. With the engines offline and the temperature regulation focused in the living areas, the cramped space of the engine room had become an ice box.

He crouched beside a control panel. His icy fingers manipulated the multimeter's probes into the stabilizer—a vital component for maintaining the arc drive's energy field. The flickering light from his headlamp cast erratic shadows, complicating the simple task.

He finally managed to take a reading and grimaced at the display. *Damn it! Still no electrical flow.* There must be something wrong with the internal circuits, but damn-it-to-hell if he knew how to fix them. Without the stabilizers, he couldn't reactivate the arc drive. And without the arc drive, they were stuck in the middle of fucking nowhere. Impulse engines worked, but it would take forty years to reach any form of habitation.

He fell back onto his butt and slammed the multimeter to the floor. The clatter echoed ominously in the cold silence. Despair surged inside him, threatening to explode.

Gaichu nudged his hand with a nose colder than usual. Terk's overwhelming emotions receded. He sighed, then ruffed the dog's head.

The engine room door flew open. The silhouette of a lean frame loomed at the entrance. "I'll kill that fucking dog!" Lixin bellowed.

Terk jumped to his feet at the same time as Gaichu, and both growled. "The hell you are."

"Look at this damn mess!" Lixin lifted something. It took Terk a moment to realize he'd taken off his shoe. "Why did you bring that stupid ass dog, anyway?"

"Ask Lady Amarante," Terk replied, knowing good and well that Lixin wouldn't be foolish enough to insult a noblewoman who had Lord Qing's ear. "It was her idea."

"I don't care who's fucking idea it was. Get this shit cleaned up."

Normally, Terk would've bristled at the chima's tone but laughed instead. Lixin snarled and clenched his fists. Terk smirked, daring him to attack. Lixin's eyes blazed even as he blanched. His sense of self-preservation won out as he turned on his heel and stormed off, muttering curses along the way.

Terk looked down at Gaichu. "Next time, go *inside* his shoes."

Gaichu responded with an eager tail-wag as if understanding the command.

Terk put the tools away, then retrieved the cleaning supplies. He wasn't smart enough to fix an arc drive, but he could pick up after his dog. Not for Lixin, though. For everyone else.

He found the half-squished pile in the main cabin. The putrid odor inspired a new urge to vomit. Using a towel, he picked up the squishy brown stuff from the floor and showed it to Gaichu. "This is why dogs should *not* travel on ships."

The pup sniffed it, then gave him a clueless look. Terk scowled but Gaichu didn't buy it. In truth, Terk was thankful his mother had insisted on letting the pup come aboard. He pretended to be angry about the mess, but he'd pick up crap all day if he needed to. Not that the stupid dog ever did anything around here other than poop, piss, and eat. But Terk secretly enjoyed the companionship.

A beep sounded from the cockpit. *About damned time.*

Terk tossed the soiled towel in the recycler and jogged inside. They'd arrived at the coordinates hours ago, but space wasn't static. Stars, planets, or space stations served as an anchor of sorts, but there were none out here. And since their contact hadn't sent out any signals, the search for their rendezvous in this vast expanse was harder than trying to find an eyelash in a pile of dirt.

Terk reviewed the sensor sweep data. Radar identified something the size of a warship. Since no thermal or radiological emissions were detected, this was either an asteroid or a vessel equipped with advanced thermal and radiation sinks.

Only one way to find out. He switched on the optical telescopes. A massive ship with a bizarre design appeared on the screen, triggering a primal fear that burst through his body like an electric shock. *No. It can't be.*

The vessel resembled a giant insect, like the aggressive chengzi hornets that'd once taken up residence in the back of Baba Airi's barn.

A cold sweat flushed through him. He clutched his chest, trying to breathe. He'd seen a ship like this once before. The chimas who traveled on it had been responsible for taking his eye.

The beep of an incoming message nearly made him piss his pants. A million thoughts zipped through his brain. *Run. But we're low on fuel... Run. Where? There's nowhere to go... Run, damn it! But they will catch us.*

Terk's vision tunneled. He could handle his father finding out he was alive, but MEGAs? Flashbacks bombarded him in no coherent order.

MEGAs prepped him for surgery. Father stood at his side, not to offer comfort but to will him into a better warrior.

He looked in the mirror and a stranger with a cybernetic eye peered back at him.

Captain Wang awoke from his own procedure only to go into convulsions because his body rejected the tech.

Senshi Yujio slumped over in a drug-induced stupor after using his implants to medicate himself.

Another memory replayed itself over and over in between the others.

Blue energy burst from his weapon as he sprayed the workers with phaser fire. Anger spewed from him like a volcano while workers screamed and tried to run. He shot them all until they lay in crumpled heaps before him.

He choked in air. His hands trembled violently.

Breathe.

The word came like a whisper.

Breathe.

A longing to heed it trickled in.

Breathe.

He took in a breath. Then another. His vision turned from black to blurry. A warm hand rested on his shoulder.

"Breathe," his mother said.

Burning tears streamed down his face. The trembling in his hands subsided. His breaths became even.

His mother grasped his hand and edged into the small space beside him. She swept the wet hair stuck to his forehead aside. "There you go. It's alright now."

He shook his head, still unable to speak, and pointed at the screen.

"Our rendezvous?" she asked.

She didn't know. She'd never seen it before—but he had. He filled his lungs and mentally grasped for control. "That's a cyborg ship," he croaked.

Dismay surged from her. She'd met MEGAs once. It was before Jori and Terk had traveled to the Depnaugh space station. They'd come to offer their father an alliance and he'd used her to determine whether they could be trusted. But she'd never seen their ship.

She gripped his hand tighter. Her emotions vanished, indicating she'd blocked them. "That's a problem," she said with far too much calm to be real. "But let's keep a level head so we can figure out what to do."

He wiped the tears from his face and nodded. She was right. He breathed until his panic retreated. When he was sure it wouldn't lunge back out, he glanced at the message. It was flagged with a text blurb reading *Operation Exodus*. This was the name of the plan that'd enabled them to escape the island. Either the MEGAs were their allies, or this was a trap.

His instincts screamed the latter. If that was the case, it was too late—they'd caught him.

Huang popped into the cockpit with a smile. "Hey! We finally found them."

Terk's anger shot forth. "Them?" He jabbed his finger at the screen. "You mean those *MEGAs?*"

Huang blinked. "I didn't know they were MEGAs, but it makes sense, don't it? Who else would be powerful enough to go against the Dragon Emperor?"

Terk clenched his jaw. "Powerful, yes. But also dangerous."

"I don't see the problem." Huang's bushy brows furrowed. "Look at their ship. Who better to protect us than someone with advanced technology?"

Terk scowled. "Do you want to become a cyborg?"

The man shrugged. Terk's mouth fell open. His mother's did the same.

"Is there somewhere else we can go?" she asked Terk.

Huang looked at her as though she were daft.

Terk intervened before the man dared to insult her. "Not unless someone knows how to fix the arc drive."

Huang flicked his hand. "I'm sure they can do it."

Terk recoiled, then growled. "You have no idea what these people are capable of."

Huang huffed. "Better them than the emperor."

"They once helped the emperor by turning his men into super-soldiers," his mother said, repeating what he'd told her when he'd first come to the island. "Then those soldiers turned on him at their command." That part was a rumor, but Terk didn't doubt it. After he'd cut out his cybernetic eye, he sabotaged the perantium emitter and made it appear as though the MEGAs had compelled him to do it. Father would have retaliated and the MEGAs might've responded in kind.

"Good," Huang replied.

Terk clenched his fists. "You're not getting it. Those people are looking to dominate us as much as the emperor is."

"I'll take my chances," Huang said. "The emperor just destroyed my home, so fuck him."

Terk gritted his teeth, but the old man had a point. Few here could fully understand the dangers, but his options were severely limited.

Huang left. His mother placed a hand on his shoulder. "Didn't you tell me they'd waited until they had your permission before giving you implants?"

He nodded.

"So long as no one agrees to augmentations, we should be alright." Her voice radiated surety but since she still blocked her emotions, he suspected she faked her optimism.

"Not me."

"Yes, you too. Hundreds of others have likely already found their way here, including Major Jingyu. You can hide among us."

Terk scoffed. "For how long?"

"This is just a rendezvous point. Maybe we don't even have to dock."

The idea sparked hope, but then he remembered the arc drive. "I can't stay here. This ship is broken." He swallowed down the hopelessness threatening to crawl up his throat.

"Terk," his mother said gently. "Look at me."

He obeyed, taking in the warmth of her dark eyes.

"And listen to me," she continued. "What happened to you was beyond terrible. But you're strong. Stronger than them. Stronger than your father. And you won't let them frighten you anymore."

She spoke it as a command, and he wondered if she was using her imperium ability on him.

"I'm not," she replied, reading his mind. "What I'm telling you is already inside you. You only need to take a hold of it."

He nodded.

"The next time you're triggered by these people, I want you to grab that anger and use it to fuel your courage. And not just any anger—the righteous anger, the anger that fuels you but doesn't control you, the anger that has turned you into a fine young man who fights to help those who need it. You can do that. I believe in you."

Truth blazed from her like a blinding light. His heart swelled. Others might've called his anger a liability, something to quash— something to be ashamed of—but she saw it as his strength.

He reached for the heat that constantly burned inside him. This anger had helped him endure so much, including his father's criticisms and abuse. Sometimes it had even spurred him into making stupid decisions. But ever since he'd been thrown into the midst of innocent people who lived a life harsher than his, he'd been working on tempering it. It was too bad that Sensei Jeruko had to die before Terk took his teachings to heart. Heeding those lessons was the least he could do to honor him.

He drew in a deep breath and opened the message. Their vessel was called the *Tatawar*—so not the same one that'd helped his father. *Still a MEGA ship, though.*

They requested a visual connection but he wasn't about to reveal his secret. He typed in a reply, giving them the general information about who they were and why they were here. Using the term *refugees* shifted his anxiety into sadness but that's what they were now.

The *Tatawar* sent docking instructions. Terk's heart jumped, but he calmly responded. *"We just need repairs to our ship, then we'll be on our way."*

Another message came in, giving him hope. He turned to his mother. "It's from Major Jingyu."

"Let me speak to him," she replied, then took his place. "Stay out of view. The MEGAs are undoubtedly monitoring us, and I don't want them to find out you're here."

Terk folded his arms. "What about you?"

"I suspect Lord Qing has already told them about me."

Terk's heart jumped. "He knows about—"

"No," she said sharply. "He doesn't know of my abilities. I doubt the MEGAs do either. Your father kept it a closely guarded secret."

"I still don't like it."

"It must be done," she replied. "Someone must convey the need to protect your identity." Before he could protest further, she tapped the comm and the major's round face appeared in a square on the bottom of the main screen. She smiled. "Major Jingyu."

"Lady Amarante! Thank goodness. We thought we'd lost you."

"I'm fine. So are many of our villagers… Thanks to our young, capable pilot."

Terk flushed.

"Really?" Jingyu's brows shot up, then he grinned. "Seems Washi picked the right man for the job."

"Indeed," she said. Terk shifted his feet as her pride infiltrated his senses. "How many others made it here?"

"More than we expected, including Lord Qing and most of the island guards." He smiled but Terk swore he saw a bit of tightness around his eyes.

"As relieved as I am to be away from danger," his mother replied, "I don't think this is the right place to be. You know what these people have done. We can't trust them."

"I'm afraid we have little choice. We need protection from the emperor and the MEGAs can provide it."

"This is crazy," she said with a foreign forcefulness. "Why would they ally with us? They must have ulterior motives."

"Indeed. They've already offered to enhance those who want it."

Terk's chest constricted at the same time his mother gasped. "No!" she yelled. "You can't allow this."

"Don't worry. It's voluntary."

"That means nothing. We both know someone they coerced into it and exacted a terrible price."

Terk's stomach churned at the reminder of how he'd murdered all those people. But that wasn't him—not really. His father had manipulated him—and the cyborgs had made it possible.

His anxiety shifted into anger. He'd die before letting those chimas trick him again.

"You're, my Lady. But I'm afraid it's out of my hands."

His mother glanced at Terk, then spoke carefully. "Docking our ship with theirs isn't such a good idea. They might recognize…"

She left it at that. Major Jingyu's brows curled, then rose in understanding. "If we don't dock, Lord Qing will question it."

Terk's heart sped up.

"But," the major continued, "someone should stay with it. And I'll make sure we only allow authorized personnel on board."

Terk recaptured his anger, clutching it until his heart slowed. The major's idea wasn't ideal, but it should work. He'd alight in their bay, keep out of sight while they repaired the ship, then get the hell away from here.

"Do we have any other options?" his mother pleaded.

"Not yet," Major Jingyu replied. "Right now, we're just focused on making sure we've rescued as many people as possible. But there's time to figure things out."

After the conversation ended, she rose. Worry radiated from her as she gave him a look that said she'd tried.

He put on a brave face. "Tell everyone we're about to dock with MEGAs and warn them of the dangers."

She placed her hand on his shoulder on the way out. He stood there for a while, staring at nothing. Trepidation threatened to well up once more, but he quelled it with his hatred for his father.

This is your fault, you chima.

17
One Enemy for Another

A chill that only Terkeshi felt trembled through him. The villagers stood before him, some with a lost look in their eyes, others with smiles of hope. His mother had tried to warn them about the MEGAs but too many considered this an opportunity.

They had no idea. He understood their desire to finally have an ability to fight against their oppression, but they were still idiots.

His mother placed a hand on his shoulder but looked out at them. "Terk has personal experience with these people. Please listen to him."

Everyone stared at him with rapt attention. No one had taken him seriously when they thought he was just a villager. But ever since his confrontation with the slavers, he'd sensed their growing esteem and appreciated it. He'd always wanted to be good enough for others to look up to him, but that had never happened back home—not with his father's disdain constantly tearing him down.

He squared his shoulders. "These MEGAs are not our allies."

The group shared looks, brows curled. Only Anxi maintained eye contact.

"We've merely traded one enemy for another," he continued.

"They're gonna help us fight!" Huang said.

"But there's a price," Terk replied harshly. "They want to turn you into robots—robots designed only to do their bidding. You'll no longer be yourself. You won't have any free will. Everything you do will be at their mercy."

Lixin huffed. "That's just a rumor."

Terk pursed his lips. That these farmers had no access to a formal news network made them ignorant. "The rumors are true."

Someone scoffed. "How do you know?"

"Because I've lived it." He'd hoped to avoid telling them anything about his past, but it had to be done. "See this?" He pointed at his eye patch.

Their attention sharpened. "Major Jingyu knows everything about me. He'll confirm MEGAs tried to make me into one of them. They gave me an implant and a cybernetic eye and planned on doing more. I went along with it at first, thinking how amazing it would be to finally have the power to kick some ass. I realized my mistake when they used the implant to…" He cleared his throat and attempted to quell the pain swelling in his chest. "They made me murder a bunch of people—innocent people like you."

Whispers filled the cabin. "Is that why you fight so well?" Yuan asked. "You have implants?"

"No. My circumstances forced me to learn how to fight. The MEGAs took advantage of that." He paused, shoving down the emotions that accompanied the memories. "The chip was an experiment. When I realized the cost, I cut out my eye."

Mouths fell open. Fierce doubt spewed from too many of them. Others looked at him like he was crazy.

"I came to this island to escape the consequences," he added, "and I don't regret it. I do, however, regret having to come to this cyborg ship. These people are helping us because they want to use us. We're just fodder to them."

"But we need to defeat the emperor. And we can't do it without help."

"We must find another way," Terk boomed. "The MEGAs are *not* our friends. I was lucky. I disabled the implant before it completely took me over. If it had, I'd be nothing but a mindless soldier."

"I'd rather be a soldier than let the emperor keep walking all over us."

"You won't be a *real* soldier," he retorted. "You'd be more like a robot."

"No more sweating our asses off in the fields!" someone yelled.

"No more worrying about slavers or Dragon Warriors!" another added.

Damn it, why won't they listen? "You won't worry about anything because you'll be brain-dead!" Terk reined in his temper and tried a different approach. "Becoming a MEGA super-soldier won't give you freedom. You'll just be another type of slave with zero freedoms, not even the freedom to care for your own family."

"That's not true. It can't be."

"Really?" Terk said with a pitch to his tone. "I dare you to ask any of those cyborgs about their life. What do they like to do in their spare time? Are they married? Do they have children? Do they even have friends?"

A few people squirmed, but not enough. Terk tilted his brows imploringly. "I've seen what these super-soldiers are like. I've seen the emptiness of their eyes and watched them just stand there for hours when they had no orders to fulfill."

"So what do we do?" Anxi asked.

Terk gave her a nod as a silent thanks for her support, but he didn't know the answer to her question. "Lady Amarante has spoken to Major Jingyu about it and he's trying to figure it out. In the meantime, I don't want any of you agreeing to enhancements. If you do, those of you who are on my team will be off it."

Lixin scoffed. "What makes you think you'll get to keep your team?"

At first, Terk wanted to smack him, but he was right. He met the eyes of all those he'd been training. "I say we continue acting like we're part of a team and maybe they won't break us up. Washi Jeruko tasked me with training you and he has clout with Major Jingyu, so our chances are good. But I'm not keeping anyone on my team who gets enhancements. If they implant something in your eye, they can use you as a spy."

"A spy?" Huang asked.

"Yes. My—" He almost said *father*. "My superior officer used it to spy on me and punish me for every minor infraction. I had no privacy."

Several throats bobbed. Terk sensed how his words had swayed most of them, but a few still radiated a stubbornness that hinted they'd go through with it anyway. Lixin wouldn't be a loss if he ended up braindead, but some MEGAs had appeared to keep their personalities. The thought of that dangerous bully having the power of a soldier made him cringe, but it was a worry for another day.

"It's important that you tell others what I've told you. Now go."

They filed out. Anxi and Yuan stayed behind.

"How come you never told us?" Yuan asked.

"Major Jingyu ordered me not to."

"I know, but we're your friends," Yuan replied, hurt in his tone.

Terk scowled to cover his guilt. "I've been raised as a soldier and soldiers follow orders."

"It looks more like a burn," Anxi said regarding the area around his patch.

"It's a long story, but yeah. After I cut out my eye, I had to hide what I'd done with a nanite mask. Then I was near an explosion and the mask burned my face."

"That must be some story," she replied.

You have no idea. "Maybe someday when we don't have so much to deal with, I'll tell it to you."

Yuan brightened. "Alright."

Terk chafed at his eagerness. Since it was borne of trust, he let it go. "Not yet. For now, get out there and try to convince the rest not to go through with this. That's an order."

"Yes, Sir," Anxi said with a salute.

Yuan merely nodded. Anxi was the real soldier. The only one with potential among his team. Well, he supposed the others had promise too, but it'd take a lot of work. If Washi still let him, he'd do it. If there was truly an organized rebellion, he'd rather serve with his friends at his side.

They left. Terk plopped into one of the cabin seats. Gaichu sat on the floor beside him and rested his head on his thigh. Terk patted him. "The same goes for you. You run off and become some sort of super-mutt, I'll disown you."

Gaichu's tail thumped, making Terk smile. "Stupid dog."

18
Detour

The spaceship tumbled on an odd axis. Darkness shrouded it like a skulking phantom. No beacons, no transponder codes or other signals, and no engine signatures issued from it. Its carcass drifted through utter blackness as though swallowed by an eternal void.

Jori stood in the center of the *Black Thresher*'s bridge in an at ease stance. He took in the ship displayed on the viewscreen but wasn't sure what to make of it. It was as nondescript as any other transport ship in the galaxy—bulky, a hefty arc drive that ensured distance rather than speed, and a bit beat up but built to withstand just about anything the universe threw at it. Except, apparently, repeated blasts from a PG-Force cruiser.

Why would they do this to a simple cargo ship? Even if they suspected the people on board of theft, the cruiser could've easily disabled them without resorting to this level of destruction.

He glanced at Doctor Sokolov, who'd learned days ago what they'd encounter but kept it to himself. "*It's better if you see it for yourself,*" he'd insisted. Jori's attempt to find out had gone nowhere. If there'd been more communications between the doctor and MEGA-Man, he couldn't locate them. His search of the main data stream came up empty as well. MEGA-Man undoubtedly had something to do with it, leaving Jori to be swept along as helplessly as that ship.

"Captain Groman was an independent contractor," Doctor Sokolov said, rising from his seat. Now that Vance's oversized central chair had been removed from the bridge, there was ample space. "He had a cybernetic eye, acquired after some sort of accident." He paused and faced Jori. "Did you know it's less expensive in some poorer societies to get a mechanical implant than it is to grow a body part?"

Although the doctor spoke the truth, Jori had trouble believing it.

"It's why cybernetics are more commonplace in the lower levels of society," the doctor continued. "The promise of being made better is a lure that entices many, including a young man whose life circumstances made it difficult for him to land a decent job."

Jori scrunched his brow, trying to imagine how a society who claimed to treat everyone equally could let such a thing happen. It made sense in Toradon where people were strictly divided into upper and lower castes, but not the self-righteous Prontaean Cooperative.

"Believe it or not," the doctor said matter-of-factly, "he got a job right after the surgery. Independent cargo haulers are always looking for workers and they couldn't care less whether they're MEGAs. He'd worked his way up over the years. Eventually saved enough money to buy his own ship. Many of the people he hired were also MEGAs. But they weren't criminals. I admit Captain Groman had violated a few Cooperative rules, but neither he nor his crew ever did anything to warrant an arrest. This here…" He pointed at the screen. "The PG-Force did it out of hate."

Jori swallowed. Although he believed the doctor, there had to be more to it. "Do you know what led up to this? Did the PG-Force just start shooting?"

"I'm not sure. But you're welcome to go find out." Doctor Sokolov inclined his head toward the ship on the viewscreen.

Jori blinked. The only way to get more information was to visit the other vessel and piece the story together from its logs. "You'll let me leave?"

"I don't see why not. You're perfectly capable." The doctor winked.

Jori considered. Visiting a ship full of dead people made his gut writhe. It reminded him of the time his father had taken him to a small space station after he'd destroyed it. But he had to know the truth.

"Ramir," Jori said to the cyborg at the operations station. "Have someone prepare a shuttle. Rodrigo?" He turned to his personal guard. "You're with me."

The man saluted with a precision as precise as a machine. Jori pursed his lips. Even though MEGA-Man likely spied through him, Jori still held a small hope that the real Rigo was in there somewhere. And it bothered him to leave him behind with nothing to do but wait.

He turned on his heel and departed the bridge. The doctor joined him, keeping to his side, while Rigo took up the rear. "I'm going with just Rodrigo here," Jori said.

Doctor Sokolov halted. "Just you two? Are you sure you don't want others to come along?"

"I'm sure." *I'll be damned if I give you a chance to manipulate this any further.*

*****

The shuttle ride contributed to several hours of aimless musings. Although the *Black Thresher* had matched the cargo ship's velocity, it maintained a safe distance to avoid the smaller ship's erratic spin. And it wasn't as simple as flying over. The process of increasing the shuttle's thrust, then slowing it down again for the approach took a lot of time. Synchronizing the rotation and lining up the shuttle for boarding required more.

Although the autopilot could've done all this, Jori attempted to divert his mood by handling all the controls himself. But being in the cockpit reminded him of his brother. The sadness that'd been hovering over him these past several months wrapped its tendrils around him like a greedy sea creature. Terk had been an expert pilot. He would've sped over here with his eyes full of a wild zeal while performing stunt maneuvers along the way.

By the time Jori had attached the skywalk to join the two ships, his shoulders hung like dead weights. It was getting harder to keep depression from drowning him when his only companions were a simple rat and a soulless cyborg.

Kiyoshi was back on the *Thresher*, but he wouldn't have minded his company right now. "Let's go," Jori said to Rodrigo.

He secured his helmet to his suit, grabbed his toolbox, then disembarked with a controlled bounce. The effects of his shuttle's artificial gravity waned as he pushed off and glided through the skywalk to the other ship's airlock. To prevent boarding, most ships went to great lengths to secure their outer doors, but the locks on an old cargo ship like this presented little trouble.

Once inside, Jori activated his gravity boots. The light from his headlamp revealed a narrow hall. Shadows flittered with his light's movement, creating the illusion of a tooth-lined gullet.

A blast door awaited at the end of the hall. It was closed but not locked, telling him a surprise attack had damaged the ship and caused it to come down automatically. If Captain Groman had expected to be boarded, he would've shut it manually and secured it. *Alright. This supports Doctor Sokolov's claim so far.*

Jori activated the emergency release button. The door clicked. With nothing to power its opening mechanism, he had to use the pry bar from his toolbox to widen the gap. Once ajar, he pushed it open further and slipped through.

Pitch blackness awaited on the other side. His lamplight created an eerie glow around him but didn't reach the end of this corridor. The oppressive darkness might've choked him had his father not subjected him to endless training. And he'd been through worse.

He eased his way down, keeping one hand on the wall for orientation. This area was as empty as the other. It was to be expected. People wouldn't try to flee a dying ship by heading toward the rear engine rooms. They'd head for safety depots or escape shuttles housed closer to the bow—the direction he headed now.

The first sign of death appeared as black clumps congealed on the walls and floor. His light revealed a bloodier version of ground meat. The gore intensified with each step. Globs of blood and tissue drifted in the microgravity as well. When he came upon a mangled body, his gut clenched as though struck with a sledgehammer. The bloody pulp belonged to a man with a cybernetic arm. His unnaturally twisted body hovered near the ceiling. Droplets of his blood floated in a mass. As Jori passed through, they stained his suit like acidic raindrops.

He swallowed down his bile. A cool sweat beaded on his forehead. He'd never gotten used to seeing such mutilation.

The next three bodies verified that the inertial dampeners had either been damaged or couldn't accommodate the barrage of energy striking the ship. Wading through the mess probably only took fifteen minutes, but it felt like hours.

He reached the hatch to the bridge. This one required his electronic tools to break into. A minute later, he was inside. Emergency power within provided a spectral illumination. The cramped space was barely large enough to squeeze in four workstations arranged in a half circle and two central chairs behind them. Strapped in the seats were the remains of bodies. He pointedly looked away and trudged to the communications station. The screens here remained active. *Good.* That'd make this easier. It made sense for the bridge to still have power. Most had redundant energy sources.

Finding the correspondence with the PG-Force ship proved easy. It'd started with a ping from a PG-Force cruiser called the *Green Falcon* and commanded by Major Darwish. Captain Groman of the *Lady Pachyderm* answered. Darwish responded with an audible demand to search the ship.

"On what grounds?" Groman asked. "I'm up to date on all my licenses."

"You're a MEGA."

"Yeah, what of it? I have a right to run my own ship. Doesn't mean you can search it without cause."

"We're at war. That is our cause."

"Bullshit. This is discrimination. Just because I have a cybernetic eye don't mean I'm a part of this damned war."

"Then you have nothing to hide."

"I don't, but you're still not allowed on my ship. I know my rights."

The conversation deteriorated from there. Captain Groman wouldn't give in. Jori willed him to comply, though he understood the man's offense at being searched without cause. He wondered whether the man was hiding something. Or perhaps he was merely scared because of all the hate being spewed toward MEGAs.

Regardless, the cruiser's actions were unwarranted. The *Lady Pachyderm* tried to leave. The *Green Falcon* fired. They gave three warning shots before turning it into a deadly and one-sided battle. As the ship rocked violently, Captain Groman demanded to know why they were destroying it rather than disabling and boarding it, but he received no response.

Jori also played the recordings from the bridge. Nothing said or done during all the chaos suggested Captain Groman was hiding something. A lump formed in Jori's throat. Doctor Sokolov was right. The PG-Force did this out of hate.

He poked around a bit more but found no evidence to warrant this wanton massacre. His horror intensified when he located the crew manifest. One of the engine workers was the second officer's son—and he was the same age as Jori's brother. He didn't look like Terkeshi. His hair was blond and unruly, and he wore a cheery smile. That this person had looked so happy disturbed Jori even more.

He closed his eyes to hold back searing tears. Hapker never would've done this. However, a Cooperative ship had. Jori had experienced firsthand that several people within its organization still held prejudice. And the prejudice against MEGAs had been raging a lot longer than with Tredons.

How long ago had they enacted the MEGA Injunction? He didn't know his history well, but it'd started when too many prominent individuals used their enhanced abilities to gain political or military power. Riots from the less wealthy members of society ensued, eventually erupting into war. It was almost the opposite of the current situation.

Despite the sour dispositions of the MEGA hunters who'd once tested him for illegal augmentations, the MEGA Injunction promised fairness. It even affected Toradon. Jori's ancestors from before that era had been enhanced, but no one in his ancestry since. He couldn't imagine how much worse his father would be if he had genetic or cybernetic modifications. At the same time, Captain Groman was merely a man with a crew who just wanted to get by in the world.

Jori clenched his fists. The solution to this mess eluded him. *"Violence begets violence,"* Zaina had told him. Yet the people on this ship deserved justice.

19
MEGA Trouble

Commander J.D. Hapker donned his newly fabricated uniform, admiring how well the sleek brown material hugged his wide shoulders without inhibiting his movements. Trimmed with subtle accents of gold along the seams, it exuded an air of authority without ostentation. Embroidered insignia made up the epaulettes, denoting a commander's rank.

So far, things had been quiet here on the space station. But it was like the profound stillness of the woods just before a storm blew in.

He would've appreciated leaving this place to return to the *Odyssey* had it not been for Captain Arden's update. Apparently, they'd had their own adventure with a MEGA saboteur and overzealous MEGA Inspectors who took their jobs of rooting out MEGAs too far. It was supposedly all being handled, but Hapker couldn't quell the foreboding drumming through him.

He used the keypad by the door to check out of his room. A short time later, he arrived at the public section of the station where a palpable mood of writhing tension made his hair stand on end. Anxious faces darted about as if bracing for imminent violence. People stuck close to the walls, only venturing to the middle of the corridor to avoid others. A quiet yet nervous energy replaced the energetic bustle that usually accompanied a place like this.

He dipped his head at a passing unit of PG-Force officers, receiving a wary nod from the corporal in return. Although they were all a part of the Prontaean Cooperative, Hapker's rank held sway over the PCC side rather than the military side. Still, this level of reservation highlighted the fear and suspicion permeating the station.

As he neared the designated docking bay, a family of four hurried by. The mother and father kept glancing back, wrought with urgency. The hairs on Hapker's neck prickled and prompted him to dash toward the unknown danger.

People rushed by with turmoil twisting their faces. Their gasps and muttered curses combined into a rumbling akin to an impending avalanche.

Hapker mumbled apologies as he nudged his way through. The closer he got to the *Odyssey*'s docking port, the hotter the air seemed. More people hustled off. A child wailed. A man with a limp flinched as someone pushed by him. Women wearing the religious robes of Chondrian monks hugged the wall and prayed. Hapker's heart thumped harder.

"How dare you!" a male voice bellowed.

Hapker broke through a crowd of whispering onlookers. A lanky man dressed in the gaudily decorated royal blue uniform of a MEGA Inspector headed a cohort of doctors and assistants. They faced off with Major Bracht and several of the *Odyssey*'s other PG-Force officers. While the members of the inspector's unit wore expressions of haughty disdain, the officers carried a demeanor of bristling severity.

"I am an officer of the law!" the inspector continued. His aged face held a sour expression while his eyes blazed with a fanaticism that Hapker associated with all those who worked for the MEGA Inspections Office.

"Your actions here have exceeded the law!" Bracht bellowed. "I will not tolerate your harassment of my crew." The ferociousness of his wild yellow mane and pointed teeth should've deterred the inspector, but zealotry had a way of instigating self-righteousness to the point of stupidity.

"Beware!" The man jabbed his finger at Bracht while addressing the onlookers. "This ship is full of MEGA lovers!"

Oh crap.

Major Bracht snarled, his taut physique signaling a barely restrained temper. Hapker darted in between, planting himself in front of the inspector. "Sir!" The force of his voice caused the other to flinch and to shut up long enough for Hapker to say more. "Stop this childish nonsense or I'll have you arrested for inciting a riot."

The man sneered. "You don't have the authority."

Hapker leaned in with a menacing glower. "You want to bet? I've got a Rabnoshk warrior here just begging for an excuse to take you down. One word from me and you'll be kissing the floor."

The inspector yanked the hem of his jacket and jutted his chin. "I am a lead examiner of the MEGA Inspections Office with the authority to oust a captain. You'd do well to back off, *Sir*, or I'll have *you* arrested."

It was true. These people had that ability, but Hapker stood his ground knowing Major Bracht must have a good reason for his actions. He narrowed his eyes and lowered his voice. "I dare you to try it."

"Begone, Sir!" Bracht said with the other PG-Force officers planted behind him in silent authority. "You no longer have any power here."

Hapker hid his surprise. Considering how the MEGAs had infiltrated their ranks, the major's reaction made no sense. The universe really had flipped on its head.

The man lifted his nose in the air. "You will hear from the Master Examiner about this. The lot of you."

Before Hapker could respond, the inspector turned on his heel and marched off. His cohorts followed, throwing dirty looks over their shoulders.

Hapker expelled his breath and faced the major with a bewildered look.

"Everyone's going crazy, Sir," Bracht said.

"I should say so," Hapker stated. He waited a moment for the crowd to disperse, shooting warning glances at those who looked like they wanted to make trouble. "The captain mentioned their overeager behavior, but don't we still need their help?"

"Their persecution has gotten way out of hand, Sir." The major replied with vehemence. "These fiends have harassed everyone who's exhibited the slightest deviation of what they consider normal."

Like how they treated Jori.

"They've propagated fear with their hate and ruined lives," Bracht continued.

Lieutenant Hanna Sharkey cocked a brow. "They even accused the major here of being one."

Bracht bared his teeth. "Based on nothing!"

Hapker ran his hand down his face and shook his head. That sounded like something they'd do. It made it difficult to determine who the enemy was.

He took in Bracht, Sharkey, and the others. "I'm sorry that happened… But it's good to see you… All of you."

Major Bracht gave a sharp nod. His posture was stiff, as always.

Lieutenant Hanna Sharkey grinned. Though her physical traits were severe—sandy hair pulled in a tight bun, solid facial features— her buoyancy radiated from her like a star. "I'm glad you're back. We missed you."

"I've missed being on board," Hapker replied. It was true, regardless of his current mood.

"Commander!" Lieutenant Rik Gresher put out his hand. His stark white teeth stood out against his darker skin. He had a wide smile almost too big for his face, but looked good on him. "Welcome back."

Hapker grasped his hand and shook it heartily. "I'm glad to see you've returned safely as well."

Gresher shrugged sheepishly. Hapker suppressed the stab of resentment, knowing it wasn't fair to blame the lieutenant for not staying with Jori. After Hapker had been transported to a medical ship for the regrowth procedure, Gresher had tried to take over as Jori's advocate, but the Cooperative authorities denied him. They'd said his lawyer would be adequate and ordered Gresher back to the *Odyssey*.

The lawyer—Hapker couldn't quite remember his name—had been exemplary in getting Jori exonerated, but Hapker hated himself for not being there. Jori had undoubtedly needed a friend. And he had needed someone to accompany him to whatever hellhole the Cooperative had sent him to.

He'd already asked Gresher in a previous communication if he knew where they'd take Jori, but the Cooperative was being tightlipped about it. It was enough to make Hapker want to roar.

After the other officers expressed their welcomes, Hapker gestured to the skywalk. "Shall we?"

"The sooner the better, Sir," the major replied, shaking his head. He took the lead, his heavy steps echoing in the segmented and reinforced tube that led to the *Odyssey*.

Sharkey walked beside Hapker, still smiling. "It really *is* good to see you, Sir." She looked like she wanted to say more but didn't.

After a moment of waiting for pressure stabilization, the entrance hatch to their ship opened. A brush of air swept out, not much different from what was in the tube but still eliciting a sense of nostalgia. Hapker took it all in, wishing he could enjoy it.

They entered the ship's skywalk platform where Captain Arden, his wife Symphonia, and Director Jeyana Sengupta waited. All wore smiles—the captain's as stoic as ever, and partially hidden beneath his dark beard, Symphonia's with a gentleness that matched the warm tones of her skin, and Sengupta's with an upward tilt he used to think reflected snobbishness.

"How'd it go?" Captain Arden asked Major Bracht.

"As expected, Sir."

Hapker straightened when the captain's eyes fell on him. Arden's smile softened, almost banishing his stoicism. "Welcome, Commander. I'm pleased to have you back."

"I'm glad to be back, Sir." He quirked his mouth wryly. "It seems I missed something."

The captain's chest heaved. "You did. There's much to fill you in on. But first, how's the arm?"

Hapker winced internally at the reminder. "Good as new, Sir."

"That's a relief."

"So what happened here?" Hapker thumbed behind him.

The captain drew in a breath. "Perhaps you should settle in first."

"Not to sound impatient, Sir, but I've been waiting around in rooms at hospitals, on ships, and at spaces stations for quite a while."

"Very well. I suppose this is as good a place as any for an informal briefing." His dark, bushy brows turned down. Symphonia rested her palm on his forearm and the two of them shared a tender yet sad look. Arden patted her hand. "I'll start with the MEGA Inspectors. Thanks to the discovery you and your young friend made, these people have embarked on a new crusade. And by *crusade*, I mean like the ones of yore where thousands of innocents were persecuted in the name of righteousness."

Hapker soured. "How many MEGAs did they find on our ship?"

"*Found* is a subjective term. Before the two real MEGAs came to light, they had already accused eight people."

"We had two?"

The captain nodded. "One was a passenger. He wreaked all sorts of havoc. Killed three crew members, I'm afraid."

Hapker's heart sank. "And the other?"

"She turned herself in, actually—before they discovered her."

Hapker cocked his head.

"Nariya Pae," the captain said. "Our director of cybersecurity operations."

"Ex-director," Bracht boomed.

Hapker ignored him. "The red-haired timid one? Really?" He never would've suspected her.

"Genetic enhancements, not of her choosing. I'm certain she's not part of the MEGA faction. She helped us capture the other. Now we're short a damned good cyber defense operator."

"And we are stuck here for a while," Sengupta added.

Arden's brows tilted, signifying he didn't like the idea of staying. "The MEGA damaged our ship, so we're undergoing a few repairs."

"There's even worse news, Sir," Lieutenant Gresher said, making Hapker's stomach knot. "Some MEGA Inspectors have been experimenting on MEGAs."

Oh crap. What a mess. Earlier, he assumed the MEGAs were the bad guys, but it seemed there'd been atrocities committed on both sides. "Is that why you kicked them off the ship?" The captain nodded. "Why weren't they arrested?"

Arden pressed his lips together. "Admiral Nielsen suspended them pending further investigation."

Bracht emitted a low rumble.

Gresher frowned, an unusual expression for the usually smiling man. "Somehow I doubt they'll get to it anytime soon."

Not with all the other disruptions going on. "What happened with Nariya?"

"I had to issue her a dishonorable discharge."

Hapker hid his surprise at the regret in his voice. "Is she still here?"

"She is. Her career is over, but I plan on convincing the admiral to allow me to keep her here—under strict supervision—as a consultant."

Hapker's brows rose. This was new—the captain pushing the boundaries of the rules. It almost made him smirk at the irony.

"A lot has changed," Arden said as though reading his mind.

"Indeed."

"And it's not over yet."

Tell me about it. Hapker rubbed his jaw.

"There's another reason we must remain at the station for a few more days," Arden added, his tone carrying a hint of bitterness. "The admiral is sending us an entire platoon of PG-Force officers."

"An entire platoon?" Hapker asked. "I realize MEGAs are a danger, but how many more could we have left on our ship now?"

"The MEGAs have their own vessels. They've been attacking our ships and stations as far as the Enkalu sector. The extra soldiers will protect us should the MEGAs attempt to board."

"Do you have any good news at all, Sir?" Hapker asked, shaking his head.

"I'm afraid not. It gets worse." The captain grasped Symphonia's hand.

Hapker swallowed the lump in his throat as her eyes watered.

"I just received word that MEGAs have abducted my sister-in-law and nephew," the captain said as though dragging the words out like an anchor burdened by seaweed.

Hapker's mouth fell open. Symphonia sniffled. Bracht looked ready to spit fire while Sengupta patted the captain's arm.

Hapker waited for more information, but Arden seemed reluctant to speak. He thought back to some of the news reports. There was so much going on. Space battles, ships attacking stations and moon bases. "Wait," he said, remembering the most recent newscast. "Your family was on that cruise liner?"

The captain bobbed his head. "They were the entertainment coordinators. The MEGAs attacked, took everyone, then left the ship drifting."

Hapker's skin turned ice cold. As much as he condemned the radical tactics of the MEGA Inspectors, they had bigger problems. The news reports hadn't said why the MEGAs were taking people, nor had they mentioned a ransom demand, but Hapker guessed the answer.

What better way to raise an army than to create one?

20
Abominations

The Brenmos outpost dominated the screen. Unlike most space stations with a gravity wheel circling a spindle, this one resembled a rapidly spinning planet. The design had the advantage of more surface area but the difference in gravity from the equatorial region to the poles might disorient some people. Not Jori. Under different circumstances, this station would be perfect for performing a range of military exercises without having to mess with the gravitational settings.

"This is where they took the survivors," Doctor Sokolov said, quashing Jori's daydream.

According to the information he'd gleaned from the *Lady Pachyderm*, three escape pods had jettisoned during the attack. He'd also found confirmation that the PG-Force had captured one of those pods. The ship's main systems failed shortly after, but he suspected they'd gotten the other two as well.

"What is this place?" he asked the doctor who stood beside him as they reviewed the information on the newsroom workstation screen.

"It's a MEGA Inspections Office."

"The whole thing?"

"Mmm, yes. They have hundreds of offices spread throughout Cooperative territory."

Jori's mouth fell open. "Hundreds?"

"Yes, but only a few like this one take up an entire space station."

Jori hesitated but asked anyway, "What do they need all this for?"

"This is one of their largest laboratories—"

"Laboratories?" Jori felt stupid throwing out one-word questions, but he couldn't wrap his mind around how devoted the Cooperative was to policing MEGAs.

"They dedicate this place to imprisoning and testing MEGAs." Doctor Sokolov tapped the console and a video popped up. It began with doctors operating on a man with a cybernetic arm. Jori's gut did a flip as they removed it from his body.

"This man didn't volunteer for this," the doctor interrupted. "The lead inspector of this station calls it *cleansing*."

Jori watched in horror as another scene took its place. This time, they operated on someone's brain.

"They removed a chip from his brain," Doctor Sokolov said. "My understanding is that he became utterly braindead after that."

Had Jori not been trying to suppress the nausea rolling in his gut, he would've argued that the chip might've already made that man braindead.

The scene changed again. This time, the camera peeked through the barred window of a steel door and into a jail cell. The small room contained only a single bed and a toilet… And a girl about his age sitting in the corner. She wore a grey gown and a withdrawn expression.

"This is Amelia," the male camera operator said. He knocked on the glass encasing the bars. The girl didn't move, not even her eyes. "Her parents genetically altered her, giving her all manner of unnatural abilities," the man added bitterly. "Including those of an imperium animi."

Jori swallowed. His mother was an imperium. Although her ability came from her ancestors, he doubted the speaker in this video would care.

"She's a danger to society," the man spit with condemnation. "An abomination."

The scene switched again. This time, the girl was on an operating table and someone else held the camera while a man wearing the decorated royal blue uniform of a high-ranking inspector watched the procedure through an observation window.

"We're hoping to reverse the genetic alterations made to this child," the uniformed man said, his voice matching the one from the earlier video—and his blazing blue eyes were just as fanatical as Jori had imagined.

"But she's so young," a woman wearing a white doctor's robe said from beside him.

The inspector sneered. "Would you propose we keep her locked up until she comes of age?"

The woman's brows drew together. "Surely we can help her some other way. Send her to a special school, perhaps."

"A natural born imperium doesn't develop their abilities until they're older, meaning they hopefully have some semblance of a conscience before they are able to manipulate others. She's already begun abusing her powers, and to ill effects."

"I hardly call getting a shopkeeper to give her candy an ill effect."

The inspector reddened. "Just who the hell's side are you on, doctor?" He towered over the woman, forcing her to step back. "These people always start out wanting something small. And once they realize how easy it is, they take further advantage. She's dangerous!"

Jori's spine tingled. The process of genetic engineering was far from simple. This girl would have to undergo multiple treatments, all while recovering in a prison not of her making. What would this do to her? He doubted she'd be the same person afterward.

A medical alarm sounded. The doctors and medics surrounding the girl's bed whipped into a controlled frenzy. A roar built up in Jori's eardrums as he looked on with horror. She was just a little girl. She shouldn't be flatlining.

Eventually, a doctor called out the time of death. The woman gasped and covered her face. The inspector himself turned away and muttered, "It's for the best."

Jori's mouth went dry. "They killed her."

"Yes," the doctor said, his sadness as deep as Jori's horror. "They tried to do too much at once, and on a child who'd already been weakened by her imprisonment."

"I can't believe the Cooperative allows this."

"They do. And they're still allowing it. Perhaps now even more so than before."

Jori's mind reeled. He didn't know what to say.

"We can stop it," Doctor Sokolov said. "This station is only a little out of the way. We can attack the station and rescue everyone who's being used as test subjects by these sick fanatics."

Jori dipped his head. If the doctor reacted to his agreement, he couldn't tell. He was too busy trying to quell the rage burning inside him.

21
Old Friends

The main lounge bustled with over a hundred people. Whether gathered at tables, clustered in groups, or forming a line at the buffet table, their conversations all buzzed with good humor. Upbeat music with a punchy bassline enhanced the lively atmosphere.

Commander J.D. Hapker leaned on his elbow against the bar counter. He put on a smile even though melancholy had infiltrated him to the marrow. He enjoyed being with friends again but this ship made him think of Jori. If they hadn't thrown this party for him, he would've spent his time investigating Jori's whereabouts.

He sipped his drink. The burn of alcohol ran down his throat, followed by a sweet, nutty aftertaste that he couldn't quite appreciate.

A woman sauntered up and touched his arm. "Hey, you."

It took him a moment to recognize Lieutenant Hanna Sharkey. She wore her hair down—a rarity. Her eyelids sparkled with eyeshadow and blue-tinted mascara. The neckline of her shimmery blouse plunged low, revealing a lack of cleavage. "Oh, hey," he said, glad for the company of a close friend. "Thanks for the party."

"I only invited a few people." A glimmery pink gloss coated her lips, making her smile seem flirtatious. "Looks like I'm not the only one who missed you."

"They're probably just here for the food." He smiled then flourished his hand at her made-up face and stylish attire. "Who are you dating?"

She laughed and coughed at the same time. "I'm not dating anyone."

"Oh," he replied as he regarded the other partygoers, wondering who she was trying to attract.

Sharkey's gaze slid downward. An awkwardness bloomed between them. Was there something she was reluctant to tell him?

Or maybe she wanted to offer him support but didn't want to dampen the mood by bringing up Jori.

"So what have you been up to?" he asked.

She brightened again, then heaved a sigh. "Well, things were stupendously boring for a while. There's not much to do between assignments, you know. Then everything went crazy."

"The MEGAs." He took another drink. "I still can't believe Nariya Pae has genetic enhancements."

"Have you talked to her yet?"

"No, but I'd like to. The captain's regret has me curious. I mean…" He stroked his chin. "He's known the people on this ship a lot longer than I have. What sort of person is she that he'd want her to stay?"

"I don't know her all that well, but she and Symphonia were always close. Still are, it seems."

"You think she knew?"

"I doubt it, but that kind of friendship doesn't just go away."

He could understand that. It was similar to the time he found out Jori was the son of the Dragon Emperor. Although he and Jori hadn't quite become friends yet, they'd gotten close enough that Hapker had accepted it without bias. "That makes sense."

"Yeah." She shrugged. "I get why it's unfair for someone with augmentations to be a part of the Cooperative, but they're still people. There must be more to all this than what the news stories are focusing on."

"I'm sure it's skewed, especially considering the behavior of the MEGA Inspectors. Who else did they accuse?"

"Jensin."

Hapker nearly dropped his drink. "Jensin? Really? Why?"

"*So talented, yet so young*," she mocked. "*He* must *be a MEGA*."

"That's it? That was their only reason?"

"Yep. Hateful jackasses."

"I'll say." He'd never given them much thought until they'd harassed Jori.

She glanced away again, her earlier buoyancy gone.

"Sorry," he said. "This is supposed to be a reprieve."

She smiled once more, making her cheekbones more prominent. "Yeah, let's change the subject. We needed a reason to celebrate, and what better reason than your return?" She grasped his hand and squeezed, her eyes tilting in a way that made him inexplicably uneasy.

Is she flirting with me? No. That couldn't be it. They were just good friends.

Lieutenant Gresher approached, saving him from dwelling on this line of thought. "Hey again, Commander." His white teeth flashed as he grinned. "How does it feel to be back on the *Odyssey*?"

"Different. I imagine it'll feel normal again when I return to duty," he replied. "How's Korbin? Are you still in touch with him?"

Gresher's smile didn't fade. "Yep. I just spoke to him."

"What's he up to? And the others? I heard they decommissioned the *Defender*."

The man's good cheer faltered. "The authorities ran us all through a gauntlet of endless questioning, and not everyone got to return to duty."

Hapker shook his head. After Gottfried's ambitious plot to commandeer the *Defender* and steal the plans for the potentially deadly perantium device, they'd all had to be vetted. He'd been transported to a hospital ship for recovery, but that didn't stop the authorities from questioning him as well.

"I think all our allies did, though," Gresher continued. "They sent Ortega to a PG-Force station. Harley was assigned to another ship, as was Singh. And Korbin…" Gresher straightened, his grin returning. "Korbin might get transferred to the *Odyssey*."

"That's fantastic! I'll be glad to have him." Hapker lifted his drink. Gresher clinked his glass to his.

"How's Chesa?" Gresher asked.

A bit of alcohol went down the wrong pipe, making Hapker cough. "Um—"

Sharkey's brow crinkled. "Who's Chesa?"

Why would she be worried? "An old friend. Well, not so much anymore. She's ticked off at me."

"You two didn't get back together?" Gresher asked.

Hapker wagged his head. "Even though Gottfried had used his imperium ability to influence her hostility toward Jori, I doubt she needed much of a push. I forgave her but had no desire to rekindle our relationship."

Sharkey's shoulders fell. "The admiral's aide was an imperium?" she asked, serious now.

"One of his many genetic alterations." Hapker suppressed a shiver at the thought of Gottfried getting inside people's heads and making them do his bidding. He gazed about the lounge, wondering if any of the other conversations were as distressing as this one.

Director Jeyana Sengupta caught his eye and headed over. Her smile was soft yet still bright. He returned it. "Thanks for coming, Director."

"I wouldn't miss a good party." She had to arch her neck to look up at him. Although her bushy black hair reached his chin, her forehead only came up to his upper chest. "So what do you think of it?"

Hapker took it all in once more. "Amazing. I didn't realize I've been so missed."

"By me more than anyone," she replied. "Acting as commander while you were gone is not a job I envy."

"Well, you've held two jobs at once." That she was the Director of Intelligence gave him an idea. He cleared his throat to give him a moment to figure out how to broach the subject. Nothing came to mind. "I don't suppose you'd be able to find out where they sent Jori?" he blurted.

"We just want to know he's alright," Gresher added.

"If the councilors wouldn't tell you…" Sengupta hesitated. "I'm not sure they'll approve of me asking around… But technically, they haven't forbidden me." She leaned in and cleared her throat. "I can reach out to a few contacts."

Hapker's chest hitched. "Thank you. You have no idea how much that means to me."

"You've grown quite attached to him. No one else here seems to see it, but I know the face of a man trying to hide his grief."

Hapker lowered his head. "I shouldn't have let them take him."

Sengupta placed her hand on his forearm and squeezed. "I hope you find him."

She left. He took another drink, this time a gulp rather than a sip.

"It *was* really crappy separating you two like that," Sharkey said.

"I agree," Gresher added. "But he'll be alright. He's pretty tough."

That's just an act. Yes, Jori was intelligent, and he could fight. But he was trying to navigate unfamiliar territory now—maybe literally as well as figuratively.

The party dragged on. He chatted with several of the officers he used to share his bridge duty shift with, including Jensin. Chief Sam Simmonds made him laugh with a story he told about his homeworld. And a growing sense of fellowship came over him when Major Bracht attempted a conversation.

The cheery atmosphere was just beginning to lift his mood when Doctor Gregson and Doctor Jerom asked after Jori, then his spirits dipped. He put on an effort to appear cheerful when Sergeant Ander Vizubi and his team approached.

"Welcome back, Commander," the sergeant said.

Hapker almost clapped his shoulder but thought better of it. Vizubi had the bearing of a man who brooked no nonsense. "Thank you."

"Of course, Sir." Vizubi made a small smile that deepened the fine lines of his face. Although he was the oldest PG-Force officer on the ship, he still radiated a silent power.

Corporal Rona Quigley quirked her mouth in a way that came across as cocky. Hapker had come to recognize it as part of her bold personality. "We're glad to have someone with even a little military experience back in charge," she said, tilting her head and planting her hand on her curvy hip.

Private Ishaq Bari flashed his dark eyes at her, then faced Hapker. "Not that Director Sengupta didn't do a good job."

"Right." Quigley replied without a hint of contrition. "No insult intended."

"It never is," Bari mumbled.

She nudged him. Her pushing against his lean frame made him step sideways. She mouthed for him to shut up and he shot her a smirk in reply.

Hapker suppressed a smile at their team camaraderie.

Private Mai Fung shook her head at them. When Hapker had first met her, he doubted someone so petite would be good at security. But he'd seen her hold her own in a sparring match against Sergeant Naran. Jori would be in awe of her swift and unrelenting agility.

"What my friends are trying to say," Sergeant Oscar Woolley said, "is welcome back."

Of all the members of Vizubi's fireteam, Woolley seemed the friendliest. He also came across as the most unassuming. Hapker never would've guessed a man with a disarming grin and light curly hair that was almost boyish could outfight every single one of these hardcore officers. The only two people on the ship he hadn't seen him beat in a sparring match were Lieutenant Gresher and Major Bracht. *Impressive for someone who attended the PG Institute to become a pilot.*

"If the past is any indication, Sir," Fung said, "you'll have your work cut out for you."

Quigley grunted. "Yeah, first a little MEGA warrior, then a MEGA terrorist. They were both MEGA pain-in-the-asses, if you ask me. But it's gonna get a whole lot worse now that all the MEGAs are showing their true colors."

Hapker bristled. "Jori's not a MEGA." *Or a pain in the ass.* "He's been tested."

Quigley narrowed her eyes as though he were daft. "They supposedly tested the admiral's aide too."

"Didn't that boy use some sort of implanted tech to take over this ship?" Bari asked.

"He's not a MEGA," Hapker said, adding a warning to his tone. "You don't know all the facts."

Vizubi's brow hooded over his eyes as he glared at Quigley. "He's saved a lot of lives. Not just the ones his father took prisoner. But those on the *Defender* too, if I heard right."

Hapker dipped his head in both agreement and as a thanks for the defense.

Quigley blathered on, oblivious. "What better way to hide that he's a MEGA than to pretend to be against them?"

"For the last time," Hapker said through his teeth, "Jori is not a MEGA."

Quigley raised her palms. "Alright. Alright. Damn. Didn't know you'd be so touchy about it."

Woolley shook his head at her. She planted both hands on her hips. "What?"

Fung rolled her eyes. "You've got the tact of a buffalo at a ball." She steered Quigley away. "Let's check out the buffet. I hear there are strawberries."

Bari shot Hapker an apologetic look and followed, as did Vizubi, though his expression also seemed to hold exasperation.

Woolley moved to follow but paused. "Sorry, Sir. She takes a little getting used to."

Hapker didn't reply. If he found Jori and brought him here, no one would throw him a welcome back party.

Things went downhill from there. He overheard other derogatory comments about Jori. He even heard a few about the stupidity of those from the *Defender* for not knowing they worked alongside MEGAs.

When the negativity became too much to bear, he downed another drink and returned to his quarters.

22
Questions Without Answers

Every visit to the captain's office provoked a distinct feeling. In the beginning, Commander J.D. Hapker found the sparse décor stale. After a while, he decided the animal carvings and scenic pictures held an inviting warmth. Today, it had a somber atmosphere. All the wooden creatures seemed to frown, and the landscapes reminded him of the places he'd never be able to take Jori.

The captain's demeanor weighed the mood down further. He sat behind his desk, looking as stoic as ever, but with a brooding tilt to his brows. "As you can imagine, it's been challenging around here," he said, finishing up his update on everything that'd happened since Hapker had been gone.

"I'm sorry about Jori," the captain added. "I understand that you're not thrilled with the outcome, but I'm sure he's safe."

Hapker nodded. "You wouldn't happen to know where they sent him, would you?"

Arden shook his head. "No. I'm afraid they've classified the information."

Hapker almost groaned in anguish. Even though it made sense to protect Jori's new identity, his heart sank. The pain twisted on the captain's forehead reminded him he wasn't the only one who'd lost someone. "I'm sorry to hear about your family."

"Thank you." The bags under Arden's eyes seemed heavier. "Did that MEGA on the *Defender* ever tell you anything about MEGA-Man's plans?"

"Not me, but Jori."

"Really?" the captain asked in a lilting tone.

Hapker waved his hand. "It's not what you think. Gottfried acknowledged Jori wasn't a MEGA but still tried to recruit him."

Arden's eyes widened. "For what?"

"Jori is the son of the Dragon Emperor. If something happens to the emperor, then the MEGAs have the means to infiltrate the Tredons. Plus, Jori has many uncommon skillsets. Perhaps they had another use for him."

The captain leaned back. "Like harvesting his genes."

Hapker ran his hand down his face and sighed. "It explains why Gottfried showed so much interest in him."

"What else did he tell Jori? Anything that'll help us figure out what they plan on doing with our people?"

"Gottfried wanted to take Jori to Cybernation. My best guess is others are being taken there too."

Arden straightened. "Any mention of turning people into MEGAs?"

"No. I'm sorry."

The captain's face fell, making him look much older than his mid-fifties. Hapker swallowed. He had no real condolences to give but tried anyway. "I'm sure the admirals and generals are organizing a rescue as we speak."

Captain Arden clasped his hands in front of him and shook his head.

Hapker lurched forward, perching on the edge of his seat. "They're not?"

"Councilor Alvia said they are doing everything they can but are overwhelmed."

Hapker ran his hand down his face again. He couldn't do anything about Jori right now, but maybe he could help Arden's family. "We can send our own people to Cybernation. Perhaps Sergeant Vizubi and his team."

"Considering they feel the need to assign a PG-Force platoon to my ship, I doubt they'll sanction me sending my officers away."

"Did you ask?"

"I meant to, but Councilor Alvia said they've already sent several reconnaissance missions there… And none of them have returned."

The councilors rarely got so involved in military matters, but the recent upheaval had them working closely with the admirals and generals. Alvia would be the most personable one to ask, but he doubted any of them had the time to consider all the requests and suggestions that were likely pouring in from their PCC captains and PG-Force majors.

Hapker frowned. "I hate sitting here doing nothing."

Arden splayed his hands in a helpless gesture. "You and me both. But we just don't have enough information to risk our people's lives."

Not even for your family? It was an unfair question. No doubt Captain Arden felt as powerless as he did.

The captain's door comm buzzed. "Enter," Arden said.

The hydraulics hissed as the door opened. Major Bracht entered, followed by a diminutive red-haired woman and Sergeant Naran.

Hapker stood. "Nariya Pae," he greeted neutrally.

"Hi, Commander," she replied meekly, head hanging.

"Have a seat." Arden gestured to the chair beside Hapker's.

Hapker pulled it out for her. She eased down and folded her hands in her lap. Her posture was straight but held an edge that betrayed her insecurity as Bracht and the sergeant planted themselves behind her.

"It's alright," the captain said to her. "You've given me more information than I could've ever hoped for, but I thought it'd be a good idea for my second officer to speak to you as well."

"Of course," she replied, dipping her head at Hapker without meeting his eyes.

Hapker filled his lungs. "I'm told you have no affiliation with the MEGA cause."

She finally looked at him, her brows furrowed in stricken lines. "None, Sir. I swear. It wasn't until after I joined the Cooperative that I discovered I had genetic enhancements."

"How'd you find out?"

"My mother let it slip. I-I was…" She wrung her hands. "I was so mortified. Believe me, I wrestled with telling the authorities. But I worked so hard. I didn't realize I was cheating. And when I went on duty later that day, my friend Salia invited me to a party. It reminded me of how much I love my work and my friends. I didn't want to leave."

A tear trickled down her cheek, moving Hapker to pity. If she was lying, she was darned good at it. He touched her shoulder. "Believe it or not, I understand. I can't imagine what I'd do in your shoes."

She wiped her nose with the back of her hand and sniffled. "I know I messed up. But I still want to help."

Hapker rubbed his chin. "You kept it secret from us, but did you ever tell anyone else?" She wagged her head, making her tight red curls sway. "No one? Not even someone who you suspected might be a MEGA too?"

"No one."

She averted her eyes so he pressed. "Are you sure? This is important. I can't promise we won't report it, but I promise we have far greater concerns right now. We need to learn more about Cybernation."

Her forehead wrinkled and this time she met his eyes. "I never even heard of Cybernation until all this happened."

Hapker eyed her. "But you told someone about your enhancements, right?"

She nodded. "Jeremy, a boyfriend, noticed I was upset and begged me to tell what was wrong, so I finally did. He was angry, but not at me. He said it wasn't my fault and I shouldn't have my life ruined because of something my parents did."

"Jeremy. Is he here on this ship?"

"No. I haven't seen him in years."

Darn. It didn't sound like he was a MEGA, but it wouldn't hurt to question him—if he were here. "Is there anything else you can tell us at all about Cybernation or MEGA-Man's plans?"

"I'm sorry, Commander. I truly don't have more information."

Hapker suppressed a groan. *A million questions. Zero answers.*

"But…" Nariya's throat bobbed. "I have an idea."

"Go ahead," the captain replied.

"Well." She wrung her hands. "We've learned some MEGAs have direct communication with each other, no matter how far away… And in real time."

Captain Arden dipped his head. "They call it the Great Commune."

Hapker straightened. "The RT-comm transceiver on this ship is as big as my bathroom. How can they possibly be in contact with each other without one? Are they using ours somehow?"

"I don't think so," she replied. "They've made their transceivers small enough to be implanted in their heads."

Hapker's eyes widened. "You're kidding! Do they have their own communication hubs too?"

"I suspect they do," Arden said. "But I'm not sure we know where any of them are."

Hapker rubbed his chin. It wouldn't surprise him. The MEGAs could've built secret communication hubs anywhere across space.

"So what's your idea?" he asked, trying to wrap his mind around it.

"Oleg is still here, right?" She looked at the captain, hopeful. "He had—maybe still has—direct contact. That's how I became aware of it. I can help reverse engineer it—under supervision, of course. It's not my area of expertise but perhaps I can figure out how to use it to get information from the Great Commune."

Hapker leaned in. "Can you really do that?"

She shrugged. "I'm not sure, but I'll try. I mean…" She wrung her hands. "There's probably other people already working on this, but I want to help."

Hapker rubbed his chin. He and the captain shared a look. "Liam Garner has talked to her?"

Arden dipped his head, confirming their resident extraho-animi who could extract thoughts had verified Nariya's allegiance.

"Then I'm open to her giving it a shot," Hapker said.

"Alright." The captain planted his palms on his desk in finality. "Let's do it."

A little of the tension in Hapker's shoulders loosened. He was no closer to finding Jori, but at least he could help rescue others.

Step one, find out where their people were being taken. Step two, virtual reconnaissance. Step three, infiltration.

If Nariya succeeds.

23
Family

Murkiness infiltrated the cockpit—or perhaps that was Terkeshi's imagination. A single green light created a soft glow as well as depressing shadows. Most of the systems had been shut off, but he left the external cameras running. Other than the appearance of an occasional robot-like worker, the bay was quiet.

He felt like an idiot hiding in here. He should be out there, making sure his friends didn't get suckered into doing something stupid. Anxi and Yuan wouldn't, but he wasn't certain about Chenwei and a couple of others.

He heaved a sigh and fought to regain a logical perspective over an emotional one. Just because his mother saw his anger as a strength didn't mean he had to let it overrule his common sense.

He'd implored her to stay here so the MEGAs couldn't use her for her status. But she worried Lord Qing would get suspicious. Besides, Washi and Michio, who'd also escaped and made it to the *Tatawar*, would protect her. Although he trusted his personal guards, he didn't trust the MEGAs.

It was her final argument that'd convinced him. "I don't like using my abilities on people," she'd said, "but I will do what I must to keep them safe."

"To keep them from making stupid decisions, you mean," he'd replied petulantly. But in truth, he felt better knowing his friends wouldn't get suckered into becoming MEGAs.

Logical or no, he still sulked. Once again, his chima father had cost him his future. He could have stayed on the *Dragon* and risen to a Dragon Warrior with Jori at his side. That could've been a decent life if Father hadn't ruined it. A farmer's life wasn't so bad either. It was hard but being surrounded by good people had made it better. Father had ruined that too. And now here he was, with no option but to hide in here like a coward.

No, not cowardice. *Prudence*, Sensei Jeruko would've called it.

The only positivity he could see through this whole mess was that Baba Airi would get medical treatment. And his mother and his friends were alive. And he had Gaichu with him. Alright, so he had more than one thing to be thankful for.

He sighed. None of these things helped him figure out what to do next. All their food, medical care, and shelter now depended on people who'd tried to turn him into a machine and make him their puppet. He could run away—or try to. But he wouldn't leave his friends behind—no matter how tempting.

A beep sounded. He glanced at the cameras. Two warriors stood outside the starboard airlock. He bounded eagerly from his seat and headed over. The gravity here was a little less than it had been on the planet and one of his strides propelled him into a conduit that ran along the ceiling. Although he'd spent his life practicing in different gravitational settings, something about the *Tatawar*'s gravitational device created pockets of instability.

He pressed the door open, not having to worry about depressurizing, and stepped back into the shadows.

Two heads poked in. "You in here?" a man asked.

"Yes," Terk replied. "I just don't want anyone else to see me."

When they came in and shut the door behind them, Terk activated the lights. The brightness made him blink. Washi and Michio stood before him. The brothers shared many similarities—dark hair, solid build, matching mustaches and patch of hair under their lips—but each had a distinctive personality. Washi, always the most solemn, radiated a pleasure at seeing Terk while his face remained placid. Michio, of course, wore a wide grin across his slender face.

Terk returned it. Damn, it was good to see them. "You're alright."

"And so are you." Michio looked him up and down with a pleased expression. "I heard you saved the villagers again."

Terk's insides swelled with pride. His father's words about emotions being a weakness made him want to hide it, but he couldn't help himself. "Yeah." He cleared his throat. "How is everyone?"

"Safe," Washi replied.

"Better," Michio said at the same time. "Some are even healthier than before they came here."

Terk shook his head. "That seems generous on the surface."

Washi crossed his arms and harrumphed. "They've sure got a lot of people fooled."

"How many have agreed to enhancements?" Terk asked, taken aback.

Michio looked away. Washi growled. "Too many."

Terk clenched his jaw. He'd really hoped they wouldn't fall for it.

"Your speech helped, though," Michio added. "No one from the *Dusty Rose* wanted any enhancements."

A little tension left Terk's shoulders. He was almost certain his mother had something to do with it as well but didn't say so. Just because Washi and Michio knew of her ability didn't mean they wouldn't be uneasy about her using it. "So what do we do?"

"We're not sure yet," Washi grumbled. "Lord Qing is kowtowing to these people like they're his saviors."

"In a way, they are." Terk glowered. "The MEGAs are taking advantage of his desperation."

Washi rubbed his brow. "Yeah."

Michio elbowed him. Washi glanced at him. Michio gave him a knowing look. Washi sighed and faced Terk. "You're gonna have to stay in here. We'll bring you food once in a while and anything else you need. Don't answer the door to anyone you don't know."

Terk scoffed. "I have no intention of going out there. The last thing I want is for the MEGAs to find out I'm alive and kill me."

"No. I don't think they'll kill you," Washi said. "They want into our territory. I suspect eliminating the emperor is their plan now, even if it'll create chaos. The lords won't bow down easily, and they'll go to war over who should be in charge next. If the MEGAs discover you're alive, it'd be easier to gain access by using you as their figurehead."

Terk groaned. "You can't be serious. Look at me." He indicated his damaged eye. "I can't take my father's place. Even without this scarring. You remember how horrible I was back home. I couldn't lead a pig to his trough, let alone thousands of Dragon Warriors."

"You weren't horrible," Michio said.

"Just inexperienced," Washi added.

Terk quirked a brow. "Thanks," he muttered.

"Regardless, it'd still create a civil war." Washi's voice rose in frustration. "And you know very well that this MEGA-Man won't let you rule anyway. That was probably the whole reason to get you to undergo cybernetic surgery—to control you."

"We can't lose you," Michio added. "Prince or farmer. You're family."

Terk's throat caught. Damn his sentiment. Becoming a farmer had made him soft. *But in a good way, you idiot.*

It was strange that these two men had once been his personal guards under his command. The roles were reversed now, but he didn't mind. And he regarded them the same way. It'd taken him a long time to realize it, but they'd been more of a father to him than his own father.

"You don't need to worry about me," he said. "I'll stay here and be careful about who I let in." *But for how long?* "What else is going on? Is the *Tatawar* waiting for more MEGA ships or are they heading somewhere?"

Washi shrugged. "The ship is on the move, but I'm not sure where it's taking us. Not even Major Jingyu knows."

Terk frowned. If the MEGAs planned on giving the rebels a base of operation, he might remain unnoticed. But that'd just tie Lord Qing to them even more.

"Keep me posted," he said, realizing it came out like an order. "I need to know what's going on, for sanity's sake. And if you come up with a plan, let me in on it."

Michio smiled. "Will do."

The man radiated positivity, but it wasn't enough. They were stuck here. Prisoners. And the longer he stayed, the greater the chance they'd discover him.

Chusho.

24
Fire Fight

Jori faced a cold sea of stars smothered by an endless blackness. Though weightless, his mood pressed down on him. He gripped the tether connecting him to the outside of the space station, thinking of it as a puppet string rather than a safety line. If only he could float away into oblivion and forget all his troubles.

Coming out here should've been an adventure, but this was no exhilarating spacewalk. Today, the expanse was a prison, one he couldn't escape no matter how far he drifted.

"Are you ready?" Doctor Sokolov asked through the comm.

"Yes," Jori replied without giving away his gloomy anxiety.

"Good." The doctor blew out a breath that amplified through Jori's earpiece. "Listen. Even though MEGA-Man says the probability of you getting hurt is minimal, I must take great care. Let the soldiers go in first."

"Understood."

Jori waited outside an emergency airlock as a pair of super-soldiers set charges. He still couldn't believe MEGA-Man was allowing him to do this. Any risk for someone deemed so important seemed too much. Perhaps this was more about gaining his trust—or maybe MEGA-Man had an ulterior motive.

It'd be smarter to stay behind. Although the soldiers with him were capable, disciplined, and would follow orders without question, he had to make sure they handled this his way.

The anticipation of battle usually elicited excitement, but trepidation tangled his insides. The warrior side of him burned for a fight, but the circumstances which brought him here troubled him. He was well aware MEGA-Man pulled his strings but fighting him proved more difficult than physical combat.

His blood boiled at the memory of all those videos made by the inspector. The man's smug face, with skin as white and as shiny as porcelain, provoked an unreasonable urge to shoot things. It was bad enough for people all over the galaxy to riot against MEGAs, but the Cooperative sanctioned the actions of these chimas. The MEGA Inspectors must be stopped and their MEGA prisoners had to be rescued.

Jori's lip curled. MEGA Inspectors—or MEGA hunters—were worse than predators. They were glory hunters who inflicted harm for no other reason than to prove their superiority, and arrogant chimas who hated MEGAs with an absurd fanaticism. He'd experienced their attitudes himself when they'd tested him. Now he had a chance for revenge.

No. Not revenge. Justice. This was a rescue mission, not an attack.

A violent rush of air shot out of the airlock hatch, making no sound but creating a force that spewed outward. Despite Jori's placement to the side, the gust pushed him away. A panicked impulse kicked in as he groped for a handhold. The tether went taut, halting his momentum. With a huff, he grabbed the lifeline and hauled himself back in.

Focus, damn it. The enemy had showed no signs of knowing they were here but would certainly know now.

"Station breached," a monotone voice reported.

Jori's heart skipped a beat as he readied himself with the squad of super-soldiers clustered around the open airlock. "Proceed," he ordered.

The soldiers charged in with strict precision. Jori waited to go last. His warrior training had prepared him for this yet he felt woefully unprepared. He almost always succeeded in simulated attack scenarios, but this was different. It was real.

An uncomfortable tingle ran through him as he recognized the reason behind his trepidation. He wasn't afraid of getting hurt. He was afraid of hurting others.

"Violence begets violence," he kept hearing Zaina say. But she'd also said some people don't deserve to live. She'd meant Vance, but didn't sadistic MEGA hunters count too?

The soldiers had already opened the second interior hatch by the time Jori entered. He activated his magnetic boots and knelt beside Rodrigo, his muscles coiled and ready for action. He trained his weapon into the darkness, waiting for a counterattack. His hands held steady, though his heart twitched like a fly caught in a web.

The lead soldiers tossed a few grenades into the intersecting hall. Multiple flashes of white exploded soundlessly while the floor quaked beneath Jori's feet. Without air, no smoke billowed, but shrapnel zipped through the corridor. He huddled behind the soldiers at the threshold carrying shields until the danger of suit penetration passed.

Sparks of light erupted as the opposition arrived and opened fire. The orange flashes of a weapon set to kill streaked from the muzzle of Jori's phaser rifle as he fired with determined fury. His soldiers did the same but with detached rigidity.

He'd given explicit orders that only those threatening them with armaments could be shot. No killing anyone who hid, ran, or surrendered. Even though he was the aggressor, fighting the station's defenders was an acceptable action. They were soldiers and by protecting this place, they were complicit in the atrocities of its occupants.

The super-soldiers killed the opposition with a calculated precision. The advanced targeting of their cyber-eyes allowed them to see through the darkness. Jori couldn't tell what his own shots struck, but pains of death filtered in through his searing adrenaline as enemies fell.

Enemies. That's what he called them now. *Am I doing the right thing?*

The firefight ended. Jori used his senses to locate opposing lifeforces and found none. The super-soldiers stormed forward. He followed in their wake, keeping his weapon poised. An eerie silence ensued as they tromped through the airless corridor. He tried not to look at the floating bodies they passed. Gloom threatened to douse his adrenaline high, so he summoned his resolve. It was too late to back out now. Besides, people still needed rescuing.

"Explosive detected," a lead soldier said.

"Neutralizing," another responded.

Smart. The enemy set traps rather than engaging directly.

After defusing the bombs, they encountered artillery bots. His soldiers eliminated them in less than a minute with their precise targeting.

Not my soldiers, damn it. They belonged to MEGA-Man and were only his until MEGA-Man decided otherwise.

They infiltrated further into the station. Defenders appeared in small groups. The super-soldiers took them out with little effort. Events passed in a blur. Jori's mind got caught in the rhythm of his breathing and the pounding in his eardrums. He didn't even notice when the station's gravity had strengthened enough to negate the need for the magnetics of his boots—or when they entered an area that still had its atmosphere.

A blast of brightness lit up his surroundings. His visor tinted before it became blinding. A boom resounded, followed by a shockwave that sent him and his men crashing backward. A red icon flashed in the upper right of his display. Something had penetrated his suit but his buzzing urgency kept him from determining if it'd harmed him. No alerts popped up so he scrambled to his feet and righted his weapon. Most of his soldiers did too, but not all.

"Two down," a super-soldier designated as B216 said. The information box on the bottom right corner of Jori's visor indicated the speaker was the one in charge now. "Proceeding."

"Wait." Jori's heart thumped as his display identified the two soldiers on the floor. *Not Rodrigo.* He glanced about and found the man standing at his back, still alive and with no sign of injury. Jori puffed. Of all the lifeless soldiers he'd selected for this mission, Rigo was the only one he couldn't bear to lose.

Leaving the dead behind, they continued onward. When they reached a hall with rooms on either side, the super-soldiers broke into them one by one to clear them. The first three were empty. Five station personnel burst from the fourth, followed by two young men with obvious cybernetics. The soldiers allowed the unarmed employees to leave and directed the MEGAs to wait for assistance.

This scenario played out twice more. As instructed, no one was killed unless they presented a viable threat. The man who wielded a wrench was disarmed while a doctor waving a scalpel was permitted to retreat. They encountered more defenders and took them all down. Jori suspected he'd feel remorse later, but battle-focus commanded him now.

After a swift march through an empty corridor, they reached their destination—a cell block crowded with MEGAs. Still in a focused daze, Jori guarded the rear while the soldiers released them. Several had to be carried. One, a woman, had half her upper face encased in bandages. He gritted his teeth, suspecting the hunters had removed cybernetic parts from her eye socket. The misgiving he'd had about allying with MEGA-Man turned into vindication.

Soon, every prisoner was out. Jori heaved a sigh. They'd done it.

They retreated, herding the MEGAs with them. As they crossed the final intersection, a man Jori had come to despise appeared. The high-ranking inspector raised a finger and spewed curses coupled with the word *abomination*. The soldiers braced themselves against his tirade but didn't fire since he had no weapons.

Jori clenched his jaw against the temptation to give orders to kill him anyway. "Arrest him," he said instead.

"Are you sure?" Doctor Sokolov asked through the comm channel.

"I'm sure," Jori replied, even though he wasn't.

"He has no weapon, but he's tortured and murdered so many," the doctor said. "He doesn't deserve to live."

Jori almost changed his mind as Zaina's words echoed in his head. But he couldn't do it, not if he wasn't armed. "Arrest him."

Rodrigo snagged the man by the wrist and flipped him about in one swift motion. The inspector's curses cut short as Rigo pinned his arms behind his back and shoved him along.

"Father!" a woman screamed. She ran forward only to run into the bulky arm of a soldier. She bounced off and landed on her butt. "My father!"

Jori's stomach clenched. It wasn't a woman. It was a girl perhaps twelve or thirteen years old.

"No!" she cried, tears streaming down her anguished face. She slammed her fists against a retreating soldier, her expression twisting with rage, demanding that he be released. "You stronzo! Give him back!"

She charged. Since she had no weapon, the lead soldier struck her in the head and knocked her out.

A young man wearing a uniform that identified him as an administrative officer rushed in. He carried a rifle with shaking hands. Fear exuded from his wide eyes as he raised it.

"No!" Jori lurched forward, intending to dive low and kick the man's feet out from under him—but he was too late. Rodrigo fired. The pain of death seared into Jori's skull. The rifle clattered to the floor and the man dropped over dead.

"No, damn it!" Jori screamed. "I was about to disarm him."

"He was a threat," Rodrigo replied.

Jori's sinuses burned as he beheld the young man's still wide yet lifeless eyes. He was just a low-level employee. Regular soldiers would've noticed the difference and not taken their orders so literally.

Jori swallowed down the bile rising from his throat. Technically, this was his fault. He should've given clearer instructions. But there was nothing to be done now. They still had a mission. A single tear rolled down, burning his cheek. His helmet kept him from wiping it away, but he wouldn't have done it anyway. That tear was the only way to honor the young man's sacrifice.

He balled his fists. "Everyone, get the hell out of here, now!" *Before this situation gets any worse.*

His throat tightened. This death would undoubtedly haunt him. So would the girl's anguish. He doubted he'd be as upset if someone had arrested his own father, but the power of her emotions suggested she cared a great deal for hers.

What if she thought these MEGAs were taking him to be tortured? Would she end up hating MEGAs even more now? Will she seek revenge? Will that young man's family?

Violence begets violence.

25
Execution

Jori lingered in the eye of a storm. A dark calm settled around him while uncertainty reigned everywhere else. Though the air was still, his skin tingled as if brushed by a cool breeze. His heart thumped in a slow, distant rhythm. Reality seemed distant. Nothing made sense.

With the lights dimmed, Jori sat at his desk and conducted an after-action review of the space station assault. Technically, it had been a rescue, but he couldn't stop thinking that he'd done more to contribute to the cycle of violence.

Kiyoshi slept on his lap, blissfully unaware. Jori stroked him now and then but nothing calmed the turmoil churning inside him.

He'd already read up on the young man Rodrigo had killed. The contents of his file didn't indicate he was a MEGA hater—just an ordinary man who had recently earned a computer technician degree and took the first job presented to him. His life had been cut short for no reason other than being in the wrong place at the wrong time. He'd tried to be a hero and it'd cost him everything.

Jori quelled the nausea roiling in his stomach and focused his energy on the man who should've died instead. General Inspector Lamberson's face took up the screen. He'd signed on with the MEGA Inspections Office ten years ago after MEGAs murdered his wife. The news article said two MEGAs attempting to rob a store killed her. Rather than give up the money, the shop owner pulled out a gun. The MEGAs opened fire, killing the owner and two innocent bystanders, including the girl's mother. Juliana had been her name and she bore some resemblance to his own mother. A photo of her with her then smiling husband and daughter brought tears to Jori's eyes.

If someone murdered his mother, he'd want revenge too. Blaming all MEGAs and ultimately torturing them didn't sit right, but what if it'd been PG-Force officers who killed her? Would he hate everyone who served in the Cooperative's military? There was a time when he considered all in the Cooperative his enemy.

He dropped his head in his palm and huffed. This was all so confusing.

The door comm buzzed. Doctor Sokolov waited outside with mild concern. After the soldiers had returned to the *Thresher*, the doctor congratulated Jori for a job well done. Rather than share in his excitement, Jori left without a word. No doubt the man was here now to ask what was wrong.

"Lights," Jori called out begrudgingly.

The room brightened, making him blink. He hesitated, then pressed the security button on his computer. The door opened with a hydraulic hiss. The doctor displayed a wan smile and entered.

"How can I help you, Doctor?" Jori asked without enthusiasm.

"I'm wondering what you plan on doing with our prisoner?"

Oh. That. They'd locked General Inspector Lamberson in the same dingy cell Vance had put him and Zaina in when they first arrived. The place almost seemed too good for him, but Jori made sure he had more comforts than Vance had afforded them.

Jori frowned. The Cooperative had an extensive process that included lawyers, judges, and rehabilitation facilities while Toradon authorities tortured and killed criminals without a trial.

"How does Cybernation's justice system work?"

Doctor Sokolov cocked his head. "I'm not entirely sure, but I have word from MEGA-Man. He says this man must be executed."

Jori's gut soured but he wasn't sure why. His only real experience with a justice system was when the Cooperative put him on trial for commandeering Captain Arden's ship. They could've just thrown him in prison without giving him a chance to defend himself. Even though he had plenty of evidence against this man's wrongdoing, it seemed unfair not to give him the same opportunity.

The doctor's throat bobbed. "And he wants you to authorize it."

Blood drained from Jori's head. "If MEGA-Man says he *must be* executed, then telling me to do it is moot."

"Perhaps *must* is the wrong word." Doctor Sokolov looked down.

Jori narrowed his eyes, trying to decipher the man's distress. "What? What did he say?"

The doctor puffed. "Well," he said as he rubbed his forehead. "He questioned why we didn't just kill them all to begin with. I explained you didn't want anyone to die unless they were fighting us. He replied that these monsters do not deserve such a consideration."

Jori's temper flared. "Did you tell him about the young man? Or about the girl? Were we expected to kill them too?"

"I-I suspect so, although he didn't name them specifically."

Jori chewed the inside of his cheek. The doctor appeared as troubled by this as he was. "You don't think this man should be executed?"

The doctor's brows shot up. "Oh, he absolutely deserves to die. But you shouldn't be the one to do it, not even by proxy. You're much too young to carry such a burden."

"I've taken lives before," Jori muttered.

"In defense." Doctor Sokolov's eyes tilted. "This is different."

"I see." *Sort of.* "So you both say the inspector should die but MEGA-Man says *I* should do it while you say I shouldn't?"

"Correct."

"And he wants *me* to do it because…" he paused, trying to put the jumble of his thoughts into words.

"Because if you do it, it shows him you are on our side."

Aha. Jori stared down at his hands, thinking. Zaina had said people like Vance didn't deserve to live. The inspector was just as bad as Vance, perhaps even worse. He should die too. But Jori didn't want to be the one to authorize it, and not because of what it meant about supporting MEGA-Man. Something about it still tweaked his conscience.

I wish Hapker was here. He couldn't see the commander condoning such a thing but maybe he'd have a better idea of how to handle this. Despite one of the doctor's earlier promises, he doubted MEGA-Man would let him reach out to a Cooperative officer.

Doctor Sokolov emitted such a powerful misgiving that Jori suspected there was more to it than that. "It seems contradictory to want me to become his ally willingly, then backtrack and make demands of me."

"I agree, but…"

"But…"

"MEGA-Man didn't say, but I get the impression he's on a timetable. I realize this makes everything harder, but his guidance has never failed me before. He says it's important for you to do this, not just to show commitment but because you must be capable of making these types of decisions if you're to be the next emperor."

Jori considered the point. As emperor, he'd have to deal with brutal wrongdoers somehow. Since Toradon had few prisons, most criminals were sold into slavery or executed. Neither option appealed to him but that was a problem for another day.

The doctor still hadn't answered his question. "But…" he prodded again.

"But I fear he doesn't understand you."

"Meaning?"

Doctor Sokolov rubbed his brow. "I believe you're destined for great things, but pushing you into this… Well, I just don't think it's right." He cleared his throat. "You don't have to decide now. Perhaps you should visit the people we rescued first."

Jori wasn't sure what to make of the doctor's hesitation, not with the hands of MEGA-Man's manipulation pressing down on him once more. A part of him wanted to rebel, but that part diminished more and more every day. He hated his predicament, but the advice to get a different perspective made sense.

That doesn't mean I have to become his pawn.

26
Political Upheaval

Commander J.D. Hapker sat before the captain once more, but this time in the conference room. He'd always disliked this uninspired place. Its unadorned walls provided nothing to distract the eye while he waited. Nor did the oval slate-grey table. And while the fancy curved-back chairs promised comfort, they made his backside ache.

Captain Arden sat at the head of the table wearing his usual stoic expression. His dark brows hooded exhausted eyes. Major Bracht perched on the chair to his right. His upright posture clashed with the fatigue that seemed to grip him as well. Or perhaps it was boredom coupled with frustration.

It'd been three days since Hapker had returned to the ship, and they were still at the space station waiting for the platoon of PG-Force officers. It wouldn't be so bad if the Cooperative had given them an assignment to look forward to. But so far, all was quiet. It had him worried, and everyone else too. The saying *no news is good news* didn't apply. Not with the barrage of terrible news that had taken over all the public feeds.

Director Sengupta arrived. She held the same harried expression as that day she'd revealed Jori was the son of the Dragon Emperor. She smiled, but it was tighter than the skin of a dolphin and didn't hold a hint of good humor.

After a wordless greeting, she tapped her MM tablet to the big screen. The monitor flickered on and a news broadcast played. The bottom-left logo of stylistic hands cradling the galaxy indicated it came from the Prontaean Cooperative's public station.

An anchorman with dark hair and wide green eyes full of perpetual surprise stood to the left of the sharp-lined and sleek Cooperative HQ building with its metallic sheen and reflective glass windows. People crowded at the bottom of the steps, their expressions awash with expectancy as they fixed their gaze on

Councilor Pham, who arrived at the podium on the landing. Stern worry etched his elongated face.

"Our chairperson, Councilor Alvia, is about to speak," the anchorman said. "For those of you just now tuning in, the Prontaean Cooperative called a press conference about an hour ago. They have yet to say what it's about. Many fear the worst as the MEGA rebellion intensifies."

Councilor Pham tapped the microphone, creating a thump that silenced the crowd faster than a mute button.

The anchorman stepped aside and let the camera focus on Pham.

"People of Asteria. I appreciate you coming at such short notice. The news you're about to hear has come as a great surprise to all of us, including Councilor Alvia. I present her to you now."

"Is this live?" Bracht asked.

"No," Director Sengupta answered. "I received the information about twenty minutes ago, and it was already an hour old by then."

Councilor Alvia approached the podium, taking care as she steadied herself with her cane between every step. It surprised him to see signs of her advanced age breaking through a normally lively persona.

She smiled but it held sorrow rather than happiness. "As you know, tensions between our society and the MEGAs have been horrendous these past several weeks. Ever since the discovery of MEGAs in our ranks, we've had an upsurge in fierce riots and savage attacks. Violence has broken out all over the galaxy. People are scared, and I understand that. And just to be clear, this fear comes from both sides. The war started by MEGA-Man and his allies has little to do with many of the MEGAs in our populace."

The crowd booed. Someone threw something toward the landing, though it didn't come close enough to the front steps to warrant a genuine threat.

Alvia put up her hands. "Please. I'm not advocating a MEGA lifestyle. I'm merely stating that not everyone who has chosen to be a MEGA is our enemy. My nephew being one of them."

A collective gasp preceded a deafening silence.

"That's right. I have a nephew who is a MEGA."

Boos resounded once more.

Alvia shook her head. "I don't know what prompted him to choose this path, but he's always been a good person. He's the type of man who puts others first by volunteering at his local food bank. He loves animals and has rescued quite a few. And he's never held a job prohibited to MEGAs."

The vocal discontent of the crowd amplified.

"Although I am against the hatred he and those like him receive, I understand the conflict of interest many of you see. So it is with great regret that I resign from my position. I'm saddened by this because I strongly believe the best way to end this war is to listen to what our MEGA citizens have to say and come up with a reasonable compromise."

"Traitor!" someone yelled, followed by others repeating the same thing until the crowd thundered with furor.

Hapker tensed. Although he had a bad taste left in his mouth after Gottfried's actions and the current incident with Arden's family, this all-out loathing against MEGAs wasn't the answer.

Director Sengupta stopped the feed. "This is official. I've verified the timestamp."

Hapker studied everyone's faces. Bracht seemed angry. Arden looked troubled, as did Sengupta.

"Councilor Alvia has always been an advocate of peace," the captain said. "This is disheartening news."

"Is compromise even possible?" the major barked. "We'd be negotiating with terrorists."

Hapker harrumphed. "I think we've established that not all MEGAs are terrorists. And how can we say that after what the MEGA Inspectors have done?"

"Their actions were reprehensible but not deadly. Citizens were killed at the Avalon space station. And hundreds of innocent people on Cardosia were slaughtered."

"There have also been deaths inflicted by our own citizens," Arden said. "I recently read a report about a family getting beaten to death because the father was a MEGA. That family included their two children."

The anger in Bracht's face slipped into shock. Hapker's gut soured. Nobody was innocent. MEGAs against MEGA-haters. MEGA-haters against MEGAs. Councilor Alvia was right. They needed to stop and listen to one another.

"We have a lot of overreactions occurring on both sides," Arden added, echoing Hapker's sentiment. "Responding with more violence is not as effective as attempting to negotiate."

"It's sad to see Alvia go," Sengupta said, diverting the dispute. "She was our only chance for a peaceful resolution."

"Who's in charge now?" Hapker asked, dreading the answer.

She hesitated. Her eyes tilted downward. "Councilor Greymore."

Hapker groaned. That man only ever called for actions that intensified friction. With Councilor Alvia resigning, he'd undoubtedly get his way. *This is not the time for political upheaval.* "There goes any chance of negotiating for our people back."

Arden slumped, mimicking his own despondency. The captain had a reputation for negotiating between two enemies. He'd helped broker peace between the Cooperative and Rabnoshk many years ago, paving the way for Bracht to hold a position as a major. He'd negotiated a treaty between Helion and Bardos, two planets with conflicting ideologies orbiting the same star. And he'd arbitrated the end of the civil war on New Rafah. To put someone like Greymore in charge was a slap in the face to what the Cooperative was supposed to stand for.

"Sir?" Sengupta said. "I realize this is shocking news, but there might be a bit of hope in it."

Arden cocked his head, his left brow tilting dubiously.

"While I commend Councilor Alvia's reconciliation attempts, I don't believe she would've accomplished it anytime soon. Councilor Greymore may take more of an offensive stance and get your family back before it's too late."

Arden's expression remained forlorn. "True. However…"

The captain trailed off, but Hapker understood. One thing he missed about being a Pholatian Protector was the idea that people could resolve everything if they just sat down with an open mind and listened to each other.

Councilor Greymore's philosophy promised an all-out attack against Cybernation. And he doubted the man would put much thought into whether any Cooperative prisoners were held there.

We can't afford to wait for Greymore to take action.

27

Police Report

The lighting of the PG-Force bullpen illuminated the chaos on the floor. Zaina Noman's nerves frayed as officers and civilian employees bustled about or labored at tiny desks crowded with screens. Victims like her either sat before those desks or waited on hard benches.

Bullpen. That's what the PG-Force officer who'd brought her here had called it. It was more like a crowded chicken coop full of chickens frightened by a fox. One person actually sounded like he was squawking as he argued with an officer. Something about his missing wife. The woman he spoke to pretended patience but the tightness around her eyes suggested she'd blow any moment.

Zaina wrung her hands as she waited on a bench set against the wall. She'd been here a good fifteen minutes already. Considering the chaos going on in the galaxy, she'd probably be here a lot longer.

She'd wait as long as necessary. It didn't matter if her eyelids threatened to fall, her backside numbed, or her tendency to take in emotions put her in a state of perpetual panic. She'd withstand every ache, pain, and emotional tumult.

Whatever it takes. She whispered the mantra over and over. It wasn't quite meditation, but it helped. Thanks to Jori, she'd gotten better at keeping her nerves from overwhelming her. She couldn't completely get over the anxiety that sizzled through her like overcooked eggs, but she pushed it down just enough that she didn't feel like running out of here screaming.

A lean woman wearing civilian clothes approached. "Are you Zaina Noman?"

Zaina jumped to her feet. "Yes. Yes I am."

The woman dipped her head, her stiff blond hair not moving by even a whisper. "Corporal Kole will see you now."

Zaina wanted to hurry but strained her pace as the woman meandered through the room. They edged down the side of the wall, dodged passersby between rows of desks, and circumvented a cluster of workstations. Finally, she arrived at the desk of a husky man with a pointed nose set in the middle of a round face. He appeared younger than her but old enough to have experience.

"Please, have a seat," he said.

Zaina took the fabric-worn chair. He asked her what brought her here today. She explained how she and Jori had fled the Avalon space station only to be held prisoner on a MEGA ship. They eventually let her go, dropping her off at a small space station. She didn't mention how the MEGAs also released the Stenson doctors since Stephen was worried the Cooperative would arrest him and his wife for their part in altering people. But she did tell him how that place didn't have much of a PG-Force presence, so they transported her here where she'd undergone an intense inspection to make sure she wasn't a MEGA.

"You were on the Avalon space station?"

"Yes. We were supposed to catch a transport to Marvdacht but—"

"All hell broke loose."

"It was horrible. No one was safe."

"MEGAs did this?"

"No. MEGA-haters started it. They attacked everyone they thought might be a MEGA. I watched a shopkeeper with a prosthetic hand get beaten."

The man leaned back in his chair and crossed his arms. The twist in his expression suggested he didn't like this contradiction of his beliefs. It was the same everywhere. *Those damn MEGAs. Freaks. Unnatural monsters.* Even if MEGAs had committed some horrible acts lately, the public's violent retaliations were uncalled for. She said as much and Captain Kole gave her a flat smile.

She continued her story, telling him about Vance and other MEGAs on the ship.

"I thought you sympathized with MEGAs."

Zaina scowled. "I didn't say that. I said the vigilante response is horrific."

"Of course."

She wanted to smack his patronizing smile right off his face but pressed on. When she got to the part about how they were turning people into MEGAs, he leaned in with a malevolent glower. "They're making more of them?"

She nodded.

"How many?"

"I'm not sure. They restricted me to only a small section of the ship. There may be hundreds or just a few."

"And they let you leave without enhancing you?"

"Yes. Apparently there are complications when they alter people who don't want to be altered. But they didn't let my charge go. They still have him."

"The boy? Why would they keep him?"

"They believe he's special. He's intelligent, but he's not a MEGA, so I don't understand. But they wouldn't let him come with me."

"Tell me more about this ship."

She did, giving him as much detail as possible without betraying the Stensons. Kole typed it all in.

"Can you find the ship?" she pleaded. "And rescue Jori?"

"We'll do what we can, ma'am."

She knew a dismissal when she heard it. "Didn't you hear what I said? They kidnapped a boy. Jori is only eleven years old."

"There are violent outbreaks all over the place," he said with no hint of an apology. "We're doing everything we can to contain it. Your information about the ship will help us. When we find it, we'll take care of things."

"What do you mean, *take care of things*?" Her voice lifted. "Do you mean you'll attack the ship even though there's a child on board, or will you try to rescue him?"

He put out his hands in a shrug. "That's above my paygrade, ma'am. I'll pass this on to someone higher up and they'll take it from here."

"Don't you care about what they might do to a child?!"

Her desperation rang throughout the bullpen but he remained unmoved. She wanted to shake him, but he was right. He was just a mere corporal.

He dismissed her. She pushed out of her chair and stomped away. Tears streamed down her face. Getting through the bullpen was like trying to navigate an obstacle course blindfolded. She could see, but everything was blurry and her peripheral vision was nonexistent. She ran into a table, a person, and something else she couldn't identify.

The way cleared but she still stumbled along.

"Ma'am?"

So much was going on that she didn't realize they were speaking to her. But they touched her arm. "Ma'am? Excuse me."

Zaina stopped, wiped her fingers under her eyes, and turned to a PG-Force officer with short hair spiked green and wearing… Were those sunglasses? "Are you talking to me?"

"Yes," the woman replied. "I heard you say a name. I have a friend named Jori."

"Jori Tran?" Zaina sniffled. "You know him?"

The woman deflated. "I'm not sure. I just know him as Jori. Is he a child?"

Zaina gasped. Her vision cleared. "Yes. He's my charge. I'm supposed to be taking care of him."

The woman straightened. "Is he about eleven or twelve years old, dark hair, carries himself like a soldier?"

Zaina's knees buckled. She clasped her hand to her mouth. "That's him," she said—or tried to say. Tears splurged anew. She grasped the woman's arm to keep from falling. Sobs wracked her chest.

The woman held her up. "You know him! How? Where is he? Is he alright?"

Zaina couldn't answer. She forced herself to breathe. With effort, she filled her lungs. Her throat rebelled, making the intake of air quiver with a painful sensation that almost tickled.

"Jori," she finally managed to say. "He's…" She couldn't get the words out.

The woman eased Zaina onto a chair. "It's alright," she said as she held Zaina's hand. "You can tell me. He practically saved my life."

"Saved you?"

The woman quirked a smile. "Yeah. He's quite remarkable for a little guy."

For the first time, Zaina noticed how big the woman's eyes were behind the sunglasses. She'd read about people with larger eyes but had never seen this before. Despite the alien appearance, this woman felt like an old friend.

"He is," Zaina replied, making a small smile in return. "He saved me too. Now he's in trouble."

The woman cocked her head. Zaina continued, "We were at the Avalon space station when MEGA-haters went crazy. We had to get out of there. We ran into someone who seemed like he wanted to help us. He led us to his ship. It turns out it was run by the MEGA faction."

The woman pulled back. "No! Like a warship?"

"Yes." Zaina lowered her head. "And headed by a psychopath who kept making Jori undergo these horrible tests."

"Oh no."

Zaina told the rest of the story about how they attempted to escape and Vance tried to kill them, but Jori managed to kill him instead. The remaining MEGAs decided he was their leader, but still wouldn't let him leave. However, Jori convinced MEGA-Man to let her go, so here she was trying to get someone to rescue him.

"Do you know Commander Hapker?" Zaina asked.

"I do."

Zaina perked up and clutched her hand. "Can you contact him? Tell him what's happened to Jori? He'll want to rescue him, right? Jori spoke so well of him. Said the commander wanted to adopt him but the Cooperative authorities separated them on purpose. Is that true?" She couldn't stop herself from rambling. Her heart, and her thoughts, ran like a speedster at full tilt.

The woman squeezed her hand back. "Yes. The answer to all your questions is yes. I can contact him, and I'll do it as soon as possible. Do you want to make a video?"

Zaina halted, hardly believing she'd gotten this far. She thought it'd be like pulling teeth—the way it'd been with the other uncaring Cooperative officers.

She peered into the woman's enormous eyes, saw a deep kindness, and nodded. "Yes, please."

"Alright. Let's do it."

28
Rescuees

Bright lights illuminated row upon row of hospital beds, reinforcing the somber mood. Over two dozen MEGAs from the Brenmos outpost had suffered injuries. Their whimpers, cries, and numbing silence discharged from every bed. Those who had a lifeforce radiated despondency. Life had kicked them down and even though they'd been rescued, they weren't sure how to get back up.

Jori waded through the crowded space with Rodrigo trailing him like a shadow. Although MEGA-Man likely used Rodrigo's eyes to spy on him, Jori couldn't bring himself to banish him. However, he'd refused Doctor Sokolov's company. He wanted to see all this for himself and make his own assessment.

None here were children, meaning the officer's son was one of the dead bodies left behind on the *Pachyderm*. His heart ached. Another life cut short because of hate. At least no children also meant the inspectors hadn't imprisoned any others like the girl with imperium abilities.

He came upon the woman with the upper half of her face and one eye wrapped in bandages. Scraggly blond hair hung to her shoulders, looking as exhausted as her other features. Her lifeforce was strong but her emotions were numb.

He moved into her field of view. "Hello. I'm Jori. How are you doing?"

Her eye flicked to him, along with a prick of curiosity. "I'm alright, I suppose." Her gaze returned to her surroundings but settled on nothing.

"That's good," Jori said, feeling awkward. "We're a little shorthanded here at the moment, but we'll help you when we can."

"Will you give me a new eye? A cybernetic one?"

Jori cocked his head. "Do you want one?"

"Hell yeah," she replied. "I want back what those bastards took from me."

Jori faltered. Despite everything, she still wanted to be a MEGA. "How long have you had cybernetics?"

"Since I was sixteen."

Jori studied her. Guessing her current age, she'd probably had them for almost twenty years. "Why?" he blurted.

She shot him a scowl. "Why not? You think you're better than me 'cause you don't have implants?"

"No," Jori replied, keeping his voice neutral despite his desire to snap back at her. "I'm just curious."

Her ire dwindled. "I don't know where you're from, boy. But where I came from, life was hard and shitty. Home life was shit, school was shit, authorities were shit. I couldn't cut it in school, so my choices were to stay home and become a drug dealer like my parents or get an upgrade and find a job out in space."

"You had to have cybernetics to do that?"

"It was the only way to get a leg up on everyone else who wants to work in space."

"What was your job?"

"Worked as a scrapper until the damned MEGA hunters came along. Stupid war. Why can't they just leave us alone? I wasn't hurtin' nobody."

"I'm sorry," Jori replied

She waved him away. "Yeah, yeah."

Jori moved on and found someone else with a part removed. A man with a missing arm sat cross-legged on the bed and stared down. His bottom lip protruded, almost reminding Jori of Admiral Belmont but with lighter skin and Vance's bulk. His blocky head rose and he scowled. "Who are you?"

Jori refrained from answering that he was the captain. No one would believe him so he simply gave his name.

"I don't remember seeing you on Brenmos."

"No. I've been on this ship."

The man's expression softened. "They rescue you from someplace else?"

"Not exactly," Jori replied. *I'm a prisoner*. "What happened to you?"

"They took my arm." The man hung his head. "It was the only thing that gave me strength. Now I got nothin'."

Jori frowned. "You still seem strong."

"Not strong enough."

"Strong enough for what?"

The man's brows curled over his eyes as he looked Jori up and down. Apparently satisfied with what he saw, he said, "Structural welding."

"Welding? Don't they have machines for that?"

The man harrumphed. "Exactly."

Jori waited but the man didn't elaborate. "I don't understand."

"Big corporations moved into our town. They used machines to build, putting hundreds of people out of work. The only way for our company to stay afloat was to offer us enhancements."

Jori's mouth curled. "That doesn't make sense."

The man's glower sharpened. "It's cheaper to enhance a few men than it is to buy and maintain manufacturing robots."

Jori's eyes widened but this shouldn't be surprising. Back in Toradon, a lot of lords and regional rulers relied on slaves for labor since acquiring machines was so expensive.

He moved on. A lifeless young woman lying flat on a bed drew him over. Her chest rose and fell and her skin was pink from the flow of her blood, but everything else about her felt dead. Not a hint of a lifeforce emanated from her.

A chubby, balding man with red hair and a bushy beard tended to her on the other side. His lifeforce wasn't as strong as Doctor Sokolov's, but at least he had one. He twisted his lips in studious thought as he examined a screen implanted on his cybernetic arm. The lines and data scrolling across the display resembled a med-scanner. A variety of medical tools took the place of his fingers.

"Are you a doctor?" Jori asked.

The man lifted his head. "Hmm?"

"Are you a doctor?"

The man's mouth broadened into a cheerful smile. "Oh. Yes, yes. I'm Doctor Phemius," he said in a voice that was almost as high-pitched as Kiyoshi's.

"I don't remember seeing you before," Jori replied. "Have you been on this ship the entire time?"

"Oh no. Not me." The doctor wagged his head but kept his smile. "I came from Brenmos, just like they did. But I saw a need here and helped." His brows drew down. "And you are?"

"Jori. I got you all off that station," he said, not meaning for it to sound like a brag.

"Ah! You're our savior, then." The man raised his hands as though praising a sky god. "Good to meet you."

Jori inclined his head at the woman. "What's wrong with her?"

"Not sure," Phemius replied. "She's alive, her reflexes react to physical stimuli, but she is utterly unresponsive. I remember seeing her when I first arrived. She was just like this then too."

"When did you come to Brenmos?"

He glanced upward and rubbed his beard with his good hand. "Oh, I'd say about twenty days ago."

So not long after Gottfried was discovered. "What did you do before that?"

The man grinned. "I was a doctor, of course."

"But…" Jori trailed off. He didn't know MEGAs could serve as doctors.

"I worked in secret, helping MEGAs like her whenever they were sick, hurt, or their tech malfunctioned."

Jori nodded. "And when the war started, MEGA haters stopped you."

"Yes, yes." The man sighed. "It's such a shame. All those good people left behind with nobody to give them aid." He brightened. "But I can help the ones here."

Jori's mouth quirked into a smile at his enthusiasm. Any thought of whether what he'd done was wrong faded away. No one here deserved what the MEGA Inspectors had done to them.

A furious shriek erupted a couple of beds down. "Give it back, you snake!"

Phemius squeaked while Jori shifted into high alert. A petite woman with no obvious cybernetics leapt from her bed. She lunged for a lanky man with a scraggly beard and messy brown hair. He responded with a laugh as he held something out of her reach. His lifeforce carried the same muted strength as Phemius' but it reeked of devious meanness.

"Give it back!" she screeched as she pounded his chest with feeble fists.

"Don't-a worry, miss." He bit into the bread. "There's-a more."

"That was mine, you creatin." She stormed to her bed in a huff.

Jori considered intervening, but the man had already taken two huge bites of her food. With a triumphant smile, he approached the doctor and smacked his shoulder. "Phemius! My-a friend!"

The doctor squeaked again and tried to turn away but there was nowhere to go. "We're not friends," he muttered in his high-pitched voice.

"Of course-a we are, Tubby!" The man poked Phemius in his side, eliciting a yelp.

Jori frowned, catching the doctor's distress and the hooked-nosed man's antagonistic glee. "Who are you?"

The man's bright blue eyes fell on Jori and his smile widened. "I'm-a Sebastian. And who are you?"

Jori stuck out his chin. "I'm the one who helped save your ass."

Sebastian snickered. "You? What did you-a do? Kick the bad guys in the shins?"

"I was the mission commander," Jori said through his teeth. "This rescue wouldn't have even happened without my authorization."

Sebastian broke into a fit of laughter. "Sure-a thing, squirt."

Jori clenched his jaw. He'd been belittled often enough at home to realize arguing would get him nowhere. That didn't stop him from fuming.

When Sebastian poked the doctor a few more times, making him whimper, Jori charged to the other side of the bed. "Stop! Leave him alone."

Sebastian's flicker of surprise quickly turned condescending. "Oooh. Or what, little one? Will you-a kick me in the shins too?"

Jori clenched his fists. "Try me."

A gleam splashed across Sebastian's eyes. "Maybe-a I'll give you a poke, too."

He pointed his finger at Jori's face. Jori snatched it and twisted, sending the man to his knees. In a blink, he grabbed Sebastian by the neck with his other hand and glared down at him. "Leave people alone or I will lock you up."

The man tried to nod. "Yeah. Yeah. Alright."

Jori let go and stepped back. Sebastian rose, rubbed his finger and neck. His face slackened like someone cowed, but Jori sensed a threat lurking beneath. Sebastian made a half-bow as though to capitulate. Jori braced himself. The man lunged. Jori cut to the side. Sebastian stumbled. Jori jabbed him in the nose with his fist. A satisfying scrunch and squelch preceded a spurt of blood.

Rodrigo swept in and yanked the man up by his arm. "You will not hurt our captain."

Sebastian's eyes widened, either from getting subdued by a child, by Rigo's announcement, or both. "Yeah, yeah. Sure-a thing. I was just-a joshing."

Rigo maintained his grip but didn't respond. Jori stared hard at Sebastian and let the silence linger. When the man's uneasiness reached a gratifying level, he signaled for Rodrigo to release him.

Sebastian wiped at the blood oozing down his chin, smearing it across his face. He cast conniving glints between Jori and Rigo, then darkened. "You broke my-a nose, you little shit."

Jori bared his teeth. "Next time I tell you to leave someone alone, you do it. Now get your ass on an empty bed and stay there until someone decides to help you."

Sebastian opened his mouth as though to protest but shot Rodrigo a wary glance.

"Rodrigo," Jori said without taking his eyes off the snake before him. "Escort him and make sure he doesn't harass anyone else."

Rigo seized the man's arm and dragged him away.

"No one gets-a the best of me," Sebastian muttered with a malicious glower.

Jori sensed the truth of his words. Many people made idle threats that they believed to be true in the moment, but something about Sebastian's lifeforce gave him chills.

Doctor Sokolov approached, wearing a smile that radiated admiration. Jori responded with a questioning scowl.

"You're a natural," the doctor said.

"I know how to defend myself," Jori replied defensively.

The doctor flicked his hand. "I'm not just talking about that. I mean with everything. You've been handling yourself quite well, from taking over Vance and Blakeley's job—"

Which is easy.

"—to planning and executing a rescue."

Where an innocent man was killed and a girl was left without either of her parents.

"Have you decided what to do with the inspector?"

The unease flittering through Jori's insides amplified. "No."

"But you agree he must be executed, don't you?"

Jori hesitated. The man didn't deserve to live yet he still wouldn't give the order. It didn't matter whether MEGA-Man would kill him anyway, Jori hated the manipulation.

The doctor sighed. "Alright. I'll give you more time."

Jori's brows furrowed as he tried to decipher the reason behind the doctor's relief.

"You know…" Doctor Sokolov emitted reluctance. "I've been prompted to remind you of the reason you should become emperor."

Jori straightened. He hadn't forgotten about his mother but they'd lured him in so many directions he no longer believed he'd be allowed to rescue her.

"You really are a natural leader," the doctor continued. "Imagine all the good you can do."

Jori scowled. "I'm not stupid enough to believe I can command legions of warriors as easily as I run a ship full of robots."

If Doctor Sokolov was offended at them being called robots, he didn't show it. "Not by yourself, no. But MEGA-Man will help you."

"If he has the power to make me the Dragon Emperor, then he can save my mother."

"Perhaps, but—"

"I'm done being manipulated," Jori said with finality. "If MEGA-Man wants me on his side, then he should start by rescuing my mother."

He pivoted on his heel and stormed away.

29
Exchanging Words

Commander J.D. Hapker pushed through an oppressive melancholy as he jogged on the treadmill. Normally, it helped him fall into a pleasant daze. Today, his mind fluttered from topic to topic like a caffeinated hummingbird. What would the MEGAs do next? When the *Odyssey* finally received an assignment, would it be providing medical care, assisting with evacuation, or would they need to enter the fight? How was Jori faring through all this?

He glanced at the ball courts. Under different circumstances, a bout of wall ball would distract him from his thoughts. Since he and Jori had grown from rivals to friends through the game, he doubted it would work today.

The treadmill inclined, adding an unwelcome resistance. To ensure everyone practiced being in various environments, they turned down the gravitational setting. It wasn't so low that people risked bouncing too high, but it was enough that he had to wear bungees to keep him on the exercise machine. Each step had a slight jounce to it that should've enabled an easy run. But his mood siphoned his energy, making him feel more sluggish than a sloth.

Too bad he couldn't immerse himself into work instead. Being stuck at a space station left them with little to do. Bridge duty wasn't necessary. There were no missions to plan. Scheduling was simple since he wasn't the only one lacking work. He'd organized a few drills and assigned a few extra safety checks, but that took almost no time.

He could go to the lounge. Symphonia attempted to keep everyone's spirits up with a different entertainment theme each day. Today was all about the Simoman culture. Funk jazz played on the stage. Fabricated food such as fried plantains, bread puddings, and crawfish dishes were served. Art, music, and dancing contests took place. However, yesterday's theme was a flop. The few who had attended slouched at their tables. It reminded him of his grade school dances.

Not even the announcement that they'd be leaving the station soon had lifted people's spirits. Departing meant nothing if they didn't have a mission. What was going on with that anyway? With the galaxy in an upheaval, he expected them to be pulled in multiple directions.

The treadmill beeped. Although he'd vowed to run for at least an hour, he turned off the machine at the forty-minute mark and detached the bungees. It'd only been two hours since he last checked his messages, but the need to check again lured him like a carcass in an animal trap.

As Hapker stepped away, a thumping clatter resounded, followed by derisive laughter.

"Cut the crap, Agni!" Private Bari bellowed. He stormed toward Agni and two other officers with his chest out, leaving behind a fallen rack of martial training gear.

Hapker rushed over.

Bari didn't see him, but still stopped short and jabbed his finger at Private Agni. "Leave me the fuck alone, you ass."

"Get lost, MEGA lover," Agni replied.

"Yeah," his friend added. "Just quit already. No one wants you here."

"Screw you. I belong here just as much as you."

Hapker put himself between them and swiveled his head to give them all a stern glower. "What the heck is going on here?"

"Just wondering why Bari hasn't been kicked off the ship yet, Sir," Agne said, lip curled.

"Why would he be?" Hapker asked, confused.

Bari didn't miss a beat. "My cousin is a MEGA, Sir."

"So?"

Agne made a face. "So it's a conflict of interest. Councilor Alvia stepped down because of it. Bari should too."

Hapker scoffed. "Councilor Alvia is a politician, forced by public sentiment to resign. Bari is a soldier. If we discharged everyone with a MEGA relative, there'd be few of us left."

"What if he commits sabotage like that other MEGA did?"

"Don't be stupid," Bari replied. "If I wanted to side with the MEGAs, I would've done it already."

"How do we know you haven't and just didn't get caught?" Agni asked.

"That's enough," Hapker interjected, using the same tone his father had used on him when he was young. "We can't afford to second-guess one another. Bari has a clean record. There's no reason not to trust him."

"*I* don't trust him," Agni replied.

"Too bad," Hapker barked. "It's not up to you, soldier. Now back off. We have enough to worry about without turning on each other."

"Yes, Sir," Agni said in a disrespectful tone. He shot Bari another sour look, then departed with his friends.

Bari glared at the man's back with a tight-lipped expression. When Agni was out of view, Bari's shoulders relaxed.

"Has this been happening a lot?" Hapker asked.

Bari huffed as though getting rid of the last bit of his ire. "We exchange words with Sergeant Naran's team from time to time, Sir." He shrugged. "We're kinda rivals. Not in a bad way, really. Just Naran can be a pompous jerk at times."

Hapker lifted an eyebrow.

Bari seemed to read his mind. "I know what you're thinking, and I'm sorry about Quigley. She's a bit…"

"Blunt," Hapker finished.

Bari laughed. "Yeah. That's a nice way of putting it. She has a talent for rubbing people the wrong way, but she doesn't do it on purpose."

Hapker wasn't sure he believed that, but he let Bari explain.

"She just doesn't think. Although I get irritated with her sometimes, I also admire her bluntness. Plus she's loyal as hell."

Hapker dipped his head, glad to have a better insight into her personality. "Team cohesiveness is important," he said. "So is a little rivalry, but I need you to report it if Naran's team gives you any more grief. I'm sure you can handle yourself, but we can't afford for things to get out of hand."

"Yes, Sir," Bari replied, his voice conveying his agreement.

Hapker smacked his shoulder. "Good man."

Bari dipped his head.

After Hapker made sure Bari and Agni stayed out of one another's way, he left the gym and returned to his quarters. Although compelled to check his messages, dread gripped him like a snake swallowing a mouse. Every time he sat at his console, it was the same thing—a swelling hope that this time he'd get the answers he needed. And bitter disappointment always followed.

Why do I keep doing this to myself? Maybe he should wait until tomorrow. But he still turned on his console. It flickered to life, revealing five unread messages. His heart picked up its pace even though they were all likely work-related.

He leaned closer to the screen. A message from his mom made him start. He clicked it and her smiling face appeared. All must be well, then. That didn't surprise him considering Pholatia's strict rules about MEGAs. Most planets restricted the activities of MEGAs to some degree, but Pholatia had one of the strongest laws of all. They forced anyone with modifications to undergo reversal surgery.

He closed the video, not wanting to listen to her begging him to give up his career with the Cooperative and come home. A message from Director Sengupta popped up, causing a painful lump in his throat. "*Sorry, no updates,*" the subject line glared. He deflated, propped his elbow on the edge of his desk, and scrolled down to the other messages.

One from Sergeant Ortega caught his eye. He was a little surprised to hear from her. She'd contacted him once while he was getting a new arm, but not since. He almost dismissed her message, not wanting to deal with another well-wisher, but the bolded word *urgent* in the subject line seized his curiosity.

He clicked it and her face appeared. Even though she concealed her eyes with sunglasses, her anxious expression was evident through the wrinkles on her forehead and the tightness of her mouth.

"Commander," she said, breathless, "you'll never guess what I just learned."

Hapker's chest hitched. Was this the news he'd been waiting for? Besides Lieutenant Gresher, she had been the last one to see Jori. Since she couldn't accompany him to his trial and they'd reassigned her elsewhere, he doubted she knew anything. However, hope encased him like a cocoon.

"So…" She related how she overheard a woman crying out for help. "Oh my God, you won't believe this. I'm not sure I believe it," she mumbled. "But she said they must rescue Jori."

Hapker's heart leapt to his throat.

"Yeah, that's right," Ortega said as though seeing his reaction. "*Jori*. Our Jori. I mean, what are the chances?"

She continued with a long-winded story full of unnecessary and excruciating details about a riot on the Avalon space station and a rescue by a MEGA ship.

Hapker broke into a sweat. First Gottfried, and now this.

"That same MEGA ship was the one that attacked the station. They took Jori and this woman, her name is Zaina by the way, as prisoners."

Another woman stepped into the camera's view. Dark bags sagged under her red-rimmed eyes like an overworked mule. She had black hair and a kind face that might've been pretty under different circumstances.

"They wanted Jori," she said, her voice laden with grief. "They knew about his abilities. The captain—his name was Vance—ran tests on him, even hurt him one time. But Jori eventually stopped him. After Vance was gone, the other crew members decided Jori was in charge. But they wouldn't let him leave. He negotiated my release, but he had to stay. He told me to contact you, which I didn't know how to do, and tell you they're taking him to meet MEGA-Man at Cybernation."

Hapker's throat tightened. Everything pointed to Cybernation. This was where he had to go. One way or another, he'd find a way.

30
Persuasion

Commander J.D. Hapker stifled a yawn. He had it all worked out. *"Don't bring me problems. Bring me solutions,"* his dad would say. So he'd stayed up through his sleep schedule to put together a plan. All the unknowns made it terribly risky, but it was better than sitting around doing nothing.

He rubbed his brows to ease the ache swelling behind his eyes. A yawn pushed its way to his jaw. Now was not the time to look like a groundhog just woken up from his winter nap. He inhaled deeply, pulled back his shoulders, and rang the comm to the captain's office.

"Enter." The captain's transmitted voice hinted at the same weariness Hapker felt.

Captain Arden slumped before the deskview screen opened on his desk. The lines around his blue eyes gave away more than his age. No doubt, he experienced the same level of uselessness as the rest of the crew.

His wife, Symphonia, stood by his side, her hand resting on his shoulder as though providing comfort—or using him as support. She greeted Hapker with a smile that held warmth while her eyes betrayed a deep sadness.

"I have something I want to run by you, Sir," Hapker said.

Symphonia stepped away. "I'll leave you two to it."

"No, that's alright." Hapker waved his hand, motioning for her to stay. "This also concerns you."

She cocked her head. Arden dipped his. "Go ahead."

He told them about Jori, including how they'd take him to Cybernation. "If this is where they're taking him, then they'll likely bring the other prisoners there as well. It's not definitive, but it's more than we had before. If our superiors authorize a full-on invasion, it might do more harm than good. I believe we should attempt to rescue our people before that happens. And before you object, I have a plan." He handed the captain his tablet. "With the platoon arriving soon, we have plenty of protection here. I'm sure we can spare a few people—enough to crew two small vessels." He caught his breath. "One could be a Bastion-class. Its stealth capabilities are comparable to a PG-Force stealth ship. Plus it has a bit of firepower, just in case. All we need to do is enhance its communications systems."

Hapker shifted his feet, ready to disobey orders and do it anyway if the answer was no. Not even the risk of receiving a dishonorable discharge or getting charged with treason could dissuade him from saving Jori.

Captain Arden pinched his lip and studied the tablet. Symphonia's eyes tilted with hope, but she didn't offer her opinion. Nor did she need to. The way she poised over her husband's shoulder with parted lips signified she wanted the same thing Hapker did.

The captain's brows shot up. "You intend on getting captured?"

"Just one of the ships—perhaps a non-affiliated transport ship you use when we need to portray a humble appearance. And not captured. I'll tell them we want to join them."

Symphonia cocked her head. "Won't they suspect subterfuge? See through your ruse?"

"Considering the level of persecution MEGAs are experiencing lately, we can't be the only ones seeking them out for protection. We just need the right people and convincing falsified records. If we're lucky, they'll take us in and put us with the others. Even if they don't, we can still gather information and transmit our findings to the stealth ship."

Symphonia pressed her hand to her chest. "But a facial recognition scan will tell them who you are."

"We'll wear nano-masks."

"But how can you be sure they won't begin alterations on you right away?" she asked, her eyes reflecting a fear of what might happen to her family.

Hapker heaved a resigned sigh. "I can't, but I'm hoping they don't have the resources to keep up with all the people they've abducted so far."

Captain Arden's forehead wrinkled up, but he didn't remark on Hapker's determination. He reviewed the tablet once more. "Let's say you get in and you're able to gather information. How will you get out?"

"We'll have bio-sensor implants. The other ship can keep track of us and use their transport pad to beam us away." *The same way we rescued Jori from his father*.

"That won't work if you're in a shielded area," Arden said.

Hapker dipped his head. "I suspect they have city shields just like we do, but it makes more sense to keep the thousands of our people—their enemies—out of their cities."

"That's a thin hope." Arden stroked his beard as though still considering it.

"Yes, Sir. But even if we can't escape, I'm confident we'll gather more information than anyone has managed so far."

Arden rubbed his forehead. "I understand your desire to go, but I won't order somebody else to take the risk."

"We ask for volunteers."

"If it doesn't work, I lose valuable crew members."

Hapker cocked a brow. "If we do nothing, you lose your family."

Arden tensed at the confrontational tone. Symphonia gripped his shoulder.

"I apologize for my bluntness, Sir," Hapker said. "But let's face it. We've been sitting by doing nothing while the council focuses on putting out fires. We have an opportunity to act."

The captain leaned back, his forehead wrinkling with a troubled expression. "I'm not a military officer, so I don't have the expertise to determine if this is an acceptable risk. So let me run this by our superiors."

"And if they say no?"

Arden studied Hapker. "You know my answer to that. I *want* to say yes. But I also have a responsibility to this crew's safety."

Hapker frowned. It was just like the captain to follow the chain of command to a fault.

"I'm not authorized to initiate a military action," Arden continued as though reading his mind. "Taking a risk like this would put me and everyone else in a compromised position, especially if we're doing it for someone Councilor Greymore already deems suspicious."

"This is about *all those* who've been abducted," Hapker said, his words cutting like a hot blade. "Besides, Jori being in the hands of

MEGAs should be another reason to act. The last thing we want is the emperor's son being controlled by a man who thinks he's God."

Arden turned white. "You've pointed that out before, and I agree. But I daresay Greymore will view it differently."

Hapker scoffed. "Probably see Jori as a traitor too. But he's not there by choice. I bet my life he's not remaining passive. If I don't go help him, he'll have to fight alone."

"And so will my sister and nephew," Symphonia added.

Arden met her pleading eyes. His silence seemed to suck the air out of the room until he broke it with a resigning breath. "Alright. But let's be smart about this." He straightened. "We try it my way first. I'll contact Councilor Greymore and present your plan."

Hapker clenched his jaw.

"I realize it's not the answer you want," the captain continued. "But it'd be better for everyone if we can convince him. And if we can't… And if we have a reason to believe he's not already organizing a rescue…" He shrugged. "I will look the other way while you do what you need to do. Deal?"

Hapker's mouth hung open as he considered. If Councilor Alvia still directed Cooperative policy, she'd say no. Although he didn't care for Councilor Greymore, perhaps this man's more hostile attitude would benefit them. And if it didn't. Well, at least he had the captain's support—and in a surprising way.

"Deal," he said.

Symphonia's shoulders sagged. Hapker practically melted in their shared sentiment.

Hold on, Jori. I'm coming for you.

*****

The bridge sizzled with anticipation. After being briefed on the proposed plan, everyone perched on the edge of their seats. Or in Commander J.D. Hapker's case, balancing on the tips of his toes.

He and Major Bracht flanked Captain Arden and faced the giant viewscreen with squared shoulders. An intense heat billowed through his body when the councilor's face appeared on the screen. How he loathed this man. It wasn't just that Greymore had likely been the greatest influence on the decision to send Jori so far away.

It sickened him that someone so full of antipathy was now in charge of an organization that spouted equal representation for all.

Having to supplicate himself made matters worse, but he gritted his teeth and let Captain Arden do the talking.

"Thank you for responding so quickly, Councilor Greymore," the captain said.

"Keep it brief, Captain," Greymore replied in his usual clipped tone. "I have a lot on my plate right now." He leaned closer to the camera and narrowed his eyes, no doubt noticing all the witnesses on the bridge. Hapker had initially questioned the captain's choice to have it here, but it made sense. Perhaps having the crew listen in would influence the councilor's decision.

"I understand, Sir," the captain replied. "I'm hoping the plan I sent over will ease some of your burden."

Arden highlighted the primary components. That the councilor hadn't read it yet became apparent when he asked for more details. They'd decided not to mention Jori. Councilor Greymore's militaristic attitude might see the boy's presence as a threat and attack Cybernation outright—especially since they still didn't have evidence that their kidnapped citizens were being taken there.

"I can get us there in about ten days," the captain continued.

"And you're volunteering for this, Commander?" Councilor Greymore asked.

Hapker jutted his chin. "Yes, Sir."

The councilor's mouth quirked. Hapker assumed if he died on this mission, it wouldn't be considered much of a loss. He quelled his resentment. Greymore not caring about his fate might contribute to his agreement.

"Who else?" the councilor asked. "You, Major?"

"Captain Arden needs me to stay," Bracht replied neutrally. He undoubtedly wanted a chance at action, but he also had a strong view about his duty to protect the crew.

Councilor Greymore almost looked disappointed. Being a Rabnoshk warrior and former enemy of the Cooperative, Bracht was another person the man didn't care for.

"Perhaps some officers you're sending us will want to go," Arden offered. "I know you wanted them here for protection, but Major Bracht is more than capable of defending this ship."

"I didn't vote to send them to you," Greymore replied. "If it were solely up to me, I'd have all the PG-Force out there on the offensive."

Of course you would. Hapker refrained from showing his disdain.

"Perhaps my proposal is fortuitous, then," Arden said diplomatically. "This mission deviates from their original assignment, but it could result in bountiful information."

"You realize that every other recon we've sent to Cybernation has failed?"

"Yes, but I wager none of them arrived intending to surrender."

"Hmm." Greymore rubbed his chin. "Your present location and the fact that you have resources we can spare makes for a much better option. Major Darwish and his platoon are due to arrive soon. If I agree to this, he will lead the mission and command the stealth ship. Commander, I'll consider putting you in charge of the surrendering ship."

Hapker didn't like the idea of not leading, but it made a little sense. Although he'd once been a PG-Force officer, his command was of a non-military expedition vessel.

"Before you get started," Greymore continued, "give me a couple of days to run it by the rest of the council."

Hapker experienced a sensation of heartened lightness. Having the support of his superiors, even someone as distasteful as Greymore, improved his chances of finding Jori.

The councilor's indifference toward the risk of losing Hapker on this mission only fueled his determination to succeed.

31
Unwelcome Visitors

Once again, Commander J.D. Hapker stood beside Captain Arden with their attention on the bridge's main screen. Instead of a sour-looking old man with white hair, they spoke to a black-haired woman with soft brown skin and a genial expression.

Nice though she seemed, Hapker wasn't fooled. General Inspector Joubert was one of the many MEGA Inspectors on a witch hunt for MEGAs.

"We're not here to conduct more inspections," she said, her voice as smooth as honey. "It's clear that our previous team went too far."

"Went too far?" Captain Arden interrupted, his face redder than Hapker had ever seen it. "Their baseless accusations have created dissent among my crew."

"I won't insult you with excuses, Captain. So I'll just say I'm sorry instead. I truly am."

Hapker found himself unbalanced by her niceness. He'd joined this conversation to add his indignation for the treatment of their crew, but she wasn't giving him a reason to vent.

"If you're not coming here to administer more tests," Arden said, "what are you here for?"

"You have two confirmed MEGAs aboard. We'd like to question them before the PG-Force takes them into custody."

"You can't," Arden blurted. "Nariya is investigating Oleg's method of communication with the Great Commune. And she's making headway."

"That's wonderful," Joubert said, sounding genuine despite the conflict of interest. "I welcome her to continue her work—under strict supervision, of course."

The captain faltered. Hapker didn't blame him. The man had opened this conversation intending to deny the MEGA hunters further interference. Nariya wasn't the enemy, he'd declared. Now his intention had fallen flat to her civility and logical refute. It was a negotiation tactic that Arden had undoubtedly used in his own career.

"Something else has come up," Hapker said, unsure why he felt compelled to stand up for Nariya too.

General Inspector Joubert tilted her head. "Pray tell."

Hapker cleared his throat and shot the captain a look he hoped signaled him to play along. "We may have a mission soon. One she can help with."

"I'm not aware of any mission," she replied.

"It's still under discussion."

"And what does this mission entail?"

"I'm not sure I can give details, but she'll be useful in two ways. One would utilize her programming skills." He gave Arden a meaningful look, then turned back to Joubert. "Her MEGA status makes her ideal for the second part by providing validity to our plan."

She pursed her lips. "And how soon will you decide on this mission?"

Arden answered, "I expect to hear from Councilor Greymore within a day or two."

"Very well," Joubert replied, eliciting a silent sigh of relief from Hapker. "If you'd be so good as to get Oleg ready for transport, we'll come pick him up now. And I'll hold off on retrieving Nariya for a couple more days."

"Thank you, Inspector," the captain said.

The comm officer ended the conversation. Captain Arden turned to Hapker with an unreadable expression. "I don't care for the idea of Nariya going on your suicide mission."

"I'm not setting out to die, Sir. I intend on finding our people." *Including Jori.* "If MEGA-Man still has spies within the Cooperative, he'll know about her. Having a MEGA with us could make a tremendous difference in our success."

"Not if he's aware she helped us. We don't know what Oleg told him."

Hapker shrugged. "She could say she was operating under duress. Maybe we made her promises but didn't keep our end of the bargain. Joubert's presence would lend credence to that."

"I won't force her to do this," Arden said sternly.

"That's fair," Hapker replied. "I agree that everyone on the mission should *want* to go."

The captain's brows protruded over his sharp blue eyes. "You'll be giving her a choice between getting arrested or going to Cybernation to join the MEGAs."

Hapker frowned. Given her situation, he wasn't saving her from the MEGA Inspectors. He was pressuring her into a dangerous mission. "Sorry, Sir. You're right. I won't ask anything of her."

Captain Arden sighed. "No. You should give her the choice. Just don't make it sound like it's that or jail."

"I'll be tactful, Sir."

Hapker's mind spun with the new possibility. If she agreed to come along, it wouldn't change the plan. It would transform it.

He hoped she'd agree to help.

*****

Commander J.D. Hapker set his jaw as he waited for the shuttle bay to pressurize. After reading the update to Major Darwish's file, he was not looking forward to meeting him. The major's most recent engagement had fallen under question. He'd been in command of a ship that destroyed a cargo hauler after they refused to be boarded. *A wartime action*, his superiors had decided. So rather than receive a discharge, they'd reassigned the major here where they hoped he couldn't make more trouble.

The green light finally clicked on. Hapker stepped out of the observation room and into the bay. The hatch to the shuttle eased down and landed with a clank. A tall and lean man with spiky blond hair stomped out. His smirk reeked of arrogance. His swagger was unmistakable. A bitterness rose in Hapker's mouth, but he forced himself to smile.

The man faced Hapker and gave a half-assed salute, all while smiling in that cocky way of his.

"Major Darwish," Hapker said. "Welcome to the *Odyssey*."

"Thank you, Sir. Can't say I'm looking forward to babysitting, but who knows?" He shrugged. "We may get some action yet."

Hapker gritted his teeth. "Let's hope that if there's any action, it's because we're conducting a rescue mission."

Darwish shrugged again, still smiling. "We'll need to make an assault to achieve a rescue, Sir. A little shoot and scoot will do us some good."

Hapker's smile slipped into a frown. "I certainly hope you're joking, soldier."

Darwish chuckled. "Just a little."

Hapker glowered as a weight of dread settled in his gut. Councilor Greymore's openness to hearing about the proposed mission had surprised him. Now he understood. Major Darwish's militaristic attitude implied more than a simple rescue would be involved. And if things didn't go as planned… Maybe Darwish was another *resource to spare*.

He clenched his teeth. As much as he itched for Councilor Greymore to give the go-ahead, he might be better off going on his own.

Hapker struck up a conversation while they marched through the ship. "I heard about your actions against the *Lady Pachyderm*."

He'd meant it as a rebuke but Darwish tilted his chin in pride. "Yeah. It felt good getting rid of a few more MEGAs. It was easy, too. Took almost no time. So much for them being superior. Right, Sir?"

"They were just cargo haulers."

Darwish harrumphed. "Working for the enemy, no doubt."

"I saw the report, Major. Everything on their ship was legitimate."

"That didn't mean they weren't also giving out information."

"You had zero evidence of that."

Darwish shrugged. "Don't matter. They were MEGAs. The galaxy is better off without them."

The blanketed hate struck Hapker's nerves. "Not everyone—"

"I hope Councilor Greymore gives the mission a go-ahead," the major interrupted.

Hapker halted. "You've been told about that?"

Darwish cocked a smile. "Of course. He mentioned it after I told him I wasn't too thrilled about my assignment here. No offense, Sir. Me and my men are just used to a little more action."

Hapker frowned. Why would a major be speaking so casually with a councilor? "How well do you know him?"

"Didn't know much about him at all until he argued on my behalf. Said I was a fine officer." Darwish puffed out his chest and grinned. "Said he was glad someone finally understood the danger these freaks present to our society."

Hapker soured. *Sounds like something Greymore would say.*

The new information slogged around in his brain. As much as he wanted the mission to be approved, Darwish's involvement troubled him.

If not for Jori, he wouldn't be as eager to go.

32
Something in Common

The lounge was dead. Not even the lively holo-band playing in the corner could revive it. The last attempt to bolster the crew had deflated like a jellyfish out of water. The decorations resembled tattered curtains. Wilted greens and cold dishes occupied the buffet table. And the dim lighting, which usually inspired a relaxed atmosphere, felt like a rain cloud threatening to burst. Only a handful of people were here today—and all were somber.

Commander Hapker sighed, wishing to be anywhere else.

"Come on." Lieutenant Sharkey nudged him with her elbow. "He can't be that bad."

Everyone deserves a chance, Hapker reminded himself. Perhaps Major Darwish was more compelling than his first impression implied. After all, the man had invited him here. *"To get acquainted before becoming a team,"* he'd said. Hapker had cringed at the thought, but it made sense.

He spotted the major sitting in a booth in the corner.

"Commander!" Darwish waved him over with a cocky grin. "Good to see ya. You too, Lieutenant Sharkey."

They sat across from him, Sharkey against the wall and Hapker to the aisle.

"I didn't realize this was a formal meeting," Darwish said, sweeping his hand down his colorful shirt patterned with palm trees and birds.

Hapker glanced at Sharkey with her everyday steel-grey uniform as crisp as ever, and his own brown commander's outfit. "Habit. Off duty or not, we never know when we'll be called on."

"You probably think us PG-Force officers on a PCC ship have the most boring jobs," Sharkey said with good humor, "but we get our fair share of action."

Darwish laughed. "So I hear! From Dragon Princes commandeering your ship to MEGAs trying to sabotage it. You all have had the worst luck."

Hapker clenched his jaw at the mention of the emperor's sons. Although he was giving Darwish the benefit of the doubt, it wouldn't work if he badmouthed Jori.

"You seem well-informed," Sharkey said with a friendly smile.

Darwish winked. "I'd be remiss if I didn't do a little research on my new shipmates."

That's fair. Hapker forced himself to relax despite how the comment irked him.

After exchanging pleasantries and ordering drinks, they chatted with the amicable wariness of strangers sizing one another up. When Sharkey mentioned the major's shirt, the conversation took a turn for the better.

Darwish tugged at the collar. "Got it on Tresslia. They're known for their beaches but I preferred the hike through their jungle."

"You enjoy hiking?" Hapker asked, trying not to look too eager.

"Oh yeah. Love it. I can't visit a planet without checking out the natural scene. Cities are great for the nightlife, but I'd rather explore the mountains, rivers, and oceans."

Hapker made a genuine smile for the first time. Maybe Darwish wasn't so bad after all.

They traded stories, the major sharing his experience hiking to the rim of a volcano, Hapker telling him about the Spire Wilderness back home in Pholatia, Sharkey laughing about how a family of raccoons had invaded her campsite. Then she told Darwish about a snorkeling expedition she and Hapker had been on. It was supposed to be funny, but Darwish's brows curled.

"Sorry for asking," he said as he glanced between them. "But... Uh... Are you two... Uh?"

Hapker choked on his drink. Sharkey turned bright red. Hapker cleared his throat and waved his hand. "No. We're just good friends."

"Ah." Darwish pulled his lips back in an uneasy smile. "Sorry."

Hapker brushed it off, though he wondered how they'd given him that impression. It had seemed odd for the major to only invite them, but he'd assumed it was because he and Sharkey were certain to go on that mission once Greymore approved it. Bracht couldn't go. Lieutenant Gresher had decided he should stay since Sharkey was going. And Major Bracht's people were still thinking about it.

Darwish cleared his throat. "I don't know why I thought that. I guess I just assumed because you—" he said, looking at Sharkey whose cheeks were flushed, "—were so quick to volunteer for the mission."

Before she responded, Hapker asked a question that'd been burning in him since his initial conversation with the major. "How familiar are you with it?"

"I know you want to go in posing as MEGAs requesting sanctuary. Bold move." Darwish wagged his head and smiled. "Though I don't get why you're so sure they're sending their prisoners to Cybernation."

Hapker leaned in on his elbows. "They wouldn't be holding all those people on their own ships for long. They must be taking them somewhere, and Cybernation makes the most sense."

"No other reason, huh?"

Hapker frowned. Was he aware of his conversation with Sergeant Ortega? Anyone with the proper clearance could access communications to and from the ship. The major didn't have it but Councilor Greymore did. But why would he bother?

"No," he replied. "Why do you ask?"

Darwish shrugged. "It's just that you're the commander yet you've done little commanding."

"What are you implying?" Hapker snapped.

"Nothing." The major waved his hands as though to ward off smoke. "Nothing, I swear."

The major's nervous laughter came across as fake but maybe that was Hapker's imagination. He crossed his arms. "These aren't normal times, as you well know."

"Yeah, I get it," Darwish said. "I meant nothing by it. Really. Just surprised is all."

Sharkey leaned in as though to intervene. "You're aware two of the captain's relatives were taken, right? Someone's got to help them. Why not us?"

"Sure. Yeah. That makes sense," the major said. "I can't wait to storm in there myself."

"The plan doesn't call for any *storming*," Hapker retorted.

"Well, not unless someone gets some good intel. Your plan has a decent chance of that." The major grinned. "And now that Councilor Greymore is in charge, we also have somebody with the balls to finally take the fight where it belongs… Right up their MEGA asses."

Hapker's spine tingled, though he couldn't say why. Was it the correlation between Darwish's gung-ho attitude and Greymore's preference for violence over peace? A strange feeling that the two men were colluding crawled through him. Perhaps they were just discussing potential war plans based on the intel Hapker intended to gather. That's what recon was for, after all.

The major still rubbed him the wrong way. They might have some things in common, but their reasons for wanting to go on this mission were vastly different. Hapker wanted to save while Darwish wanted to kill.

He swept his tongue across his teeth as his dislike for the major reemerged.

33
Blackout

An unnerving silence descended upon the bridge as a mind-blowing scene played out on the main viewscreen. Commander J.D. Hapker clenched the armrests of his chair, helpless as five MEGA battleships bombarded the nearby F-172 communication hub. The enormity of this cataclysmic destruction halted all thought and motion and stifled his breath.

This hub wasn't the only one in danger of being destroyed. Reports were coming in from all over the galaxy. Despite the complications of coordinating space-time, the MEGAs conducted a concerted attack on hundreds of communication hubs at once. Many had already stopped transmitting, leaving the fate of those within their service areas unknowable. The magnitude of this ruination left Hapker speechless. Blackouts in space could last months or even years.

It'd be like going back to the ancient Earth days of the Pony Express. Instead of horses, ships using their arc drive for FTL travel would have to transport messages over long distances. This tactic would undermine the Cooperative's ability to coordinate a counterstrike. They might as well fall into the void of a black hole—one way in and no way out.

A blast of bright energy burst from the main section of the hub. The live feed ended, leaving a blank screen that seemed to swallow him whole. The silence of the bridge amplified, creating a surreal experience of being frozen in time.

"Oh, shit," Officer Chandly muttered.

His intrusion prompted a cacophony of voices. Some crew members added their own curses. Others gasped or cried out in dismay. Hapker glanced at the captain, just as lost for words as himself.

The nearest communication hub had already been obliterated, leaving them at least two weeks away from another one. And who could say whether that one wouldn't get destroyed next?

Other than those at the space station, they were all alone. Sending quantum-entangled transmissions was no longer possible, hindering their ability to order supplies or request help. If MEGAs abducted more people, it would take months before the authorities learned of it. MEGAs could create an army and conquer the galaxy before anyone even realized there was a problem.

"Real-time communications are down," Officer Brenson said from his comm station.

"What do we do now?" Jensin asked.

All heads turned toward the central command chairs, eyes both devastated and beseeching. Hapker had no answer. The captain's brows furrowed in thought, but his mouth remained closed.

After a pained stillness, Arden opened the ship-wide comm. "Emergency meeting. All senior officers to the main conference room immediately."

Apprehensive glances skittered about the bridge. The brittleness of everyone's features threatened to crumble. Rather than just the usual small advisory council, the captain had called every resource from the medical doctors to the science and technology officers. Under different circumstances, Hapker would've considered it overkill.

He and the captain were the first ones to the conference room, but it didn't take long for others to arrive. Director Sengupta rushed in with a harried expression. Chief Sam Simmonds' nose seemed redder than usual, distraught beyond mere worry. Major Bracht arrived sans his usual fortitude, concern wrinkling his brow instead. An edginess replaced Lieutenant Gresher's perpetual confidence and Lieutenant Sharkey's eyes flicked about.

Then came the medical doctors, the top-ranking science officers, the Chief of Operations, Communications, and Navigation, followed by Hamada, the Chief Technology Officer.

There weren't enough chairs for everyone, so a few people stood along the walls. Lieutenant Gresher gave up his seat for the older Chief Hamada. The chubby man took it graciously. His small eyes drooped with long-term fatigue.

Hapker suppressed a groan when Major Darwish arrived. Unlike the others, he strutted in with an undisturbed air. He even had the audacity to smile as he leaned against the wall and crossed his arms and ankles.

The captain eased into his seat as though weighed down by a two-ton pack. "I assume you are all aware of the situation?"

Everyone nodded unenthusiastically. "Director." Arden flicked his hand at Sengupta. "Numbers please."

Her shoulders sagged. "From what information I gathered before everything went dark…" Her throat bobbed. "They attacked two hundred seventy-five communication hubs at once… And not all attacks come from the outside. Some sabotage occurred from the inside."

The nape of Hapker's neck tingled.

"Of those," she continued, "forty-two had stopped transmitting before ours did. Add this to the twenty-seven taken out over the course of the past few days."

"Do you know which stations went down?" Arden asked.

"Yes."

"Are there any active ones close to us?"

She wet her lips. "The closest one not yet disabled is over twenty days away. But it wasn't looking good at the time I received their last broadcast." Her eyes tilted as she took in all the surrounding faces. "The nearest hub that had reported no attack is over two hundred thirty days from here."

A collective gasp swept through the room like a tidal wave.

Hapker blew out a breath to ward off the oncoming wooziness. "How far is it from Asteria?"

"It's farther than we are," Sengupta replied, her voice muffled by the thudding in his eardrums.

"And we're at least seventy days from base," the Chief of Navigation added.

Hapker dropped his chin in his palm. Seventy days to reach the Prontaean Cooperative home base in Asteria. So much could happen between now and then. Rescuing those on Cybernation seemed more imperative than ever—except their resources were more limited. "Is there a closer sub-base?"

The downturn of her mouth held zero hope. "On Verona, but that planet was attacked a few days ago. Last I heard, most city shields had fallen."

"What do we do?" Lieutenant Sharkey asked.

Darwish straightened. "We go fight those bastards!"

"This isn't a military ship," Hapker snapped.

"We rescue people," Doctor Gregson offered.

Darwish sneered. "I'm all for saving folks but if we don't stop those fuckers, they'll just go around shooting up more hubs and habitations."

The room erupted with both agreement and dissent.

"We don't have that capability!" Sengupta yelled uncharacteristically. "Those hubs had defenses yet the MEGA warships still ripped them apart like they were nothing. The *Odyssey* doesn't stand a chance against that kind of firepower."

Darwish threw up his hands. "Great. Our enemy's out there tearing us up and I'm stuck here babysitting."

Hapker clenched his teeth to keep from smacking him with a slew of insults.

"I agree with the doctor," Captain Arden boomed as he shot Darwish a glower. "We help people, starting with those stationed at the nearest communication hub. And while we're there, we also assist with fixing it."

"We're not equipped for that level of repairs, Sir," Chief Sam Simmonds said.

"True," the captain replied. "But we won't be the only ones wondering what our next move should be. Other ships will go there with the same intent."

Hapker lifted his brows. That was actually a good idea.

"What if the MEGAs are still there?" Doctor Canthidius asked.

"It's a possibility," Arden said. "But they've achieved their objective. They'll likely head elsewhere to inflict more damage."

"Or kidnap more people," the Chief of Operations added.

Hapker's insides clenched. "Sir," he said to the captain. "We have another option—one we can do in addition to repairing the hub."

The captain dipped his head. Hapker gave the others a wary glance, especially those not usually a part of these conferences.

"Proceed, Commander. I trust everyone here," Arden replied although his eyes twitched at Major Darwish.

Hapker shared the sentiment. If the major and the councilor intended to use his intel for a side mission, they wouldn't be able to implement it now. Only those present would be aware of their decisions from this point. "Well, Sir. Since Councilor Greymore can't get back to us about our other plan, I say we proceed."

"I agree, Sir," Bracht said. "We can't guess what his answer would've been, so we make our own decision."

Hapker dipped his head in thanks for his support. "The source of all our woe resides on Cybernation. If we gather enough information, we can carry it to the right people, coordinate a rescue—" *Before our citizens get turned into MEGAs.* "—and plan an attack."

"Hell, yeah!" Darwish whooped. "Attack those bastards, just like they've attacked us."

Lieutenant Sharkey eyed his overenthusiasm. She'd shared Hapker's suspicions that the major knew far too much to not be working with Greymore. She'd also reminded him it was common for the PG-Force to have overlapping plans. Hapker had mixed feelings about not being included in it, but he didn't let it bother him as long as it allowed him to search for Jori.

Greymore or Darwish hadn't been informed of one aspect of the plan because it was just a concept. Hapker turned to Chief Hamada. "How is Nariya coming along with figuring out how the connection to the Great Commune works?"

The man rubbed his eyes and Hapker realized why he'd looked so tired. He must've been working as hard on this as Nariya. "It uses entanglement, like ours. But utilizes a much more powerful entanglement generator—or generators. I suspect there's many hidden throughout the galaxy, but there'd have to be one where MEGA-Man resides too since Oleg could communicate with him."

"Have we figured out how to make a transceiver like Oleg's yet?"

"Yes, but it's not functioning as expected."

"Why not?"

"Well, no external system is attempting to establish a link with it, so we're not receiving any data. And we can't transmit to anyone without knowing their identifier. With nothing incoming or outgoing, it's ineffective." Hamada cleared his throat. "However, she's been seriously considering your proposal... About going to Cybernation. She has a plan for deploying a spyware virus."

"Can a virus operate over quantum entanglement?" Simmonds asked.

"It can't intercept entangled messages. The virus operates at the local level, accessing messages once they've been decrypted. That's why she needs to go to Cybernation. She's hoping their hub will initiate a handshake protocol, giving her the opportunity to inject the spyware."

Hapker propped his elbow on the table and leaned in. "And she's willing to go?"

The man's chin wobbled as he bobbed his head. "She seemed eager after watching all those hubs go down."

A surge of optimism sizzled through Hapker's body. He directed an imploring gaze at the captain. "We have to do this, Sir. Since the Cooperative will have a harder time organizing a recon, it's become more imperative that some of us take the initiative."

"I agree," Bracht said. "We may not know the locations of all their entanglement generators, but one must be on Cybernation. Getting information about it can eliminate MEGA-Man's direct influence on this rebellion."

It's gone way beyond a mere rebellion.

"Let's do it!" Darwish interjected again. At least he didn't curse this time. Not that the situation didn't warrant blasphemy, but it certainly made the man look like an immature fool.

Hapker suppressed a sigh, hating that he agreed with this man. His earlier suspicions about him waned. If the major was still excited about this plan, perhaps he and the councilor didn't have something else going on after all.

"Do you volunteer then, Major?" Arden asked.

"Hell, yeah! I was hoping we'd get the go-ahead."

Hapker narrowed his eyes as his misgiving resurfaced.

Darwish lit up like a child at an amusement park. "Can't wait to kick some MEGA ass."

Hapker's jaw tightened at yet more juvenile swearing.

"This is a recon mission," the captain warned.

"Sure thing." Darwish shrugged.

An uneasy sensation wriggled through Hapker's gut. He considered refusing the major's help, but his desire to find Jori won out. "Alright," he said, looking at Hamada. "Let me ask Nariya, assuming you can spare her."

Hamada blinked. "Um, yeah. We've sort of come to a dead end."

"Major," the captain said to Bracht. "You ran this by a few of your people, correct?"

"Yes, Sir," Bracht replied. "Sergeant Vizubi's squad expressed interest. I will verify."

Oh good. Of all their squads, Vizubi's had the most experience with covert missions.

Arden folded his hands and tapped his two index fingers to his lips. "You realize you won't be able to pass on real-time information to anyone? That means you must escape."

"We take three ships, Sir," Hapker said. "I'll be on the one that surrenders. Major Darwish can lead the other two. Once I transmit enough data, Darwish can send one ship back to you."

"That's a great idea," Darwish said. "And if the information is actionable, I'll use the other ship."

Arden hesitated. "I don't like risking our people—or our ships."

"We'll take every precaution, Sir," Hapker replied, though he couldn't speak for the major.

The captain dipped his head. "Get confirmation from Nariya and Sergeant Vizubi's team."

"Yes, Sir." *Finally.*

34
Strikes & Bites

Euphoria propelled Jori into motion. His pulse increased with the pleasantness of exertion. The treadmill spooled under his feet, sometimes inclining, sometimes slowing or quickening. It wasn't as challenging as jogging through a simulated obstacle course, but he relished the warming of his muscles and the cool sweat beading on his brow.

Although the area in front of this machine generally played a virtual scene, Jori watched a Prontaean Cooperative newsfeed. An earlier blurb had hinted about an attack on a space station, and he wanted to hear their perspective of Brenmos.

After a half dozen accounts of the political upheaval caused by Councilor Alvia's resignation, the disruption in intergalactic trade, and reports on further MEGA uprisings, the bulletin finally came on. Jori stopped the treadmill and gave his full attention.

A woman with fiery red hair and a small, serious mouth took up the screen. "The details of a vicious assault on the Brenmos space station just came in."

Jori grunted. He should've known they'd twist this around and ignore all the lives saved.

"A ship identified as the *Sublime Liberty* waged an unsolicited attack on the station, killing twenty-three people."

Sublime Liberty was the *Black Thresher*'s fictitious name, but the word *unsolicited* stoked his ire. Of course they ignored the *Green Falcon*'s slaughter of *Lady Pachyderm*'s innocent crew.

The inspector's daughter came on the screen. Her light-colored hair was in disarray and redness rimmed her eyes. "They abducted my father." She sniffled. "Who knows what those monsters plan to do to him. We have to get him back before they kill him. Or worse—turn him into one of their abominations."

Jori's stomach did a somersault. Her words, brimming with a hate as intense as her father's, promised vengeance.

"My father has done so much to help our community, but they took him. And they murdered so many of his employees."

Jori clenched his fists.

"By *they*, you mean MEGAs?" the newscaster asked.

"Those savages killed my mother, too!"

The newscaster returned to the full screen and summarized the girl's tragic history and how she was an orphan now. That word made Jori's gut twinge. He was an orphan too, but not because of MEGAs. Because of his father. Still, he knew what it was like to be alone.

He wasn't sure whether he'd care if someone had killed his chima of a father. The girl's plight saddened him, but her father had tortured innocent people. He needed to be stopped but the Cooperative wouldn't do it. Keeping him in a cell on this very ship was better than what he deserved.

The more Jori thought about what the man had done, the more his blood boiled. Something Sensei Jeruko once said gave him a sense of vindication. *"Your choices have consequences."* The inspector had chosen his path. His resulting death was his own fault. Yes, the girl had lost her father, but the galaxy was better for it.

Someone needed to tell people the whole truth. Perhaps he could record the stories of their rescuees, share their medical data, and have MEGA-Man hack into the Cooperative's stations and broadcast them.

"Breaking news!" the newscaster said as she pressed her hand to her earpiece. "It seems the MEGAs are taking their war to another dangerous level. We just received a report that several communication hubs throughout the galaxy are under attack. Twelve… No. Make that thirteen." She turned as though talking to someone offscreen. "What? Ours too? You're kidding." She paled. "Ladies and gentlemen. I don't know how much longer we'll be on the air. Our hub is experiencing a hostile takeover led by MEGAs."

The blood drained from Jori's head so fast, he almost fainted. It was a brilliant tactical move that'd blind the Cooperative. But the implications chilled him to the bone. Those hubs weren't just machines operating independently in space. People lived there. So did their families.

"Cowards!"

Jori flicked off the news. Heat flared in his chest. This entire war was stupid. Why couldn't everyone stop and listen to one another before taking such drastic action? His idea of broadcasting the truth could've worked, but it was too late.

This attack wasn't fighting for the rights of MEGAs. It was a takeover, not a plea for justice. MEGA-Man was as bad as the Cooperative.

"Rodrigo!" Jori called to the man keeping guard a few meters away.

"Captain," Rigo replied, giving his full attention.

"I want to speak to MEGA-Man right now."

"I am unable to comply."

"Why the hell not? You have access to the Great Commune."

"It's not permitted."

Jori gritted his teeth. "Answer the damned question. Why not?"

"It's not permitted."

Jori growled and marched out of the gym, intent on confronting Doctor Sokolov. He kept up a brisk pace all the way to the conveyor. As he waited for the car, he tapped his foot and imagined all the things he would say to his manipulative captors.

The conveyor opened, but before Jori stepped into it, a surging panic struck his senses. Kiyoshi was in trouble. The sensation was distant. He discerned the direction but not the location, so he closed his eyes and concentrated. Phemius was there and he was frightened. Sebastian's glee clashed with it, and Jori could almost see his stupid, sly face.

Jori estimated their whereabouts. When he opened his eyes, the conveyor had already left. *Damn it!* He called for it once more, then focused on Kiyoshi. As with the test with Vance, he extrapolated the situation. Although he couldn't see what was happening, something about everyone's emotions told him that Sebastian had Kiyoshi by the tail and was waving the rat in front of Phemius. *That chima!*

Jori pressed his fingers to his temples and willed the rat to be brave. *Stay calm,* he said in his head, wishing his furry friend could hear him. *Calm down. I'm on my way.*

Kiyoshi's panic subsided. *That's right,* Jori told him even though he knew it was a coincidence. He pictured Kiyoshi's stomach muscles contracting as he folded upward. *That's right. Stay calm and pull yourself up to his fingers. Then bite that chima!*

Sebastian's emotions spiked in pain. Kiyoshi smarted too but then he radiated salvation. Jori imagined Sebastian had dropped him and now the rat was free and on the run.

Jori snapped open his eyes. *Did I help him do that?*

When the rat returned to him, he scooped him up and peered into his little black eyes. "Either that was a coincidence or *you heard me.*"

Kiyoshi twitched his nose, giving nothing away.

35
Rampage

Jori plopped into his office chair. His relentless fighting on the holo-program had propelled him to level eleven but did nothing to appease the fury raging inside him. He dropped his head in his hands and growled. The heat wafting off his face burned as hot as his temper.

How did an organization claiming to be as benevolent as the Cooperative allow an institution like the MEGA Inspections Office to exist? And how could MEGA-Man, who had a legitimate cause, return such ruthlessness by committing murder? Jori had thought he'd left all that behind when he escaped his father.

After several hours of fighting, he still hadn't figured it out. But that wasn't why he'd stopped. Sebastian had made trouble again, this time by damaging the gymnasium's entire electrical system. The idiot had assumed cutting out the lights would give him an advantage, but Jori sensed him lurking about and gave him another bloody nose.

He needed to learn more about this conniving snake, so he went to work, accessing both the Great Commune and reports downloaded from the Cooperative's MDS.

Two accounts battled each other like opposing weather fronts. One side painted a bright blue lake dazzled by the sun while the other portrayed a storm-induced sea hiding a treachery of sea monsters. Jori shook his head, trying to make sense of the conflicting information.

According to Cooperative records, Sebastian was wanted for questioning in regard to three separate murders. None of the acts had been committed directly. Equipment had been sabotaged in each scenario. Two of the people killed were high-profile targets while the third was a co-worker who hated Sebastian and had just filed a complaint of harassment against him.

Files from the Great Commune gave a different story. One said Sebastian discovered an insidious plot and saved a community of MEGAs. Another recounted how he'd rescued two MEGA children.

Jori's heart told him the Cooperative's report about Sebastian's murder-filled sabotage was more accurate than MEGA-Man's heroic praises. But how could he trust the word of either of them?

He slumped into his chair with a huff. How the hell was he supposed to decide which side to take when both factions skewed the facts in their favor? If the differences were so vast on a player as minor as Sebastian, how much worse was the bigger picture?

A terrible agony bloomed in his skull. Jori gasped and leapt from his seat. The pain of death didn't overwhelm him but only because it came from a far end of the ship and from a MEGA with a muted lifeforce.

He darted out the door. "Rigo," he said to the guard outside. "With me."

While running, he tried to determine more about the developing situation. The victim was only vaguely familiar—a MEGA who maintained the ship's fabricors. But Jori couldn't tell how he died or what had caused it.

Although likely too late, he tapped his comm. "Doctor Phemius? Are you available to help someone?"

"Oh. Yes, yes. What do you need me to do?"

"Level two, section five, near the secondary recycler, I believe. I'm not sure what happened, but they're in serious trouble."

"Oh my," Phemius squeaked. "I'm on my way."

Jori almost told him he'd meet him there but another sharp pain penetrated his senses. He clutched his head and stumbled. Even though this lifeforce was also muted, they fought harder to survive. This time, he recognized them. Her name was Phoebe and she must've been using her emotion chip because she practically screamed through his skull.

Jori puffed in and out, trying to regain his own senses. With Rodrigo' help, he stumbled into the conveyor. "Level two, section—" Pheobe wasn't in section five. "Section three."

Three was about fifty meters away, telling him the blast doors hadn't been activated by an emergency. Someone was doing this, but who?

"Rigo," he said. "How many weapons do you carry?"

"I have two phasers."

"Give me one."

Rodrigo handed him the weapon from his right holster. It had four settings ranging from a mild yet crippling shock to a brain-frying zap. Since he didn't know what he'd face, he left no room for error and flipped it to its highest setting.

Phoebe died, leaving a lingering sensation that made him want to vomit. He used the small reprieve to spread his senses further. A black and bitter hatred struck him like a lightning bolt. *General Inspector Lamberson.*

Chusho! How the hell did he escape?

As soon as the conveyor opened, he bolted out. The man had gone another thirty meters and he moved fast. Jori pumped his arms and sprinted after him, leaving Rigo behind.

"You!" he called out when he caught sight of the inspector. "Stop right there or I'll shoot."

The man turned about with a dark expression and a sneer. His emotions staggered. "A MEGA child?" His hatred returned. "It doesn't matter. You're still an abomination."

Jori snapped into a tactical stance and aimed his weapon between the man's eyes. He could've lowered the phaser's setting, but the image of those this man had killed combined with the darkness spewing from him decided him. "You're a monster. Return to your cell or die."

The inspector bared his teeth in a snarling smile and stomped over to Jori, gripping a hefty industrial-sized wrench. "You can't stop me, boy."

"Halt! Or I *will* kill you, you chima."

The man quickened, his evil grin spreading wider. Jori's heart leapt but he squeezed the trigger. The blast struck the man's forehead, halting him in his tracks. Smoke wafted from the wound as he dropped to the floor.

Jori flinched as the pain of death burst in his skull. It evaporated quickly. He glowered down at the body, expecting remorse but experiencing numbness instead. Shouldn't he feel something? Relief at eliminating a man who had tortured and killed so many? Guilt for being the one to take his life? Stupidity for giving in to MEGA-Man's wishes? *Violence begets violence but some people don't deserve to live.*

An external terror erupted, breaking him from his thoughts. Phemius was in trouble. Urgency propelled Jori back the way he'd come, his battle-focus leaving little room to wonder what was going on and where the hell Rigo had gone.

Phemius' emotions didn't reflect an active infliction of pain but Jori kept his weapon primed just in case. He came upon one of the murdered MEGAs and averted his eyes from the blood oozing from her smashed skull. Phemius' medical kit lay next to her, its contents scattered across the floor.

When he reached a hall that ended at a storage freezer, he stopped short. Phemius' muffled whines coupled with his pounding reverberated through the thick metal door. Its handle hung loose with a long screwdriver stabbed into it.

"Sebastian," Jori growled.

He removed the tool and yanked the door open. Phemius fell out, dropping to his knees with a wail. Jori attempted to help the hefty man up to no avail. He held his arms over his head and huddled on the floor.

"You're alright, Phemius. You're out now."

"He tried to kill me," the man cried.

"Who?" Jori asked, even though he suspected the answer.

"Seb-sebastian," Phemius blubbered.

"What the hell was he doing down here?"

"I don't—" The man wailed. "—know."

Jori gritted his teeth, trying to subdue his exasperation toward the doctor and his outrage leveled at Sebastian. "What did he say?"

Phemius didn't reply.

"Tell me what happened," he said in a firm but coaxing tone.

The man hiccupped, then sniffled. "I saw him in the hall and asked if he could help me." He eased up to his knees and wiped the snot from his nose. "B-but he shoved me in the freezer instead."

"Which direction did he come from?"

"I-I don't—"

"Think!"

Phemius looked around, then pointed. "There."

Jori clenched his jaw. That led to the jail cells. Did Sebastian let the inspector out? If so, why? A sinking feeling nearly brought him to his knees. Sebastian, MEGA-Man's agent. Would he release the inspector at MEGA-Man's bidding?

Manipulated again, damn it.
Rodrigo appeared, ambling at a normal pace.
"Where have you been?" Jori snapped.
"I was ordered to stand down."
"What?!" Jori balled his fists as everything fell into place. "By who?" He made a slashing motion. "No. Don't tell me. MEGA-Man gave you that order." His head exploded with rage. "That fucking chima set me up! He wanted me to kill the inspector, didn't he?"
Rigo remained motionless.
Jori planted himself before the cyber-soldier and glared in his cybernetic eye.
"You say you want me on your side," he said to MEGA-Man, who was surely watching, "but you keep doing shit like this."
Rodrigo didn't respond. Jori growled and stormed off. "Find Sebastian and throw him in the inspector's cell," he called out.
He wasn't certain whether Sebastian had let the man out, but locking Phemius up in the freezer where he could've died was a good enough reason to lock him up.
What is it with these half-brained MEGAs?
He still didn't feel any remorse for killing the inspector. Zaina was right, some people didn't deserve to live. But damn MEGA-Man to hell for manipulating him into doing it.
Chima.

36
Azure Horizon

The diaphanous sheet adhered to Commander J.D. Hapker's face. It tickled as though thousands of pharma ants crawled over his skin. A cooling sensation brushed his eyeballs. The nanite mask plugged his mouth and nostrils, making him squirm in his chair. Before his anxiety turned into panic, holes opened around them. The tingling dissipated. He blinked, quirked his lips, and wrinkled his nose. If the mask was still on, he no longer felt it.

Officer Erikson handed him a mirror. The reflection of a dour man with thick jowls stared back at him with marked determination. The bags under his now blue eyes added ten years, as did his black and white hair. He touched the new beard that somewhat disguised the natural crookedness of his mouth, his illusion doing the same. This was still him, yet he couldn't shake the unsettling wrongness. The sensation was worse than his new arm.

"Are you sure no one will detect this?" he asked.

"I am certain," Erikson replied. "This is top-of-the-line covert technology. It's imperceptible to electromagnetic scanners, and it fools both retina and facial recognition software." He opened Hapker's hand, which had been fitted with a nano-glove earlier. "Your fingerprints are disguised as well but beware of subdermal or DNA-based authentication scans."

Hapker shook his head. "This is still better than I expected." He'd always assumed only criminals used nano-masks, but it made sense for authorities to use them for deep covert operations.

Technicians from the space station had created the identity of Herra Arbour to root out a black-market dealer. Although that mission had ended some time ago, they kept him on file. Hapker wore him now. It was possible MEGA-Man or his spies knew he wasn't real, but his reputation would lend credibility to their story.

So would Nariya's presence. With surprising help from General Inspector Joubert, they engineered a fake escape during her custody transfer from the *Odyssey* to the space station. Records showed a ship disguised as a luxury star-clipper owned by Herra Arbour arrived at the station shortly thereafter. Now that ship was in the *Odyssey*'s docking bay.

Nariya's escape only existed as a digital trail, and the complexity of this plan worried him. He kept imagining a rock tumbling down a hill turning into a mudslide. However, seeing his new face bolstered his confidence.

He leaned toward the woman in the chair next to him. "What do you think?"

Lieutenant Sharkey fingered her curly, mousy-brown hair. "It's so strange. I know this is me, but I feel like I'm looking at someone else."

Private Mei Fung crossed her arms. "Which is why I don't keep looking at myself." Despite her rounder face and fatter nose, the intensity of her small physique made her seem the same.

Corporal Rona Quigley's surly attitude still matched as well. Her lips curled as she reworked her new unruly brown hair. "I look like a drug-addled whore."

"At least you look your age." Sergeant Ander Vizubi examined the fabricated undershirt that provided armor while also giving him a rounded gut. Rather than grizzled hair and a stubbled chin, he now had white hair and a short-cropped beard. Like Hapker, he used an existing identity—Thomas Appleford, Herra Arbour's butler.

Private Ishaq Bari checked his reflection, turning side-to-side with a smile. "I like how mine looks." His nose was longer and his brows thicker, somehow lending a level of sternness to his previously disarming features.

"You would," Sergeant Oscar Woolley replied as he ran his hand over his bald head, undoubtedly having second thoughts about his choice to shave off his hair rather than change its color.

"Why do we need to put this crap on now?" Quigley asked.

Hapker ignored her sour tone and answered with tact. "Because Officer Erikson isn't going with us."

"But how am I supposed to bathe?"

"The old-fashioned way," Bari replied. "With water and a damp towel."

"That's correct," Erikson said. "You can do everything you normally do except take a sonic shower."

Nariya arrived, her body bearing an unbendable tension. Her eyes widened as she took them all in.

Hapker met her with a dip of the head and dismissed her guards. "Are you sure you want to do this?"

She blinked, then gave a small smile. "Yes. I'm sorry. I'm just nervous."

He detected no hesitation but pressed anyway. "If they fall for our ruse and take us in, we may not get out again."

She bit her lip and stared down at her feet. When she lifted her head, her eyes locked onto his. "I'm not ashamed of who I am. But as someone altered without permission, I want to discourage it from happening to anyone else."

Quigley's lips curled into a patronizing frown. "You realize we're ultimately upholding the injunction limiting the rights of MEGAs, right?"

Nariya shifted her feet but stood her ground. "Not everyone who's a MEGA is a threat."

"Why get augmentations if not to seek an unfair advantage?" Quigley's tone carried an accusation even though she was aware of Nariya's circumstances.

"Some people just want to survive," Nariya replied.

Her words made surprising sense, but Quigley scoffed.

"Hey." Bari nudged her before she said something snotty. "Leave her be."

Quigley shot him a sour look but let it drop. Whatever the woman's unbending opinion, at least she hadn't put up any resistance to Nariya partaking in this mission. Hapker also noted how Bari had a way of tempering her mood. It wasn't by any warning or threat, which meant Quigley held a certain respect for her junior officer.

Major Darwish entered with his usual cockiness. "Hey, wow! Y'all are like a squad of rank-and-file civvies."

Hapker suppressed a groan. The optimism boosted by the fellowship of Vizubi's team crumbled with the major's arrival. Although the man had his own cohesive following, his bullish attitude grated on his nerves. Even Bari grimaced while Woolley rolled his eyes. At least Darwish and his two squads would be on separate ships.

"Gotta kick some ass," Darwish said, "so let's get going."

"We're not there to fight, Major."

"Yeah, we—" Darwish's face flipped to realization in the blink of an eye. "Yeah, right. Recon."

Hapker frowned. *What was he about to say?* He hoped the major wouldn't get too overeager and turn this into a fight. Not for the first time, Hapker wished he could oversee this mission himself. But the chain of command was tricky in this situation. Darwish served directly under Admiral Patel but his assignment to this PCC ship meant he answered to Hapker's and Captain Arden's authority. This became more muddied once they left the *Odyssey*. This was technically a military operation. And though Hapker had acted in a military capacity during the Thendi defensive, his leadership here was debatable.

Once again, he was thankful he'd be on a separate ship. Let Darwish command the Bastion-class ships. Hapker along with Nariya and Vizubi's team would take the star-clipper.

After gathering supplies, they met in the bay where all three vessels waited. The clipper was a decent little ship that'd been seized by the PG-Force some years ago. Renamed the *Azure Horizon* and given a fake transponder code, it was the perfect vessel to lend credibility to their story. It didn't have any firepower, but it was fast and equipped for stealth from its past use in smuggling. With the flip of a switch, its microcapsule coating would turn it black and absorb signals rather than reflect them. It also had a thermal shield that prevented it from showing up on infrared. And its low emissions would make it difficult to detect by other means.

The Bastion ships resembled dreary ostriches next to a sleek falcon. But they were just as fast and had similar camouflage and shielding. Plus, they had weaponry. Hapker hoped they wouldn't have to use them.

He entered the *Horizon*, toting his suitcase. Since he—or Arbour—was the registered owner of this vessel, he looked for the master suite. He found the largest and most garish room easily enough and sighed at the giant four-poster bed with its thick and downy comforter.

The dresser was just as uselessly fancy. He unpacked the fabricated clothes a wealthy man like Arbour would own. The silky charcoal jacket was something he'd wear at a fundraiser hosted by his parents back home. But the bright blue ruffled shirt he was supposed to don underneath it made his eyeballs hurt. Thankfully, he'd have on an enviro-suit during the trip.

On the way out from his quarters, he caught two voices coming from the ship's common area.

"I just don't like him," Quigley said.

"Why not?" Bari asked.

"Come on. You heard about the incident where he was kicked out of the PG-Force, right?"

Ah. She must be talking about me. Hapker halted and clenched his jaw.

"He disobeyed a direct order," she continued, "and let a notorious murderer get away."

Hapker's gut twinged. He thought he'd come to terms with his actions, but this criticism bothered him.

"Kimpke was on a civilian ship," Bari replied, echoing Hapker's thoughts. "Innocent people would've died if he'd obeyed."

"I still don't trust anyone who doesn't follow orders."

Bari barked a laugh. "You're the *queen* of disobeying orders."

"I am not!"

"Yeah, then how come Lieutenant Anghel reassigned you— twice?"

"Because he was a dick."

Hapker imagined Bari rolling his eyes.

"Seriously," Quigley said. "Major Darwish should lead the infiltration."

Hapker almost stepped out but held back when Bari scoffed. "Seriously? You mean that hothead who murdered innocent people in the name of war?"

"They were MEGAs," she replied.

"They were people."

"Whatever."

Bari groaned. "I think your prejudice is grossly misplaced. The commander seems competent… And much more level-headed than Darwish."

"Commander Hapker has no business leading this mission. He's not even a real military officer."

That's it. Hapker stormed out. "Corporal Quigley!"

She whispered a curse and slowly straightened into an attention stance. "Sir."

"No one is forcing you to be here," Hapker boomed. "If you don't like who's in charge, leave."

She worked her jaw. "We were just talking, Sir. I didn't mean anything by it."

"You are a corporal. *Gossiping* with those under your command is unprofessional and threatens to undermine the operation."

She glanced at Bari, who cocked his eyebrow at her. With a clearing of her throat, she looked down and muttered an apology.

Hapker slowly exhaled, dispelling some of his anger. "Are we going to have a problem, Corporal?"

"No, Sir," she mumbled.

He lifted his brows. "You don't sound sure."

She snapped her eyes to his. "No, Sir," she said more forcefully.

"Good. Now get back to it."

He left the crackling silence behind and exited the ship. Vizubi and Sharkey busied themselves with a pre-combat check on the various weapons. Since they needed to appear as authentically civilian as possible, none of them were military-grade. That just meant they required additional scrutiny and those two were the most qualified to do it.

Captain Arden arrived. He took his time, chatting with each of them individually, offering them safe travels and good luck. He did the same for Hapker but reluctance filtered through his voice.

"What is it, Sir?" Hapker asked.

The captain hesitated. "Sergeant Vizubi and his team can handle this mission on their own, you know."

He doesn't want me to go? The sentiment gave him pause. He'd only been commander of this ship for a short time and he'd spent much of it elsewhere. "I have complete faith in them, Sir," he said. "But I need to do this."

Arden sighed. "And I need my commander. I wish you'd stay."

"I wish I *could*, Sir. Even though this is the best crew I've ever had the honor to serve, I can't abandon him. Not after I promised to protect him."

"I understand," the captain replied solemnly. "But the chances of you running into Jori are slim. It'd be like accidentally coming across a rogue planet."

"I'm not just looking for Jori."

"True. But even locating our own people is a long shot."

"It doesn't mean we shouldn't try, Sir."

Arden's expression shifted from agreement to doubt. "I only wish it wasn't my people who had to do it. I realize you were once a PG-Force officer. And I'm certain Vizubi's team can handle themselves. But you're going in blind."

"I know."

"Just don't take any unnecessary risks."

"No, Sir. That's Darwish's department."

The captain grunted. "I don't like that man. He seems like the trigger-happy sort."

Hapker folded his arms. "I couldn't agree more. But we're the ones going in. Not him."

"True enough. But still be careful. As much as I want to save my family, I don't want to lose my best officers in the process."

Hapker's emotions surged with an appreciation. "Will do, Sir. We'll meet you back on board soon."

I hope.

37
Destination

Boredom sank in like a stone into the viscous hydrocarbon ocean of Biyu. Terkeshi reviewed the information on the tablet once more. Since no one had come to fix the stabilizer yet, he wanted to figure it out himself. The visual aids were somewhat helpful, but the technobabble jumbled together into an incoherent mess. He released a long-winded groan. If only he had something else to do.

He lounged sideways on a crash couch in the cabin with his legs thrown over one side and a pillow cushioned against his back on the other. This would've been the most comfortable place on this cramped ship if not for Gaichu laying on top of him. Damn, the dog was getting heavy. He must weigh twenty kilos by now.

Rather than move him, he caressed his ear. *Spoiled mutt.*

A beep sounded. He flinched and Gaichu jumped down, barking. Terk focused his senses and detected Washi's austere and troubled lifeforce. He leapt out of his seat and bounded to the entry hatch, eager to see for himself that his old personal guards had made it here safely too.

Washi entered with slumped shoulders. After the door closed and the lights turned on, he handed over a tablet. "We've arrived."

Terk swallowed as he studied the planet on the screen. It looked like any other inhabited world. Blue, brown, and green marbled with wisps of white clouds. The only thing to distinguish it from Meixing was its larger land masses and smaller polar ice caps.

"Which planet is this?"

Washi's throat bobbed. "Cybernation."

"What!" Terk's hands broke into a tremor. The tablet crashed to the floor. "No fucking way!"

"I'm afraid so."

Invisible claws seized Terk's chest and squeezed. He dropped to his knees as his vision darkened. *A ship is bad enough, but a whole fucking planet!*

Washi grasped him under the arm and helped him to his feet. "Stop this and summon your anger. It'll help you fight off your fear."

Terk took in some breaths, but they were short and sharp.

"Use what those chimas almost did to you," Washi continued, "to think about what you'd like to do to them."

Terk tried, but what was the point of imagining stabbing their metallic eyes out when it was one person against an entire planet?

Washi gripped both Terk's shoulders and made him face him. "I know it seems hopeless, but I have a plan. We can still get out of this, but I need you to focus. Find your anger. I know it's in there. Use it."

Terk choked out a sob.

"Damn it, boy! Get your shit together!"

The imitation of his father's voice and words sent a shock through Terk's system. A fire ignited inside him. He focused on it, willing it to spread into a conflagration.

His breaths came easier. These chimas had already hurt him once. He wouldn't let them do it again. It didn't matter how many there were. He'd fight them all into oblivion.

When the threat of blacking out receded, he clenched his fists and faced Washi. "What's your plan?" he asked through gritted teeth.

Washi handed him two pieces of cloth—a large, faded black one and a smaller one colored with bright, dizzying patterns. Terk frowned. "What the hell are these?"

"Wear them. This one—" He pointed at the black piece. "—is a hooded jacket. The other is a shirt from Lord Qing's niece. Use it as a mask."

"What for?" Realization struck him like lightning. He staggered back. "Wait, I need to go out there?"

Washi grasped his shoulders again to keep him in place. "Listen to me. It will be alright. This is actually an opportunity."

Terk's temper exploded to the surface. "Yeah, an opportunity to get captured!" He shook free of Washi's grip.

"Just listen, damn it!" Washi's brows furrowed into a glower.

Terk folded his arms and waited to hear this brilliant plan that'd undoubtedly get him turned into a machine.

Washi heaved a sigh. "From what we've been able to discern so far, they'll herd us off this ship together. We'll conceal you among us."

"Concealed?" Terk flung his hand out at an imaginary MEGA. "Do you have any idea how powerful their cybernetic eyes are? Even with most of my face covered, their recognition technology will figure out who I am."

"I said listen!"

Terk snapped his mouth shut and scowled.

Washi groaned and rubbed his brow. When he reined in his irritation, he met Terk's eye and softened. "The colorful material will confuse identification software by creating visual noise."

Rather than interrupt, Terk shot him a questioning look.

Washi waved it away. "I have experience in this type of situation."

Terk lifted his brows.

"But never mind that," Washi continued. "The important thing is that you can leave with the rest of us. We'll wait for an opportunity and create a diversion while you slip out."

"How will I know where to go?" he blurted, realizing it was a stupid question since Washi wouldn't know either.

"Anywhere but where *we* are. On the outside, you'll have a chance of getting out of this—and maybe you'll find a way to get us out of it too."

Terk pressed his lips together. He'd have better luck capturing the wind.

"This is the best we can do," Washi said, his eyes tilted apologetically. "They want us off their ship."

"The *Dusty Rose* isn't theirs."

"No, it's Lord Qing's and he's allowing them to keep it here until they repair it."

"I'll hide here while they do it."

Washi shook his head. "They know you're here. If you don't leave with the rest of us, they'll be suspicious and investigate."

Terk huffed. "Chusho."

"It'll be alright," Washi said. "Use part of your hood to cover your eyepatch. Turn away when they look at you."

"That won't be suspicious at all," Terk mumbled.

"It's all we've got, so just stick close to us. We'll be watching your back."

"What about Gaichu?" Terk flicked his hand and the dog who sat at full attention beside him like a little fluffy soldier.

Washi shrugged again. "Figure it out. You should've left the mangy thing behind."

"He's not mangy," Terk replied defensively.

Washi's mouth quirked, almost into a smile. "You've gotten quite attached to the farmer's life, haven't you?"

Despite the gravity of his situation, Terk played along. "Yeah, well, I haven't had a mad dragon breathing down my neck every second. And this mangy dog here is a much better companion than anyone on *that* damned ship."

Washi nodded appreciatively. "You've changed. And for the better at that." He smacked Terk's shoulder. "Keep the dog close. We'll do what we can to make sure no one has a problem with it."

With him, Terk wanted to say. Gaichu was a he, not an it.

"We'll arrive in twelve hours," Washi said on his way out.

Gaichu nudged Terk's hand with his wet nose. Even though the pup had no clue why Terk was so upset, he radiated sympathy.

Terk ruffed him between the ears. "It's about to get interesting," he said, knowing full well it was a massive understatement.

38
Diversion

The blinding white walls of the corridor kicked Terkeshi's heart into a patter. Walking through the *Tatawar* reminded him too much of the moments before his surgery. It was more than the cleanliness of this place, or the cool air that sent shivers down his sweating body. What if they realized who he was? What if they forced him to undergo another procedure?

Dread dragged him toward the crushing darkness of a black hole. He itched to make a run for it. Every fiber of his being screamed at him to get the hell away from these people before it was too late.

He clenched his fists. *Not yet!* There was no escape when trapped in the confines of a MEGA ship.

He diverted his thoughts by paying attention to his surroundings. The hall wound to the right in a gentle curve. No intersections or offshoot doors broke up the monotony. He might as well be walking in circles.

With no visual distractions, he focused on sounds instead. The plodding of a dozen footsteps reverberated like discordant drums. Washi and Michio didn't speak, but whispers from the villagers buzzed in his ears. Nearly everyone exhibited unease, whether through words, expressions, or emotions, and it fueled his own.

The only one at ease was the MEGA leading them. Her wavy blond hair bounced as she walked. The pride she radiated hinted that she believed herself to be their rescuer.

Since she had a strong lifeforce and no obvious cybernetics, he suspected she had genetic augmentations. If that were the case, perhaps some of these villagers could avoid getting turned into super-soldiers. He doubted they'd be given much of a choice, though. It seemed more realistic that the MEGAs had sent this woman to disarm them. She certainly helped to keep his fears from spilling over into panic.

The hall ended at a closed hatch. A clank resounded, making Terk flinch. *It's just a damned door, you idiot.*

The hatch ascended with agonizing slowness. His imagination took off in anticipation of meeting cyborgs on the other side, but he forced himself to breathe easy. He'd run into them eventually. Might as well get used to being around a bunch of soulless freaks.

He shifted his feet and craned his neck to peer inside. Each incremental rise of the door revealed nothing, but his heart still fluttered.

"Here we are!" The chipper woman swept her hand toward the fully open hatch and the empty room beyond. "This is the transport room. Just get on the platform over there and I'll send you to a temporary haven on the planet."

"Send us how?" Yuan asked.

"It's a molecular disassembly and reassembly device," the woman replied. "It'll disassemble your matter to an atomic level, transmit it, and reassemble you into your original form."

The villagers gasped. The most technical thing they'd ever seen was the *Dusty Rose*. A transport device was mystical sorcery in comparison.

Terk swallowed. He hated these things. Given a choice, he'd rather take a shuttle. It didn't matter that traveling via a small vessel carried more statistical risk. A device that took him apart and put him back together made his skin crawl. *What if it recognizes my damaged implants and repairs them?*

No. That can't happen. These devices were complicated enough without having to fix things too. Or so he hoped.

Gaichu whined. His apprehension matched Terk's own. Did transports work on animals? *Don't be ridiculous.* If they worked on foodstuff, equipment, and something as molecularly complex as people, they'd work on a dog. But would they allow a dog to come with him?

"It'll be alright," he whispered to the pup. "Just stick close." If the MEGAs were eager for more converts, they'd indulge him. And if not, he'd have an excuse to leave.

An empty pit settled in his stomach, but he waited in forced stoicism as the first half of the people stepped onto the platform. After they phased out, he pushed through his reluctance and joined the next group up. Gaichu followed him with the same hesitation even though he likely had no idea what was going on.

Before Terk had a chance to brace himself, the MEGA woman activated the transport. The nervous tingling in his Terk's body intensified. The scene before him faded, then shifted into a new view. Despite how fast he reassembled, it took a moment to reorient himself.

Adrenaline shot through him, sharp and hot. Four stony soldiers with cybernetic eye implants and bionic limbs met them. Terk's brain registered them as lifeless statues since they had no lifeforce and stood too still. But his fight-or-flight response kicked into overdrive, knowing full well these beings were alive and deadly.

He tried to breathe, but it was as though someone gripped him by the throat. His thoughts ran rampant. *They know who I am. They've come for me. I need to get the hell out of here!*

Something pounced on his thigh, followed by a wet and insistent nudge to his palm. Gaichu's whine intruded on his panic, giving him an opening for a coherent thought. *"I want you to grab that anger and use it to fuel your courage,"* his mother's words from the other day played in his head.

He gritted his teeth and brought up the image of someone who sparked his most deep-rooted anger—his father. Emotions stronger than his fear swelled inside him. His ragged breaths evened out. His heart slowed.

He opened his eye and forced himself to study the super-soldiers. One was as wide as a senshi warrior while the woman next to him had a wiry frame. She had dark skin while the man behind her was pale. The fourth man was short in stature and had a bald head. Despite their varied physical traits, they all wore shiny steel armor and empty expressions.

Anxi shot Terk a worried frown. Whether it was because of his near-panic attack or she also didn't like the looks of them, he wasn't sure. Gaichu echoed their concern with a nervous growl.

"This way," the largest soldier said. He turned on his heel and headed for the exit. The other three soldiers herded Terk and the group after him.

Terk stayed close to Washi and Michio, and Gaichu stuck close to him. The corridor here was just as sterile and unadorned as the one on the ship, but straight. Terk kept an eye out for an intersection, but there were none. His breaths quickened.

"We'll find a way," Michio said, his optimism lending Terk courage.

A door appeared on the right. A glimpse inside its window revealed enough sterility to resemble a surgical room, but he forced that thought out of his head. Soon, more doors lined the hall. Some had windows, some didn't. Some required a keypad entry while others had a manual handle lever. The soldiers surrounding them prevented him from succumbing to the temptation of checking for unlocked doors.

They came upon an intersection. As the soldiers led them to the right, Terk peered in the other directions. All were identical with a few doors along the way. They passed more intersections. He glanced at Washi and Michio, wondering when they'd create the diversion so he could slip away.

Washi shook his head. Terk tilted his as though to ask why the hell not. "Recon," Washi whispered.

Oh. Right. It made sense.

He detected several familiar lifeforces nearby, including his mother's. Most people radiated a mild curiosity coupled with boredom, but his mother emitted worry.

They turned another corner and he saw why. The villagers and a few unfamiliar faces waited in a straggled line. Were they waiting to get prepped for surgery? He shook his hands to expel the prickly sensation from his fingers. *Get a hold of yourself.*

"What's going on?" Washi asked the soldiers who'd blocked their retreat.

They didn't reply.

"Anyone know what's happening up there?" Michio called out.

A farmer further up yelled back. "I think they're scanning us."

"For what?" Michio asked.

The man shrugged.

It was better than Terk's first thought but not by much. He shot Washi a look asking if they could please act now. The two of them surveyed their surroundings. This hall led to other intersections, but they were all guarded by soldiers. There were doors too. Terk nudged Anxi and inclined her head at the nearest one. She tried the handle and it clicked. Terk's heart jumped.

She eased it open and peeked in. "Storage."

"Close the door!" a soldier bellowed.

Terk flinched.

Anxi shrugged and shut it. "Just curious."

"You could slip inside one," Michio whispered in Terk's ear.

Terk's breath caught. "If they have security cameras, they'll figure out where I am and I'll be trapped."

"Stay only long enough for them to scan us," Washi replied. "Then you can come out and find someplace else to go."

"No. I need to get out of here." Assuming there was a way out.

Michio nodded. "A diversion still makes sense. Perhaps at that intersection up there."

Terk dipped his head in reply.

The line moved slowly. Several minutes ticked by. His heart thumped. A tightness formed in his chest. His nerves twitched. The people inched forward, closer to the intersection. A pair of soldiers guarded each side. Their bulk presented both a deterrent and a barrier, but he got a good look beyond them. This hall was the same as the others, with a few doors along the way and another intersection further down.

He wiped his hands down his pants and tilted his head at Washi and Michio. They responded with a nod. He nudged Anxi, giving her the same signal. She passed it on to their team. Their boredom switched to nervousness, but their determination signaled their readiness.

"Gaichu," he whispered. The dog perked his ears up. "Stay close," he commanded. A flicker of understanding ran through the dog's high alert emotions.

Terk looked at Yuan, the catalyst, and mouthed the word *go*.

"I want to go home!" Yuan yelled. He turned away from the intersection and tried to run beyond the soldiers at their backs.

"This isn't right!" Anxi bellowed. She dodged after him.

Yells resounded as his team followed suit. Washi and Michio took part as well, using their warrior-built muscles to add to the frenzied retreat. Those caught slowed their struggling since the point wasn't to escape, though they feigned terror to keep up the pretense. Others managed to break through. Soldiers pursued them, including two of the four guarding the intersection. With those remaining two observing the disruption, Terk and Gaichu slipped by and sprinted down the hall. Gaichu matched his stride.

They reached the crossway and turned left. Thankfully, the corridor was empty. Terk strained his ears, but no footsteps followed in his wake. His pace didn't slow, but his heart did. After another turn, he started checking doors. The first two didn't open. The third did. A light flickered on, revealing a storage room full of laboratory supplies.

He backed out and tried the next door. No lights came on. The darkness promised better hiding, but it was too small. He had to find some place bigger that would allow him to move around and hide whenever needed.

The fifth door led to a stairway down. He took it. Gaichu stuck close, his nails clicking along the way. Terk panted, as did the pup. Since only their footsteps echoed through the stairwell, he kept going down until the last flight ended at a short hall and a door.

He peered through the small square window. The gloominess on the other side promised lots of camouflaging shadows. Crates upon crates created narrow aisles. He spied a spot higher up that'd make a great vantage point. A couple of bots rolled around, but their sensors were likely only the minimum needed for moving supplies.

Perfect. He turned to Gaichu. "This is it, buddy. This is where we'll stop and figure out what to do."

That next step would be harder.

39
Awry Arrival

Cybernation. It had an official name, but no one called it that. Like many other inhabited planets, it had sparkling blue oceans, rich brown and green continents splashed with vast deserts, and frosty white polar caps. And the left half of the planet that lay in shadow glittered with broad patches of city lights.

"That's deceptively ordinary," Commander J.D. Hapker said from a seat suffocating with its endless safety features.

"I'm not sure whether it's promising or ominous," Sharkey replied from the crash couch beside him. He couldn't see her. Not with the adaptive headrest and cushioned neck-brace keeping him facing forward. The tallness of their chairs meant he didn't see Sergeant Woolley in the pilot's seat in front of him either. Private Fung, the co-pilot, operated her console barely within view.

"Let's hope for the former," Vizubi said from the chair behind him.

"There's their communication hub." Woolley tapped the control panel and the screen zoomed in on the light side of the planet where a giant object orbited in the thermosphere.

Quigley whistled and Hapker concurred. The hub's size wasn't the only thing that held him in awe. Although it appeared to have many of the same components of a Prontaean hub, its foreign design was a marvel of advanced technology. At its center resided a cylindrical module that likely contained the quantum core chamber, entanglement generators, and a habitable section for the workers.

Extending from it like the spines of a sea urchin with octopus-like sucker-endings were expansive solar and antenna arrays. The module exterior was further equipped with energy generators, cooling fins, and radiators to dissipate heat.

Hapker gripped his armrest. The hub's level of sophistication made him wonder about the planet's defenses. Although they'd activated the ship's cloaking functions, no stealth technology was perfect. Getting detected before they were ready would raise the MEGAs' suspicions.

No one spoke. Tense moments ticked by as their passive sensors gathered information.

Woolley gasped. "Oh my God."

The image on the screen changed again. This time, the focus was on a humongous ship-building station.

Hapker gasped. Corporal Quigley cursed. Nariya squeaked. The others were stunned into silence.

Like the hub, it had a central module with spines sticking out. It featured a longer and thinner shape. A series of radial structural beams terminated in docking platforms rather than arrays. The design reminded him of the delphinium flowers his mother grew, only uglier—and much more terrifying.

Hundreds of docks contained ships in various stages of construction. At least ten times that many were vacant. Hapker swayed as his mind tried to grasp the multitude of ships sent to attack the Cooperative's communication hubs. And they were still making more.

"Do you think this is why they need more people?" Bari asked. "To man all those bastards?"

Hapker's neck prickled. "That and pushing us into their definition of evolution."

"Their sensors just swept by," Fung said. "No sign that they've spotted us."

"We'll intercept with Lumpy in seven minutes," Woolley said.

The screen flickered to display a grey blob pocked with deep shadows. Lumpy, the nickname given by Quigley, was one of the planet's many natural satellites. It was three miles across—big enough to hide all three of their vessels yet too small and too far away for the MEGAs to bother equipping it with sensor arrays.

The speed at which Lumpy approached from their rear set Hapker's teeth on edge. He felt like an impala about to fall prey to a lion—a giant black lion since it came at them from the night side.

Just when he was sure it'd crash into them, Woolley lined up beside it and matched its trajectory and velocity.

"*Lionfish* and *Blue Octopus* in place," Major Darwish announced through a tight-beam transmission.

Darwish had used camouflaging animals to rename their Bastion-class ships. That he'd also chosen deadly sea creature names suggested he hoped to go to battle.

His nerves jittered as they waited for the opportune moment when Lumpy passed between the planet and their star. If all went well, the MEGAs would assume the star's energy had hidden them rather than their stealth tech.

After an hour had gone by, his leg was jouncing.

"We're ready," Woolley said.

"Alright everyone," Hapker called out. "Here we go."

Woolley took them out from behind the satellite. Hapker tried to restrain his nerves as the minutes crawled.

After twenty-five minutes where it seemed they were no closer to the planet, Woolley called out, "They see us."

A ping preceded an incoming transmission. "*Azure Horizon.* This is Anoteros Security," said a monotone voice. "You are entering restricted space. State your purpose."

Woolley answered, "Hey, my friends and I need help. We recently escaped a bunch of rowdy MEGA haters only to get chased by MEGA hunters. Everyone is going crazy, thinking we're the bad guys. Can you help us? Please, we don't have anywhere else to go."

Hapker quirked his mouth. The man did a good impression of a civilian.

"Are you MEGAs?"

"Five of us have genetic enhancements but no cybernetics. Two sympathize with the cause, and hunters are falsely accusing another of being a MEGA. We're all targets here, desperate for refuge. Please. You've got to help us."

"Identify all occupants."

"Sure thing," Woolley replied. He tapped the panel and sent the prepared information.

Several minutes passed before security responded. "Why do you have five unregistered persons on your vessel?"

Hapker blew out a breath. At least his and Vizubi's fake identities had held up.

Woolley scoffed. "So MEGA hunters can't track us. But now that they're getting bolder, we're scared." Woolley's voice grew sharper. "It's bullshit that we're always looked down on when we're so much better. And well, damn it, it's about time someone is finally standing up to them."

Hapker was impressed with Woolley's performance. All the rehearsing in the galaxy couldn't account for real-time nerves.

"Permission granted to approach the planet. Sending vector coordinates. Do not deviate. Escort One will intercept in two hours. Confirm receipt."

"Got it. And thank you," Woolley said with pretended sincerity, then ended the communication.

"They didn't ask about Nariya," Sharkey said. "That means there are still MEGA spies on the space station."

Quigley groaned. "Just how many damned people are MEGAs?"

Hapker agreed with her sentiment. All this time, they'd thought MEGAs were the minority.

Fung harrumphed. "Enough to mean this war won't end anytime soon."

A chill ran down Hapker's spine. "Nariya," he called to the operator seated behind him. "Have they initiated a handshake protocol with your transceiver?"

"No, Sir. I'm concerned we may need to initiate it ourselves."

"Can you do that?"

"Not without the correct authorization code."

Darn. That meant they'd have to find another way to insert the spyware. "Keep trying."

"Yes, Sir."

As the flight progressed, they used spectroscopic, infrared, and other passive sensors to gather data. General information about defense satellites and land-based weaponry streamed in. They pinpointed hundreds of armed ships in orbit. A map of the planet's surface was generated along with the location of suspected power generation facilities, large-scale factories, and radio communication centers.

Hapker's insides buzzed with anticipation. As far as he knew, none of the PG-Force recon ships had ever gotten this close. The information they fed to Darwish would be invaluable when it came time to rescue their people.

If their people were even here. The most dangerous part of the mission was yet to come—they didn't know what to expect once they were in the MEGAs' hands.

*****

Twenty more minutes and their escorts would complete their turn and match their course. Commander J.D. Hapker had long since given up on restraining his wandering thoughts. The mixture of boredom and anxiety gave no room for quiet contemplation.

His crew mates didn't seem to have the same trouble. He heard no tapping of fingers, no shifting of feet, and no soft noises to indicate they were as restless as he was. Nor did they have any desire to fill the silence with idle chatter.

This was no doubt a mark of their experience. In another circumstance, he would've had the same focus, but he was too close to this. Although he'd told the captain he wasn't doing this for Jori, Jori was his driving motivation—and it was driving him to distraction.

"Sir!" Woolley called out, making Hapker's heart jump to his throat. "Hundreds of ships just appeared on our screen."

"What do you mean *appeared*?"

"Like they just came out of stealth… Oh crap! They're ours!"

Hapker tried to lurch forward only to be stopped short by his harness. "Ours?"

"Ours. Battleships, cruisers, destroyers, and dozens of support ships."

What the heck? "Open a channel to the *Blue Octopus*."

"Done."

"Major Darwish! What's happening out there?"

"Thanks to you, Sir, we've got enough information to wage war on these bastards," the man drawled.

"War?! That wasn't the plan!" *At least not yet.*

"Actually, Sir… It was."

An inferno blazed in Hapker's chest. He should've known. "How in the hell did you coordinate this with the hubs down?"

"Our strike was already underway, Sir," Darwish said in a condescending tone that made Hapker wish he could reach through the comm and punch him. "We were just holding off until your arrival."

Greymore used us as bait! Hapker was too angry to feel the sting of betrayal. "How'd you know we'd still come?"

"We didn't, but it was in the strike force's best interest to wait and see."

A flood of cold heat swept through Hapker's body as he realized his predicament. "What about us? Now we can't check if our people are down there."

"I'm sure they are. After we kick some ass, we'll go down and get them. For now, just take a step back and let us big boys—" Darwish's ship alarm cut him off.

Hapker cursed under his breath. If he turned around now, it would look suspicious. Maybe they could play ignorance. "Woolley, what's our status?"

"Our escort is almost here." Woolley changed the screen to a digitized version of events. Their two ships showed up as white blips aligning with the *Azure Horizon*. Behind them, the mass of green PG-Force blips matched the numbers of the red MEGA blips dispersed around the planet. "I'm not sure what they think of us now, though."

"Contact Anoteros Security. Assure them you knew nothing about this."

"They won't buy it," Woolley replied.

"Do your best. It's our only chance."

"Hey!" Woolley announced into the comm with panic stricken through his tone. "Holy shit, guys. What's going on out there? A bunch of ships just popped up on my radar."

They waited in tense silence as the PG-Force closed in on the planet and the MEGA ships rushed to meet them. *Damn it, Darwish.* Hapker's team wasn't just bait. They were the sacrifice. If he survived this, he'd kill that cocky slimeball.

"Should we retreat, Sir?" Woolley asked.

"No way," Fung blurted. "They'll either assume we're a part of this or we'll get caught in friendly fire."

"She's right." Hapker dug his fingers into his armrest. "We're not in a Cooperative vessel. Woolley, send Anoteros another message. Tell them we're activating our shield for safety reasons."

Hapker's nerves frayed as they waited in agonizing silence. The *Horizon* had slowed during its approach but those heading into battle had no such speed restrictions. The two sides clashed. Despite the battle only being visible in digital form, a collective gasp escaped the crew.

The trajectory data displayed for the escort ships changed. The uncertainty of their intentions wriggled in Hapker's gut. "Remain steady," he told Woolley. "Stay on course and keep playing the role of innocent bystanders."

"Our shields are down!" Darwish yelled through the comm. "Oh fuck! We're hit! We're—"

Hapker's blood turned to ice.

"Oh shit," Woolley cursed under his breath, echoing Hapker's sentiments.

But that wasn't all that set his nerves blazing. "Are we on the command net?" Hapker asked.

"That son of a camel!" Woolley said. "He remoted us in."

Dread fell upon Hapker like a hammer. If the MEGAs detected an energy signature from this transmission, their cover story would fall apart. "Close it, now!"

"Our shields are—" The panicked voice of another ship commander cut out.

The ensuing silence seemed to suck out all the air. Seconds passed but it felt like hours.

Woolley gasped. "Uh oh, Sir. It looks like our escorts are activating their weapons. And they're no longer lined up to ride alongside us."

"Crap," Hapker replied in an uncharacteristic curse. "Break away. Get us the hell out of here."

Woolley didn't respond in voice but the *Horizon* shifted, its inertial dampeners barely keeping up. A tremor ran through the ship. Their ship's icon brightened with the strike of an energy cannon.

"Shields down to ninety-three percent," Fung announced.

"Evasive maneuvers!" Hapker bellowed.

The ship jerked to the side. Even with the cushions on Hapker's headrest wrap, his brain rattled. Nariya yelped. Quigley cursed. Vizubi grunted. Fung wore a determined grimace.

"Shit!" Woolley opened the comm. "Stop! We're not the enemy. We came here to get away from those bastards!"

Anoteros Security didn't respond. MEGA ships came at them from all sides. Woolley steered the *Horizon* every which way, giving Hapker vertigo. Shields fell to seventy-two percent as more firepower struck them. The ship shuddered, rattling Hapker's teeth.

The screen showed them heading to the planet. Woolley veered away only to have to turn back again. Were they being herded?

They sped onward, outrunning all but the two escort pursuers. Most of the MEGA ships must've already been out beyond the planet because they encountered fewer vessels as they approached the ionosphere.

With the escorts still firing, Woolley rolled the ship, sending Hapker's stomach into a vicious turmoil. The shield levels kept dropping. Thirty percent now. A terrifying dread infiltrated to his marrow at the thought of failing Jori once again.

"Head for the planet," he ordered. "Avoid land-based defenses if you can."

"Is that wise?" Vizubi asked.

"There's no other way out of this," Woolley replied as he made a course correction.

Nariya released a strangled cry. Hapker clutched his armrests.

The ship quaked. Hapker bit his tongue, then activated his mouth guard. An alarm sounded, buzzing like an angry hornet. The rocking intensified. An electric burning odor filled the cabin. The form-fitting features of the crash couch extended around his forehead, chin, and neck but didn't prevent his brain from quaking inside his skull.

Woolley switched the screen to a live front view. The landscape sharpened as the ship jetted toward the planet. Shorelines that once looked smooth turned into jagged detail. The ship lurched as another energy blast struck it. The scene spun. Hapker squeezed his eyes shut.

"Stabilizing!" Woolley called out in a high pitch as though the words had to squeeze through tightened vocal cords. "The enemy is falling back."

The convulsing eased into a rattle. Hapker opened his eyes. The view outside wobbled but no longer spun. And it had taken on a bluish tint, indicating they were entering the thermosphere.

The g-force increased. Oxygen hissed into the cabin. His suit inflated around his legs and abdomen. He used breathing techniques to help him withstand the accelerated forces.

The blueness outside morphed from a dark navy to a brighter hue. Browns and greens of the planet's surface became more distinct even as distortions fluttered from the heated air around their hull. A deafening roar quaked throughout the ship as Woolley decelerated. Hapker braced himself against the invisible weight pressing against his chest.

A boom resounded and the ship pitched sideways.

"We lost retro-burn thrusters!" Woolley shouted.

"We're about to crash!" Nariya wailed.

"Engaging maneuvering thrusters," Woolley responded.

"Will that be enough?" Quigley asked.

Woolley didn't answer, either because he didn't know or because he was too busy flying the ship.

A bright blue sky flashed between flickers of cloud cover. The *Azure*'s hull groaned from the increased air friction. It zoomed toward the surface at breakneck speed. A white-topped mountain range fronted by a lush forest loomed ahead. Woolley leveled out the ship. The ground zipped by beneath them. When they met the mountains, jagged peaks seemed to reach for them like greedy claws. Just when Hapker was sure they'd crash, the land opened into a spread of tan. The *Azure* descended swiftly toward the waves of desert sand until he could make out individual dunes.

The ship quaked. His stomach heaved. Creaks made by stressed metal split his eardrums. They were still going too fast.

"Hold on!" Woolley shouted.

A tremendous jolt reverberated through Hapker's entire body. Then everything went black.

40
Desert Town

Blackness swirled. A fog shrouded Commander J.D. Hapker's brain as his awareness floated in nothingness. The sensation offered an odd sort of comfort, but curiosity drew him toward a ghostly image much like an inverted bruise. Pressure built with each wave of consciousness and culminating into a throbbing pain. Muffled voices grew into familiar words.

He opened his eyes to darkness and jerked in panic. A sharp hurt stabbed into his thigh.

"Hold still, Commander," a woman said. *Lieutenant Sharkey?* What was she doing? Why was she here?

He blinked, focusing on a blurry light until it became more distinct. A glow lit Sharkey's face as she held a flashlight. Her hair had come out of its bun and strayed in random tangles. *What happened?* Why was her hair such a mess? And why was it so dark?

She knelt before him, her light aimed down at his leg—the leg that radiated the pain. He jolted as the memory of the crash slammed into him. "Is everyone alright?"

"Stay still," she said. "I need to stop this bleeding."

Hapker touched his thigh and winced. A gooey stickiness coated his fingers.

Sharkey pressed down on his wound, making him grunt. "To answer your question, we're all fine. Sergeant Woolley is one hell of a pilot. And our seats protected us. But the crash broke some things from the cockpit, giving you and Woolley a few cuts."

"We're on the planet?" Hapker looked around, but the cabin was too dark. Not even emergency lights had come on.

"Yeah." A gurgled swish coupled with his pain ebbing in coolness indicated she'd added medical foam.

After she wrapped his wound, he groped for his harness release and clicked it open. He pressed his palms onto the armrests and pushed himself up. She tried to press him back down, but he deflected her arm. "We need to get out of here. They'll be coming for us soon."

He put his weight on both feet and tested his injured leg. A twang shot up, but it wasn't as bad as expected.

"Can you walk, Sir?" Sergeant Vizubi asked, making Hapker flinch since he hadn't known the man was behind him.

"I believe so."

Sharkey held his arm until he found his balance. He took a tentative step. His side burned as though someone had stabbed him. He checked it. Not finding any blood, their predicament motivated him to push through it. Vizubi's silhouette moved back as he felt his way down the aisle. The interior lightened as they progressed through the ship.

He continued to the exit. Sharkey kept her hand on his upper arm, offering guidance. The pain in his thigh became more tolerable with each step, but he was glad for her help. "Where's everyone else?"

"Outside," she replied. "We've already scrubbed our communications with Darwish. Now we're assessing damage and gathering supplies."

"And Private Fung is scouting the area," Vizubi added.

Hapker's burst of pride at their efficiency held a taint of guilt. "How long have I been out?"

"Not long, Sir."

Her tone didn't hold any worry, so he accepted her at her word. "Do we know what's going on with the battle?"

"Not a clue. But as much as I hope we're winning, I want that asshole to suffer."

"I feel exactly the same way," he said vehemently.

"He let us come here knowing we'd probably die," she replied through her teeth. "If the battle doesn't kill him, I will."

"Not if I get to him first."

A sliver of light beamed inside. Hapker fluttered his eyelids until they adjusted to the brightness. A flood of hot dry air whisked by him. He reached the exit and met a broad landscape of rippling sand, Sharkey hovering at his side like a mother hen as Vizubi led them out.

Quigley and Bari sorted supplies under the meager shade of a thruster, their nanite disguises still in place. Woolley came over from the front of the ship, his eyes roving over the hull. A bandage wrapped around his forehead, either because he had a good-sized injury or he needed to cover his damaged mask.

He seemed in better shape than the *Azure*, which resembled a half-burned log. Black streaks marred the surface, thicker at the nose and tapering to a few bruised spots at the rear. Dozens of pock marks ruined its once sleek complexion.

"Anything broken off?" he asked Woolley.

"This baby maintained its integrity, but the thrusters are shot."

"Can we fix them?"

Woolley shook his head. "Not here."

Hapker swallowed, his throat scraping against the dryness. He dipped his head and followed Sharkey and Vizubi to the supply pile. Nariya sat in the sand nearby, legs crossed and shoulders hunched as she squinted at her tablet.

"Any luck?" he asked.

"None, Sir," she answered without looking away from the screen. "I don't think our transceiver will work. But since we're here on their planet, maybe we can find another way to deploy the spyware."

Hapker didn't ask how she planned on doing that now that their plan had crashed and burned in a blaze of inglorious failure. "We may have company soon, so hide that."

She removed the thin data transfer device containing the spyware program from the tablet and slid it into a nanite-concealed pocket adhered to her side. Erikson had thought of everything for appearing as ordinary as possible. And not just the nanite masks or DTD compartment either. He'd created personal comms that went inside their ear canal and were invisible to most body scans.

He activated his comm using the non-invasive neural interface. "Comm check," he ordered.

Everyone, including Fung who he hadn't seen yet, responded without stopping their work. He tried contacting Darwish as well but got no response. He hoped the man had the foresight to share their frequency with the other PG-Force attackers, but it seemed unlikely. Everything had happened much too fast.

He filled his lungs and expanded his chest. They could survive this. Step one, find a secure place to hide. Step two, figure out how to contact the PG-Force. Other options were to help Nariya plant her virus or continue looking for Jori and the Cooperative prisoners. All these required the same action—to get the heck away from here.

He had a good team. Their mission could still succeed.

A thunderous whoosh reverberated through the cloudless sky. Hapker glanced up, shielding his eyes from the bright sun. "Sounds like incoming aircraft," he called out. "Let's get moving!"

Nariya scrambled to her feet. The others hefted packs of supplies over their shoulders. Hapker went to grab one too, but they'd all been claimed.

Fung darted from around the ship, beckoning with a sweep of her arm. "This way!"

Everyone picked up their pace, bootsteps kicking up sand and keeping them at an awkward trot. The motion aggravated the ache in Hapker's leg, but he endured it as Fung took them up the slope of a giant dune.

"Here, Sir," Bari said, handing him a phaser.

Although someone had already checked the weapon, Hapker gave it a quick inspection as he lumbered upward. Despite the throbbing in his leg, he kept up.

The roar of the jet neared. Hapker glanced over his shoulder. The airship seemed to come right for them. *Crap.* "Drop and roll!" he yelled.

Everyone obeyed. If the enemy used infrared targeting, the hot sand would disguise them.

Crackling reverberated from all sides as energy blasts cooked dozens of sand circles. Hapker covered his head, protecting himself from the hotter air burning around him. The smell of ozone tweaked his nostrils.

The jet whooshed by. Hapker clambered to his feet, ignoring the sand that clung to his face. "Everyone alright?"

"Good, Sir!" Sharkey called. The others replied the same.

Vizubi pulled a small silver pendant out from the front of his shirt and kissed it. Under different circumstances, Hapker would've been curious.

They scrambled onward. The jet veered around for another pass. Hapker praised their luck that it was just one jet. Surely the enemy was too busy with the battle to bother with a crashed ship. He glanced to the heavens where a distant fight between the PG-Force and MEGAs took place and wondered if his unintended sacrifice would pay off.

The roaring jet charged at them once more. Hapker pumped his arms and legs. The adrenaline coursing through his veins dulled the pain in his side and leg. They scrambled up another dune. *Please don't fire missiles*, he prayed.

The increased rumble of the jet sizzled his nerves and sent his heart into a sprint. He considered using the same tactic as before, but the top of the dune was so close.

"Here!" Fung shouted. She jumped over the rise and disappeared.

The others followed, vanishing in the blink of an eye. Hapker didn't register what'd happened until he reached the summit and found himself on the precipice of a wall. He sprang from the edge without thought and plummeted into freefall.

His feet smacked rubble and sent a sharp pang through his injured leg. A horrendous boom thundered above. Rocks and sand spewed around him, sending them tumbling. Shards struck his back. He covered his head and balled into a crouch. A wave of heat hot enough to curl his hair rolled over him.

The jet shot by, its engines bombarding his eardrums. Hapker squinted his eyes against the billowing grit. "Everyone alright?" he asked through the comm.

They all replied, even Nariya who sounded stressed yet determined. They moved on, hands shielding their eyes.

The dust thinned. Before them lay a small, ramshackle town. He glanced behind him. The ridge he'd jumped over was a wall. It wasn't that tall, but it kept the bulk of sand at bay.

The ground here was still sandy but dotted with more rocks and patches of shrubs. Dilapidated buildings in various states of disrepair indicated the place had been abandoned. The team raced over to a slanted building, half stone and half cream-colored composite material. A sign dangled from a chain above an uncovered doorway. Metal parts littered the interior and exterior, hinting it might've once been a repair shop. Vizubi and Quigley ducked inside and did a quick sweep while Bari and Fung guarded the outside.

"Clear!" Vizubi called.

"Stop," Hapker said before anyone else went in. "They're bound to suspect we came here. We can't sit around and wait for either a bomb or a ground force to find us."

Fung pointed with a head tilt. "We can try that."

Beside a nearby crumbled building sat a rusted vehicle. It had ribbed tires perfect for driving on sand, a bed for hauling, and an open yet reinforced cab. Its blotched tan paneling matched the desert. Come to think of it, this entire place blended with the sands. The passing jet would surely see it but perhaps it wouldn't show up on observation satellites. Whoever had set up this town didn't want to be noticed.

"Anyone know how to drive one?" Bari asked.

Vizubi jogged over, keeping his phaser rifle low but ready. Everyone followed. A lizard skittered by, darting into a crack of what had once been mud.

Bari and Vizubi inspected it. "It looks good," Bari said.

Hapker peered inside. Sand dusted the dash, seats, and floor. It couldn't have been sitting here for more than a day.

"Check around," Vizubi ordered.

His team obeyed. Hapker stayed, looking under the seats and in the storage compartments. He found a few odds and ends, but nothing useful. "I don't see a way to activate it."

"It requires a key of some sort," Vizubi said, "but I can probably figure out how to start it without one."

"How?"

Vizubi glanced about. He reopened the metal box Hapker had gone through and pulled out a screwdriver. "This will work." He shifted his rifle over his shoulder and scooted into the driver's seat. Bending to the side of the steering wheel, he stabbed the screwdriver into what Hapker guessed was a keyhole. He smacked the handle with his palm and drove the shaft in. Then he turned it. The engine cranked with the sputter of a dying man.

Hapker held his breath. Vizubi tried again. The vehicle rumbled to life. At the same time, the roar of the jet returned. He ducked low, pulling Nariya down with him, while the team abandoned their task and took cover.

The jet flew by without firing, likely because the pilot didn't know what to shoot at. A hot desert and an assortment of metal objects, including this vehicle, probably interfered with infrared scans.

"Get in the truck!" Hapker said into the comm. "Let's get out of here before they return with bigger weapons."

"Where do we go, Sir?" Vizubi asked.

"Anywhere but here. We'll come up with a better plan when we're in the clear."

The team darted over, ducking low. Hapker guided Nariya into the back. Sharkey jumped in beside her. The others climbed into the bed while Hapker took the front passenger seat.

"You can drive this thing?" he asked Vizubi.

"Most vehicles follow the same general concept, Sir. I'm sure I'll figure it out."

Hapker pointed at the screwdriver. "How'd you know how to do that?"

Vizubi investigated the dashboard. When he tapped something on the floor, the truck jerked into motion. "The most basic type of lock is a tumbler lock, which uses pins. The screwdriver shoved them aside."

"Someone's just emerged from the building on our right, Sir," Bari said. "He looks pissed."

The owner of the vehicle. Hapker willed down his guilt. He couldn't let himself worry about the man who was now stranded in the middle of the desert.

Vizubi sped away, leaving a spray of sand behind him. They bounced in their seats as he weaved around the broken buildings. When they cleared the town, he drove faster.

Hapker listened for the jet but didn't hear much over the rumbling of the engine. The sky looked empty too, but not the ground they'd just driven over. "Don't go too fast. They might notice all the sand we kicked up."

Vizubi slowed. He craned his head and peered upward. "You all see anything?"

Everyone glanced about but no one could confirm.

"Maybe they went back to get a bigger bomb," Quigley said.

"Way to stay positive," Bari mumbled.

"Let's hope we're long gone by then," Hapker replied.

They drove until they happened upon a paved road. No sand covered it, suggesting frequent use. Vizubi turned onto it, likely thinking that the jet pilot wouldn't be able to distinguish them from their own citizens.

Hapker finally took in a full breath. His reprieve only lasted a moment.

Now to find someplace secure and decide on our next move.

41
Unmods

The bright yellow sun harangued them like an overeager drill sergeant. Commander J.D. Hapker would've wiped the sweat from his brow had the stifling heat not already evaporated it. A sticky grit coated his exposed skin while the rest of him felt like a damp towel left in a sauna. Sweat drizzled down his spine and pooled at his waistband, his underarms were as slick as mucky pond water, his inner thighs chafed like wet sandpaper, and his shoes squelched with every step. He'd hated giving up his enviro-suit with its thermal regulation system, but blending in with the populace took priority.

He hefted a pack, thankful to Vizubi's team for having the foresight to stuff them with both provisions and their personal items. Too bad he hadn't thought to bring a hat or sunglasses. His face would look like a fat tomato soon if he didn't find some shade.

They'd opted to keep their weapons but hid them on their person as well as possible. Hapker wore his under Arbour's green and blue striped shirt. It wasn't a good color for reflecting the sun's heat. Nor did it provide any camouflage. But its looseness allowed for both weapon concealment and airflow.

Quigley slammed the vehicle door shut. "Do we really want to abandon our only way out of here?"

"The owner might've reported it stolen," Hapker replied. "We should get as far away from it as possible."

Bari tucked his phaser in his pants under his shirt. "I know we decided we'd have better luck hiding in a crowd, but we're bound to stand out."

"Keep an eye out," Vizubi said. "If you have a chance to snag some local attire, go for it. Just don't get caught."

"What about facial recognition technology?" Quigley asked. "I mean, I we have masks and all, but they have our fake files."

"Let's hope this place is too poor for that," Fung replied.

"We all understand the risks," Hapker said. "Hiding out in the middle of nowhere will get us nowhere."

He took in a lungful of hot, stifling air and peered at the city. A cluster of high-rise buildings stood in the center like sunbaked sentinels while here, just within the outer edge of the city limits, sand encroached among ramshackle shops and abodes.

The plan was to find a place here to hide out, such as an abandoned building. They'd venture out from time to time, mingle with the populace, and gather intel. With any luck, they'd either learn the location of their people or come across a local communications station.

Everyone stayed close as they ambled down the cobbled street like they belonged. Narrow alleys shot off from a crowded boulevard. At first glance, it looked like pure pandemonium. A hodgepodge of small-time vendors packed the sidewalks. Hundreds of people teemed through the corridor together with buggies, scooters, bicycles, and even a donkey-drawn cart.

The smell was an overwhelming mixture of savory food from the vendors and fetid garbage clumped along the curbs. A corresponding clamor assaulted Hapker's ears. Yelling, laughing, motorized vehicles, and unidentifiable clangs and clatters accentuated the buzzing undercurrent.

Shade seemed the biggest currency as the carts and stalls with the most customers were the ones shaded by timeworn umbrellas and canopies. The entire scene melded into bland color. The vendors tried to stand out against the endless sandstone buildings, but their wares held little excitement and their displays had long since faded into chipped paint and weathered textiles. Even the people's clothing was drab. Most wore loose light-colored robes and unadorned headgear.

Oddly, none of them had any obvious cybernetics.

Hapker and the team stood out like zebras among a herd of wildebeests. Fortunately, a bright shirt here and a fancy blouse there indicated other strangers came here too. An occasional finger pointed at them. A trio of women huddled close and whispered, their eyes furtive. An old man with sallow cheeks ogled them as he passed. Two men manning a stall folded their arms and glared. But most people went about their business as usual.

"Everybody's looking at us," Quigley muttered.

"Not everybody," Vizubi replied.

"This won't work," she said. "We look like idiots."

"Cut it," Vizubi ordered in a low tone to avoid drawing attention.

"We're exposed out here, Sir," she grumbled, also keeping her voice down. "We need to find someplace to hole up—and quick."

Hapker shot her a scowl. "We're not out here sightseeing, Corporal," he whispered sharply.

Her eyes darkened but she wisely didn't reply.

Hapker gritted his teeth. Her challenges were getting more persistent. Despite the stressful situation, it was unacceptable.

He motioned them off to the side where a pile of garbage encouraged the city dwellers to keep their distance, then faced her with a glower.

"If you have any alternatives, Corporal, share them—constructively." He held a stare until she looked away, then turned about, ready to head off once more.

Vizubi lingered with Quigley. "Corporal," he said to her in a private tone. "Lose the attitude."

"I just don't understand why we're listening to a PG-Force washout, Sir," she replied.

Hapker whirled around once more. "That's enough, Corporal." He struggled to keep his voice low. "We all contributed ideas for our next move. Just because I didn't choose yours doesn't mean you get to pout like an insolent child."

Her lips pressed into a tight line as her eyes burned.

"He's right," Vizubi added. She shot him an incredulous look. He ignored it and faced Hapker. "My apologies, Sir. I *do not* tolerate this sort of behavior. If you'd like, I'll address this further."

As the target of Quigley's disrespect, it was Hapker's place to reprimand her. However, punishment wasn't practical in these circumstances. Vizubi had already earned her respect. Perhaps she'd be more likely to straighten up under his scrutiny.

"I'll give you a few minutes." He stepped away, but not out of earshot. It was too crowded for that, and they couldn't risk getting separated. "Make it quick."

Vizubi turned to her with his arms crossed. "Corporal, what the hell is your problem?"

She shifted her weight from one foot to the other. "We wouldn't be in this mess if it wasn't for him, Sir."

"Bullshit. You volunteered for this—the same as us."

"But he's not… He's not *one of us*," she replied, slightly supplicant. "Not anymore."

"You don't know all the facts of that situation. Standing up to a superior officer who gave an immoral order takes courage," Vizubi said. "And before you get the idea in your head that you're being brave by challenging him, let me tell you right now that what you're doing is *childish belligerence* and we don't have time for that bullshit."

Hapker's brows shot up along with his respect for Sergeant Vizubi.

Quigley hung her head, looking genuinely remorseful. "I'm sorry, Sir. I guess the major's betrayal really got to me. If the commander was still a PG-Force officer, he might've been told the entire plan."

A trickle of understanding filtered in. Hapker had wondered the same thing.

"I doubt it," Vizubi said with a sour twist to his lips. "Darwish is a glory-hound who only looks out for himself. He needed a patsy and we were it."

"You're probably right, Sir," she replied meekly.

"I know I'm right, and so do you. So I don't want to hear another insolent remark out of you again. Is that clear?"

"Yes, Sir," she repeated.

"Alright. Let's go."

She caught Hapker's eye and dipped her head, looking sufficiently chastised. Hapker returned the gesture, letting go of his inclination to hold a grudge.

They continued down the street, obnoxious noises surrounding their prickling silence. Private Bari eventually broke it by asking whether a particular alley was a feasible place to disappear. But like the alleyways of just about every culture, depraved souls lurked there. The last thing the team needed was to get trapped in a narrow walkway surrounded by cutthroats.

Bari stepped up beside Hapker. "Sir?"

"What's up, Private?" he replied, keeping his voice low.

"Our people are being taken, presumably to turn them into you-know-what," he whispered.

"Presumably."

"So if they need subjects, why not use their own population? I mean, that's assuming all these people aren't genetically enhanced."

"That's a good question, but I don't have an answer."

A round man a hand shorter than Hapker stepped before them. "You're not from around here, are ya?"

"What gave it away?" Fung asked, sarcasm laced through her tone.

Hapker maneuvered in front of her, giving her a disapproving glare, then faced the man with a smile. "No. We're just passing through."

"Passing through, eh?" The man chuckled. His belly jiggled and his beady eyes twinkled knowingly.

Hapker's spine tingled. "Yeah."

His wariness must've shown on his face because the man's expression turned down into seriousness. "The MEGAs put out an alert for you, but don't worry. Most folks here won't learn of it."

"Why not?"

"Well, you're in luck." The man smiled once more, bubbling his cheeks. "You're among unmods."

"Unmods?"

"Yep." The man swept out his hand. "The people here can barely afford tech. So no radios or video receivers—and definitely no implants."

"But isn't this a MEGA planet?" Sharkey asked.

"It's ruled by MEGA-Man and his MEGA cronies, but that don't mean we're all MEGAs. A lot of us are against augmentations, but there's not much we can do about it when the only way to get a decent job is if you have special abilities."

"Huh?" Quigley said, cocking her hip in one direction and her head in another.

Hapker agreed with her sentiment. It sounded like the mirror image of the Cooperative.

He took in the man before him. For someone claiming difficulty in getting a decent job, he sure dressed well. The fabric of his clothes had a nice sheen and a ribbon of color along the cuffs and collar. His even-tanned skin was smooth—unlike the leathery faces of many others here. Was he a wealthy merchant, a government official, or something else?

"But you have tech," he stated, referring to the man's knowledge of the alert.

The man shrugged. "Just a tablet. I can afford a little more than most folks. But I ain't no MEGA." He scowled, giving Hapker hope he could be an ally.

"So why help us?"

The man smiled. His small black eyes narrowed in a way that almost looked shrewd. "I want to help you. I got me a trailer you can hide in."

Hapker glanced at his team. Either this was fortuitous—or it was a trap. Sharkey's eyes roved over the man, signifying she believed the latter. Nariya leaned in as though hopeful. Everyone else's faces remained blank, giving nothing away.

Hapker studied their surroundings. They didn't know the city well enough to figure out a good place to hide, and the more they wandered around here, the greater the chance of being spotted by someone else aware of the alert.

Despite their desperate situation, he remained wary.

"I know there's a battle going on up there." The man pointed to the sky. "This world ain't right. Maybe by helping you, you can help me."

Hapker's gut twisted with misgiving. "How?"

The man flicked his hand. "Don't worry. I'm not asking ya for anything. I'm just thinking that if you're here, you're here for a reason. And mayhap that reason will get us both what we want."

"And what's that?"

"An end to our oppression."

The man spoke with such earnestness that Hapker was inclined to believe him. But he wasn't about to trust just yet. Besides, he and his team were posing as MEGAs. Did this man assume they weren't or was that in the alert? They were in trouble regardless.

He turned to the others. "Thoughts?"

"I don't trust him," Quigley said.

"You don't trust anybody," Bari replied.

"Yeah, well." She shrugged.

Hapker fixed his gaze on her. "If you have a better idea, now's your chance to speak up."

"We're screwed no matter what we do—Sir," she added with belated respect. "Might as well."

Enough of them nodded with agreement that Hapker returned to the man. "Alright. We'll take you up on your offer."

"Right this way." The man motioned his hand. "My name's Ferdi, in case you're wondering."

Hapker thought he caught a gleam in the man's eye but couldn't be certain. His insides squirmed like a salted slug, but a glance at the crowd made him keep going.

"Herra," he said, barely remembering Arbour's first name.

Ferdi weaved around the people to the edge of a square, then led them through a dilapidated building. Hapker felt better inside, but not by much. An enclosure could mean a trap.

The shop was only a little cooler. It contained a clutter of fabricated kitchenware and appliances placed haphazardly on shelves or stacked on the floor. Ferdi took them to a door at the back. He poked his head out, then waved for them to follow. Sharkey and Vizubi followed him out, phasers concealed but ready. When they gave the all-clear, he and the others exited into a dark alley.

Trepidation wound through his insides. Ragged walls pressed in around them. Light from the sun barely reached here, creating an oppressive gloom.

"My vehicle's over here."

"Can't you just hide us somewhere?" Sharkey asked. "A basement? A broom closet?"

"The cybers are thorough," Ferdi replied in an annoyed tone. "If they find you, you'll have no way out. I'm offering to get you away from here."

Hapker eyed the shadows created by junk piles and garbage bins. "And where will you take us?"

"Someplace a bit more open but also with more hiding places that are shielded against the cybers' sensors." Ferdi's gloating smile increased Hapker's apprehension.

A cat leapt off a dumpster with a hiss. It darted off, then disappeared into the shadows. Hapker trod warily through the pungent trash littering the tight alley as the feeling of getting caught in a trap intensified.

Ferdi led them to another alley where a battered truck blocked the way. The vehicle was wider than the one they'd left behind. Its once-white enclosed trailer bore a thick layer of grime while the red paint on the cab had mostly chipped away to reveal dull grey.

Hapker eyed the cracked windshield and an outer mirror affixed with tape. The vehicle tilted to one side, its skewed front bumper underlining its questionable reliability.

A round woman wearing a desert-styled robe colored with a faded flower pattern hopped out of the cab. "Who are they?"

"Friends. Cybers are after 'em," Ferdi replied.

The woman scanned them with narrow eyes and shot Ferdi a questioning look. Something must've passed between them because her demeanor flipped like a switch. "Back here," she said with a friendly smile. "There's room in the trailer. Not much, so you'll have to squeeze tight, but we'll get you away."

The team held their phasers close and scouted the area. Ferdi opened the trailer, revealing a mess of junk. Hapker eyed it, wondering how the eight of them would fit.

"I hear something," Fung said into the comm. She hovered against the corner at the end of the bisecting alley. "Possibly footsteps—and lots of 'em."

Darn it. Hapker indicated for the others to get in despite the misgiving crawling through him. He got in too, his leg and side shooting him a mild protest.

Vizubi pulled himself up with a grunt. "I don't like this, Sir," he whispered.

Sharkey came in next, vaulting like a graceful dancer. "Something's off. He says he's against MEGAs and all, but he's taking an awfully big risk for a few off-worlders."

"Agreed," Hapker said. "I'm open to suggestions."

He joined her in regarding the surrounding buildings. None of the windows were low enough to reach. And the walls, though rough stone, had little purchase to climb. "There's a door there." He pointed. "And there."

"We don't know what's on the other side," Sharkey replied as others squeezed in around her.

"Ferdi might," Vizubi added, grunting again when Bari stepped on his foot.

Hapker sighed. "Either way, we'd have to trust him."

"Definitely MEGAs," Fung said into the comm. She left her corner and dashed over. "Five of them heading this direction, and they're on the hunt."

"We fight." Vizubi replied with a resigned frown.

Sharkey wore the same dubious expression. "Yeah, but all we've got are cast-off phasers. Who knows what those MEGAs have."

Hapker ran his hand down to his chin. Fung's harried features as she lunged in last into the truck decided him. "We stay in here."

"Alright now," Ferdi said, his head swiveling from them to the other alley as he grasped the tether at the end of the hatch. "I gotta close this." The panic stricken on his face retracted some of Hapker's suspicions.

The door slid down with a metallic clunk, sealing them in darkness. Nariya whimpered.

"This is a terrible idea," Quigley grumbled.

"Agreed," Hapker replied. "But if we engage in a fight, they'll figure out where we are and alert others."

"Fighting is better than cowering in here like trapped rats."

"Speak for yourself," Bari said. "At least here we have a chance."

"If that fat bastard doesn't betray us." She squirmed. "Damn it. I've got Woolley's pits in my face, someone's leg between my butt cheeks, and this place smells like burnt grease and monkeys."

"Thanks for the visual," Bari mumbled.

"Will you two quit wasting air," Fung added. Hapker could almost see her rolling her eyes.

The truck rumbled to life. It jerked into motion, making Hapker step back onto someone's foot. The ride jostled and his leg twinged, reminding him of his injury.

"What's our next move, Sir?" Sharkey asked.

"Let's see where he brings us."

"I have a suspicion it won't be anyplace good," Fung said.

"I'm inclined to agree, Private." But this was their only viable option, and they all knew it.

The ride smoothed out, making Hapker suspect they were on a highway. After an uncomfortable silence, the vehicle slowed, then stopped. His heart pattered as several minutes crawled by and no one opened the hatch.

"What do you think is going on?" Woolley asked.

"A checkpoint?" Sharkey said.

"Could be," Hapker replied. "Stay quiet." He gripped his weapon as his eardrums pounded. Muffled voices from outside turned everyone inside into statues. The odor worsened with their combined tension, stifling his breath.

Finally, the truck got moving again and the ride smoothed out once more. Hapker relaxed as much as the strained circumstances allowed.

"Anyone else have to go to the bathroom?" Bari asked. "Or itch their nose?"

"Shut up," Quigley responded. A half second later, "Damn you, Bari."

He emitted a low chuckle.

"Shush," Hapker hissed. Some people dealt with stress through humor, but this wasn't the time.

The truck slowed to a stop once more. Just when he suspected they were stuck at another checkpoint, the hatch slid open. He shielded his eyes against the blinding light.

"Well, shit," Sharkey said, echoing his dread.

A dozen soldiers outfitted with various cybernetics stood outside with phaser rifles aimed at them. Vizubi and the others snapped their weapons up too.

"Stand down!" the biggest soldier bellowed. His metal arms bore fine segments like snake scales. The same with his fingers, which hinted at a flexibility and precision that real hands didn't have. His sleeveless steel-grey uniform displayed more adornments than the rest, marking him as the leader.

Misgiving plummeted to the bottom of Hapker's gut. All that trouble they went through to escape and now here they were at a standoff. However, the MEGAs hadn't opened fire on them. Perhaps they didn't want them dead after all.

"Not until you explain yourself," he said. "We came here to join your cause and you shot us down!"

"You're with them," the cyborg replied without lowering his rifle.

"Who? Those PG-Force ships that appeared out of nowhere? We had no idea they were there." Hapker let the truth of his words ring out, hoping one of them had the ability to sense it the way Gottfried had.

The cyborg didn't respond. Silence stretched as his face remained void of any emotion. Hapker only hoped the man was having a conversation through a communication implant with his superiors.

"You will lower your weapons," the cyborg finally stated.

"And then what?"

"We will take you to our processing facility."

Hapker swallowed. That's what they'd wanted all along. Nothing had gone their way since the moment they'd arrived, so he prayed this time would be different.

"Stand down," Hapker ordered. The team complied without complaint, though Quigley's mouth curled with distaste.

Ferdi appeared, wearing a gloating smile.

"What the hell?" Sharkey said to him.

Ferdi shrugged. "I may have fibbed a little."

"But I thought you were an unmod."

"I am but I don't wanna be. Turning you in gets me and my wife here moved closer to the top of the upgrade list."

"Bastard." Quigley hopped down and spit on the ground before his feet. Her brow scrunched so hard, Hapker suspected she'd lash out. He almost wished she would. It would serve the man right.

He jumped beside her instead, winced from the pain that shot up his leg, and grasped her shoulder. "I hear the MEGAs want to make everyone like them," he said to Ferdi as he placed himself between him and the angry corporal. "So why not just wait? I'm sure their list can't be that long."

"It is when they have a galaxy full of subjects who are more worthy than us desert rats."

Bari hopped down. "But that doesn't make sense. If they consider you inferior, wouldn't it be a good reason to enhance you?"

Ferdi darkened. "I have no clue what MEGA-Man has against us, boy. All I know is we gotta wait on some damned list."

After everyone got out of the truck, the soldiers performed a methodical search. They took their weapons and relieved them of their belongings—all while Ferdi and his wife beamed with pleasure.

"What will happen to us?" Hapker asked.

None of the soldiers responded as they patted them down and cuffed them. When they were done, they lined up in columns and stared straight ahead. Their stony faces reminded him of the MEGA soldiers on the *Defender*—but more lifeless. He shivered.

The soldiers led them to another vehicle, this one the opposite of the other in every way. It looked like a giant bullet with a swiveling turret on top. And its smooth armored paneling shone as though it had just come out of the factory.

Hapker swallowed, feeling like he was walking to his execution.

42
Interrogation

Echoing bootsteps and chinking metal created a foreboding atmosphere as the otherwise soundless MEGA soldiers escorted their captives down a stark white hall. Like a robotic assembly line stamping together parts, they marched. Their bristling weaponry and unrelenting focus sent chills down Commander J.D. Hapker's spine.

The extent of cybernetics embedded in the soldiers dried his throat into a parched desert. They had auditory enhancements of various designs planted over or replacing their ears. Some were small while others looked like palm-sized earmuffs. Their biometric optics were just as diverse. One or both eye sockets contained glass or metallic lenses shaped like ovals or circles. Only one soldier appeared to have flesh and blood eyes, but the way he stared straight forward without blinking made Hapker suspect they were manufactured.

Or maybe he's an android. The man next to him certainly resembled one. While most soldiers had at least one mechanical appendage, he had arms and legs constructed of titanium pieces fit together like the scales of a snake. He even had a razor-edged dagger embedded into his forearm, and what looked like an energy weapon attached to the other. If this was MEGA-Man's idea of evolution, humanity was in serious trouble.

While no two soldiers had the same cybernetics, they all carried identical top-of-the line phaser rifles. Their uniforms matched as well—each a polished metal grey that hugged their frames like an extra skin.

The cyber-soldiers led them through a security door and into a long, wide hall. No windows or doors lined the way, only an empty white corridor that seemed to go on forever. A cylindrical cleaning bot rolled by, but otherwise they were the only ones trespassing this pristine place. It made him sick to think about how many MEGAs were in Cooperative territory wreaking havoc, but fewer MEGAs here increased their chances of success.

After a monotonous and ominous trek, they came upon a long rectangular window. A stone-faced MEGA with more cybernetic headgear than Hapker had seen thus far sat on the other side, eyeing them with detached scrutiny.

He willed his heart to slow, reminding himself that this was what they'd wanted. This hall might lead to the Cooperative captives. Or perhaps they'd be taken to a place for Nariya to plant her virus. Better yet, maybe he'd run into Jori. His chest tightened with hope.

The soldiers led them through a giant contraption segmenting the corridor. Hapker held his breath as an almost indiscernible hum ran through him, indicating it was a larger and more sophisticated scanner. What if it detected their nanite masks? Or their comms? Or Nariya's DTD? So much of their mission depended on luck.

If the scanner had found anything, no one pointed it out as the soldiers led them through another security door into a holding area. A series of clear plasti-glass doors lined either side of the walkway, each with a corresponding keypad. Inside each cell was as bright and clean as everything else they'd seen here.

And all were empty, causing Hapker's heart to fall. *No Cooperative prisoners here*. He hoped they hadn't already been turned into MEGAs.

The soldiers steered Nariya and Sharkey into the first cell. They weren't rough about it, but Nariya squeaked when they abruptly released her and caused her to stumble. She rushed back around only to have the plasti-glass door shut her in. "Let me out!" she cried with panic stricken through her face.

Sharkey placed her arm over her shoulder. Only the fine lines created by the tightening of her facial muscles gave away her emotions.

Hapker watched helplessly as the soldiers locked the others in, two-by-two. The crew each wore a different disconcerted look— even Quigley, though she tried to hide it with a scowl.

He attempted to jerk his arm out of the grip of his cyber-armed captor. "This isn't necessary. We came here for your help." The soldier didn't waver. "I want to speak to whoever is in charge here. We're your allies, damn it!" he cursed uncharacteristically.

They shut Bari in last, leaving only Hapker. Rather than put him in another cell, they led him around to the exit.

"Where are you taking me?" he asked.

The soldiers didn't answer. Hapker swiveled his head, throwing a bewildered look at the crew. Vizubi replied by crossing his arms and scowling. Sharkey planted her palms on the glass. Her brows furrowed with worry as she watched him pass by.

Apprehension seized his chest. An image of him stretched out on an operation table getting his limbs replaced with robotics urged him to resist, but he had to keep up the guise of wanting to become a MEGA.

"Where are you taking me?" Hapker demanded anyway, prepared to fight regardless of how he was supposed to want to be here.

The soldiers brought him back to the wide, empty corridor. Rather than walk down it, they stopped and faced a section of the wall. Before he could ask what they were doing, it slid away to reveal a room.

They tossed him inside. He nearly stumbled into the only chair. It was simple with a flat seat and no armrests, but his heart jumped into a pulsing rhythm anyway. He found his footing and rushed to the exit only to have the wall slide back into place. The finality of it clutched his throat.

A pure white room surrounded him. Every wall was seamless, including where the door had been. He didn't even see a recess for lights, though the space was as bright as daylight. The only thing in here beside himself was that simple metal chair, sitting there like a lonely puzzle piece.

"Sit," a voice said.

Hapker glanced about, trying to find the source. A window appeared. His breath caught.

A man with a high forehead and long chin sat on the other side, wearing a flat smile. "Sit."

Hapker swallowed as his heart thudded like drums of doom. He eyed the chair with askance before easing himself into it. He worked the dryness from his mouth and tried to remember what he and his crew had rehearsed. If the MEGAs questioned them separately, they had to tell the same story. They also needed to avoid lying in case a MEGA had the same sentio ability as Gottfried.

"Why am I here?" he asked. "Me and my friends came to you, hoping you'd take us in, but we got shot down instead. Is this how you treat all your allies?"

The man ignored the question. "Who are you?"

Hapker couldn't say without his lie giving him away. "We already sent you that information."

The stone-face soldier seemed to accept his response. "What are you doing here?"

"We told you that too."

"So you did. But if that's so, why did you bring an armada?"

"That wasn't us," Hapker replied vehemently, glad to not have to dance around his words. "We had no idea they were there."

The man leaned forward with narrow eyes. Hapker repeated that truth in his head and stared back.

"Then why do you have weapons?"

"You mean our phasers? Precautionary. We knew from the moment we left we might face danger."

Hapker resisted the urge to squirm beneath the man's gaze. *Coming here was a bad idea*, he thought. *They won't accept us.*

"Our citizen seems to think you're unmods," the man said.

"He made that assumption on his own. We just went with it because we were desperate."

"Your words ring true, but the timing of your arrival raises some concerns."

"Is that why you attacked us?"

The man dipped his head.

"So now what?" Hapker asked.

"We will question you further… At another time… When this battle is over."

So the battle is still going on? He hoped the Cooperative would win but cut that thought short before it solidified. *Best not to think of this now, in case he's also a mind-reader.* He shifted in his seat. "Until then, why not treat us as guests rather than prisoners?"

The man cocked an eyebrow. "Can I trust you?"

"Can I trust *you*?" Hapker countered. "Listen, I'm not the best at negotiations or peacemaking, but treating those who come to you for help with a little dignity will go a long way."

The man's flat smile returned. "Once again, your words ring true. I will see what I can do."

Hapker's mouth fell open. He snapped it back shut as hope swelled in his chest. "Really?" It seemed too easy, but if they took them to an area with less security, then maybe luck had finally turned in their favor.

"You raise a valid point," the man replied. "The cooperation of as many people as possible is crucial to our success, so we'll do what we can to make you and your friends more comfortable until we reach a full understanding."

Hapker would've shouted out with glee had misgiving not crawled through his insides.

43
Inside Their Heads

A pang grumbled in Terkeshi's stomach. He wet his mouth—or tried to. This storage room was great for hiding, but not much else. Why hadn't he stuffed his pockets with rations before leaving the ship? *Stupid.*

He'd had too much training to forget the need for food, water, and shelter. It didn't matter that he was on a ship rather than a planet.

All these crates and not one of them contained foodstuff. How did cyborgs eat?

He should be out there searching, but his hunger conflicted with his fear of running into lifeless soldiers. He'd trained against virtual opponents, but his ability to detect lifeforces was such a big part of who he was that he'd never been as good at it as Jori.

A hardness formed in his gut at the thought of his dead brother, and it reminded him to check on his mother and friends. Since he didn't need to leave the safety of this place to do that, he set aside the other issue and concentrated on them instead.

Locating the general direction where everyone had gathered was easy. His mother's lifeforce leapt to the forefront, not because it was strong but because it was familiar.

A warmth spread over him. Her emotions shifted, indicating that she knew he was there. Since she also had the ability to read minds, he sent a question about her wellbeing. She emitted a mild unease. Too bad he couldn't hear her thoughts in return.

Wait. Maybe there's another way. He willed himself into her, half expecting her to put up her mental defenses. But a gentle tug pulled him in, followed by a full embrace.

Splashes of color spread across his internal vision. The shock of finding himself as his mother almost made him hop right back out.

"It's alright," she said out loud, her voice muffled oddly. "I was hoping you'd try this. Can you hear me?"

He mentally answered an affirmative.

"Good." Her pleasure radiated pride. "Can you also see what I see?"

"*Yes,*" he replied in his head. "*I can't believe this works,*" his monkey-brain thought.

She laughed softly. "It's certainly a unique ability. You're a sentio but not an imperium or extraho, yet somehow something more."

His heart swelled. He set aside the boost to his ego and focused on the situation. "*What's going on there? Where are you?*"

"We're in a huge auditorium."

She turned, showing him the vast space crowded with people. She scanned those he knew first. Some rested on blankets on the floor while others sat together in groups. Although an undercurrent of uncertainty ran through them, they appeared at ease.

She moved on to the other areas. Toradons weren't the only ones camping out. People from different planetary origins gathered around their own temporary set-ups. The diversity reminded him of the Cooperative except none wore PG-Force or PCC uniforms.

"Many of these people were abducted," she said. "Mining colonies, cruise liners, space stations. From all over. MEGAs come through here now and then to ask if anyone is interested in converting. No one is being threatened or hurt, though."

"*Is anybody agreeing to augmentations?*"

"Several," she replied. "Fortunately, it seems the MEGAs don't have enough facilities to accommodate all the requests right away because there's a waiting list."

Chusho.

Her emotions spiked with a reprimand. "*Sorry,*" he said, realizing she'd heard his curse. "*What about the ones who won't convert? Will they let them go?*"

"I haven't learned of anyone being allowed to leave. Major Jingyu has asked those very questions, but they merely smile and skirt the question with nonsense about evolution."

Terk's gut soured.

"In the meantime," she continued, "they're making sure we're comfortable and have everything we need."

Eagerness jerked inside him. "*How? Do they have food fabricors?*"

"Yes, but they also bring us fresh food."

That means they have a kitchen somewhere.

"Probably so," she said in reply to his side-thought. "It's brought in by several serving bots from over here." She turned in a direction that his senses determined was about a hundred degrees to the right from where he was in relation to her.

He sighed inwardly—maybe outwardly too, though he couldn't tell in this state.

"Be careful," she said despite him not making a coherent thought about his grudging resolve to go search for food.

"*You too*," he replied. "*I'll check on you now and then for updates.*"

"Please do." Worry spread through her, along with a comforting sensation that he interpreted as well wishes.

He returned to himself and opened his eye. Gaichu rested his head on his lap and thumped his tail. The first time Terk had moved his consciousness to someone else, the pup had burst into a yapping so frantic that Baba Airi had come running. Gaichu had since learned it wasn't anything to be worried about but refused to abandon his side until he came back.

Terk patted his head and sighed. "Alright. Let's get some dinner."

Taking the first step to leave the storage area was the hardest part. He kept imagining super-soldiers with no lifeforce patrolling the halls. But once he was out, he couldn't stop moving.

Sneaking from intersection to intersection broke him into a cool sweat. The corridors were eerily vacant, but this only made him more anxious. It was like a ticking time bomb with no sign of when it'd go off.

He approached the next crossway with light steps. His vision focalized as he inched along the wall. Gaichu stepped in front of him just before he reached it.

"Move," he whispered and nudged the pup's side.

Gaichu ignored him. His ears perked forward as a low rumble escaped his throat.

Terk halted. His senses detected nothing. He tilted his head, trying to listen. At first, the only sound emanated from a whisper of air from a nearby vent. Then came a faint rhythmic thudding. The nature of these empty halls made it difficult to determine which direction it originated from, but Gaichu faced the corridor to his left.

As the tromping amplified, Terk eased back the way he'd come. Fearing it'd reach him before he returned to the previous intersection, he tried a nondescript door. It clicked open. He peered inside and met darkness. *Unless MEGAs hang out in closets, this should be safe.*

He expelled a breath and slipped in. Gaichu followed. A light flicked on automatically. He spun about, finding only shelves of soft blankets and similar items. Some were thin, some thick. By the precise way they were folded, he suspected they were newly fabricated. The sheer number of packed shelves hinted that the people the MEGAs held in their auditorium were just the beginning.

Gaichu growled at the door. Terk pressed against it and clasped the handle tight, hoping the thing or things outside wouldn't enter. Cadent thuds grew louder as several footsteps approached, causing the door handle to vibrate.

His muscles tightened as the sounds neared. Sweat poured down his face. His heart threatened to burst.

As quickly as they'd come, the footsteps receded. He swallowed the dryness from his throat but waited until Gaichu relaxed and looked up at him.

Terk slumped against the door and slid to the floor. Gaichu climbed into his lap and nudged a wet nose into his hands.

"How did you know they were there?" he asked as he rubbed up and down the dog's neck.

Gaichu only licked him in reply.

An idea brightened. *What if... No, it couldn't possibly work. He's just a dog.*

He gave it a shot anyway and concentrated. His awareness flung into the pup with little effort. His perception shifted in such a profound way that he wondered if something had gone wrong. It wasn't only the faded brownish yellows or the muted blues of his vision. A myriad of other sensations flooded into him so quickly that his brain struggled to process them all.

Clanging, rustling, thumping, ticking, and other noises Terk couldn't put a name to drifted in. Gaichu's emotions didn't change, giving him the impression they were too distant to be a concern. Then there were the smells. He'd noticed the cleaning smell throughout this entire facility, but it was amplified through Gaichu. And although the sharpness of it dominated, other odors filtered in.

The floor had a manufactured stink, as did the printed shelving. Even the linens held a synthetic scent. He smelled himself, too. Terk would've described it as pungent, but Gaichu felt contented by it.

Another stench trickled in—one that grabbed Gaichu's attention. His ears perked and he stared at the door as though he could see through it. He couldn't, but the sounds and even the trace scents filtering in gave him enough information to know a threat approached. Terk discerned footsteps and an odor akin to him but twisted with wrongness.

Terk remained in Gaichu's head, knowing the pup's alertness would tell him the right time to act. When the scents and sounds faded, Terk came back to himself. He blinked away the odd sensations.

Gaichu returned to his lap and licked his face. Terk rubbed his ears. "I'm gonna have to quit calling you a stupid dog, aren't I?" Gaichu's clueless look made him chuckle. "Never mind."

He left the closet and continued the search. Taking cues from Gaichu allowed him to sneak through the corridors with greater ease. His heart rate normalized, his muscles loosened, and the tremendous weight that had been bearing down on him lessened.

The next hallway terminated at a wide set of double doors. Both had windows but he couldn't see much from this angle. Gaichu let out a growl and retreated. Terk followed him until they were back around the corner, but he didn't leave just yet. He jumped into Gaichu's head and took in the sensations. The human wrongness struck him, but the odd sounds intrigued him. Nothing like footsteps reverberated beyond. It was more like a simmering gurgle. Could this be the kitchen?

None of the noises indicated people walking about. His clenching stomach won out over his fear. He came back to himself and peeked around the corner. After staring for nearly a minute and seeing no movement from the other side of the door, he tiptoed over. Gaichu whined.

"Just a quick look," he reassured the pup.

Terk swallowed the lump in his throat as he neared. The windows were only about thirty centimeters square and slightly above eye level. He wondered why until he got close enough to see they opened. Ventilation for a kitchen made sense.

His mouth watered in anticipation. He rose on his tiptoes and peered through.

His throat clenched and blood drained from his head, leaving him with an intense chill that infiltrated down to his bones. This was no kitchen, but it was definitely some sort of preparation area.

Row upon row of tall tanks spread out over a giant space. Each one contained a body suspended in fluid. Tubes extended from their orifices. Wires connected to heads and chests. None of them moved. Nor did they have lifeforces. Yet he knew those bodies lived.

Their diversity hinted that they'd once been individuals. Now they were being turned into a collective force, confirming his worst fear.

His stomach hardened as though someone had dropped a stone into it.

"Fuck!"

44

A Vision of Loveliness

The moment they'd been hoping for spread out before them. A diversity of people camped out in the vast auditorium. Many huddled in shelters built of random plastic or metal parts. They'd propped up blankets using broken pipes or other items, creating additional private spaces. Despite the crowd, some groups also constructed a junk-heaped border around their tiny communities.

Commander J.D. Hapker estimated at least a hundred individuals just within his field of vision. The sultry odor of bodies and the cacophony echoing throughout the space hinted at hundreds more. He gaped, the sight both overwhelming and promising.

Lieutenant Sharkey leaned in and mumbled in his ear, "I hope the captain's family is in here somewhere."

"Me too," he replied. *And perhaps Jori as well.* "Even if they're not, I bet these people also need our help."

Their MEGA escort, who seemed less cybernetic than most, pointed to a corner. "You'll find textiles such as bedding and clothing over there. And should you wish it, items you can use to partition your own space." The MEGA indicated the rear of the auditorium. "Bathrooms and showers are there, equipped with everything you need from toothbrushes to soap. And we serve meals over here every six hours."

"What if we need something else?" Bari asked. "Who do we talk to?"

"We've anticipated all your needs."

"Really?" Quigley's mouth twisted dubiously. "What about a razor… Or fingernail clippers?"

"In the bathroom cabinets."

"Okay, yeah." She folded her arms and cocked her hips. "What about lip balm?"

"You don't need that."

"I do if I've been stuck in a desert all day. What about anti-fungal cream for my feet?"

"What we've provided will suffice."

The ridges between her eyes deepened and one side of her mouth curled in distaste. "Yeah, but what if I really need something else? Like medicine?"

If her confrontational attitude ruffled him, he didn't show it. "First aid supplies are in the bathroom cabinets."

"And if I need help beyond first aid?"

"You will have to make do, miss."

Vizubi shot her a scowl before she could argue further. She frowned and turned away in a huff.

Hapker agreed, realizing it wasn't the first time today. She might be abrasive but only because she was saying what everyone kept to themselves.

Although not having any MEGAs around made their mission easier, this didn't seem any better than a cell. It had more amenities, but he doubted all the people in here were honest. With no MEGA soldiers, PG-Force officers, or other military or police enforcing order, things could get out of hand.

Several groups guarded piles of stuff, making him suspect many of the supplies provided by the MEGAs were being hoarded. A barter system had likely developed, with the most successful and stronger pilferers controlling distribution. Depending on the type of people they were, allocation would be imbalanced. Fights, raids, and other disputes would arise—if they hadn't already.

But there was no point in debating their situation with this man. "Thank you," he said instead.

The MEGA dipped his head and took his leave.

"So now what?" Quigley asked.

"Duh," Bari replied. "We do what we came here for."

She rolled her eyes. "Yeah, but what do we do when we find them? We lost our contact, remember?"

"One step at a time, Corporal," Hapker said. "Spread out, two-by-two. Find the captain's family. Keep an eye out for Cooperative officers as well, but don't approach them just yet. MEGAs are likely spying on us, so maintain cover."

"Let's avoid using our comms too," Sharkey added.

"Agreed." Considering the unusual tech the MEGAs had used thus far, he wouldn't be surprised if they had the means to pinpoint any type of transmissions. "Meet back here at this pillar in one hour."

"Yes, Sir," Vizubi replied, then turned to the others. "Most folks will keep to themselves in a situation like this, but there's always those who'll push people around to position themselves better. So if someone confronts you, just nod your head and agree. We don't want any trouble."

Hapker expected him to give Quigley a pointed look, but he eyed everyone with equal sternness. Perhaps the respect she had for him didn't warrant direct attention.

Vizubi paired up with Fung, Bari went with Quigley, and Woolley took Nariya. Sharkey accompanied him and they headed to the right side of the auditorium. Many despondent faces peered at them as they passed, but none offered a greeting—not even a wordless acknowledgement. Some eyed them with suspicion and sidled closer to their belongings. And a few gave them a hopeful glint, perhaps looking for protectors.

No one looked familiar, but this place was huge. Like the interrogation room, light from everywhere yet nowhere illuminated the space. The walls were just as white as the other places in this facility. The floors, not so much. Tread marks, bits of trash, and splotches of food or other tidbits marked it up. Thick pillars created a grid pattern throughout, allowing him to keep track of where they searched.

Sharkey elbowed him. She smirked and pointed to a makeshift shelter where two voices grunted from inside. Either the couple had paired up to pass the time or the barter system included the trading of favors. He hoped for the former, but since no one seemed in distress, he left it alone.

An old woman approached him, desperation etched in her eyes. "Do you know anyone who can help us?" She pointed behind her to two women hugging their knees, one older and the other in her teens, and both skinny.

Hapker sagged. "We just arrived. I'm not sure how this place works yet."

"How long have you been here?" Sharkey asked, her tone carrying empathy.

"A couple hours." The woman wrung her hands. "But we don't know what to do. They didn't tell us anything, just dumped us in here."

Sharkey talked with her a bit, offering words of comfort, then indicated the areas the MEGA had pointed out earlier. The woman nodded unenthusiastically, then returned to the other two he assumed were her daughter and granddaughter.

He and Sharkey moved on. None of the faces seemed familiar. It was like a sea of assorted fish but less lively.

A short figure with black hair caught Hapker's eye and made his heart jump. He veered toward him with a quickened pace. Sharkey must've seen him too because she craned her neck to get a better look.

The boy turned around. Hapker halted, disappointment punching him in the gut.

Darn it. It wasn't Jori.

"You really think he's here?" Sharkey asked.

Hapker sighed. "I don't know." If the MEGAs had plans for Jori, he doubted he'd be here in this common area. But that didn't stop him from hoping.

Sharkey touched his forearm, her eyes tilted in sympathy. Hapker shoved his sadness aside and kept searching.

They came upon a bedraggled group of tall and skinny men and women. They had dark hair and narrow eyes that reminded him of Jori, but their hollow-cheeked faces looked more careworn. Their clothes were tattered and dirty and seemed to be made of homespun cloth rather than fabricated material. Overall, they appeared more down-and-out than anyone else here and he wondered where they'd come from.

A vision of loveliness stood among them, stopping him short. The profile of a tall woman with jet black hair in a bun tended a little girl. Her gentle hands offered compassion and concern. She wore a plain pale dress, ragged and dirty at the hems, yet she still had a majesty about her that tugged at his memory.

She lifted her head and caught his eye. His breath hitched. Could it really be her? All the way out here?

She stood upright. A bewildered frown creased her face. She wouldn't recognize him with his nanite mask, but could she identify him by his lifeforce?

"What is it?" Sharkey asked.
"Her." Hapker inclined his head at the woman.
"Uh, yeah. I guess she's kind of pretty."
"No… I mean yes. But that's not what I mean."
"What is it then?"
"I'm pretty sure that's Jori's mother."

45
An Alliance

Commander J.D. Hapker's heart stopped. Of all the people in the galaxy, Jori's mother was the last person he ever expected to see. Whether coincidence or fate, he didn't care. Either the universe had a plan or this was a cruel joke.

He approached the woman, entranced. A broad-shouldered man stepped in front of him with a glower. "This area is off limits."

Hapker blinked. This black-haired man with a dimpled chin partly covered by a goatee looked familiar. His eyes widened. The uniform wasn't the same. His once polished synthetic armor was gone and replaced by one with faded careworn material that fit too tight in some places and too loose in others. But he knew this man's face well enough. "Washi? What are you doing here?" The last time he'd seen the man was on the *Dragon* warship. Did that mean other Dragon Warriors were here too? Surely not. A quick inspection of Washi's worn uniform hinted at a more complicated story.

The man frowned. "Do I know you?"

Hapker laughed. *Of course. The disguise.* He leaned in and whispered. "It's me. Commander Hapker. I'm wearing a nanite mask."

Washi darkened. "You got Jori killed," he said in a rumbling voice.

Hapker threw up his hands. "What? No." The warrior advanced. Hapker stepped back. "He's alive."

Washi halted. His scowl remained but transitioned into a question.

"He's alive," Hapker repeated. "Our doctor grew him a new heart. He's as strong as ever."

The warrior's mouth moved but no sound came out. His eyes watered. "A-alive?" He glanced about, looking behind Hapker and elsewhere. "Where is he?"

"I don't know," he said. When the warrior bared his teeth, Hapker pressed out his palms in a *wait* motion. "I think MEGA-Man has him. He's on this planet somewhere… Or will be."

"What?! You were supposed to protect him."

"It's a long story. I was injured. He was taken from me."

Washi's glower slipped into a stricken expression. Uncertainty etched his forehead.

"How are you here?" Hapker asked.

"Thanks to you, I was exiled."

Hapker frowned, his confusion winning out over his contrition. The emperor wouldn't have exiled Washi here, so something else brought him here. He glanced at the hollow-cheeked men and women behind him. "Are MEGAs kidnapping Tredons too?"

Washi growled. "The emperor forced us to flee our home. These MEGAs are supposedly our allies."

Hapker's jaw dropped at the implications. How many were here of their own accord? And how many would willingly become MEGAs?

"You *can't* ally with these people," he said.

Washi's eyes blazed. "Believe me. This wasn't my choice. We came here out of desperation, not desire."

Hapker ran his hand down his face. Acting like a savior to gain allies was better than kidnapping them, but still concerning.

"What do they want with Jori?" The warrior crossed his arms.

"He's exceptional." Hapker planted his hands on his hips and bit his lip. "I suspect they intend to use his DNA. Now that I see you here, I wouldn't be surprised if they plan on using him for his connection to the Tredons as well."

Washi blanched. "They'll try to turn him into a cyborg too."

"They won't," Hapker said even as his mouth went dry. "I've gotten the impression that they need him to be willing. And he will never agree."

The warrior's lips twisted into a snarl. "I know someone else who I thought would never agree. But they bullied him into it." Hapker was about to ask who, but Washi turned away. "Stay put," he said, then marched off.

He quelled his anxiety and waited. All the people here were tall and dark-haired like Tredons, but there were two distinct groups. One consisted of bulky men wearing uniforms like soldiers, though mismatched and worn. The other comprised skinny men and women wearing dirty and tattered clothes. Even Tredons weren't immune from MEGA-Man's quest for domination.

Washi returned. The regal woman brushed by him and grasped Hapker's hand. Her eyes glittered with both eagerness and anguish. "He's alive? He's really alive?"

"Yes," Hapker replied, squeezing her hand. "Alive and well, last I saw."

Her expression relaxed with relief but her brows still tilted inward. "But you said MEGA-Man took him?"

"He did. But I don't think he'd hurt him. He's special somehow."

She covered her mouth and tears streamed down her eyes. "My boy," she said in a pained whisper that pierced Hapker's heart. "My dear sweet boy."

"I came here to get him back." Hapker looked down at his feet. "But I failed. Two-thirds of our team is dead and the rest of us are stuck here."

A hardness took over her features. "We'll find a way."

Washi leaned in over her shoulder. "No matter what it takes, we'll find a way."

"We'll work together," Hapker replied. "An alliance."

The warrior dipped his head. "An alliance."

She jutted her chin and squared her shoulders, reminding him of Jori. *So this is where he gets his strength from.*

He smiled, his hope restored.

46
Prisoners of War

Cybernation first appeared as a glowing spot of light in the distance. Hours passed before the details emerged. Eventually, the planet took up the entire viewscreen, displaying a glittering blue sea and an earthy, plant-rich continent. The only thing marring it was the white swirling mass of clouds making its way across the equatorial ocean.

Jori stood in the center of the bridge with his hands clasped behind his back and tried to mask his own storm. It wasn't just Sebastian's behavior or MEGA-Man's machinations. It was everything. He shouldn't be here. Even after running away from his father, he had no control over his own fate.

Doctor Sokolov stepped beside him wearing a worshipful smile. "It's so beautiful."

Jori twisted his mouth. Under different circumstances, he would've been eager to visit a new place.

He glanced at the stats on the bottom right of the screen. In about twelve more hours, he'd make landfall and meet the ultimate MEGA. What would happen once he got there? What would he do when he faced MEGA-Man? The temptation to curse him out was great, but foolish. The doctor had said Jori was important to the cause, but what if that meant he could also be a hindrance to it? MEGA-Man would surely recognize this and eliminate him if he stepped out of line. He had to play this smart, but how?

"What's wrong?" Doctor Sokolov asked. "You've been scowling all day."

First Vance, and now Sebastian. That snake admitted no wrongdoing, but Jori's sensing ability gleaned the truth. "*I-a only do what I'm-a told,*" the chima had said, which was bullshit considering what he tried to do to Phemius. What was it about implants that made these people so sadistic? But he didn't say so out loud.

The doctor looks down at him with brows drawn. "Is something upsetting you?"

Jori worked his jaw but still didn't speak.

"I noticed Sebastian is locked up, and I've been meaning to ask you about it."

"Let me guess. You don't approve."

"Oh no. That's not the issue at all. I'm just curious about what happened."

"He let the inspector out of his cell," Jori replied through gritted teeth.

"Are you sure?" Doctor Sokolov radiated dismay. "Why?"

"I suspect MEGA-Man had told him to do it."

"That makes no sense. He didn't want that man to go free."

"No, he wanted him dead. He manipulated the situation so I'd kill him."

The doctor blanched. "Oh my. I'm so sorry."

Jori harrumphed. The sincerity of the doctor's apology didn't erase the bitterness in his mouth.

"I mean it," Doctor Sokolov said. "This shouldn't have happened."

"Damn right it shouldn't have."

"I shall have a word with MEGA-Man about this as soon as we arrive," the doctor replied in an uncharacteristic fierceness.

"And tell him what?" Jori snapped. "I don't get him. Why is he doing this to me? How can he say he wants me on his side, then trick me into doing things I don't want to do? I won't be like my father, damn it!" Tears spilled from his eyes, unbidden. "I want my mother, but I can't be what MEGA-Man wants me to be."

Doctor Sokolov patted his shoulder. "I know."

"You know, so why doesn't MEGA-Man?"

The doctor heaved a sigh. "I'm not sure. I-I think…"

"What?"

"I'm worried that he's looking at this whole situation too logically. People don't always make their choices based on logic. We're emotional beings."

"I'm not emotional," Jori muttered, then realized too late that it was a lie.

"You're not a robot either." Sincerity radiated from Doctor Sokolov like a sun. "I'll speak to him. Help him understand. Please don't give up on us. Our cause is just, even if we're not going about it in the best way."

The doctor squeezed Jori's shoulder, reminding him of Commander Hapker. A bit of his anger dissipated, but not all.

To keep his mind from spinning into an inferno, he sat at an empty workstation and scrolled through the various reports. Despite the hurricane growing over the open ocean, the planetary weather patterns were unremarkable. Like most habitable planets, it was cooler near the poles and hotter at the equator with a moderate climate in between.

Jori moved on to the *Black Thresher*'s performance levels. Everything seemed fine. With a ship full of MEGAs and well-programmed bots, issues rarely occurred. He'd investigate the arc drive later to find out why its field regulator had dropped below optimal, but two percent wasn't enough to warrant immediate attention.

The blandness of the status reports did nothing to stave off his anxiety so he investigated other aspects of the planet. Conducting recon was second nature, even if it wouldn't do him much good in his current situation.

He started with a low planetary orbital scan using lidar. It detected ships, satellites, and hundreds, possibly thousands, of anomalous materials.

What? He ran a full energy sweep. His heartrate ticked up as he waited for the results. And when they came, he gasped. The residual energy and heat signatures coupled with the pockets of radiation and ionized gas clouds indicated a battle had recently taken place.

He enhanced the optics scan and investigated the debris. Ship parts ranged from an exterior panel to a detached ship's thruster. His neck prickled as he traced its trajectory back to a Fortis-class destroyer.

The PG-Force was here.

There were also frigates, an Auxilia-class destroyer with extensive impact craters along its hull, a Ductor-class destroyer venting atmosphere, a Potens-class cruiser with a jagged hole in its side, and even an Impetus-class battleship that had an odd-shaped vessel attached to it. The *Black Thresher* identified it as a MEGA Lamprey-class assault skiff, which meant MEGAs were boarding that ship.

"What the hell?" Jori said aloud to no one in particular.

Doctor Sokolov looked over his shoulder. "What is it?"

"It looks like the PG-Force waged a full-scale attack on the planet… And failed."

The doctor's brows shot up. "Are you sure they failed?"

"Considering the number of their ships destroyed compared to your own, I'd say yes."

"Call in and ask for a report."

Jori sent a query. They responded with a detailed sitrep. Jori read through it, his astonishment increasing with each sentence. It confirmed what he'd already discerned—that the PG-Force had attacked in force and suffered devastating losses. Although they'd arrived in stealth, the MEGAs had known they were coming and were prepared. How they knew, Jori couldn't discern.

All PG-Force ships had either fled or been neutralized. Several were so damaged that survivors were unlikely. Others had surrendered and were now being boarded for prisoner extraction.

Jori gulped. Taking prisoners kept the enemy from repairing their ships and starting the battle anew. He would've also considered it humane if he ignored MEGA-Man's intentions.

Doctor Stenson had once told him that they didn't force people to undergo cybernetic upgrades since it resulted in a higher percentage of hosts rejecting the implants. But would MEGA-Man take a risk on the enemy? After all, the alternative was killing them all anyway.

Chusho.

"This is very upsetting," Doctor Sokolov said.

Jori clenched his jaw. "Damn right it is."

"How could they do this?"

"It's not just them who's doing it, and you know it," Jori retorted.

The doctor frowned. "Yes, but surely you understand by now that we had to stand up to our oppressors."

Violence begets violence.

How had it gotten so out of hand? Laying the blame at the feet of chimas like Vance and Sebastian seemed like the answer until he thought about Major Darwish and the inspector. And there were good MEGAs like Doctor Sokolov and Phemius. Plus decent people such as Commander Hapker and Lieutenant Gresher in the

Cooperative. The same extremes even applied to his own people—like his father compared to Sensei Jeruko.

Ugh. Why is everything in the galaxy so damned complicated?

47
Indecision

A vast sky spanned overhead, blue and dazzling with no hint of the devastation lying beyond it. On land, two rows of short, uniform buildings lined the roadway like tall, horizontal steel bars. No identifying signage distinguished one section from the other. Neither did the identical entryways, which came at regular intervals as the car drove down a street with no signs or traffic lights. The only variations to the entire scene were the robots and MEGAs who walked or rolled down the sidewalks. Even then, they all moved at the same casual speed like organized data packets.

Jori swallowed against the dryness in his throat and fought against the temptation to fidget in his seat. The car he rode in should've been comfortable. The seats were perfectly curved, their soft grey color promised tranquility, and the fresh odor of the interior signified a luxurious cleanliness. But the smooth drive only highlighted his anxiety. Although he sympathized with what MEGAs were fighting for, he still felt he was being delivered into the hands of the enemy.

"It's perfect," Doctor Sokolov said with a reverent smile as he gazed out the window.

Rodrigo sat in the rear-facing seat across from them, his expression as blank as ever.

Jori twisted his mouth. "Perfect?"

"Yes. Notice there's no harried workforce, no arguing patrons, no impatient drivers."

No laughter. Compared to the ragged streets in Toradon territory, the doctor was right. But the big city he'd visited on the Cooperative home planet had a vibrant feel to it. People smiled, children played, and life seemed to flow in smooth optimism. This place was so boring, it might as well be dead.

"We're lucky the PG-Force didn't reach here." The doctor's pleasant emotions slipped into seriousness. "To sully this peace with war would've been sacrilegious."

"It's funny how you consider war sacrilegious," Jori muttered.

Doctor Sokolov's brow tilted but didn't respond.

Jori disliked how the Cooperative brought war here as much as the doctor did. It was one thing to fight against MEGAs who attacked their cities and space stations. But coming here signified they wanted to indiscriminately destroy MEGAs. *It's their own fault they got killed.* He wished the entire dispute would just end. It wasn't his war yet it snatched him in its clutches like a raging monster.

He knotted his hands into fists then stretched out his fingers, trying to release the anticipation building up inside him. He still hadn't decided on how to react when he faced MEGA-Man. Being agreeable without committing to anything would give him more time to figure out what to do. But if he kept letting himself get swept along, he'd end up like a hapless leaf in the rapids that got carried over the edge with no way back. He had to be strong and ask the right questions until he figured this out.

I wish Hapker was here. He'd know what to do.

An enormous, white-domed structure came into view as they reached the rise of a gently sloping street. He knew little about architecture, but its size seemed impossible. How did it not cave in on itself? The closer they got, the more fantastic it appeared. It had to be thirty kilometers in diameter and at least one kilometer tall, maybe more.

He wiped his sweaty palms on this thigh then pointed. "What's that?"

"There's our destination," the doctor replied with a smile. "The MEGA Complex."

"It certainly looks complex. How did they build it? I don't see any seems or structural support."

"That's just the energy shield."

Jori's jaw dropped, unable to wrap his mind around a shield so opaque that it looked solid white. "How?"

Doctor Sokolov shrugged. "No idea. Amazing, isn't it?"

More like unsettling.

When they arrived, Jori discerned the illusion but he still couldn't see through it. The doctor brought him to a sublevel entrance guarded by two imposing MEGAs who made no move to stop them as they passed.

A wide set of doors opened, seemingly of their own accord. They walked through into a tunnel that sloped back upward. The doors on that end opened too. The path led outside where the blue sky shone above. Jori gaped at the shield, how it appeared white from the exterior view but clear from the inside.

Before them lay a broad lake with water so blue it looked artificial. Its metal-lined shore was flawlessly curved. Their path continued straight ahead and served as a bridge to a man-made island. Jori overlooked the sprawl of square buildings taking up most of the island and gawked at a palace of grand proportions. Its metallic structure dazzled under the light radiating from the immense ball of blue energy resting amid three prongs at the top of the tallest spire.

The metallic path continued upward in an impossibly sleek slope, leading to the colossal palace gate. "How do we get up there?" he asked, imagining his feet sliding backward with each step.

The doctor waved his hand at a spherical car that hovered above the ground.

Jori eyed it with a frown. "How does it do that?"

"I suspect from magnetic repulsion." Doctor Sokolov pointed at a pair of parallel bars set along the side of the path.

Oh. The MEGAs aren't magic, you idiot.

As they rode the car up, Jori discerned geometric shapes embossing the walls of the palace. At first, they looked like random squares and triangles. But within each shape were more shapes, making it appear to be constructed of a million mazes. He got dizzy trying to trace them.

After exiting, he paused to take it all in—and to quell the thumping in his chest. It was a palace, but since he didn't detect any lifeforces inside, it might as well be a mausoleum.

He wet his mouth and walked with the doctor to the imposing double doors. As before, two cyber-soldiers guarded each side and the doors opened automatically. Beyond the threshold was a long, wide hall. It led straight ahead, but the walls patterned with dizzying geometric shapes made him stagger. It was like being swallowed by some sort of energy-based alien monster.

The hall ended in another grand set of doors. The MEGAs guarding here were even more advanced than the others. They stood over two-and-a-half meters tall and had more muscle than the largest senshi warrior. If not for the bit of flesh showing on their cheeks and chin, he would've assumed they were men in mech suits or robots.

The doors slid open with a whisper despite their meter-thick bulk, revealing a grand room with a throne-like platform at the rear. Instead of a throne, it housed two spiraled metallic obelisks which flanked a three-pronged structure cradling a smaller blue-energy sphere.

Jori's mouth hung agape. Not even the most powerful lords in Toradon were this ostentatious. He would've ridiculed the excess had it not had such a profound effect. This was the home of the most advanced MEGA in the galaxy and Jori was but a flea on a blackbeast's back.

"Welcome," a deep male voice boomed.

Jori jumped. A spectral blue face appeared in place of the energy sphere. The attributes were all human—a man with sallow cheeks and a long chin. His sunken eyes bore heavy bags, making Jori believe this was or had been MEGA-Man's actual features. Yet it was still too impersonal.

He hid his irritation and faced the mirage with a military mien. "What is this? I was told I'd get to meet you in person."

"I am here."

"The hell you are. All I see is a holo-image."

"You will meet my physical self when I am certain of your full allegiance."

Jori curled his mouth. "How do you expect me to give you my full allegiance when you hide yourself?"

"Much is at stake."

"Damn right." Jori flared his nostrils as his intent to play nice fled. "You're asking me to follow you like a blind fool. But I'm not blind. I've witnessed the horrors inflicted by the Cooperative and the MEGA Inspectors but I've also seen the atrocities committed by your minions like Vance. That chima fired on a space station full of innocent people!"

"Our cause is just."

"I agree," Jori replied. "But your execution makes you no better than your enemy. I won't fight with someone who murders people in order to get their own way. That's why I ran away from my father."

"Casualties can't be avoided."

"That's a load of crap. You obviously have recordings of what the MEGA Inspectors have been doing. You should broadcast it— get others to sympathize with you."

"There will still be casualties. MEGA hunters and their ilk will continue to persecute us."

"That blood is on their hands. It won't be on mine."

The blue man flickered. "So you side against us."

Jori's chest hitched. "That's not what I said. I believe your cause is just. I just think you're going about it all wrong. If you want people to support you, you have to do it in a way that won't inspire them to resist you."

MEGA-Man didn't respond. His image floated on nothingness with a blank expression. Jori swallowed. "I am still considering siding with you. But the death of innocents must stop."

"I will consider it."

Jori's eyes popped. Did he truly have that much sway over someone referred to as the ultimate MEGA? Surely he couldn't be that important. He filled his lungs and let out a long exhale. "And I want to find my mother… As soon as possible—before my father kills her."

MEGA-Man smiled. "Agreed."

Jori's heart lurched at his immediate response. Did that mean he'd rescue her? His pulse raced. Could he really get her back?

He didn't quite believe it. This was all too easy… And troubling. If MEGA-Man saved his mother and promised not to hurt any more innocent people, would he finally agree to join him?

But what about the MEGA Inspectors and those like Major Darwish? Then again, what about MEGAs like Vance or Sebastian?

Something Zaina had said once played through his mind. *"What's right or wrong has so many nuances. It's up to us to weigh them and do what's in our hearts."*

His heart told him it was wrong to side with this freak, but he'd play along for a while longer if it saved his mother.

48
Reunited

The sun's rays blazed through the window of the suite. Its attempt at cheerfulness only emphasized the austerity of Jori's new prison. He had a desk but no computer, an armchair facing a blank grey wall, and a basic kitchenette and bathroom. The space was a little larger than his old room on the *Dragon* warship but still felt claustrophobic.

No one had forbidden him from going out to explore, but what was there to see and do back here in the uniform steel city full of listless cyborgs? He had access to a map of the area but it showed no gymnasiums, no parks, nothing to offer relaxation or entertainment. Not even asking a few MEGAs helped. Only manufacturing facilities, laboratories, and administrative offices surrounded him.

He massaged his forehead, attempting to alleviate the ache caused by a lack of sleep. Last night had been a restless pursuit of disjointed dreams. His mother, his brother, Commander Hapker, Sensei Jeruko, everyone he cared about had flitted through his head then disappeared, leaving him with an empty pit in his stomach that hurt worse than the time his father had stabbed him. MEGA-Man's holo-image had haunted him too, promising him a great destiny. But what good was destiny if it meant being alone?

Kiyoshi stirred. Jori opened his cage and let him out. The rat scurried out, lifted his head, and sniffed. Since Jori had already given him the opportunity to explore, he didn't venture off. His emotions radiated eagerness as he ran over and tackled Jori's shoe. Jori sat cross-legged on the floor and wrestled him with his fingers. A smile formed as Kiyoshi squeaked with delight. Jori's loneliness diminished, but only a little.

When the rat was done, Jori retrieved a new toy he'd made from old wire conduits and other discarded materials that hadn't gone to the ship's recycler yet. It was an ugly tangled mess, but Kiyoshi would enjoy exploring all the tunnels and compartments.

One compartment would undoubtedly be too difficult for him to get into, but Jori had a plan. It was the only one containing treats, so it didn't take long for him to find the sealed entrance. Jori allowed him a little time to investigate before helping him. He closed his eyes and concentrated until his ability focused deeply into Kiyoshi. Then he imagined the rat putting his paw into a hole, grasping a tiny lever, and pulling it up.

Within seconds, a click sounded. Jori's jaw dropped. Either Kiyoshi was smarter than he thought or he'd just told him how to open the door.

But how can that be? His mother's skills enabled her to send mental commands to others, but this was an exceedingly rare ability. From what Jori understood, a sentio-animi, who could detect emotions, was the most common type of reader. After that came the extraho-animi—a thought reader. The imperium-animi was the most powerful level, being capable of both extracting thoughts and implanting them.

How had Jori skipped the second tier and gone straight to imperium? And was he able to command people or only animals? He'd have to try.

As if on cue, Doctor Sokolov's lifeforce permeated his senses. He focused. The doctor had just entered the conveyor and he was excited about something. *What are you so happy about?* Jori asked, hoping his ability would help him read the man's mind. The only thing he determined was when the man reached his section of the building.

Using the same technique he used on Kiyoshi, Jori imagined Doctor Sokolov stopping. He also ordered him with his thoughts. It didn't work. The doctor arrived at his door and rang the doorbell.

"Enter," Jori snapped. Maybe Kiyoshi figuring out that mechanism was a coincidence.

Doctor Sokolov swept in with a grin. He practically danced on his toes and winked. "MEGA-Man has a surprise for you."

"What kind of surprise?" Jori asked, eyes narrowed.

The doctor rubbed his hands together, his glee making him uncharacteristically giddy. "I don't want to spoil it but I promise you'll love it."

Jori side-eyed him. "It's not something stupid like he's agreed to make me his top lieutenant if I get upgrades."

The doctor's expression fell. "My goodness, no. Nothing like that. This is so much better."

"Tell me," Jori commanded, attempting to use his newfound ability.

"Nope." Doctor Sokolov winked. "You'll just have to wait and see."

Damn.

"Come on. I have a car waiting," the doctor said.

Jori hesitated, but not for long since the alternative was to stay here and do nothing. He followed Doctor Sokolov out and to the car. As always, Rodrigo joined them. The vehicle took the same boring street lined with two rows of monotonous buildings. Jori propped his chin on his fist and stared out the window, wondering if he'd ever get to leave this planet of his own free will.

They turned down a new roadway. At first, the scene looked the same except with no doors and no MEGAs. But once beyond the rear edge of the vast structure, everything changed. It was as though someone had switched from one VR setting to another.

Brick, wood, and concrete buildings jumbled together like toppled shipping crates. Trash gathered in piles by dilapidated doorways and along the curbs. The few people ambling about wore tattered clothes and surly frowns—and they had lifeforces.

"They're not MEGAs?" he asked as he pointed to a trio of men hanging out on a stoop covered by a crooked awning. Their faces looked haggard and their lifeforces radiated a tired defeat similar to the shokukin and slave castes back home.

The doctor put on a pitying frown. "No. They haven't accepted our ways."

"So you make them live like this?"

"We don't make them. They choose this life."

Jori scowled. It seemed more likely that MEGA-Man suppressed those who disagreed with him.

Depression set in as they drove on. He was sure it came from the populace. Their misery must be why people like the doctor believed augmentation was the best course for humanity. If it could still be called that afterward.

Beyond the city was a wasteland of dirt and dying shrubs. A half hour passed before they reached an extensive white building. The windowless one-story structure spanned for at least a kilometer in either direction.

They came to a gated entrance. The doors opened automatically and they drove in without slowing. The drive sloped down under the structure into a dark expanse held up by concrete pillars. Only a few vehicles parked along one wall and not a single person or bot was about. Most of the MEGA inhabitants were likely out fighting the cooperative, making every place Jori had visited on this planet thus far eerily desolate.

After leaving the car, they took the conveyor and exited into a long, white hall that intersected more hallways. It wasn't much different from the *Black Thresher*. The cyborgs here were just as diverse—and as lifeless. None paid him any mind.

An oily lifeforce wafted near. Jori wrinkled his nose. *It can't be.* The sensation came from the intersection to the right. Jori separated from Rodrigo and the doctor to pursue it.

"Where are you going?" Doctor Sokolov asked.

"I need to see something," he growled.

"Whatever it is, it can wait."

Jori ignored him and kept going. The doctor followed, his emotions piqued, and Rigo trailed behind. They weaved around MEGAs until Jori spotted the snake. He halted and ground his teeth. "What the hell is he doing here?"

Rodrigo halted into what Jori called his standby mode. Doctor Sokolov caught up, his eyes narrowing as he scanned ahead.

Sebastian put on a smug smile and waved. Regret added weight to the doctor's sigh. "Ah. I was ordered to release him."

Jori clenched his fists. "Why?"

"He will go on an important mission soon."

Jori flared his nostrils. He bit down so hard that his jaw ached but it was better than releasing the string of curses pushing against his teeth. His stomach churned at the same time. If the Cooperative records held any truth, people would die suspicious deaths.

No benevolent government would use someone like this to achieve their mission. This proved what he suspected all along. MEGA-Man wasn't concerned about justice. He merely wanted to push his ideology at any cost.

Doctor Sokolov placed a hand on his shoulder. Jori slapped it away. Sebastian threw a derogatory gesture and headed down another hall. Jori remained rooted to the floor as a flood of fire and brimstone boiled inside him.

"I'm sorry, but MEGA-Man said Sebastian has a very special skillset and is needed for an important mission."

"His *skill set* involves sneaking about and killing people."

The doctor's throat bobbed. "I'll speak to MEGA-Man about this."

Jori harrumphed. "Didn't you already talk to him? You had to know releasing him would piss me off."

"I tried to tell him." Doctor Sokolov's guilt stoked Jori's fire further. "But… He wouldn't budge."

"Of course he wouldn't. He's an emotionless freak." Jori had always been told that emotion was a weakness, but a lack of emotion seemed worse. No way would he support this.

"He just wants to help people."

Jori wheeled on him. "*Wants* to? Or are his decisions based on algorithms and predictive analysis?"

The doctor's brows drew together. For once, he had no counterargument. "You're right. I'm beginning to see your perspective." Guilt exuded from him. "It felt wrong to release him. I should've listened to my conscience."

"Why didn't you?" Jori pressed.

Doctor Sokolov's eyes tilted imploringly. "You must understand. I've served MEGA-Man for many years and have never known him to use people like Sebastian. Everything I've done for him has worked toward helping others. He's never asked me to harm the innocent to do it. But…" His eyes flicked to Rodrigo, who still waited a few meters away. "Something is wrong," the doctor whispered. "Either I've been blind or something has changed."

Although his words rang with sincerity, Jori's ire persisted.

"I will speak to MEGA-Man again… More forcefully. I swear it." The doctor put his hand on Jori's shoulder once more. This time, Jori didn't push it away.

"For now, please come with me. Our surprise awaits."

"I'm in no mood for any more surprises," Jori muttered.

Doctor Sokolov's lips curled up into a small smile. "Trust me. You'll love this."

Jori quirked his brows. He'd never trust MEGA-Man's agents but gave in. They met up with Rodrigo and continued onward through the white hallways.

After another turn and through a security door, a familiar lifeforce tickled Jori's senses. His heart fluttered. The pulsing in his ears intensified as he drew in the essence of the familiar lifeforce. *She's here. She's really here.*

He took the lead, panting as though racing through an obstacle course. Tears formed in his eyes. His hands shook and his fingers tingled. His throat dried. He couldn't get there fast enough.

At first, she emitted apprehension. But she must've sensed him too because her emotions flipped into a mixture of amazement, relief, and immense happiness.

Jori's tears broke free as he sprinted off. His senses led him to a room where he dashed in. His mother waited there, wearing the most joyous smile he'd ever seen.

"Jori!"

"Mother!"

They ran into each other's arms. He buried his head in her shoulder and bawled. He couldn't believe it. It was her. She felt real, both physically and mentally, and she smelled just like he remembered.

He clutched her hard, absorbing the moment. She did the same, neither taking a chance on letting go.

"The commander told me you were alive," she whispered in his ear, using their secret language.

Jori pulled back, eyes wide. *Hapker?* "He's here?" he asked, speaking the same cryptic lingo even though Rodrigo and the doctor stood out of earshot.

She nodded.

Jori's heart, already swollen with the joy of seeing her, swelled further. "He came for me." Tears fell anew.

She knelt before him. Cupped his head in her hands and kissed his forehead. "We're all here for you."

Doctor Sokolov beamed. He didn't need to understand their secret language to appreciate Jori's high spirits.

Jori pulled the necklace from beneath his clothes and held it out to his mother. Her eyes glittered with tears and her hand trembled as she took it from him. "I remember this. You gave it to me when you were just seven years old." She held it to her breast. "The memory of that day is so vivid."

"For me too." Jori wiped the wetness from his cheeks. "I found it after Father sent you away."

She embraced him. "I cherished it then, but I'll cherish it even more now."

Jori hugged her tight, afraid to let her go—afraid to lose her again. Though a war wrought with malice raged around them, this moment drained away his fears, banished his loneliness, and overflowed him with warmth.

But it wouldn't last. Not as long as they were stuck on this planet.

49
Letting Go

Jori remained lost in time as his mother held him. Eventually, her embrace slipped away. She knelt before him, clasping his hands with a touch as soft as flower petals. Her eyes radiated the warmth of a spring sun and her smile filled him with peace.

"I'm so glad you're alright." The thankfulness flooding through her glowed on her face. "What happened after you got separated from the commander?"

Jori told her about Zaina, the riot on the space station, and how he ended up on the *Black Thresher*. Not wanting to worry her, he glossed over the details of his encounter with Vance, but said the doctor seemed like a decent man.

He spoke using their secret language when he didn't want certain information overheard. Since she was an extraho and an imperium, he could've shared all this with her using his mind, but Doctor Sokolov might find it strange if he didn't talk.

"What about you?" he asked. "What happened after Father sent you away? How did you get here?"

"Life on the island was so peaceful. Oh. I missed you so much, of course." Using their secret language, she added, "I think even your brother found some peace there… That is, after he got over having to clean pig pens." She smirked.

Jori's breath caught. "Terk…" he swallowed. "Terk was there too? Is he here now?"

She nodded. Her eyes shining with joy. "I have both my sons back." She brushed her fingers down his wet cheek.

"B-but I was told he was killed." *Killed by my sabotage.*

"Your father thinks he was. But he escaped."

"How? What happened?"

"After he destroyed the ship housing the perantium emitter, he flew away amid the debris."

So I didn't cause it. His knees buckled. She caught him before he collapsed. He sagged against her cherishing her tenderness, then found his feet again. "Is Sensei Jeruko still alive too, then?"

"No, but Washi and Michio are… And they're here too."

She discreetly told him how his father had attacked the island and how Terk had saved her and the others from their village. Then she related the commander's story, how he'd woken to find Jori gone, that the Cooperative had kept his identity and whereabouts a secret, then how he received a message from Zaina.

Jori's heart skipped a beat. "Is she alright?"

"As far as he knows, yes."

Next, she told him how Hapker had come here with a small team to look for him but they'd shot down his ship when the PG-Force appeared. She must've sensed his worry because she added that he'd arrived in a civilian ship and wore a nanite mask to hide his identity.

"We're all sharing a big area now," his mother said. "More than just us. Lots of people from all over the galaxy."

Heat flared in Jori's chest. "Is MEGA-Man turning them into machines?"

"So far, only those who are willing."

Jori pulled back with a curl to his lips. "Who'd want to be turned into a MEGA?"

"People who are helpless—like our citizens oppressed by your father."

Jori's heart sank. "MEGA-Man wants me to take his place—become the Dragon Emperor."

Her emotions plummeted. She took a moment to collect herself. "I've always thought you would be the best thing for our people, but not like this."

"I know." Jori looked down at his feet. "MEGA-Man might let me be in charge for a while, but he'll ultimately control me."

She cupped his chin in her palms. "No. You deserve a good life. We'll find a way out of here—you, me, Terk, and the commander—and leave all this behind us. Some other day we'll figure out how to deal with your father's madness."

Jori's shoulders relaxed, thankful he wouldn't need to let MEGA-Man use him to take over Toradon. With his mother here to help him—

He snapped his gaze over to the doctor. "What happens now? Do I get to stay with her?"

"Most certainly," Doctor Sokolov said with a smile. "She will return with us."

Jori's heart leapt with joy, but then shrunk when he remembered Hapker and his brother. "Why can't I go with her?"

The doctor's mouth turned down into a troubled frown. "Um, well. I'm not sure that's the proper place for you."

"But it's where my people are."

"Yes, I know. But… But my orders were to have you stay in the suite."

So MEGA-Man has more control over me. Jori struggled to conceal the ire roiling through him. After all, this shouldn't surprise him. Since it seemed Terk was more responsible for his mother's rescue, he still had no reason to side with MEGA-Man. Yet she'd be in danger if he went against him.

"Can we at least visit them?" Jori swallowed the anxiety crawling up his throat. Being with his mother meant everything. But he couldn't leave the others behind. He needed them as much as he needed her. MEGA-Man probably knew of Washi and Michio but not his brother or the commander. This gave Jori an advantage—but only if he could communicate with them.

Uncertainty furrowed the doctor's features. "I'm not sure. I'll ask."

That the answer wasn't an immediate yes made Jori's mouth go dry. He aimed a defiant scowl at the doctor and waited.

The doctor's eyes flicked. "I-I don't have a way to ask him at the moment."

"That's convenient," Jori mumbled. He turned toward Rodrigo. "MEGA-Man," he called out to the silent cyborg standing like a statue on the other side of the room. "I know you're observing all this so answer me. When you retrieved my mother, did you tell anyone there why you were taking her?"

"No," Rodrigo replied.

Jori fumed. "Then they're probably thinking you're doing something terrible to her. How do you expect people to ally with you if you're taking them by force? Let me talk to them, tell them we're alright."

"We will tell them." Rigo's voice was as monotone as usual, but Jori suspected MEGA-Man was the one speaking.

Jori scoffed. "They won't believe you, but they'll believe me."

"Have you chosen our path?" Rigo returned.

An unpleasant tingle ran down Jori's spine. To say yes would be a lie. It might also cast him in a direction he couldn't turn back from. But he couldn't say no either. "I'm still deciding," he replied reluctantly.

"I gave. Now it's your turn."

Rodrigo's voice didn't change, but Jori detected the demand in the words. Dread knotted in his gut. "I need to see more before I decide. I want to study the implants, know how they work." *And figure out why some people lose their lifeforce while others don't.*

"You're stalling."

"I'm hesitant," Jori snapped. "You're asking me to take sides in a war that's killing innocent people."

"Very well. Your request is reasonable. But your mother will return to your people to inform them of your status, and she will stay there until you have committed."

"What?! No!" A pain worse than when his father had plunged his blade into his heart pierced Jori's chest. "You just said she could stay with me!"

"We will allow her to come see you again."

His mother's emotions plunged into despair but she stood tall and jutted her chin. "I won't leave him."

"If you agree to receive a simple implant, you may stay."

"No!" A cold shock blasted through Jori's insides. "Not until I complete my studies."

"It is decided."

Jori clenched his fists. He wanted to scream and argue but he doubted it would do any good. Reasoning wouldn't work either since he had little bargaining power. His throat hardened. He just got his mother back. Letting her go would break him.

Forcing the words from his mouth, he said, "Fine. She returns to our other people but I still get to visit with her."

"Agreed."

His mother gripped his shoulder. "Jori, no!"

"You can't come with me," he croaked. She wagged her head, fear gushing from her like water from a broken pipe. His own emotions wanted to burst but he firmed his jaw. "You must stay in contact with them."

The doctor glanced back and forth between them with a furrowed brow. "Surely this isn't necessary. Joining with us gives you everything you want. You want to be with her, don't you?"

"Yes," Jori replied, barely keeping his voice from cracking. "More than anything. But not yet." *Not until I can figure out how to save everyone.* The burden of this task threatened to suffocate him. But all those he cared about were here—and separating from his mother might be the only way to keep communications open.

Doctor Sokolov shifted his feet. "Well, if that's what you want."

That's not what I want at all. "Just for now."

"Alright. I'll make the arrangements."

Jori suppressed his anguish and summoned his will. MEGA-Man might think to use her against him, but Jori could flip it to his favor. *I'll do what you say, but only if I get to keep visiting my mother.* He'd still be obligated to do MEGA-Man's bidding, but at least he'd be able to collaborate with everyone.

If that MEGA-chima keeps his word.

This entire situation was more complicated than a game of Galactic Dominions. So far, he just had a start of a plan. End MEGA-Man, end the war, and publicize all the horrific records kept by the MEGA Inspections Office.

It would take guile. It would take strength. And it'd take every bit of skill Jori and his family and friends could muster. And they had to do it before MEGA-Man turned everyone into cyborgs.

"We'll find a way out of this," his mother whispered, her brown eyes firm.

Jori willed himself to believe it too. If only he didn't have to leave her first. His eyes burned as he choked back the tears and released her hands. In his mind, she reached down and screamed as he fell into an abyss. The empty pit in his stomach returned and clenched painfully.

It's the only way.

50
The End?

Doctor Sokolov faced MEGA-Man's blue holo-image. "It's working," he said, trying to sound happy. "Jori was absolutely thrilled to see his mother."

"Do you think he will side with us?"

Sokolov hesitated, still unsure of where the boy stood. Saying yes felt like a lie and saying no would put Jori in danger. "He's becoming more compliant every day. If you agree to also stop the killing, I have no doubt he'll become a loyal agent."

"No. We must fight. Convince him that this is the right path."

Sokolov's mood plummeted. Before he'd taken on this mission, he was certain this was the right course of action. Now, he wasn't so sure. Every time he presented an infallible argument, Jori flipped it on its head. All the while, MEGA-Man responded in ways that proved Jori was right. *Such as setting that poor boy up to kill the inspector.* What kind of heartless being would do such a thing?

"Of course," he replied despite his misgiving. "Um, it might help if you dealt with Sebastian. Jori saw he was free and is furious."

"Sebastian is on a mission."

"Yes, I understand. But surely you have another agent to send."

"It's decided but tell the young prince that I will deal with him."

"But—"

"It's decided."

Sokolov deflated. He'd promised Jori he would be more forceful when he spoke to MEGA-Man about this, but keeping the promise proved difficult. If he didn't act like he agreed with all this, MEGA-Man would replace him with someone like Gottfried or Vance.

He had to keep pretending—for Jori's sake. "Understood," he replied with a fake smile. "I have some great ideas on how to encourage him."

"Well done, Doctor Sokolov. Your service is invaluable."

Sokolov bowed. "Thank you, Sir. It's been my honor." His stomach roiled at how hollow his words felt. "Um, speaking of honor. I'm wondering if…" He paused, trying to formulate his request. "I'd like to visit you in person," he blurted. "I've served you well for a long time and it would make me exceedingly happy to meet the man behind the scenes."

"Your loyalty has been unwavering," MEGA-Man replied. "You may enter my chamber."

Before Sokolov could ask where it was, a hole in the wall opened. His heart pounded like a hammer at the prospect of meeting his hero—or maybe not his hero anymore. Reluctance overtook him, but he pushed himself beyond it and headed through the door and into a dimly lit space.

A dusty odor of ageless rot curled his insides, reminding him of a tomb. Hundreds, if not thousands of processors took up the room, their thrumming almost like a heartbeat. He trod through the widest aisle, which was barely wide enough to accommodate the width of his shoulders, and made his way to the light source.

When he found it, his heart stopped. A shriveled old man sat in the small space before him. More than old—decayed. His skin was dark like leather, wrinkled in some places but pulled tight against his skeleton. He had no hair left—or eyes. The doctor struggled to recognize the face he knew so well from the hologram. Tubes protruded from every orifice and wires splayed out from his skull. Some even ran through his chest.

MEGA-Man's body was nothing more than a shell. Part of him lived on in these computers, but his soul was dead.

Sokolov tried to swallow but his throat constricted. He shrank away, his shoulders caving in. A shudder rippled through his body and chilled his bones. The room spun at the realization of what he'd been fighting for. It wasn't for evolution or equal rights. It had nothing to do with humanity at all.

He dropped to his knees as his faith shattered into a million pieces.

Did you enjoy this novel? Leave a review. Authors love reviews!

Next:
Find out whether our three heroes will defeat the ultimate MEGA in the final book of the series, Warriors United: Book Seven. Coming in early 2026!

Sign up for my newsletter by visiting my website, DawnRossAuthor.com, and get great deals!

By signing up, you'll receive an exclusive short story and get access to the first few chapters of the first four books.

Connect with Dawn Ross online:
DawnRossAuthor.com
Twitter.com/DawnRossAuthor
Facebook.com/DawnRossAuthor
Goodreads.com/author/show/441861.Dawn_Ross
Patreon.com/DawnRossAuthor

Books by Dawn Ross:

<u>**The Dragon Spawn Chronicles**</u>
StarFire Dragons
Dragon Emperor
Dragon's Fall
Isle of Hogs (a novella)
Warrior Outcast
Dissonance (a novella)
Orphaned Warrior
Fated Warriors
Warriors United
Spire Wilderness (a novella)

Connect with Dawn Ross online:
DawnRossAuthor.com
Twitter.com/DawnRossAuthor
Facebook.com/DawnRossAuthor
Goodreads.com/author/show/441861.Dawn_Ross
Patreon.com/DawnRossAuthor

About the Author

Dawn Ross currently resides in the wonderful state of Kansas where sunflowers abound. She has also lived in the beautiful Willamette Valley of Oregon and the scenic Hill Country of Texas. Dawn completed her bachelor's degree in 2017. Although the degree is in finance, most of her electives were in fine art and creative writing. Dawn is married and has a wonderful son. Her current occupation is part time at Meals on Wheels. She is also a mom, homemaker, volunteer, wildlife artist, and a sci-fi/fantasy writer. Her first novel was written in 2001 and she's published several others since. She participates in the NaNoWriMo event every year and is a part of her local writer group.

www.ingramcontent.com/pod-product-compliance
Lightning Source LLC
Chambersburg PA
CBHW071456110726
47908CB00003B/635